FRANKLIN HORTON

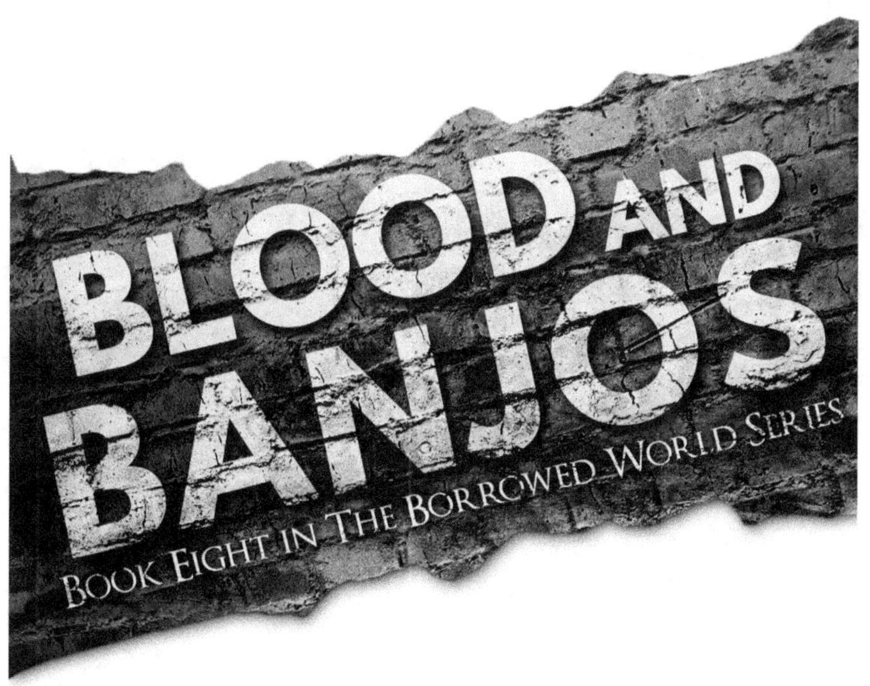

# ALSO BY FRANKLIN HORTON

**The Borrowed World Series**

The Borrowed World

Ashes of the Unspeakable

Legion of Despair

No Time For Mourning

Valley of Vengeance

Switched On

The Ungovernable

**The Locker Nine Series**

Locker Nine

Grace Under Fire

Compound Fracture

Blood Bought

**The Mad Mick Series**

The Mad Mick

Masters of Mayhem

Brutal Business

Northern Sun

**The Ty Stone Series**

Hard Trauma

**The Way of Dan Series**

Burning Down Boise

**Stand-Alone Novels**

Random Acts

# ABOUT THE AUTHOR

Franklin Horton lives and writes in the mountains of Southwestern Virginia. He is the author of several bestselling post-apocalyptic and thriller series. You can follow him on his website at franklinhorton.com.

While you're there please sign up for his mailing list for updates, event schedule, book recommendations, and discounts.

# BLOOD AND BANJOS

# PROLOGUE

A Refresher

The story of The Borrowed World begins with Jim Powell and his group of coworkers attending a meeting in Richmond, Virginia, when a terror attack rocks the nation. The wide scope of the attacks, primarily directed at infrastructure targets, leads to a cascading systems failure that soon affects utilities and communications. Attacks against oil refineries impact available stockpiles and refining capacity, forcing the U.S. to grind to a halt.

Among this group, there are mixed feelings about the best course of action, but they arrive at the decision to begin their journey home before things get any worse. They don't get far into their journey before they lose a coworker to violence when tensions boil over at a truck stop due to fuel restrictions. Unable to find any place to refill their vehicle, they are soon reduced to walking down the interstate highway. They're not alone. Rest areas, truck stops, and highway exits are filled with stranded, desperate travelers.

They eventually split up, with two of their party choosing to trust the government's FEMA system to get them home. The remainder of the group, led by Jim Powell, decides to set off on foot. Jim had been a prepper for many years and had long been worried that he might one day have to walk home from Richmond. He'd developed a plan for that possibility, packing gear and planning a route he could travel on foot if that was his only option.

His friend and coworker Gary was also a prepper and carried his own bugout bag. Another of their party, Randi, was not a prepper, but a feisty grandmother with grit and determination. She wasn't interested in waiting around for the government to save her either. Like Jim and Gary, she wanted control of her own destiny.

Back at home, in the absence of their stranded loved ones, their families struggled. Each faced difficulty as the majority of the nation lost power, cell service, and law enforcement. Communication became sporadic, then failed entirely. Thieves and predators operated with impunity. Jails were turned out, the criminals now aware that there would be no legal recourse for their actions.

Jim's family struggled with desperate neighbors willing to steal to survive. They also struggled to remember how to run the home in Jim's absence, since he was the one responsible for so many of the emergency preparations. If not for a detailed emergency manual he'd built for them over the years, they wouldn't have been able to find or operate many of the emergency measures he'd put in place.

By the time Jim made it home, his parents had moved in with his family. Almost immediately upon his arrival, he was forced to kill a man threatening his family and it would not be the last life he took. It was one of many. As his remaining coworkers reached their own homes, only violence and trouble awaited them. One by one, each took Jim up on his offer to come reside in the valley where his family made their home. Over the course of their struggles together, they became a clan. They helped each other and worked together to improve their odds of survival.

In the midst of a cold winter there was a flicker of hope. There were signs that electrical power might soon be restored to parts of the country. People were ecstatic until they realized there were strings attached. Power would initially only be restored to large "comfort camps" in each community, which locals could enter *if* they turned in their guns.

It was a divisive issue, turning families against each other and splitting communities, but the price for power was too steep for Jim. Angered that power generated locally, with local coal, was primarily being routed to the Northern Virginia and Washington, DC area, Jim struck back. He chose to flood the power plant by damming a nearby river. While he succeeded in seriously damaging the plant, his actions had repercussions beyond any he could imagine.

Rumors spread in the community that he was behind the attack. Jim tried to curtail the gossip, afraid it would endanger his family, but it was impossible to contain. Many people had been willing to turn in their guns for comfort. They were angry that Jim had made this bold decision without them. Some said he condemned the weak and elderly to death.

As a result, flyers were spread over the region offering a reward for Jim. He was labeled a terrorist, an insurgent, and an enemy combatant. People came for him, attacking his valley and his home in a desire to collect the reward of food and ammunition. Attacks came with increasing frequency and ferocity. Even folks within his isolated valley began turning on him. Seeing no route to safety, Jim and his group launched a desperate campaign to fake his arrest. The scenario turned into a violent fiasco that brought even more death and destruction to his hometown. When it was done, Jim was left hiding on his property like a trapped animal, questioning the decisions he'd made.

Had he saved his friends and family or doomed them?

# 1

----

JIM WAS WALKING THE DUSTY, debris-strewn road through his valley when he met the group of strangers. He was on his way to Lloyd's house, a musician friend who'd joined them in the valley not long after Jim got home from Richmond. Jim didn't hear the strangers coming and he wasn't used to meeting people on the road. He simply came around a corner and there they were, maybe two hundred feet ahead of him and walking in his direction.

He mumbled a few curses but couldn't think of a single counter-measure that wouldn't appear suspicious. He couldn't leap into the bushes and hide. He couldn't turn and run. He couldn't haul his rifle off his back and threaten them.

He'd changed his appearance as best he could, trying *not* to look like the photo of him that had widely been circulated on the flyers that branded him an insurgent. Most of the town should believe he was dead but he couldn't be sure of that. He didn't want to take any chances.

He'd grown his short beard out into a longer version that put him in touch with his inner hillbilly. His hair had always been short but after that whole fiasco in town he'd shorn it down nearly to his scalp, using some manual clippers he'd borrowed from Lloyd. The musician had been a barber before the collapse, though Jim never trusted him to cut his hair. He'd known him too long.

Lloyd had laughed his ass off at Jim when he first saw him like that. "You should have let me do it. You look like some hipster trying to get a job as a barista at Starbucks."

Jim had snarled at him. "The difference between me and that hipster is that they'd try to use their words to hurt you. I'll deliver a words-and-whoop-ass combo meal. If that's what you're hungry for, keep running your mouth."

Along with the changes to his hair and beard, Jim wore dark glasses and a floppy straw hat that shaded his face. Pete thought he resembled Billy Gibbons, the guitarist from ZZ Top. Jim took that as a compliment.

Since he couldn't dodge the folks headed toward him on the road, he'd just have to keep his head down and hope for the best. If they spoke, he'd nod and keep going. The longer he stood there talking, the more opportunity they'd have to figure out who he was. He couldn't let that happen. Jim Powell was supposed to be dead and he wanted to keep it that way.

Without making a big deal of it, Jim moved his hand to the pistol grip of the M4 hanging across his body. Before he was close enough for them to hear, he flicked the safety off. It was best to err on the side of caution.

They were seventy feet apart now. The strangers were two men with what Jim guessed to be their teenage sons. They weren't from the valley and Jim didn't recognize them. The men carried hunting shotguns and their sons carried .22 rifles. Jim wondered if the men had come back here to hunt or were they here on other business? They could have been visiting one of the other families in the valley.

Even if this was a social call, they'd carry weapons. Everyone traveled with weapons these days. It was the only way to stay safe and even that was no guarantee.

These strangers could also be looking for him, wanting to confirm the rumor that Jim Powell, the man who'd brought so much grief and destruction to his community, was really dead. Did the townspeople still think there was a price on his head?

Surely after all that happened in town on the 4th of July people would understand there was no reward to collect. Those who'd seen what transpired that day would have seen him shoved into a helicopter and hauled off. That didn't mean people didn't harbor resentment against him because he'd deprived them of electricity and comfort camps. Some hated him for that.

If people came for him, it was as likely to be out of that hatred as anything else. This county had a public enemy now and Jim Powell was that man. He was the vessel for their hate. Everyone wanted someone to blame for all the grief and hardship that had befallen them. Jim was all they had.

At forty feet, the men were looking at him, trying to make eye contact. They were within hailing distance. Politeness and rural custom should have them smiling and greeting each other by this point. Jim did none of those things. He kept his head tipped to where he could see their movements, their guns, below the brim of his hat. His aloofness probably put them on edge, but he was fine with that. These weren't regular times. Everyone was on guard these days. People weren't the same relaxed, casual country folk they'd been a little more than a year ago. They were hardened survivors now, less trustful of their fellow man.

"Howdy," one of the men said, slowing.

Jim didn't speak, just nodding as he'd planned. He walked right by the group, within feet of them, but didn't make eye contact. The next part of the interaction bothered him even more. He had his back to them now. He could feel the armed strangers watching him, wondering about him. He heard them whisper among themselves.

He was certain they were calling him a rude asshole, but that label had lost its ability to bother him long ago. He'd been an asshole before the world had fallen apart. Since then, he'd only gotten better at it. His actions toward these strangers, his *asshole-ness*, surely wouldn't be enough for them to identify him. He couldn't be the only asshole in these parts.

He forced himself to put another hundred feet between them before he glanced over his shoulder. When he did, he found the group had gone on about their business, seemingly unconcerned with him. In the retelling of their excursion, he would be nothing more than a rude and abrupt footnote.

Shortly, Jim climbed a fence to the right of the road and cut across the field to Lloyd's place. It was actually Buddy's old house and their entire clan ached from the loss of the kind old man. Jim couldn't help but think Buddy would have steered him in a better direction had he still been alive. He might have kept Jim from acting in such a rash manner—making decisions and taking steps from which there was no backing up. For the short time they'd had him there, Buddy had been the one man who could talk Jim off the ledge when he was ready to slit throats and sling lead. Without him, Jim was unre-stricted. He was more prone to asking forgiveness than permission, even when having acted with such finality that there was no forgiving.

Jim had to traverse this field to approach Lloyd's place from the back. The Wimmer family lived within sight of Lloyd's place, though thick summer foliage helped to break up the direct sightlines. It was still risky. The Wimmers were a large family and they owned much of the land around Lloyd's place. They were always outside farming or hunting. They'd gotten along with Jim's people at one time but there was a lot of resentment now. His clan had killed one of them for abducting a child. Even though the killing was justified, blood was thicker than reason.

The house the sheriff had been living in was also within sight of Lloyd's place, but Lloyd said he'd moved out, as he'd promised. When Jim had told the sheriff what he was going to do in town, that he intended to fake his death, the sheriff wanted no part of it. He also said he'd be leaving the valley as soon as he was able to. He reminded Jim that he'd come there to help keep the peace and instead found himself immersed in a violent world he wanted no part of. Jim wished him the best but knew he'd find no more peace anywhere else. The sheriff longed for a world that no longer existed. He wanted law and order, wanted people to have respect for their fellow men. All of those things were in short supply.

Jim hoped Lloyd was home. A couple of months ago he'd have called him on the radio before making the hike but he couldn't do that anymore. His voice might be overheard by people who wanted him dead. He was disgusted by the state he found himself in. He was in the valley he'd called home for much of his adult life but didn't dare show his face or talk on the radio. For a man already pissed off at the world, this only further stirred the pot.

"Lloyd!" Jim called, stomping up the porch to announce himself.

With no air conditioning, all the windows were open on the hot summer day. Jim didn't hear an instrument being played so he assumed Lloyd was either asleep or not home. He banged on the metal screen door, the noise loud enough to wake the napping or the dead. "Lloyd!"

"Simmer down," Lloyd growled, his voice coming from an unexpected direction.

Jim spun. He walked to the edge of the porch and saw Lloyd ambling down from the outhouse, hitching his suspenders up onto his shoulders.

"What are you up to?" Jim asked.

Lloyd frowned and gestured back toward the outhouse. "I'd think the answer would be obvious, even to someone with your obvious mental deficits."

"That comment would piss me off if I wasn't already pissed off. Randi with you?"

Lloyd shook his head. "She's taking this gardening thing seriously. That's all she does anymore. Then she passes out around dark."

"She's living the farming life."

"I call it 'hoeing around' but she doesn't think that's funny anymore. Farming ain't for me, though."

"Well, not everyone's cut out to be a drunk, banjo-playing fool either."

"It's about damn time someone appreciated that fact," Lloyd said, climbing the steps to the porch. He pointed to the front door. "Inside or outside?"

Jim wavered for a moment before replying. "How about back porch? It's too damn hot to be inside but I can't risk sitting here by the road. It's too public."

Lloyd went inside and Jim followed him through the door. Lloyd made a detour to pick up a banjo, then a second detour to pick up a jar of red liquid packed full of cherries.

"For medicinal purposes only," Lloyd said, holding the jar aloft.

"What's the ailment today?"

"I claim allergies. What's the matter with you?"

Jim faked a cough. "Asthma."

"That's a good one. I used it yesterday."

"Don't you ever run out of ailments?" Jim asked.

Lloyd shook his head seriously. "They're all chronic, recurring conditions. It's a tragedy really."

"Indeed." Jim held the back door open for him, then took a seat on a metal glider.

Lloyd settled into a wooden ladder-back chair. It had once been painted white and the paint was now peeling off to reveal the past lives the chair had lived, one in green and another in blue. "You pass those people headed down the road? I saw them when I was headed to the johnny house."

Jim plucked a cherry from the moonshine jar with his fingers and tossing it into his mouth. "Yep, but I kept my face hidden. I'm going to have to quit using the road. It's so much faster than going through the fields with everything grown-up, but I just can't risk running into people."

Lloyd took the jar and fished out his own cherry. He washed it down with a sip from the jar. "You could have run into the Wimmers or someone else who hated you. It's a long list. I always thought you should have tried to be a nicer person. Being an asshole has caught up with you."

"It's caught up with me many times in my life. This is only our latest visit."

"It's going to get worse," Lloyd said, settling back into his chair and giving the banjo a strum.

Jim gave his buddy a curious look. "Why?"

Lloyd adjusted one of the tuners, repeatedly twanging a single string until he had it where he wanted it. "The Wimmers are fixing the bridge to town."

Jim sat bolt upright. "Excuse me?"

Lloyd nodded. "One of them told me yesterday. They've been cutting logs off the hillside above the road and using horses to get them in place. It may even be done already."

"Well, that's just great. What's the point of that?"

"They said they've got more cattle than they can manage. They want to sell some off before winter. They've got corn planted and tobacco in the ground they want to sell too. It's hard to blame them for that."

Jim picked the cherry jar up off the floor and helped himself to another, his mind racing as he chewed. "I understand from an economic standpoint but it sure makes this valley harder to keep secure."

"Maybe they think there's less of a need for security. Maybe they think the worst is over and they're ready to start rebuilding what's fallen apart."

Jim looked grim. "I have no confidence that this is over. Part of me feels like it's only the beginning. What we've seen already, with the government wanting to attach aid and power to turning in guns, is a sign of things to come. I'm not ready to accept that kind of America."

Lloyd grinned. "You just going to keep blowing shit up until they come up with a version you like?"

"If I have to."

Lloyd was afraid his friend was a lost cause. "You aren't done pissing people off, are you?"

"Not by a long shot."

**2**

———————

# T*he Valley*

Jim left Lloyd sitting on the back porch, playing his heart out to a field of cows, birds, and the odd rabbit. The couple of moonshine-spiked cherries Jim had eaten did nothing to improve his mood. In fact, they only enhanced his irritation with the state of things. He was walking home through a field of waist-high grass and that pissed him off because it filled his shoes with grass seeds and made his sweaty arms itch. A variety of burrs clung to his clothing. A scowl on his face, he stomped through the grass as if he could scare it out of his way. As he walked, he pondered his situation.

Should he pull up stakes and move his entire family somewhere else? He couldn't imagine doing that. His farm wasn't perfect but he'd spent years putting things in place that made life easier for them. The entire house could be heated with his wood stove. The home had a gravity-fed water system that kept water flowing through the pipes, even if it didn't have a lot of pressure. They could flush toilets and use the sinks, an advantage a lot of folks didn't have.

He also had the spring house with a spring box, the closest thing available to natural refrigeration. While the home itself didn't have solar power, he had a few solar panels that allowed them to keep rechargeable devices operating. Plus, he had the fortified cave at the back of the property.

The idea of moving was ridiculous. Even if he found a better place, how would he get there? How would he be able to make improvements to a new place under these powerless conditions? Then there was his tribe. His clan. The friends he'd surrounded himself with. Was he just going to walk off and leave them?

The valley had some people like the Wimmers, with whom he didn't have a close relationship. In fact, their relationship was now fairly hostile. There were other families like the Weathermans and the Birds with whom he had a friendly relationship but didn't hang out with every day. They supported each other and had each other's backs, but it wasn't the kind of relationship he had with the people who formed his inner circle. That was Lloyd, Alice's son Charlie, Randi's family, Gary's family, and Hugh. They were his people. They were his tribe. For better or worse, they were all in this together.

But were they? Was it right to drag them down with him? The same could be said of his family. Was it right for him to risk their lives because he was public enemy number one?

He stopped and fished a water bottle from a pouch. He took a long pull, trying to replace some of the moisture the high-octane moonshine had pulled out. The water was warm and he'd have much preferred a dipper straight from the spring. That would be his first stop when he got home. Maybe he'd hold his head under the pipe and see if that did anything to extinguish the fires raging in his head.

He was mid-drink when a shotgun blast destroyed the midday calm. A flock of starlings erupted from a maple tree ahead of him. There was a second blast and then Jim was running. At the edge of the field, he entered an isolated forest, an island of trees surrounded on all sides by pastures. Logging roads laced through the remaining timber. Jumbled slash piles of stumps and trash logs were scattered along the path.

The roads had once been maintained but now weeds were taking over. Scrappy wild roses with their pink and white flowers tore at Jim's legs. Blackberry vines raked across his upper body. He tried to brush them out of his way but one caught his cheek. Another snagged his neck, the cut burning as sweat ran into the torn flesh. Stinging nettles grew thick, nearly at the height of Jim's elbows. Each time he brushed against a leaf, he felt the burn. His arms grew red and irritated, the outside of his body becoming a reflection of the turmoil that was going on within him.

There was another shotgun blast. Jim was certain it came from his place now. He wanted to use the radio and ask what was going on but he didn't chance it. What if it was a snake or a rabid skunk they were dealing with? He couldn't expose himself for something that trivial. What if it wasn't though?

He topped the low ridge and started down the far side. In winter, he could see his house from here but now the thick leaves of poplars, maples, and oaks formed a green wall through which he only caught snatches of the world beyond. He kept to his jogging pace, his rifle held across his body to keep it from beating him to death as he ran.

In another eighty yards, he was halfway down the hill and a gap opened in the tree canopy. He paused and squinted. Sweat ran into his eyes, burning as he tried to blink it away. He pulled out a cheap monocular and studied the scene in his yard. His family was standing in the front yard with Hugh, studying something on the ground. Jim couldn't make out what it was, but he was less alarmed now. Everyone appeared safe. If there had been a threat, it either passed or they'd dealt with it.

Jim stowed the monocular and got moving again. In about three minutes, he was crossing his yard like a lost prospector staggering into an oasis. The humidity and exertion had done him in. He'd sweated through his clothes and was gasping open-mouthed, trying to breathe through the soupy air.

Ellen hurried toward him. "You okay?"

Jim took off his wide-brimmed hat and dropped it. He paused in the shade of the maple that dominated the front yard. He gasped one question. "Shooting?"

Ellen took Jim by the arm, apparently more concerned with him than whatever had taken place in his absence. Hugh pointed to something on the ground. Jim stared at it but couldn't figure out what it was. It looked like a kid's toy that had been run over by a car. Pete and Ariel were walking around the yard picking up more pieces and adding them to the pile.

"What is it?" Jim asked.

"Honey, it's a drone," Ellen said.

Jim looked at Hugh for confirmation.

Hugh nodded. "It *was* a drone. I was on my way down here to check in and see if you guys needed any help in the garden. I thought I heard a hummingbird but I didn't see one. Then I decided it must be a swarm of bees. It wasn't. When I caught sight of it, I could tell it was a drone hovering over this general area of the valley."

Jim moved closer to the pile and studied the pieces. He dropped to his knees, set his rifle to the side, and picked up a few of them. "You know anything about this stuff?"

"It's a consumer-grade drone," Hugh replied. "You can get them anywhere but they're not cheap. It could be someone that lives in the area or it could be the cops. It could have been something some kids stole and were playing with. It doesn't look military but who knows. It could have been anyone."

"You think it could be coincidence?" Pops asked.

Jim was shaking his head in disgust. "It was in my yard."

"It could have been looking for you," Hugh conceded. "But we don't know that for sure."

"It might be coincidence," Ellen said. "Like Hugh said, we don't know that it was here for you."

"But we don't know that it *wasn't*," Jim said. "I don't like it. I don't like this at all. Does it mean there are people still looking for me? Was our production in town not convincing? Did we go to all that trouble —all that risk—for nothing?"

"The fact this thing went missing might draw some attention," Hugh pointed out. "The owners might come looking for it. The good thing is that no one likes a drone flying over their place. With the state of the world, they can complain all they want and no one is going to be able to do a damn thing about it."

"Are these pieces trackable?" Jim asked. "Have you destroyed everything?"

Hugh nodded. "I checked it. Everything is dead. I'm going to bag the pieces and hang them on a fence post on the road into town. Thought I might also leave some menacing message in the bag with them. Maybe that will scare them off."

"It could have been random," Ellen said.

"I can't take that chance," Jim said.

His wife stared at him. "What can you do any differently than what you're doing now? You're already living like a prisoner on your own property."

Jim stared at the pile of shattered electronics in his yard. "It's just going to get worse."

"How do you know that?" Ellen asked.

"The Wimmers are rebuilding the road into town. I just found out from Lloyd. The road is going to be open any day now and more people will be coming through the valley."

"But why?" Ellen asked, her voice pleading.

"Commerce obviously," Pops said. "It was only a matter of time before farmers wanted to get things moving again. They've got a product and there's demand. They might as well sell it."

"You could blow the bridge up. *Again*," Pete said with a wicked grin.

Jim smiled back at his son. "There's no point, Pete. They'd just build it back. Plus, they think I'm dead. Intentionally sabotaging their efforts would either make them suspicious or they'd blame someone in our group. We can't risk that. We have to let them keep going with it."

"More people in the valley means more theft," Ellen said. "There will be sightseers. There will be people scoping out things to steal.

That's why we blew the bridges in the first place. That's why we put guard posts along the road."

They'd quit manning their observation posts along the valley road since Jim's supposed death. Mostly because they needed all hands working on the various crops they were trying to raise. Pops and Randi were in charge of the gardens but they had every able body working in them. It took a lot of hands to keep deer fencing in place and the weeds down. Then there was the harvesting, processing, and preservation of the vegetables.

"We could put people back in those lookout posts?" Pete suggested.

Ellen shook her head. "We can't spare the people. We need everyone in the gardens."

"Speaking of which, I have rounds to make," Pops said. "Where's my assistant?"

"Here!" Ariel said, dumping the last of her drone scraps in the pile and taking Pops' hand.

When Pops and Ariel were gone, Jim looked around. "Where's Nana?"

"We have canning going," Ellen said. "She's watching it."

"Well, let's clean this drone up and go to the barn. We need to talk."

**3**

———

T *he Valley*

JIM DUMPED his Nalgene bottle of lukewarm water onto the ground as he walked, then swung by the springhouse to refill it. A plastic pipe jutting from the wall dumped fifty-eight-degree water into a concrete basin in a constant stream. Jim took a long pull from the bottle, then refilled it before joining Hugh, Ellen, and Pete in the barn.

Pete and Hugh were sitting on upturned five-gallon buckets, talking about deer they'd seen lately. Ellen sat on a rusty folding chair, her arms and legs crossed anxiously. Jim took a perch on a hay bale with one broken string. The rolling doors on both sides of the barn were open to catch the faint breeze moving on the sweltering day. With its dirt floor and cavernous spaces, the barn always felt cooler than the rest of the world and it was appreciated on the August day.

Jim liked the barn. He took it in as he sat there, like a man revisiting the old neighborhood where he'd grown up. He'd always felt comfortable there with the tractor, the mower, and the animal feed. A blue barrel held shovels, rakes, and other implements of destruction. The poplar interior walls were decorated with old pulleys, pieces of hand-wrought hardware, and a few hubcaps from antique cars. There were buckets of chains and a shelf with the various things needed to keep equipment running—lubricants, starting fluid, fuel treatments, and grease. A pile of old doors leaned against one wall. Hooks on another wall held tractor pins, a big hammer, and a roll of air hose.

"I need to get out of here for a while," Jim said.

The group stared at him blankly but he waited patiently, giving them time to process what he'd said.

"What exactly do you mean by that?" Ellen said after a long moment.

Hugh was the only one who seemed to know where this was going. He looked unsurprised, watching Jim with an owlish expression. Jim knew the look. Hugh was waiting to see how Jim was going to talk his way through this without his wife smacking him upside the head.

"It's unsafe for me to be here right now," Jim said. "Unsafe for me and for all of you. There are too many people out moving around, too much activity. Inevitably, unless I stay in the basement like some kind of troll, someone is going to recognize me. Word is going to get out and you'll all be at risk again. I don't want that to happen. I don't want to go back to the way I felt earlier this summer, wondering if we were going to be attacked at any moment."

Ellen had that look on her face. She didn't like what she was hearing. "It could be months before life slows down here. When the days get shorter and the air gets colder people will start staying inside more, but not until then. You're talking two or three months."

"I realize that," Jim said. "Two or three months is probably what would be required."

Ellen didn't want to have this conversation. She wanted her husband to stay at home, wanted her family to stay together. "And what are we supposed to do without you? How are we supposed to get by?"

"You'd be fine. It's not like the early days of the collapse when you all were struggling and alone. You have a community now and everyone here knows the routine. You guys know how to run the house, you know how to respond to situations, and you've got all these folks who are part of our family now—Hugh, Randi's family, Charlie, and Gary's people. All of them would help."

Pete held up a finger. "You didn't mention Lloyd."

"I'm not sure he's any help," Jim said.

Ellen raised an eyebrow in acknowledgment. "He tries. Sometimes. Bless his heart."

"You've got a houseful of people," Jim said. "Charlie's been staying with Randi's family a lot but I'm sure he'd be willing to stay up here more if you needed him to."

"If you don't mind me staying in the shop, I'd be glad to come down and stick around at night," Hugh offered. "I don't think you're going to run into any trouble but it would be an extra set of hands if something did happen."

"That's a kind offer," Jim said. "I appreciate that, Hugh."

"I'm down here most of the time anyway, helping with the crops. I could help Pete and Charlie with the firewood situation if they had any trouble. I'd just need to head up to my place every so often to make sure the bears aren't wrecking the joint."

Jim looked at his wife, raising an eyebrow to see if she was willing to consider the offer. The fiery look in her eyes said this was far from over.

"You and I have some talking to do in private, Jim Powell."

He understood it wasn't over yet. "In this case, our private business affects all these people. That's why I asked them to be here."

"I get that, but are you seriously planning on a three-month camping trip in the woods by yourself? I won't hear from you? I won't know if you're dead or alive? How do you think that's going to affect your family?"

"Any means by which I could check in with you only presents further risk. If I come back to visit, I risk being seen. If I get within radio range and reach out to Hugh, I risk being heard. I feel like if I go, I have to stay gone until the weather turns colder."

When Ellen replied, there were tears in her eyes. Her cheeks were flushed. In those indications that she was conceding, Jim found no victory. He felt awful. He was again reminded that the actions he'd taken had led them all to this point. This was his fault.

"As shitty as the last year has been, there have been good parts," Ellen began. "We weren't buried in our individual lives. It used to be that you were always at work or working here on the farm. The kids were engrossed in electronics. I was either at work, running them all over the place, or trying to keep the house from descending into chaos. The highlight of this whole mess is that we've been a family again. We've worked as a family and we've rediscovered each other. One day the world will get back to normal but we've had this time that no one can take away. Despite the challenges, I'll always remember that as a gift."

Jim was nodding as she spoke. "I get it. I've felt the same way. It's like we were transported back to a simpler time. I've enjoyed parts of it too. You and I talked about that in the beginning. I felt a lot of guilt because in some ways I wanted the world to reset. Then, when it did, people died. People suffered."

"You didn't cause the world to reset, Jim," Hugh said. "I wanted it too but I'm no more responsible for it happening than you are. This was terrorism and we weren't the terrorists."

Jim smiled at the irony of Hugh's words. "Some people seem to think I'm a terrorist now. They hunted me down like a terrorist. Some would like to see me executed like a terrorist."

"That will fade over time, Jim. In our grandparents' day, and even before that, when people got into trouble they often had to go away until things cooled off. It was the way things were done," Hugh said. "My mom's grandfather shot a man who pulled a knife on him at a barn dance at Finney. It was justified but his family wanted to kill my great-grandfather. He went to Cincinnati and lived for a couple of years before coming home. He got some hard looks when he came home and there were some words exchanged, but the fire had burned out."

"This fire may never burn out," Jim said.

"There are things you can change and things you can't change," Hugh said. "You can't control whether this fire ever burns out or not. If you want to get out of here for a while, I fully support that decision. I'll do whatever you need me to do."

"I appreciate that."

Hugh gestured at Pete. "Let's get out of here for a while and let the grown-ups talk."

Pete got to his feet and Jim noticed that he seemed taller than he had even a day earlier. He was at that stage where kids changed fast, beginning to resemble the adult they would become.

"You a kid too?" Pete asked Hugh.

Hugh winked. "Always, bud. I'm never getting old."

When they were gone, Jim got up and started pacing. He was never good at sitting when there was thinking to be done. He was startled when Ellen shot up from her chair and flew at him, arms wide. She wrapped them around him and held him tight, her face pressed against his chest. Jim held her there, feeling her tears soak through his already damp t-shirt, warm against his skin.

"This is a shitty idea, Jim."

"Do you have a better one?"

"No," she said, the words distorted by her anguish.

"Do you understand why I need to do this?"

"Understanding doesn't help. It doesn't make me feel any better."

"I'm not sure I have it in me to make you feel better about this," Jim said. "I only know that I couldn't live with any of you being hurt because people were hunting me."

"That stupid drone may not mean anything."

Jim shrugged. "Yeah, but it might mean something. If I'm back in a few months, I can stay on the farm all winter and do a lot of my work outside at night. Who knows what things will be like by the time warm weather returns next spring? Maybe there will be enough order restored that people won't care about me anymore."

Jim fell silent, not believing the words even as he said them. He didn't feel confident in the restoration of order and what that might mean for anyone's safety. He had no faith in things ever being the way they used to be. It all depended on who was left standing when the powers in Washington finished their game of dodgeball.

"I'm going to head over to Gary's place in a few. I want to let him know what's going on. On the way back, I'll track down Randi and let her know the deal."

"Well, if I can't talk you out of it, when are you going to leave?"

"Tomorrow night," Jim said. "I'll ride out around dark. That gives me tonight and tomorrow to get my supplies in order."

"Where will you even go?"

"I want to get up on Beartown Mountain and scout out a bugout location for us in case we absolutely can't stay here any longer. I'll probably head to Laurel Bed Lake from there. After that, I don't know."

Ellen nodded against Jim's chest, her head bobbing slightly. "Okay."

"I need you to be strong. I need you to help the kids feel comfortable with this. I'll need your confidence to get through it because it's going to be tough on me too. There will be a lot of time to think. Too much time to think."

"These will be my last tears for your decision, Jim Powell. From this point, it's all about counting the days until you're home again."

Jim hugged his wife harder, trying to wring those last tears from her.

## 4

T *he Valley*

THE NEXT MORNING, Jim was up early squaring away his gear. He'd made his visits yesterday to Gary's family and to Randi. Both promised to regularly check on Ellen and see if she needed anything. Jim had no doubts that this was the case. With gardening season in full swing, his clan interacted daily. They'd started gardens at each house, utilizing the old garden spots that the previous residents had used for decades. They all pitched in at each other's houses, finding that working together made the days go faster. Weeding and watering weren't such drudgeries when you could carry on a conversation to pass the time.

Jim had decided the previous night that he'd be taking a horse and a packhorse. They had several animals now. Some had been found wandering in the hills, starving and covered in burrs. Others had been taken in skirmishes over the past year. Having a horse would allow him to travel faster and live more comfortably than if he was attempting this journey on foot. He'd be able to carry spare ammo for his weapons and take a few conveniences.

He didn't have any traditional saddlebags or horse packs, but he had a couple of high-volume packs they'd taken off the dead. He'd found an English riding saddle in an abandoned barn and used that as the basis of his system. No one wanted to ride with that saddle so he might as well adapt it into something useful. He hooked the two backpacks together at the shoulder straps and affixed them to the saddle. They would ride high and balanced on the horse, the saddle keeping them from sliding to either side.

Being an organized and methodical packer, Jim had the items he was taking laid out on the porch so he could see everything before he packed it away. He was constantly weighing which items he'd need and which he could leave behind. He had water filtration and plenty of cooking gear, including a lightweight grate from an old charcoal grill that he could cook over. He even took a cast-iron skillet, something he'd never carry on a backpacking trip. He had a small jar of lard and hoped to find some fresh fish or rabbits to cook. He had a tent, a hammock, two tarps, and plenty of rope. There was an ax and a machete. There was a fire-building kit with plenty of tinder and several methods of getting a blaze going.

Jim was taking the M4 he carried each day. He had a cleaning kit and a spare parts kit for it. He took a lot of loaded magazines and five hundred loose rounds. They were heavy and he split them between each pack but it was the minimum amount he felt comfortable taking. If he needed more than that, he'd have to make a trip home to restock. He carried his Beretta 92 because he was comfortable with the weapon. He'd carried it for years before the Army ever adopted the M9 and he never had any issues with it. He only had a couple of spare mags for it but he carried several boxes of ammo.

After a lot of waffling, he decided to wear his plate carrier with the plates in it. A man on a horse was a tall, visible target and there were a lot of people out there who'd kill a man just to see what he was carrying. Armor wasn't a guarantee of survival but it would allow him to breathe easier.

Fixed across the front of the plate carrier was a handgun Jim didn't usually carry unless he was backpacking. It was his 10mm Glock 29. It was a decent weapon for black bears and the mountain he was ascending was thick with them. Although Jim had hiked all over the eastern US, the majority of his scary bear encounters had been in the mountains close to home. After dealing with one persistent bear that refused to go away, Jim had purchased the 10mm to carry with him on future trips. He had two boxes of heavy cast bear loads for the weapon and they were going with him.

He packed a set of good binoculars and some of the military nightvision they'd liberated in battles with better-equipped men. It was a far sight better than the "toy" nightvision he'd used on his trip home from Richmond. The cheap stuff was better than nothing but you couldn't walk or fight with it.

Jim was checking his spread of gear against his written list when he heard whistling in the yard behind him. He found Lloyd ambling toward him and, oddly enough, he wasn't carrying a musical instrument slung over his back this time.

"What's up?" Jim asked.

"I'm going with you."

Jim was taken aback. "Excuse me?"

"I said I'm going with you," Lloyd repeated. "I'm going stir crazy in this damn place. Randi told me you were getting away from here for a few months and I want to go."

"Why?"

Lloyd took a seat on the steps, leaning back against a porch post. He wiped the sweat from his forehead with the tail of his shirt. "This has been hard on me. Harder than I've let on. At the barbershop, I saw people every day. I was talking to people all day. Several nights a week I was out there playing music and meeting more new people. I'm not used to sitting around by myself. I'm used to having new blood and I'm going nuts."

Jim considered his friend's words. "This won't be an easy trip. There will be months of camping, dealing with the bugs and the weather. There may be trouble."

"I can deal with the trouble if I'm out there doing new things. It's eating at me here. I hate this feeling of sitting around waiting for the next shootout. I hate having to be on guard against attack all the time. As I've said many times, I'm a lover and not a fighter."

Jim grinned. "I thought Randi said you were neither."

"Any response I could offer would be ungentlemanly and therefore I'll let that pass."

That cracked Jim up. "What does she think of this idea of you going off on an adventure with me?"

"She gets it. She understands I need the break. She also thinks we'll both have a better chance of surviving if we go as a team."

Jim gave him a doubtful glance. "I'm still waiting for the part about how hauling your ass along with me improves *my* odds of survival. You drink too much and train too little. Just what do you bring to the table?"

"Companionship," Lloyd said. "I can also pull a shift if we need to keep watch."

"So far you're running neck and neck with a dog. That all you got?"

Lloyd screwed up his mouth as he searched his mental resume. "I can provide comic relief. I'm well known for my sense of humor."

Jim conceded the point. "Okay, maybe you're slightly better than a dog but your impression of your sense of humor is over-inflated. You're funniest when you aren't even aware of what you're doing."

"In other words, when you're laughing *at* me and not *with* me?"

Jim smiled and pointed at him. "Exactly!"

"That doesn't lessen my contribution to the expedition, does it?"

Jim considered. "I guess not."

"Then can I go?"

"I'm leaving at sundown tonight. You'll need to be ready then if you're going. Pack carefully and make sure you have everything you need. I'm not babysitting you. If we get up on that mountain and you aren't prepared, you can march your happy ass back home."

"Are we walking or riding?"

"Riding."

"Can I borrow a horse?"

Jim sighed deeply. "Yes."

"And a pack?"

Another sigh. "Yes."

Jim led him across the yard to the storage building that the family called The Daddy Shack. There was even a sign on the door to that effect. It was where the family stored their camping and outdoor gear. Despite the fact that the family was using much of their camping gear to survive everyday life now, the contents of the building had not dwindled. In fact, there were piles and piles of gear stacked in the building. The spoils of war.

Life in the valley had not been peaceful. They had fought off invaders intent on stealing cattle. They had fought off bounty hunters there to kidnap Jim for the reward. They had killed United Nations soldiers and private military contractors in their mission to flood the power plant. With each fight, they collected weapons and ammunition, they collected coats, packs, and gear. Everything was split between the various families of the clan and this was where Jim kept his loot.

He sorted through a stack of backpacks and selected one for Lloyd. It was high volume but cheap. It wouldn't matter so much since he'd be strapping it to the back of his horse and not wearing it on his shoulders. Jim handed the pack over to his friend, then tugged a thick garbage compactor trash bag off a roll.

"You can't trust the waterproofing on a pack like this. Line it with this bag to keep your gear dry."

Lloyd shoved the plastic bag into the pack and held it aloft, like a victory trophy. "Thanks! You won't regret it."

Seeing Lloyd's excitement made Jim feel bad about giving him so much shit, but he wanted to make sure Lloyd knew what he was getting into. This wouldn't be a picnic, but Lloyd didn't seem to care. Jim had to admit he liked the idea of having a companion on the trip. It would make things a bit less lonely. It might keep him from becoming too pensive and depressed.

He had to be careful and not give the impression he was excited about the trip though. Ellen would be pissed if she got the idea he was going off on a fun adventure and leaving her to take care of things. While he was excited on one level at getting out of the neighborhood, this would not be a vacation. It would be an uncomfortable throwback to his trip home from Richmond when he was constantly consumed with fear for his family's safety.

His only comfort was in the fact that his friends and family had grown in their level of preparedness since then. They'd all become warriors. From his children to his wife to his parents, from Gary to Randi to Charlie—they were all survivors who could think on their feet and handle any situation life threw at them. Except for Hugh, of course. He'd always kind of been that way. Years ago, when the world was still peaceful, he was always a little too intense. Now there was no one Jim would feel more comfortable entrusting his family to.

$$5$$

## T *he Valley*

As the sky reddened with the sunset, the hazy August evening glowed with golden light. Everything took on that magical quality that kept you outside, unable to tear yourself away from the closing of the day, the end of the show. The air was still and the creatures of evening were coming to life. Frogs chanted from the creek. Crickets sawed at their own symphony. Owls hooted from scattered perches on the mountainside, their sound traveling like an accusation.

A fire crackled in Jim's fire pit, Pete feeding in small branches in an effort to drive the bugs away. The river brought its blessings and its curses, mosquitoes being among the latter. It was a somber moment. They were waiting for Lloyd's arrival. Randi had walked a horse up to his place earlier.

"If we have to wait on him to carry his stuff down here he'll never show up," she complained. "He'll fall over and get stuck on his back like a turtle."

Her daughters were at home with her grandchildren. It was the same with Gary's family. Only Gary and his son-in-law Will came to see Jim off. This wasn't out of any animosity or lack of concern. Both families felt it was a personal moment, a goodbye that those less connected with Jim had no business being part of. Jim would have been fine with it either way. He wasn't a people person but, for better or worse, they were all bonded now. They shared even when it was uncomfortable.

Everyone around the fire was lost in their own thoughts. Ariel, often a standoffish child, wouldn't leave her father's side. She wasn't happy about his decision. She didn't understand the nuance of the situation. To her, it was Daddy going away after he promised he'd never do that again. The only consolation he could offer was to point to the distant Beartown Mountain, the green crest that loomed over their backyard, and offer to take her there one day.

She'd asked him to take pictures and for that reason alone he was taking his worthless iPhone and the solar charger that kept it powered. The availability of that phone and the pictures it contained was a double-edged sword. Looking at pictures of his family on that original desperate walk home from Richmond had been motivating, but it had also opened chasms of pain and longing. Seeing pictures of the things he and his family had done had made him feel blessed at one moment and a failure at others.

Sometimes it made him wonder why they hadn't been out camping every weekend. Why had he not spent every second with them doing the things they loved to do? But life couldn't be that way. Other things had to be done and people forgot about those responsibilities in the warm glow of memory. They forgot about the daily hassles, the exhaustion of raising small children, and the pressures of work—all those little things that kept them from playing all the time.

"I hear them," Ellen said.

Jim cocked an ear and picked it up as well, the clop of hooves on the hard-packed farm road. A year ago that sound would have been the crunch of hooves on gravel but the earth was swallowing the stone. Grass and mud were reclaiming the earth from Jim's efforts to shape it. He rose from the wooden bench where he sat with his daughter, giving her tiny shoulders a squeeze before he stood. His horse and the packhorse were already loaded. They stood tied to the fence, occasionally shifting or switching their tails at bugs.

Jim hugged his wife and was pleased that she didn't seem upset. She was already switching gears, ready to assume her new responsibilities in his absence. She had to push emotion aside and be strong. She was strong, of course. He'd always known it and she'd consistently proven it, but that didn't mean his absence would be easy. They'd been there before and no one wanted to revisit that dark period. Jim's only consolation was that things would be different this time. She had support and community. She had backup.

Lloyd came into view, leading his horse. Randi walked alongside him. Everyone stopped to watch them approach. The pair paused at the fence and Lloyd tied his horse a few posts away from Jim's. Before joining the group, he gave Randi the same kind of weak hug you might give a little old lady who made you a pan of brownies.

Not impressed with the gesture, Randi grabbed him and pulled him into a kiss. When she broke it off, she noticed she had an audience. "What the hell you all gawping at?"

Jim snickered and cued up a remark, then thought better of it. There was nothing he liked more than giving Randi grief, but she'd probably punch him. He didn't want to spend the night riding with internal bleeding.

"You have something to say?" Randi asked, noticing Jim's expression.

"Not a word," Jim replied.

Randi nodded with satisfaction. "That's what I thought."

Jim said his goodbyes to the rest of his family. His dad assured him he'd take good care of everyone and keep an eye on the gardens. His mom was short, not pleased with the prospect of her son riding off into the wild blue yonder. She frequently found herself questioning his decisions.

He hugged Pete and reminded him of how proud he was of him, then did the same with Alice's son Charlie. He shook hands with

Gary and Will, then even had a hug for Randi. He returned to his wife and kissed her goodbye, then stood there pondering. "Is there anyone I've forgotten?"

Ariel gave him a frown. "Me, loser."

Jim grinned. "Oh yeah." He pulled Ariel up into a tight hug.

"Don't forget my pictures," she said.

"I won't."

He put her down and she looked away. She wasn't ready to cry but he could tell she was sad. He'd drawn this out long enough. "Let's hit the trail, Festus," he said to Lloyd, referring to the drawling deputy from the old western, *Gunsmoke*.

"Sure thing, Marshal Matt," Lloyd drawled, falling into character and limping toward his horse.

Jim fought the urge to repeat his round of farewells. This was painful enough already. He walked toward his horse feeling the eyes of his loved ones on his back, untied the long lead for the packhorse, then untied his own mount. He climbed into the saddle and rode toward his family. He and Lloyd would be leaving through the back gate, cutting through the field toward Rockdell Farms rather than using the road.

Passing his family, he offered waves and smiles that felt completely ridiculous when weighed against the step he was taking. He was hit with a surge of doubt and second-guessing himself. Hell, wouldn't it be better for him to simply hide in the basement? At least then he'd be there for his family and could help them if he needed to.

He couldn't do it, though. He hoped they understood this was how it had to go. He needed to give it time to cool off. If there were people out there determined to keep looking for him, he had to give them time to satisfy their curiosity. Eventually, someone would find a position where they could watch his house and he wouldn't be there for them to see. Word would spread and people would forget about him.

Or so he prayed.

Pete ran ahead and opened the narrow gate that separated the yard from the pasture. It was a new addition Jim had put in place since foot traffic had changed the way they moved around the property. The driveway was no longer the main way in and out. People took shortcuts. Jim smiled and thanked his son when he rode through. As the last orange crescent of sun dropped below the ridge, Jim turned and waved at his family.

Without waiting for their returning waves, he spun his horse and trotted off. Behind him, he heard Pete swing the gate shut, then the rattle of chain as he fastened it. Jim stared ahead. He'd traveled through this very field more times than he could count over the last year. Never had it felt like this. Never had it left him feeling so unsettled.

Lloyd began singing Gene Autry. *"I'm back in the saddle again. Out where a friend is a friend."*

Jim groaned. "I can put up with a lot of shit, but I'm not spending three months listening to cowboy songs. I ain't in the mood."

"I brought my banjo. You rather hear a banjo tune? I can play Dueling Banjos."

"I'm more concerned about whether you remembered a gun or not."

Lloyd pulled up alongside him, giving Jim his first close look at his packing efforts. Lloyd's pack was cinched behind the saddle. A soft banjo case was strapped atop that. Lloyd had a pump shotgun hooked over the saddle horn. With his demonstrated lack of marksmanship ability, a scattergun was a solid approach.

"You brought more shells for that?"

"I've got two hundred or so mixed shotgun shells. Stuff we took off the dead."

"I'm assuming your .32 pistol is on you somewhere?"

Lloyd shook his head. "Nope, you hurt its feelings. You've insulted that .32 for the last time. I left it with one of Randi's daughters. I'm carrying Buddy's old Colt 1911."

"That's a solid choice, Lloyd." Jim dabbed at a fake tear. "It's like you've finally grown up. I'm so proud of you."

"About damn time."

After a few minutes, they passed by Randi's house. No one was out. They continued on through the fields, following a path barely visible in the tall, uncut hay. A little further along they topped a rise and were able to see down onto Gary's house, the place that used to belong to Jim's old friend Henry.

They descended the hill above Gary's place to a creek that ran behind his house. It was the feature of the property that his grandchildren found most entertaining. Many summer afternoons Ariel would join them to wade in the creek and catch crawdads. The mothers and grandmothers found it relaxing not just because it occupied the children but because it was nice to see them playing and happy.

The salmon-colored clouds high above them reflected in the still pool of the dark creek. Just beyond the swimming hole, the pair rode through a gap in the fence and climbed onto the road. This was the same spot where they'd fought the folks from Washington County. Those people had initially come to the area to buy cattle, then decided it might be a good place to resettle. The only thing they needed to do was drive out the locals.

The locals, Jim and his neighbors, weren't thrilled about that prospect and it ended in violence. Signs of that battle remained. A few burned-out vehicles were scattered along the roadside. Trash from their encampments littered the field, much of it picked over of anything useful.

They didn't stay on the road, simply crossing it to resume their progress following alongside the lazy creek. They were on Rockdell Farms property, the fields vast and clear. They were untended now, the cattle wild and the hay uncut for the first time in two centuries. This was old country, long-populated and touched by the hand of man. With a lapse in efforts, it took no time for the world to begin erasing man's presence. Weeds and grass grew to hide the scars, gravity tugged at the structures, and rain and wind eroded.

In another mile they crossed the second and last paved road between them and their destination. It was Route 80, a modern road that followed an ancient path over Clinch Mountain. Native Americans had used it for trading and for obtaining salt from nearby

Saltville. In fact, all these lands had hosted centuries of villages and hunting parties. Each year when the fields were plowed anew, relic hunters scoured the soil for arrowheads, spear points, fish hooks, paint pots, and various other remnants of the Native American presence.

Not long after crossing Route 80, the terrain changed from flat bottomland to the rolling pastures that made up the foothills of the mountain. They saw no one and smelled no fires. There were no homes for miles in any direction, which was part of why Jim had chosen this route. They stuck to the existing farm road so they'd be able to use the gates when they hit interior cross-fencing.

The light faded and stripped the color from the world. The land went from green to gray, only the sky able to retain its tinge of blue. The farm road climbed and rolled, taking them higher with each passing mile.

"I hope you know where you're going," Lloyd mumbled.

"Don't tell me you're getting tired. You ain't doing nothing. Your horse is doing all the work."

"I'm holding on."

Jim snorted. "To your sobriety? Your sanity?"

"Both, and it's wearing me out."

"There's a place I want to see. Maybe a twenty-minute ride from here. We'll overnight there. It's secluded."

6

Beartown Mountain

As the pair of riders climbed in elevation, the foothills about them rippled with ambling geographic convolutions. Who knew why these mountains had formed this particular way in their ancient upsurge from the core of the Earth? In some ways the logic of mountains was no more decipherable than that of men, their inspiration often lost and obfuscated with time. As with men and mountains, sometimes the monument to their existence was plain and featureless, an ordinary life. Other times, it stood so bold and glaring upon the land that one could not turn away.

When this particular mountain rose from the mantle of the Earth, it did so without thought to being there three hundred and twenty million years later. It did so without regard for how people would look upon it and the emotions it might provoke. Yet people did look upon its towering presence and they cast their own judgments.

It was often the same with the cruelty and ill deeds of men, the impacts of an individual life that remained when the flesh was long buried and gone. The words spoken, the actions, could shape lives for generations. Those actions themselves sometimes became monuments, the legacy of the departed. They rose above the plane of an otherwise featureless life to become the peak from which everything else was viewed. One decision could become the feature that defined everything. The single point which overshadowed every other year, every single moment, and every word a person ever uttered.

Sometimes those accomplishments, those peaks, were moments of heroism, where someone rose above the fray to save lives. Other times it was a person becoming a leader at a time when there was a void to be filled. Those mountains that stood within a life could also be negative. Like the ill-planned coupling between incapable, incompatible, and incomplete humans who turned their children out like dogs to fend for themselves in the world. Like the blurry barroom decisions that resulted in drunken fatalities and shattered families. Like the suicide that cursed generations with the perception of mutual shame and a free-floating sense of responsibility that, like a balloon with no string, no one understood how to take hold of. One moment, one decision rising above all others.

Jim's life had become such a thing itself. It was a composite of little things that altered the landscape around him. There was the decision to live a prepared lifestyle before the collapse and the decision to surround himself with a clan of friends afterward. There was the decision to fight violently against those things that he saw as wrong. It was the amalgamation of all those decisions that put him in the situation he was in now.

Above all those things, all those choices, was the most drastic choice he made, which was to interfere with the process of restoring power to his community. It was a small choice he'd undertaken in a big way, leaving the power plant itself in such a state that it might take years to restore under ideal conditions. Was that how he'd be remembered? Was that how his children and grandchildren would be remembered? Would history smile on him for his adherence to old ideals of freedom or would his descendants be scorned as traitors for impeding progress?

Jim navigated the gloaming with minimal visibility now, depending entirely upon the prowess of his horse. He was headed to a place he'd never been and had indeed only speculated about with the aid of binoculars and a crude ninety-year-old map he'd seen in a book. He'd often been tempted to skulk into the mountains beneath the cover of darkness and come to this place, but he'd never done so. It was not his land, not his secret.

They topped a rise and descended into a dark basin. The trail was a deep rut carved by the sharp hooves of thousands of cattle. Exposed limestone rippled from the ground like the remnants of dinosaur skeletons. Then the air changed around them and the horses stopped in their tracks as if they'd known all along that this was where they were going.

Aware that the basin in which they stood sheltered them on all sides, Jim clicked on his headlamp. The wide mouth of a cave opened before them like the yawning maw of a lost whale. The ground beneath their horses had been chewed to bare dirt by the hooves of cattle and was now baked into a scarred brick by the summer sun. The cave entrance was fenced to keep the cattle from wandering inside. Several *No Trespassing* signs hung from rusty strands of barbed wire.

A second light clicked on and Lloyd muttered, "Wow."

"Wow is right."

"That's a big cave."

"It's not just any cave," Jim said, barely concealing his excitement, his reverence for this location. "I've waited years to see this place."

"How the hell did you even know it was here? I grew up in this town and never heard of this cave."

Jim slid off his horse, leading it and the packhorse to a dwarfed and twisted tree, the bark scrubbed loose by hordes of scratching cattle. "Research. I've always been interested in the history of this valley. It has a long history of early settlers and there were eons of Native Americans before that. One day I came across an old article talking about the custom of cave burials in some areas of southwestern Virginia."

"Cave burials?" Lloyd asked, a wary tone in his voice. He reluctantly climbed off his horse and tied it to a different tree. He leaned back, crossed his arms, and stared at the cave with a little more trepidation.

"Yeah, most tribes in this part of the country buried their dead in the ground. A small segment of local tribes or clans, for reasons we still don't understand, laid their dead out in caves. It's an isolated thing. Only a few counties around here have them. It's something more common in the desert southwest where the bodies would mummify in caves. Here they just rot."

Lloyd played his light across the wide entrance as if he expected to find bones staring back at him. "You're telling me *this* cave was used to bury people?"

"Oh yeah. This is the granddaddy of burial caves, Lloyd. The Smithsonian was here in the 1930s and they estimate there were over three hundred graves in there. The skeletons had already been jumbled up by that time so it made it difficult to get an accurate count. Relic hunters had been inside for decades to scavenge anything they could find. In this community it was common to find skulls on mantels or on a kid's dresser."

"That's creepy."

"Seems that way now but it wasn't at the time. This cave was a popular destination for young people whose families worked at Rockdell Farms. It was a huge operation at the time. They had their own schools and towns. Besides swimming and baseball, exploring caves was part of their recreation."

Lloyd was unconvinced. "I can't believe I never heard of it."

"I've talked to other people who grew up here and never heard of it either. It wasn't always a secret but it became one over time. It's protected now, or at least it was before things fell apart. There are supposedly trail cameras around here to make sure no one tampers with anything."

Lloyd chuckled. "I think we're safe. Besides, with all the shit you've already done, what's a little trespassing?"

"Good point. You ready to take a look inside?"

Lloyd's eyes grew wide. "So much for being safe. You really want to go in there?"

"It's something I have to do."

Lloyd gave an ushering gesture. "Lead the way."

Four irregularly-spaced strands of barbed wire stretched across the opening, tacked to leaning cedar posts. Jim ducked between the strands and held them apart for Lloyd. He carried his rifle, not so much out of concern for what might be inside the cave but for the possibility that something might be waiting for them when they came back out.

As is frequently the case with caves, the entrance in no way foretold what lay inside. Jim had seen some impressive-looking caves that dead-ended just beyond the portal. That was not the case here. Just inside the entrance, the floor began to gently slope away from them and the ceiling rose higher. The floor may have been a single, solid slab at one time but over the course of eons massive tables of rock had fallen from the ceiling and lay scattered like blocks. There was a sense of vast space around them that was almost extraterrestrial.

"It's the size of a football field," Lloyd mumbled. "Maybe several football fields."

"That's what I'd read," Jim said. A flutter around his head startled him and he caught the flicker of a bat in his headlamp. "Shit!"

"It's time for them to head out for the evening," Lloyd said. "The place is probably full of them. A cave this size could have thousands. Hundreds of thousands even."

It was indeed the case. As they continued deeper into the earth, tiny bats the size of rodents dropped from the ceiling and flitted toward the entrance. Soon the floor began to level out. There were more slabs the size of tables and some naturally-occurring ledges of stone ran along the wall. Then they began to see bones. Jim's light hit a pile the size of a campfire, the bones yellowed but distinctive. There was no mistaking what they were.

"I'm no doctor, but that's more than one person," Lloyd said. "That's a lot of damn bones."

Jim agreed. "I read about this too. Looters picked through the graves for skulls and the remnants of old shell necklaces. Anything they didn't care about got tossed to the side. Back in the 80s or 90s a local tribe got involved in trying to protect the site. With no way to reconstruct what it was supposed to look like, they decided to leave everything the way it was and focus on keeping it from being further disturbed."

Lloyd played his light around the chamber. "This is some spooky shit. Imagine this place filled with torches while they did some ancient burial ceremony. Can you imagine being a fly on the wall for that?"

"Makes you wonder who they were," Jim said. "Were they Cherokees or Shawnees? Those guys were active in this area. Was it some isolated, remnant tribe with weird customs whose history has been lost to time? We like to think we understand the past but we really have no fucking clue. We only know bits and pieces."

They poked around for more than half an hour, finding that the vast chamber seemed to be the extent of the cavern. If smaller tunnels were leading off, they required crawling or scrambling in a manner that Jim wasn't interested in. The two touched nothing and took nothing, though Jim did remember to snap a few pictures with the iPhone he'd brought along.

"I'm ready to go," Jim finally said, shoving the phone in his pocket.

"Good. I'm starting to get creeped out. I feel like I'm being watched."

Like the bats before them, the pair fled the cave. They climbed the slick floor carefully, not anxious to be injured so early into their adventure. When they were out, Jim went to his horse and got a drink of water. "You want to stay here for the night?"

Lloyd looked back at the yawning mouth of the cave, then out into the darkness. "Let's go a little further. I'm not all that tired."

"Chickenshit."

"Call me what you want," Lloyd said, getting wound up. "I'm not waking up in the middle of the night surrounded by pissed-off Indian ghosts. You know they gotta be riled up over their missing heads and relics. You want to have to answer for that?"

"That's fine. I guess I got a few more miles in me." Jim took up the lead of his packhorse and climbed onto his own mount. "I hope you brought a teddy bear or something because this ain't the last scary sight we're going to see out here. You're going to have to hitch up your panties and toughen up."

Lloyd climbed onto his horse, groaning from the effort. "What is this? You got some kind of morbid tour lined up for us? Ghosts and cemeteries?"

"Not in particular," Jim said. "But I might have an itinerary."

"You going to tell me about it or keep it a surprise?"

"Eh, I think I'll just keep you in suspense. Don't want you getting scared and running home to Randi."

"Glorious," Lloyd groaned. "Just glorious."

They managed to push on for a couple of more miles before they began to get punchy. They rode in the dark, not wanting their headlamps to broadcast their position on the high pastures of the mountain. There was enough moonlight to keep them headed in the right direction but the gentle rocking motion of the horses lulled them into sedation. While the ride itself hadn't been particularly exhausting, it came on top of an already long day. Normally Jim would have been in bed hours ago.

They stopped for the night on a shoulder that jutted prominently from the mountain, near the tree-line. It was an exposed position that would have been lousy if they'd intended to have a fire. It was too late to bother with one though. They unpacked their horses and hobbled them for the night so they could graze.

Lloyd wasted no time stretching his sleeping bag out on a ground cloth. "I'm going to bed."

Jim rolled out his own sleeping gear, then retrieved his binoculars from his pack. "I'm going to take a look around before I go to bed. You can see for hundreds of miles from up here. I want to see if there's anything interesting out there."

"Knock yourself out," said Lloyd. "I don't want to see anything but the inside of my eyelids."

Jim walked about forty feet from their camp, closer to where the edge of their shelf began to slope back down the mountain. He sat down, propped his elbows on his knees, and held the binoculars to his eyes.

Beartown Mountain was the seventh highest peak in Virginia and the forty-first highest in the eastern US. Jim had hiked up there several times before but from a different direction. The route they were currently using was on private property, part of the massive Rockdell Farms holding. Jim had only been up there at night once before, when he was a kid in Boy Scouts.

It had been cold and snowy, probably way more of a hike than a bunch of kids in thin boots and Sears' winter jackets should have been out doing, but they'd made it. They collapsed exhausted on top of that solitary peak as their scoutmaster pointed out the dozens of small towns and highways visible from there. Jim could still remember that feeling, having never seen so far before. It was like seeing constellations of stars laid out on the Earth itself.

Later, as an adult, Jim had hiked the mountain for the challenge of it and it had indeed been a challenge. He'd approached the mountain from the back, coming up through the Clinch Mountain Wildlife Management Area. It was the single roughest day hike he'd ever taken. He'd once read that Beartown was one of the most inaccessible peaks in Virginia and perhaps one of the toughest hikes in the east because the public land around the mountain had no access trails. No one but bear hunters ever went up there. It was an unforgiving morass of thickets, cliffs, and bears.

The route to the top required a map or GPS with advanced land navigation skills. There were steep knife-edge ridges where a climber had to kick steps into the earth and pull themselves along by tugging on scrubby brush. There were odd boulder-strewn canyons that looked out of place on top of the wooded peak. Then there were the mazes of rhododendron so intense and disorienting that a hiker could easily panic in their clutches. It was the kind of miserable experience that only outdoors people understand, the way you can love a trip that totally breaks you down and makes you hurt for weeks.

None of those highways his scoutmaster had pointed out so long ago were easily located now. There were no streams of white headlights and glowing red taillights. There were no glowing domes of light reflecting off the clouds, as the distant towns had once produced at night. In normal times, he'd have been able to spot his town and several small cities from up there. He'd have been able to spot coal mines and factories working twenty-four hours a day.

There was none of that now but there were indeed pockets of light out there. There was life in the world. Most of it was just faint flickers—likely a lone bonfire, a burn barrel at someone's watch post, or a group of people still up for one reason or another. He could see the city of Bristol on the Tennessee and Virginia border. There was a large pocket of light there and Jim wondered if it was one of the comfort camps, like the one the government had tried to establish in his community.

Jim knew that his efforts would not stop the progress of the world at large. Electricity was coming back and people were so hungry for it that he had no doubts as to the many ways in which they would prostrate themselves for it. Many saw no freedom worth the nights of darkness and the lack of refrigeration. They would kneel before the gods who brought light and give them anything they wanted in return. Their souls, their children's souls, and everything in between.

Jim shifted his view to his valley. He saw no lights at all but could make out the general area of his home in the tufted grayness of the moonlit terrain. He hoped his family was all safe and sleeping, but he expected Ellen was not. He could feel her out there in the darkness worrying about him. He understood that. Despite his best efforts he seemed to often be the source of worry for those who loved him. That was the hardest part of being married he found, that surrendering of freedom. That awareness that his actions were never without conse-quence to other people.

Jim didn't know if he'd be able to look onto his sleeping family in the same way tomorrow. He and Lloyd would likely top the mountain and move deeper into the forest. He said his goodnights to each of them and went off to his sleeping bag.

7

———

T*he Camp*

Sharon woke with the crow of the first rooster and saw that it was not yet light outside. Had the night not been so insufferably hot she probably could have rolled over and gone back to sleep. Instead, any part of her body not stuck to her damp nightgown was stuck to the damp sheets. It was typical of the Appalachian Mountains this time of year. Nothing ever felt clean. Not the bed, not your clothes, and not your body. Without the convenience of electricity, keeping all those things clean was harder than it used to be. A year ago it was two showers a day and laundry once a week. Now, like a lot of other values, standards of cleanliness had shifted.

She pushed herself up and looked toward the window with its thin curtain stretched on a rusty rod. Outside, the dark of the night was diluted with a hint of the coming day, like a splash of cream in a cup of strong coffee. There was plenty that needed to be done and this was the time of year to do it. That made it even harder to go back to sleep. They had good weather and long days. Despite that, everything took longer than she wanted and she never accomplished everything she set out to do each day. Her list was never done.

It wasn't so much the impediments to her own mobility that slowed her as the circumstance itself. She felt a duty to teach as she worked. When she handed out assignments, she showed each child how to perform the task, then carefully explained why they were doing it. That took longer but it felt like the right thing to do. She didn't know how long it would be before order was restored to the world, but even if things did get back to normal, who was to say something similar wouldn't happen again down the road.

Sharon wanted these children to know how to survive, both for now and for the future. She wanted them to have every bit of knowledge that she had in her own mind. While she was by no means an expert, she knew a few things. She also knew how to look up information and thank God they'd had a decent library there.

Of course, mastering survival and homesteading skills wasn't why these children were with her. Their parents certainly hadn't sent them to summer camp with the intention they'd come out as skilled survivalists. They'd come there to learn traditional Appalachian music. These were kids who had an inclination for the banjo, the guitar, the upright bass, or the mandolin. Some even played the autoharp or the dulcimer. Others liked to sing the mountain ballads or dance to the traditional tunes. A year ago they were junior musicians, not homesteaders. Now they were both.

Sharon wasn't a musician herself but was the program director for the camp. She scheduled events and managed the staff, brought in the instructors, and kept an eye on every aspect of the camp experience. She made menus, scheduled deliveries, and bandaged skinned knees. She picked up kids at the airport and sent them on their way when camp was over. She'd been doing this as a summer job for over twenty years now and it renewed her in a way that nothing in her life ever had before. Being at the camp, among those kids, cleared her head to return to a year of teaching school within the tight confines of the traditional educational system.

She much preferred the experience of being at the camp to sitting in the classroom. There had been many times she wished she could live there forever, but she was insightful enough to understand that the magical feeling of summer was fleeting. It was the transitory nature of the experience that contributed to it feeling so special. Every two weeks the pool of children changed and she got to relive the magic of camp through new eyes. Then, at the end of summer, the last of them went home and the camp sat idle all winter, awaiting their return.

Until last year.

As the world crumbled around them, Sharon did her best to get children where they needed to be. She coordinated rides and worked the phones in the early hours after the terror attacks. She counseled child and parent alike, trying to keep everyone calm. Despite her best efforts, however, not everyone made it home. Within days of the attacks, the phones no longer worked and the fuel no longer flowed. Flights continued to depart, though she could no longer get children there to board them.

She had eight children between the ages of nine and fourteen remaining at the camp. For some, she'd been unable to track down their parents or their emergency contacts before the phones went dead. Through a long fall, a cold winter, and a damp spring she'd waited for the parents of these last children to show up, but they never did. At this point, she had to assume the worst. They weren't coming.

She was aware the world outside of their pastoral oasis was a harsh and unforgiving place right now. The children understood that too. She'd been honest with them in her assessment of what was taking place in the rest of the world. She'd learned from her own life, from an accident that left her unable to walk, that you didn't give people false hope. Honesty and practicality were the best approaches. This was what the world had thrown at them and they had no choice except to confront it head-on. They had to roll with it, meet life's challenges and overcome. If she could teach them anything, it was that.

She kept the children busy and she filled their days with work and structured play. She kept them working on their music lessons, both as individuals and as a group. They taught each other and they studied reference books. Through their own labor and with the assistance of the camp's owner they survived.

Sharon twisted and swung her legs to the floor. She stretched and yawned, fighting the temptation to lie back down and find another hour of sleep. She knew it would never come and the time spent laying there waiting would be wasted. It would be an hour she'd never get back. An hour she might need later.

An inflatable solar lantern sat on her nightstand and she turned it on, wincing at the harsh intrusion of artificial light into her peaceful world. She reached for her wheelchair and rolled it closer. Yesterday's clothes were piled in the seat and they weren't so dirty that she couldn't get another day out of them. As she pulled them on she caught the smell of dried sweat on her t-shirt. It was the same musty smell that pervaded every corner of her life right now and likely would for another month at least. Sweaty clothes, sweaty sheets, and sweaty bodies. When she was dressed, she pulled a headlamp onto her ratty straw cowboy hat and headed out of the cabin.

Sharon wasn't the only adult on the property. The camp was located on a thousand-acre farm and the owner, a bluegrass musician named Oliver Poteet, had built the summer camp on fifty acres of it. The farm belonged to his parents, who raised cattle and tobacco but had also instilled a love of traditional music in their son. He'd convinced them to let him build the camp in the 1960s when the hippies were rediscovering hillbilly music.

Over fifty years later, Oliver was an old man in his eighties and his summer camp was an institution in music circles. Each summer they had sessions for adults or children, as well as weekend workshops for those who couldn't get away for an entire week. They had musicians-in-residence who would come teach in exchange for the opportunity to hang out in the mountain setting at no cost. There were dozens of cabins, toilet and shower facilities, a dining hall, a library, gardens, creeks, and a pond. They hosted square dances and jam sessions that were the stuff of legend.

Although some of the facilities had been upgraded over time, the place was pretty rustic. As a result, much of it was not easily accessible to folks with mobility issues when Sharon first started working there. Initially, Oliver hadn't understood all of the challenges that people with physical differences faced but Sharon helped him with that. She gently guided him through improvements that made the camp a place everyone could enjoy, whether they walked, rolled, or navigated the property by some other means.

Her cabin had a ramp that was thirty years newer than the rest of the structure. It connected to a boardwalk that allowed Sharon to get to the dining hall without having to push her way over a rutted path of tree roots and exposed rocks. The boards made a hollow echo as her chair rolled over them, like a finger dragged across a xylophone. At the base of the ramp, she hooked a right and was soon beneath the wide covered porch that surrounded the dining hall.

She went inside. They didn't lock the doors these days. The camp was a mile off the nearest road and they didn't get much company. They'd never had a problem with theft. The camp was hidden in the inner recesses of the farm, requiring that you pass Oliver's house to get there. The occasional visitor, escorted by Oliver, showed up to bring them the gift of some supplies. Usually some canning or meat they'd butchered.

Other times they might see a hunter crossing the property. Waves were exchanged but no one ever approached. Sharon knew some people still showed up to check on Oliver, but not nearly so many as before the collapse. As a musician he had many friends, but it was not a good time to travel. It was sad to admit but Oliver was getting to that age where most of his friends and family had passed on.

Inside the dining hall, Sharon headed directly for the kitchen. Had she been at home she'd have headed for the coffee pot, but they'd been out of coffee here since last fall. She'd had a lot of herbal tea over the winter, but the last thing she wanted now was to pour hot water into her already warm body. She picked up a glass jar in which fresh mint leaves the children had picked along the bank of the creek had been steeping overnight. She tucked the jar into her lap and moved from the kitchen to the dining room, lit an oil lamp, and removed a notepad from the pouch hanging from the side of her chair.

Every day started with a list. She reviewed the things they'd accomplished the day before, which was never as much as she'd hoped, and added new things to her list that had occurred to her as she lay in bed at night. Food preservation was always on the top of their list. Another fall and winter would be upon them soon and they'd go into it more poorly-equipped than they'd been a year ago. They'd eaten their way through the leftover camp supplies; the big number ten cans and the bagged rice, all the pasta and canned sauces. They wouldn't have that as backup this year. Survival would be about their own resourcefulness. It would be about the supplies they laid in and how well they preserved them.

8

———————

# T *he Camp*

Nearly two hours later children began straggling into the dining hall. Once one of them woke up, the rest came to life as if some sort of chemical signal passed between them. The oldest of the girls, twelve-year-old Kay, took responsibility for making sure the girls were ready and prepared for the day. Sharon had put her in a role similar to being a counselor at the camp. Their counselors for the children's sessions normally had to be sixteen but these were unconventional times.

Sharon assured Kay it would be good training since she'd already expressed an interest in being a counselor in the future. "Just do your best. Make sure they have what they need. Make sure they're comfortable. If you need help, ask me."

In the boy's cabin, fourteen-year-old Nathan did the same. He kept the morale up and made sure the boys changed their clothes when required. This time of year, keeping the children bathed and their clothes clean was less of an issue. They simply went swimming in their dirty clothes, splashing around in the creek until they were clean.

They were all back to living in the cabins for now because Sharon felt like it contributed to the feeling that this was just camp and they were normal kids having a normal summer camp experience. Last winter they'd all moved into the dining hall with its wood stove and insulated walls for obvious reasons. They spent the cold months feeding the fire and pretending they were at a slumber party.

Keeping morale up on those long, dark evenings had been quite the challenge. The children practiced their instruments and had lessons every day, worked puzzles, and played board games. Sharon made them read books from the camp library in an attempt to keep their general education from suffering. Despite her career as a classroom teacher, she did everything she could to make the camp *not* feel like a classroom.

Sharon had breakfast laid out in the kitchen by the time the children showed up. It wasn't the kind of breakfast kids would find at most summer camps. There was no sausage, bacon, or eggs, no biscuits, pancakes, or little boxes of sugary cereals. There were no juice boxes and tiny cartons of milk. All of that was long gone and they were back to the bounty of the Earth.

"Who wants to get the yogurt this morning?" Sharon asked.

"I will!" Jenny bolted out the door before anyone could protest.

A cold mountain stream ran past the cabin. They'd taken an old cooler and drilled the bottom full of holes with a hand drill. Cold stream water ran through the cooler all day, allowing them a basic level of refrigeration. They had a variety of goats that had once served as nothing more than entertainment at the camp. Now those goats provided milk, which in turn allowed Sharon to make cheese and yogurt.

While they waited on the yogurt, kids helped themselves to blackberries, strawberries, chunks of cantaloupe, slices of apple, and ripe summer peaches. It was a bountiful time at the camp and it warmed Sharon's heart to be able to provide for the children in such a way.

Last winter they'd often struggled to find a meal that everyone liked but that wasn't an issue now. The fruit, topped with yogurt and honey, was a favorite for everyone. They were attempting to dehydrate berries now to preserve for the winter but Sharon had never done it before. She was uncertain if they'd survive storage.

Jenny was back in a few minutes with two crocks. One held plain yogurt and the other a flavored variety that Sharon was experimenting with. While the children ate, Sharon studied her list.

"It looks like another hot day," she said. "We're going to work for a while, then we'll take a break and play in the creek so you can cool off if you want. Then we'll work some more, eat lunch, and then take a break in the early afternoon so everyone can practice their instruments. How's that for a plan?"

"What do we got to do today?" Tara asked. She was the youngest of the kids and the most insecure with the situation. Despite Sharon's assurances, she was always afraid she'd be assigned some task that she couldn't do. She was lacking in confidence and Sharon was working hard to bolster it.

"Most of us will work in the garden this morning," Sharon said. "Everything is coming ripe at once. We need to pick tomatoes for tomato sauce, ketchup, and tomato soup. We'll cook everything up this afternoon and do some canning tonight."

"It's hot inside," Jenny said. "Do we really have to can tonight?"

"There's nothing we can do about that, is there? Everybody is going to want ketchup. Everyone is going to want tomato soup this winter. The only way we'll have those things is if we cook and can them."

The children already knew that. Everyone understood the canning had to be done but no one was excited about doing it. It required cooking on the woodstove in the already hot dining hall and it could be unpleasant. Sharon wanted to build an outdoor canning kitchen but she hadn't gotten around to it yet.

"Nathan, you and Stevie are going to go collect peaches. I need you to get two full buckets each. Then check the eggs and make sure the chickens have water."

"I wanted to check the eggs this morning," Jenny said. "I like it when they're still warm in your hand."

Sharon smiled at her. "That's fine. When you finish breakfast you go do that." As much as Sharon depended on her lists, flexibility helped keep everyone sane. She picked her battles. Sometimes the list had to be adhered to and other times it did not. If Jenny wanted to get eggs, she'd let her go.

With the planning out of the way, they ate their breakfast and talked. Sharon had several prompts to get them talking if everyone was trapped in the doldrums. She'd ask about any interesting dreams anyone had. At dinner every evening, she made each person bring a story about something interesting they'd seen during the day. It could be a pretty leaf or a weird bug, an unusual bird, or an animal they didn't normally see. It wasn't just about distracting the children; Sharon was interested in building their observational skills and teaching them mindfulness. However, she had an ulterior motive even beyond that. In these dangerous times, she wanted them to be cautious, and that required being constantly aware of their surroundings.

When they were done, each person cleaned their own plate and utensils, each washed their cup. Before leaving the kitchen, they dipped them into a solution of bleach water to help sanitize it, then put them in a rack to dry. This system had worked for the camp for years and Sharon saw no reason to change it now.

They met as a group on the back porch of the dining hall and Sharon reviewed their assignments with them. She reaffirmed the safety procedures. No one was to be left alone or go anywhere alone outside of the main camp area, which consisted of the dining hall, cabins, and garden. If they saw a stranger they weren't to speak with them. They were to run and find her if she was close, or run and hide if she was not.

"You tell us this every day," Tara said, rolling her eyes.

Sharon smiled. "And I will continue to do so because I care about you and want you to be safe." She poked Tara in the belly for emphasis, the child giggling as she pulled away.

As everyone wandered off to their jobs, gathering the supplies they needed, Nathan went about the first task he performed every day. In addition to goats, Oliver kept some ponies around for the children to pet. As a resourceful farmer, used to improvising, he'd figured out in the early days of the disaster that Sharon could harness one to her wheelchair and use the small animal to pull it around like a cart.

In an ideal world, the measure wouldn't have been necessary but the world wasn't ideal. Some of the places Sharon needed to go around the camp didn't offer smooth, wheelchair-friendly surfaces. She was a strong woman and could muscle her chair into a lot of places, but that wasn't the best use of her energy. Why exhaust herself rolling over uneven ground when the docile ponies were perfect for it?

They'd settled on a friendly animal named Honey, but it had taken them a while to perfect the rigging. Eventually Oliver, Nathan, and Sharon came up with a good system. Sharon perfected it over the winter. She made a good nylon harness with buckles and Velcro. It clipped onto her chair with a couple of carabiners, turning it into a miniature buggy. It turned out to be a game-changer in terms of getting her where she needed to go on the property. For the two decades she'd worked there, she'd relied on a gas-powered golf cart for that task. That cart now sat abandoned in the high weeds behind her cabin.

"What are you getting into this morning?" Nathan asked, securing the last buckle and stepping back from the pony.

"I'm going to go check on Oliver. He wasn't feeling so good when he left here yesterday. You reach a certain age and you can't tolerate heat like you used to."

"Is that age fourteen?" Nathan asked with a grin.

Sharon smiled and shook her head. "Not hardly."

9

The Valley

ELLEN WAS down at the barn preparing for a day of canning. There had been a day when it was an indoor activity, conducted in an air-conditioned kitchen with all the modern conveniences. That was no longer the case. They needed a wood-fired stove for sanitizing jars and sealing the canned foods. Performing that operation inside rendered the house uninhabitable.

Early in the spring, Jim had set up an old woodstove near the barn just for this purpose. They had plenty of water there from the nearby springhouse and there were folding plastic tables for cutting vegetables and staging supplies. The rusty old woodstove was set up beneath a lean-to attached to the barn, keeping them from having to work directly in the sun all day. A chimney made of thick steel well-casing directed the smoke through the roof. As far as apocalyptic canning kitchens went, it wasn't a bad setup.

Nana and Ariel were organizing jars so they could be washed and sanitized. Ariel was less than excited about the task, but Ellen made it clear that her presence was *required*. Everyone had to pitch in to help. Everyone had jobs to do. It was the only way they'd survive the winter with enough food to eat.

Ellen was building a fire in the recesses of the broad stove when she heard a horse approaching. She turned and shaded her eyes. Hugh was coming across the yard toward them. He tossed a hand up in greeting.

"Morning, folks. How's everyone doing?"

Ellen smiled. "We're good. Just getting ready for a day of canning."

"Passing on the skills to a new generation, I see." He nodded toward Ariel.

She crinkled her brow at him. "I don't want to can. I want to play."

"Work first, play later. That's how I was raised," Hugh said.

"You sound like my daddy," Ariel said.

"And your mommy," Ellen added.

"And your grandmother," Nana pitched in.

"Sounds like you're outnumbered, little girl," Hugh said. "Best go along with it. There'll be time to play later."

Ariel didn't appear convinced.

"What you into today?" Ellen asked. "Here to lend a hand with the canning? We could use it."

"Afraid not. Going into town with Gary and Debra. We've heard that farmer's market has really grown this summer. They want to see if they can trade off a few things."

"I'm glad you're going with them. That didn't go so well last time. Turned into a gunfight, as I remember."

"Yeah, we'll be ready for trouble, but hopefully everyone is more interested in trading than fighting. Gary's leaving Will in charge back at his place. Charlie is going with us. He said he had a few things that belonged to his parents that he wasn't going to need. He wanted to see if he could trade them for something more useful."

"Any of it stuff we can use?" Ellen asked.

Hugh shook his head. "Nothing that would benefit us. There are some collector knives that aren't really made for use but would be helpful if you didn't have a knife at all. He's also got some oddball hunting ammo that doesn't fit any of our weapons, some heart medication that belonged to his dad. A few other things."

"He and Pete are helping Randi and Pops with the garden at her place," Nana said. "At least that's where they said they were going."

"I'll head over that way then. Anything you need from town?"

"A milkshake," Ariel said. "Vanilla. And maybe some French fries."

Hugh laughed. "If I could buy one and get it back here before it melted, I'd be glad to do that."

"I don't know of anything we need right now," Ellen said. "I don't have any vegetables I'm ready to trade either. I'm going to try to can everything we raise."

"Good enough," Hugh said. "Pete is going to be riding a patrol while we're gone. You should be able to get him on the radio if you need him."

"You guys be careful," Ellen said.

"Always." Hugh tipped his hat and rode off.

He circled Jim's house and cut through the narrow gate in the backyard. That would deliver him to Randi's house faster than returning to the road. It was a private, direct path between the two homes. After a short ride, he found everyone gathered in the garden. As he got closer, he saw they had serious looks on their faces. These were not happy gardeners. These were pissed-off gardeners.

"What's going on?" he asked, dismounting and tying his horse off to a fencepost.

"Coons!" Randi said with disgust. "The damn trash-pandas got in our corn. They wrecked entire rows, pulling off ears and trampling the plants."

"Yeah, Mack Bird had some get in his chickens. He's not happy with them either," Hugh said.

Charlie frowned. "I want to put out traps."

"I already told you once, you trap one of my daughter's cats and you'll be the one getting skinned," Randi warned.

"I've got some trapping books at my place," Hugh said. "There might be some options for live traps."

"Coons are vicious," Pops said. "Most cats and dogs don't want to fool with them. They'll pretend like they didn't see them and go the other way."

"Mack was going to put that thermal scope of his on a .22 and lay in wait for them. Maybe he'd let you borrow that setup if you use your own shells. You could sit down here at night and wait for them."

"We've got to do something," Randi said. "Even if I have to camp out in the garden myself I'm not losing all this corn. This is too important."

"There may be some live traps floating around the valley we can borrow," Pops said. "I had one at my house but it's all the way across town. It might as well be on the moon."

"Are you ready?" Charlie asked Hugh.

Hugh checked his watch. "Yeah, we need to meet Gary and Debra at the foot of Jim's driveway. They're probably waiting on us already."

"Where you headed?" Pops asked.

"Charlie is going into town with Gary, Debra, and me. We wanted to check out the farmer's market again. Hopefully, we'll get a better reception this time. Between us, I'm curious to see if I overhear any gossip about Jim. We need to know if people are still looking for him or it's passed. I thought it was over but that drone spooked everyone a little."

"I hope it's passed," Pops said. "This whole mess is about to be the death of his mother. She can hardly take all this worry."

Charlie headed for his horse, tied up under a tree in Randi's yard. Pete wasn't far behind him.

"And where do you think you're going?" Pops asked.

"I told Hugh I'd ride a patrol in the valley while he was gone," said Pete. "Just keep an eye on things."

"That's good. I'd prefer you not go into town if you don't have to."

"Fine with me," Pete said. "I have no interest in town."

"Nor do I," Randi said. "Nothing there but trouble and heartache."

Pete, Hugh, and Charlie saddled up and headed for Jim's house, leaving the two gardeners in their hot, humid domain. Hugh nudged his horse and caught up with Pete, already ahead of him.

"You keep an eye on your grandfather," he said. "This heat is hard on older folks. He'll push himself because he knows we're depending on him, but he may push himself too hard. Make sure he's drinking enough, and that he takes breaks and gets out of the heat. Maybe even convince him to drink an electrolyte mix."

"I'll do that," Pete said. "I'll arrange my circuit so I can catch him every hour or so."

"Good man," Hugh said.

When they reached Jim's house, Pete pulled off. "I'm going to see if my mom needs anything before I start patrol. You guys be safe."

"You too," Hugh said.

Hugh and Charlie continued down the driveway. In the distance, they could see Gary and his wife waiting on them in the shade of an old cedar tree. Charlie carried a backpack tied to leather strings on the back of his saddle. Inside were objects he'd decided he no longer needed. He had memories of the people he'd lost—his mother and father, his grandmother. He had a new life now. A new family and new friends. He didn't need to be weighed down with a bunch of crap that meant nothing to him. If he could get something of value for the wreckage of his old life, things that may help him now, he'd gladly trade it off.

**10**

———————

T *he Valley*

During their ride, they talked to dispel the nervousness each of them felt. None of their clan had been into town since the 4<sup>th</sup> of July, the day they supposedly turned Jim over for the bounty. That had turned into such a shit show that no one was anxious to show their face in town again. There was all the shooting, they may have blown up a few things. People might have died. They couldn't live in hiding forever though. Life had to go on.

For nearly a year they'd been forced to use the back way into town, cutting through fields and crossing a small river, because Jim had blown up the road. His reasoning had been solid at the time. There were people in vehicles wandering into the valley and stealing cattle. Menacing people. He wanted to put an end to that and protect his valley, so he packed a drainage culvert with explosives. The blast took out a large chunk of the road and made it a lot harder to get into the valley.

Until now.

The Wimmer family had worked this valley for nearly two centuries. They were farmers and were ready to resume commerce with the townspeople. It was the way of farmers since the beginning and they weren't about to let the little matter of societal collapse hold them back. They'd settled the valley in a time without electrical power and their people had thrived. They would do so again, electrical power or not.

Conducting commerce with the town meant reopening the road into the valley and the Wimmers had made it happen. With axes, they cut tall hardwoods from the hillside and felled them into the roadway. With determination and brute strength, they jockeyed the logs into position until they'd spanned the gap Jim blasted out of the road. Long spikes made of half-inch steel rebar pinned everything together into a serviceable bridge.

The results of the reconnected roadway were obvious to the party of four on their journey into town. Shortly after leaving Jim's driveway they ran into people they didn't recognize, a pair of bicyclists wearing backpacks and sidearms. Hugh had intended to keep going but the couple stopped in the middle of the road, forcing conversation. The man threw a friendly wave at the riders as they neared.

"Hey, we just bartered some corn from the Wimmer family. Anyone down this way trading?"

"No," Hugh replied with no attempt to match his friendly demeanor.

"You sure about that?" the man asked. "No one?"

"You should probably just turn around," Hugh continued. "There's nothing for you down here."

The man became indignant at that. "It's a public road, buddy. There's no reason we can't keep riding and find out for ourselves."

"Nope, there's no reason you can't. Until you step off this roadway and approach someone's house to ask about trading." Hugh shrugged. "Then you'll figure out why I tried to get you to turn around. One of you is going to die and the other is going to be pushing two bikes back to town. Which of you will it be?"

Hugh didn't wait for an answer. He nudged his horse and pushed on, forcing them to move. No one else in the party made eye contact with the cyclists. They left them behind to carefully consider their next move. When they were out of earshot, Hugh got on his radio and warned Pete to be on the lookout for them.

"They have a little attitude," Hugh said. "Be careful."

They passed several more parties and chose not to engage with any of them beyond a nod. They didn't slow or stop, didn't respond to questions or greetings. Unfriendliness worked to their advantage. It sent the message they wanted to convey. It let the visitors know that they weren't welcome, at least as far as *some* of the valley residents were concerned.

"People must have been waiting for this bridge to open," Charlie said. "I've never seen this many people on the road."

"I guess it's something new to do," Hugh said.

Shortly before they hit town, they reached the log bridge and came to a stop.

"They put a lot of work into this," Debra noted.

"It's solid," said Gary. "You could drive cattle across it or pull a wagon."

"Or even drive a truck," Hugh added. "If you had one to drive. That's the part that worries me."

Charlie stopped on top of the bridge while the others rode on across.

Hugh stopped and swung his horse around. "What is it?"

"We could burn it," Charlie said, no touch of humor in his voice. "It's wood."

Hugh grinned. "Who do you think would get the blame for that, Charlie? They'd immediately think of us."

"It was just a thought," Charlie said, clucking at his horse and falling in line behind Debra.

Hugh watched the boy pass, hoping he wasn't serious about that idea of his. There was something about that boy sometimes, a dark turn to him that Hugh was uncertain if anyone but him saw. Maybe it was because he spent more time with him or perhaps he just knew what to look for, but it seemed the losses he'd experienced had affected him. Charlie had something seething inside him that could be dangerous if it showed its face. It could simply be a stage he was going through, part of processing his past, or it could be something he'd struggle with for his entire life. There was no way of knowing.

The rest of the ride went quickly. Minutes after the bridge they passed the river crossing they'd been using all winter. Just beyond that, they turned up the access road to the superstore. After the shooting that happened there earlier in the summer—which Gary and Debra had been part of—the open-air market that had popped up there had fallen out of favor. A new site had sprung up in town.

The new market was in a large parking lot adjacent to the county government offices and it took the group about fifteen minutes to ride over there. Aptly enough, it was the site of an established farmer's market prior to the collapse, though much of the infrastructure was useless now. The bathroom facilities didn't work and the electric outlets served no purpose. Only the long shelters found use, offering protection from the elements for those who got there early enough to claim a spot beneath them.

Since most people had lost track of what day of the week it was, this market had no schedule. There were people there every day of the week. Since it was the only thing going on in town, it was the epicenter of commerce and the hub of daily activity. Even those not in the market to buy or sell came there just to see what was going on and to hear the latest gossip.

When the riders reached the entrance to the parking lot, they paused to study the scene before them.

"There's more people than I expected," Debra said.

"Same here," Hugh agreed. "That's hundreds of folks."

"I didn't know what to expect." Gary glanced around the group. "How should we handle this?"

Hugh looked at Charlie. "You have stuff you want to trade, right?"

"Yeah."

Hugh pointed to the yard of an abandoned dental office. "How about we tie the horses off at the east corner of the parking lot. There's grass there. I'll stay with them while you all do your trading. I'll be close enough that we can group up if things go south."

"Don't you want to look around?" Debra asked. "We can switch out if you do."

Hugh shook his head. "I'll be fine."

Everyone was in agreement that this was as good a plan as any so they got moving. As usual, folks on horses drew attention. They were the one-eyed men in the world of the blind, holding a better hand than those stuck walking. Such visibility always carried the risk of attracting the wrong kind of attention, of being targeted by those needing transportation or desperate for the protein a healthy horse might provide. The valley folks were well aware of that after a year of traumatic experiences. Everyone had weapons on display, rounds chambered, and plenty of backup mags in case things got sparky.

Some eyes in the crowd followed them as they rode to the abandoned dental office and dismounted in the parking lot. They never knew if people were watching out of curiosity or if it was something more than that. It was the way of things anymore.

Hugh collected the reins and tied the horses off to a couple of decorative parking lot lights. He liked the location from a tactical standpoint. There were no high shrubs or other obstructions to his visibility, and he had a good view of what was going on at the market.

He sat down on a concrete parking block and pulled a pouch of deer jerky from a cargo pocket. While he chewed, he watched his people get swallowed by the crowd. He didn't need to see them. They had their radios. Hopefully, if shit got real, they'd remember to use them.

## 11

T *he Farmer's Market*

Gary, Debra, and Charlie decided to split up in the crowd. Though there were other people there carrying guns and others who'd arrived on horseback, there was something in the demeanor of the three valley folks that made the crowd part for them. Certainly everyone in the crowd was hardened now. Everyone had suffered and was struggling to survive, but there was something different about these members of Jim's group. A wariness. An edginess. A willingness to escalate and pull the trigger that must have been apparent even to those who only glanced at them.

Debra had bundles of herbs she wanted to trade for things on her list. The mint she'd picked along the creek bank made good teas. There was catnip she'd found growing wild, mullein, and yarrow. She'd handwritten notecards that were attached to each bundle telling how to prepare them and what they were good for. Her needs were baby clothes, diapers, and hygiene items.

Charlie wandered off on his own to peruse the tables of goods. Other vendors had thrown out blankets in the parking lot and laid out items they hoped to parlay into something they had a greater need for. The first booth Charlie stopped at belonged to an older couple selling old-fashioned honey candy. Charlie had never had it before but it was the first sweet treat of any kind he'd seen for sale.

"How much?" he asked.

"I get a .22 shell for two pieces," the woman said. She wore a long denim skirt and had hair down to her waist. Charlie knew women dressed like that because of a certain church they attended, but he couldn't remember which one.

"Ain't got no .22," Charlie said. "Will you take .25?"

"That a bullet?"

"Yeah, it's a bullet."

The woman conferred with her husband for a moment and he stepped over to speak to Charlie. "Ain't much call for .25 ammo."

"Until you meet a man with a .25 who ain't got any bullets."

The man tilted his head to concede the point. "How many pieces was you wanting?"

Charlie thought on it for a moment. "A dozen."

"I'll take a dozen rounds of your .25 caliber for a dozen pieces of candy," the man said, giving Charlie a hard trader's stare.

"That's twice the .22 price."

"And I may be sitting on those .25 rounds for a long damn time before I move them. I can sell .22 all day long and get a good trade for it. Can't remember the last time I even saw a .25 pistol."

The .25 rounds in Charlie's pack weren't doing him any good. They'd belonged to his dad, to a gun no one even remembered. It wasn't likely Charlie would ever own one in his lifetime so he thought it prudent to take what he could get for the ammunition. "I'll take it."

He removed his pack and fished out the ammo while the woman wrapped the candy in a clean white sheet of copy paper. Charlie shook out the ammo and waited patiently while the man counted the rounds. The woman held the candy in both hands, not ready to turn it over until she got the nod from her husband. When he was satisfied with the count, he signaled his wife to hand over the goods.

"Thank you," Charlie said. He stashed the candy in a side pocket of his pack and slung it over his back.

Moving down the row of vendors, he wove through the crowd, listening to people haggle over items that would have been trash before the collapse. Camping gear that wouldn't have sold at a yard sale now brought a premium price. Seventy-year-old hand tools, relics of a bygone era, were now highly sought-after. Even old worn-out shoes were in demand now that no one could get new ones. The standards of what made something "worn out" had changed considerably.

Charlie stopped at a booth where a hand-painted sign announced "Heirloom Seeds." The table was packed with baggies and tiny pill bottles. Each had a label scrawled on it with marker. "What kind of seeds are these?"

A red-cheeked man with a chaw of tobacco regarded Charlie. "All kinds."

"What's *heirloom* mean?"

The man spat onto the ground. "A lot of the shit you get at the store now is hybrid. Can't grow nothing from the seeds that come from that. My family always harvested their own seeds from the crops they grew and I learnt how to do it. I've got a good supply so I'm trading some off. This is what you need now since you can't buy new seeds."

Charlie had heard Randi and Pops discussing this very issue. A lot of what they were growing in their gardens this year was from hybrid seeds they'd scraped together from their own homes. It left them uncertain about what they were going to do next summer. Taking some of these seeds back to the valley could be a big help. "What you get for them?"

"Each pack has fifty of whatever the label is. Normal price is five .22 shells a pack but I also take other stuff too."

"I got .25 shells," Charlie offered.

"Well, I ain't a pimp and this ain't the 1960s. Ain't nobody carries a .25 anymore. What else you got?"

His attitude pissed Charlie off but he bit his tongue. This was a trade he needed to make. Charlie took off his pack and stared down inside it. "Got a stack of knives, a couple of old zippo lighters, a rifle scope, and a couple of tiny tool kits."

"What kind of tool kits?"

"Them little kind like you used to get as a gift when you bought something stupid, like subscribing to a magazine or something. A little pouch with pliers and a screwdriver that takes a bunch of bits. There's a crescent wrench in there too. One of those tiny ones."

"Knives, you say?"

"Pocket knives mostly," Charlie told him. "Got a fillet knife too."

"I tell you what, how about I give you all these seeds on my table for everything in your sack of goodies there."

"And how about you kiss my ass," Charlie said. "I may be a kid but I ain't stupid."

The man spat again and narrowed his eyes at Charlie. "I don't give a damn if you're a kid or not. You talk to me that way again and I'll knock the shit out of you."

"And you'll die before your fat ass gets around this table," Charlie said. "You want to trade or not? Now, I figure folks are needing rifle scopes awful bad now since there's more people hunting for their food. How about I give you the scope for what's on the table?"

"No fucking way."

"I'll give you the scope and two of the tool kits."

The man chewed on it. "Throw in the fillet knife and it's a deal."

"I'll take it," Charlie said, digging into his pack and removing the items he'd offered, placing them on the table.

The man slid the seeds across to him and Charlie carefully packed them into a side pocket. "Whereabouts you live, boy?"

Charlie finished packing the seeds away. He hauled his rifle up and slung it over his shoulder. "Why you asking? You planning on coming for dinner?"

The man gave a broad grin, strands of tobacco stuck between his stained teeth. "You never know."

"I don't advise it. My people ain't the friendly sort," Charlie replied. "But I *will* see you around. I'd like to buy some more of those seeds."

"Bring something worth trading and we'll do it again."

Charlie hit several more booths and traded off nearly everything he'd brought to barter. It was only a small drop in the bucket of the things he intended to get rid of. He had sacks of it at Randi's house and more at Pete's. It felt good to get rid of some of it. He headed back to the dental office and found the rest of his group waiting for him, discussing the market.

"How'd you do?" Gary asked.

Charlie grinned. "Not bad."

"We did okay," Debra said. "I traded all my herbs, but I'm not real impressed with what I got for them. A handful of tampons, a dozen diapers, and a few sample packs of baby wipes that are probably dried out already."

"What did you get, Charlie?" Hugh asked.

He had a hard time containing his excitement. "Probably a thousand heirloom seeds from one feller. I got some candy for the kids, two unopened packs of some big-sized diapers, and I got three boxes of them things Debra was just talking about."

Debra cocked an eyebrow. "Baby wipes?"

Charlie looked off, pretending he was studying a bush. "No, them other things."

"Tampons?" said Gary.

"Yeah, that's it."

Hugh smiled. "Charlie, it sounds like you made a good haul, but there ain't a thing in there that's just for you. Did you only get stuff for other people?"

"You all say we're a tribe," Charlie held his hands out. "I got stuff for the tribe. I figured I'd just throw it all in the pot and you all could figure out how to split it up between you."

"You don't want to be responsible for handing out tampons and diapers?" Debra asked.

"I reckon we better be getting home." Charlie untied his horse and climbed into the saddle.

Debra climbed onto hers and pulled alongside Charlie. "I'm sorry. I was just teasing you. I'm really impressed with what you did. That's thoughtful of you."

"You all have been good to me," Charlie said. "Reckon I should return the favor. That's all."

"I'm proud of you too, Charlie," Hugh said, feeling halfway bad about the things he'd thought on the way in. Maybe the boy had a dark side in there somewhere but perhaps he was entitled to after the things he'd been through. He definitely had a sweet and thoughtful side too. Eventually, one side would either win out or temper the other. That came with age.

**12**

---

*liver's House*

Oliver Poteet's farm had been in his family for nearly one hundred and fifty years. Over that time they'd raised cabbages and beets, tobacco and cattle. They'd sold timber and made charcoal. They'd prospected the ground for coal, natural gas, and even gold. If there was a way to squeeze a dollar from dirt, they'd tried it. In return, they were good stewards of the land. They kept it healthy, balancing periods of regrowth and healing against the resources they took. They cared for the land and the land cared for them.

Oliver's proudest accomplishment during his tenure as the landowner was the camp. As he'd retired from actively farming the land, he used other means to keep money coming in for his favorite project. He leased sections of his property for grazing, growing, or cutting hay; continued to sell timber; and he allowed hunting clubs to pursue deer, bear, and turkey in his rich forests.

When his only son died, leaving him without an heir, Oliver had his will changed. He set the camp apart as a non-profit organization and left everything he owned in a trust to keep the camp going after he passed. The farm would continue to operate as it had under his guidance and all proceeds would go toward raising more generations of Appalachian musicians.

The farmhouse Oliver lived in was built not long after his ancestors purchased the farm. It had been expanded several times in order to provide additional space for growing families, but somewhere beneath the walls lay the original chestnut log cabin. There were places where you could tell if you knew what you were looking for. Places where a wall was noticeably thicker than the others or where a doorway was unusually low. Like many older homes in America, it had come into existence in a world without power, conditioned air, and running water. Now it would quite possibly go out in the same manner.

Oliver's bedroom had once belonged to his parents. He was born within those four walls and in that very same bed. He'd found getting old in the same house in which he had so many memories to be a strange experience. There was no avoiding the past. Even though his last few years there had been spent alone, his wife and son buried in the family cemetery behind the house, the place often felt...*active*. It was like life, or some semblance of life, continued on around him yet apart from him. He'd hear the voices of people who'd once shared the home with him. In fact, he could swear he often heard them speaking directly to him or calling to him from another place within the house.

Sometimes he thought he saw them too. He'd be walking down a hall and catch a glimpse of his mother carrying laundry from one room to another. He'd smell his father's pipe. He'd turn from the woodstove to see his brother sitting in an overstuffed chair like he was enjoying the fire. During the long, quiet days he'd experienced since the collapse, Oliver spoke to the dead more than to the living. It was truly an odd thing to be so old that you teetered between worlds, uncertain to which you belonged anymore.

On this particular morning, as Sharon worked on her list at the camp, waiting for the children to awake, Oliver's eyes fluttered open. Most days he got himself ready and was waiting for Sharon when she showed up to check in on him. Depending on how he was feeling, he might walk back to the camp with her or they'd just sit a spell on his porch and talk. He'd tell her little things he knew about how to get by without power. He'd explain things she might do to help them survive, wanting to help in the only way he could now that his body was withered and useless.

He'd tried since the early days of the disaster to get her and the children to come live with him in the big house but she refused. There was certainly room for them in the vast old house. Oliver had given Sharon a hundred reasons why they should move in and she'd thrown back a hundred reasons that they shouldn't. She wanted to keep the children in their routine. She wanted to keep them in their familiar surroundings. Sometimes he thought the real reason was that she didn't want to impose on him. Other times he suspected it was because the camp was where she found the strength to go on. The place was special to her and she wasn't ready to surrender it.

He'd worked on her for a year, trying to build his case, to no avail. Just yesterday, he'd come up with a strategy he thought might have a fighting chance and he was going to throw it at her before cold weather returned. He was going to appeal to her pity, and claim he needed them to get by, that he was too old and frail to make it without them. She might suspect he was lying, or at least trying to manipulate the truth, but she'd give in this time. He just knew it.

Now it was too late.

That morning he awoke confused, feeling different than the morning before. He couldn't put a finger on it but he was *off* some-how. Instinct took over, the habits of a lifetime. He'd done the same thing each morning for over eighty years and that impulse drove him onward. He made to swing his legs out of the bed but they wouldn't swing. Trying to figure out what was going on, he tried to push himself up to a sitting position and was unable to do that either.

As he lay there in the darkness, trying to wade through his muddled thoughts, trying to spot the truth hiding in the grass of confusion, he felt dampness on his cheek. He went to wipe it away but could barely move his arm. It wouldn't do what he told it to do. With the utmost concentration, his body trembling from the effort, he raised his hand up in front of his eyes and saw the hand gnarled into a useless claw, curled like a fiddlehead fern in the spring.

He understood in a vague sense what was going on now. This was the very thing his own father had died from. It had to be a stroke. A vessel in his brain had blown out like a weak hydraulic hose on an old tractor. What happened now? How long would he lay there before he died?

He noticed then the vague outline of figures along the wall. It was a death vigil. Why would Sharon bring those children in here to watch him die? Had she been tending to him and he'd forgot that fact in his delirium? Then he noticed that the figures were not children and the woman closest to him was not Sharon.

It was his wife.

She was wearing a dark dress that he recalled from their son's funeral. Her gaze was strangely impassive, her eyes holding neither sympathy, nor love, nor understanding. She could have been an insect watching him from the branch of a tree, a crow from a fence. With the same expression, Oliver's son Bailey stood at his mother's side, his hand resting supportively on her shoulder. To their left, Oliver's parents stood watching too. He made eye contact with his father and received a nod, a gesture perhaps intended to offer support or indicate an understanding of what he was going through.

Oliver grunted and managed to push himself closer to a fetal position. His eyes screwed about wildly in their sockets and he saw more people, the walls packed like spectators at a sold-out show. He saw his brother Don who'd been crushed when the old Farmall tricycle tractor rolled with him. He saw his Uncle Tim who'd been killed in a logging accident and his cousin Duke who'd drowned in the New River.

There were so many children he wondered where they'd all come from. He'd never seen the house so full of them. Then he realized they were the *lost* children, the babies stillborn or miscarried. They came here through crib death or croup, through internal problems unknown to the old country doctors and midwives. He saw the scarred face of Louisa, the great-aunt who died at four years old, her dress catching on fire while her mother made lye soap. Oliver had never laid eyes on the child before, her death predating him by decades, but she'd forever been the reason his mother wouldn't allow him close to fires. Oliver understood that these faces in the room weren't just family. They were the mythology of family. They were the legends and the stories. They were the architects of an entire system of belief. They were his history.

A sound caught Oliver's attention, wheels on wood. His first thought was a gurney coming down the hall for him. Maybe the ambulance was here? The undertaker? Was he already dead?

Oliver's door swung open. Unable to straighten his body to see in that direction, he twisted his eyes upward, trying to see who'd come for him. The rolling came closer and a face hovered into view. It wasn't a gurney. It wasn't the cold steel table of the undertaker. It was Sharon and her face held perhaps the saddest smile Oliver had ever seen.

"Oh, Oliver," she said, a single tear tracing its way down her dusty cheek.

# 13

B*eartown Mountain*

JIM AWOKE TO A LOW, throaty growl. He'd first thought it was Lloyd snoring, then worried that it was a coyote, but it sounded bigger. He didn't immediately open his eyes, not sure he wanted to give away that he was awake.

"Maximus!" a man snapped.

The dog quit growling and stepped away, unrushed. Knowing he couldn't play possum forever, Jim listened to the dog's steps. Beneath the blanket, his hand snaked toward his Beretta. He cracked an eye open and spotted a man sitting on a horse regarding them. No weapons were visible but Jim couldn't be certain he was alone. He could have help somewhere out of Jim's line of sight.

Jim made his move. He flipped his unzipped sleeping bag off his body and leveled his handgun on the rider. The stranger did not react, as if this was the logical progression of things, but the dog wasn't having it. At Jim's movement, the massive Anatolian

Shepherd bared its teeth and growled again. Jim responded by aiming at the dog. Right now it seemed the more dangerous of the visitors.

"Call him off," Jim warned. "I'll kill him, then I'll kill you for making me kill him."

"Max," the rider said. "Easy boy."

The dog settled onto its haunches and glared at Jim. He'd seen that look before. It wasn't the first time a dog had called him an asshole.

The man on the horse pushed his hat back and wiped his forehead with a sleeve. "He wants to know why you're in his territory."

"Tell him I'm sorry," Jim said, not sounding like he meant it. "I didn't know anyone was still working the farm."

"Tell him yourself. He's sitting right there."

Jim frowned at the dog, deciding it was too early to be sitting there having a conversation with a strange dog. He shot a glance at Lloyd, who hadn't stirred. He was still out cold, his sleeping bag pulled over his head. Jim guessed from the angle of the sun it was around 7 AM. "Who are you?"

"My name is Gandy. I'm the head shepherd for Rockdell Farms."

Jim was sleepy, his back stiff, and there were a lot of pieces of information that didn't compute. "There are shepherds around here? And Rockdell Farms is still operating?"

"Could you lower the gun, mate? I've got a rifle and a pistol too but you don't see me going around waving them at people, do you? It's just bad manners."

Jim acknowledged the point by lowering his weapon. "Sorry. It pays to be cautious these days."

"Hence why I'm up here and not down there," Gandy said, gesturing toward the lowlands with a toss of his head. "And yes, there are shepherds around, just not many. We don't all carry staffs like Little Bo Peep. Rockdell Farms had nearly ten thousand head of sheep. With that many, they thought it best to get a real shepherd. I trained in Scotland and lived there for a number of years. They recruited me to come over here and run their operation."

Jim didn't know what to say to that. "You're still tending sheep? After all that's gone on?"

"Rockdell Farms isn't operational anymore but what am I supposed to do with myself? I'm a shepherd with a big flock of sheep. I brought them up to the high camp for summer like I normally do."

"You alone, Gandy?"

"I'm alone right now but there are others back at camp. Some of the other Rockdell folks came with me. Some of their families. There was too much shooting and craziness down below. It was making everyone a mite uncomfortable. Too many people dying."

Jim winced. "Yeah, I was probably responsible for some of that. Actually a lot of it. Things haven't been easy."

"Sounds like a fucking war sometimes," Gandy said.

"With good reason. It *has* been a war at times. We can't catch a break." Jim cast another frustrated glance at Lloyd. He couldn't believe his friend hadn't woken up even with an entire conversation taking place right beside him. If this was his customary level of vigilance, they were screwed.

"We haven't had that much trouble up here in the high country. Most people are too lazy to come up this far unless they're on horseback. We've seen a few hunters and that's about it. You guys hunting?"

"No, I live in the valley over that way." Jim raised a hand and pointed toward his home in the far distance. "My buddy and I are getting away for a bit."

Gandy followed where Jim was pointing, then raised an eyebrow. "That's where a lot of the shooting comes from. Not all of it, but quite a bit."

"Yeah. That's part of why we needed a break." Jim stood, nudging Lloyd until he eventually stirred. "Get up, dumbass. We got company."

At the mention of company, Lloyd stuck his head out of his sleeping bag and squinted at Gandy. "Who the hell are you?"

Jim shook his head in frustration. "Get up, Lloyd. Catch up with the conversation. If he was a bad guy you'd already be dead."

Gandy nodded curtly. "You both would."

Lloyd tossed back his sleeping bag and sat upright. He was far from awake but at least he was semi-vertical.

"Maximus and I were out checking the herd. Our camp is on the south ridge, above The Loop, if you ever want to stop by. Just announce yourself because some of our folks are kind of jumpy."

"Like me?" Jim asked.

Gandy smiled. "Exactly like you."

"We might do that. We took this route because I wanted to see the burial cave."

"Ah, I've been in there myself. A bit spooky, isn't it?"

"Maybe, but it's fascinating. I always wanted to see it. We're going to hit the top of the mountain today and camp out there for a few days. I wanted to check out some of the old plane wrecks. There's another cave I'd like to see if I can find it."

"Which one?"

"There's an old story that some deserters from the Civil War lived in a cave up here until the war ended. I wanted to see if I could find it."

Gandy furrowed his brow. "I've seen a few caves but I don't know anything about that. There's a nice one on the south face of the mountain that might be the one you're talking about. I've only been in there once but it looks like it's been well-used over the years. On the maps the place is called Raven Rock or Raven Cliffs. Something like that."

"I'll look for it."

"Best be looking for bears, too," Gandy warned. "They're thick as grasshoppers right now."

"We'll be careful. How did your sheep fare over the winter with no feed and no place to sell them?"

"We lost quite a few." Gandy frowned. "Coyotes, dogs, bears, and a lack of supplemental feed. The herd did better than I expected though."

"They've got a market going in town," Jim said. "I expect you'd do well if you wanted to take a few head down to sell."

"Hadn't heard tell of that, but not much news reaches up this far."

"I don't know the details. I've even heard that some businessman is going to do an auction in his front yard. Livestock and whatever crops people have to sell. You should check it out."

"If I go looking for the market, who do I say sent me? I didn't get your name and I don't know many folks down there."

Lloyd burst out laughing, the first indication he was coming to life.

"What's he laughing about?" Gandy asked.

"Yeah, about that. You'll probably get farther if you *don't* mention that I sent you."

"I don't even have your name, mate."

Jim shrugged. "It's best that way. Come to think of it, you should probably forget you ever saw me."

"Ah, entanglements," Gandy said. "I've had a few in my day too. No worries."

"You ever heard of that book about how to win friends and influence people?" Lloyd asked.

"By Dale Carnegie," Gandy said. "Yeah, it's a business classic."

"Well, my buddy there never read it. In fact, he seems naturally inclined to do just the opposite. If he were ever to write a self-help book it would be on how to *lose* friends and *kill* people," Lloyd said.

Gandy cackled, looking from Lloyd to Jim. "Is that right?"

Jim nodded, seeing no reason to deny it. "Afraid so."

"My friend also seems to think that no problem is too great to be solved as long as you kill the right person," Lloyd went on.

"He was awful quick to whip that gun up," Gandy said. "I guess I should feel lucky he didn't kill me?"

"You probably should," Lloyd agreed. "It's his go-to solution for everything."

Jim frowned. "Okay, enough about me, Lloyd. If you got the energy to sit there and flap your jaws, you've got the energy to get up and ride. Let's move it."

An amused Gandy made eye contact with Lloyd. "Your friend here is a bit testy. How long have you two been on the road together?"

Lloyd checked his pocket watch. "Maybe ten hours?"

"Jesus," Gandy replied. "If you get a chance, stop by my camp on your way home. I want to know how this ends."

Sensing that the only threat remaining was to his dignity and not to his life, Jim dropped to his knees and shoved his sleeping bag into the waterproof stuff sack. When he was done, he folded his ground cloth and tucked that beneath the straps of the stuff sack. He grabbed his saddle off the ground and went to toss it on his horse.

"Well, I'll leave you guys to it," Gandy said. "Nice to meet you and thanks for not killing me."

"Yeah, no problem," Jim said. "You stay safe."

Gandy clucked his tongue. "Come on, Max."

The dog reluctantly fell in behind Gandy's horse, looking as if he had unfinished business with Jim.

Lloyd rubbed his eyes with his palms. "Damn, it's early."

"Your tongue is obviously awake already. You can't seem to quit rattling it."

Lloyd reluctantly rolled off his sleeping bag and began packing it up. "I don't know why you're so defensive. You *are* quick on the trigger."

Jim ignored the comment. He got his horse squared away with a bridle, blanket, and saddle, then got the packhorse ready. When both animals were saddled, he lashed on his gear.

"You bring coffee?" Lloyd asked, stretching as got up, sleeping bag tucked under his arm.

Jim scowled at him, then heaved a loose water bottle in his direction. "Mix in some dirt and use your imagination."

Lloyd dodged to the side, the bottle barely missing him. "You know, there really is something wrong with you. You need therapy, or at least a regular-sized human heart instead of that stunted mouse-sized heart you got." He bent over and picked up Jim's water bottle, then began to lower his zipper.

"Don't you do it!" Jim warned. "You piss in that bottle and this won't end well."

Lloyd tossed the bottle back to Jim. "I thought you knew I needed to go. I thought you were being helpful."

"You should know better than that. When have I ever been helpful?"

Lloyd scratched his head dramatically. "I might have to think on that." He wandered off to water a rock.

Twenty minutes later, they were riding uphill through high alpine-like meadows. Every few minutes they were compelled to stop, turn around, and reexamine the world below them. From this high vantage point they kept seeing new things, new places, and it stirred up old memories. Sometimes it wasn't so much the things they saw as the things they no longer saw. The places that were part of them, or at least had been part of an earlier version of them, that had been torn down to make way for something else.

Jim could see the vacant lot where The Hub used to be. It was a cluttered variety store run by an industrious old character who sold a bit of everything. There was the location of the old Rack-N-Snack where you could get a bag of potato chips and shoot a game of pool. There was the old putt-putt course and the skating rink, both of which fell victim to the rise of shopping malls as a form of entertainment.

"Sure are a lot of things that have been burned down," Lloyd said, taking a peek through Jim's binoculars. "There's burned-out buildings everywhere."

"It's the hillbilly way. We kill people and burn their shit down."

Lloyd threw an accusatory look at him. "Some of you have clearly mastered the skill."

"Sticks and stones, Lloyd. Now I'd suggest you shut up and save your energy. We got places to go."

# 14

liver's House

WHEN SHARON SAW Oliver in his bed, the twisted expression and the terrified eyes, she knew exactly what was wrong with him. She'd seen it before. It was a stroke. Her heart surged and swelled, tears filling her eyes. She went to his side and took his hand. It was all she knew to do. She'd known people who'd had strokes before. Some had lived for days, others for decades longer, trapped in the uncooperative husk of their bodies. Those people had advanced medical care and life support though. She had nothing like that to offer Oliver.

She held his hand until she saw the panic subsiding, talking to him the entire time. "We'll get through this, Oliver. Don't worry. We'll take care of you. We'll keep you comfortable. Do you know what's happened to you?"

He was unable to move his head but she took the look in his eyes and the intelligent, accelerated blinking as an answer.

She gave him a tender smile. "I think you've had a stroke."

His eyes glued to hers, acknowledging her comment. She noticed his gaze peeling off, scanning the walls of the room. She wasn't sure if it was an involuntary movement or if he was seeing something there that she couldn't see.

"I have to get help, Oliver. I want to move you into a more comfortable position but I can't do it by myself. I need to get Nathan to help me. It's going to take me a little bit to get back to camp, then return with someone. Will you be okay while I'm gone?"

She could swear that for a moment his expression said something like 'Are you nuts? Of course I'm not going to be okay.' The sense that this was his intended response was so pronounced that she had to respond to it. She squeezed his curled hand, feeling like something of warm and overstuffed leather. "I'm just trying to figure out if I can leave you behind for a bit. It might take me an hour to get to the camp and back. Do you need any water?"

He didn't blink this time, which she took as an indication that he didn't. She hoped she was guessing correctly.

"Then I'm going to head to the camp. I'll be back here as soon as I can."

Oliver wasn't paying any attention to her. He was looking back to the walls of his room, at something she couldn't see. She released his hand and tugged his homemade quilt up over it. She scanned the walls before she left, curious as to what had Oliver so engaged.

She hurried from the room and rolled down the hall with its high ceilings and dark maple wainscoting. The front of the house had a high porch that was not accessible with her chair so she usually came and went through the kitchen. It was a big room designed for a large family. The cabinets were white metal, the sink cabinet made of porcelain-covered steel.

The floorcovering was an old 1970s vinyl flooring that probably laid in half the kitchens in the area. Most of those other homes had probably updated their flooring, but Oliver never had. It seemed a waste to the practical Oliver to remove perfectly good flooring just because it was a touch outdated. It wasn't so perfectly good now. There were holes beneath the legs of the kitchen table and chairs, and thin spots worn in front of the stove and sink where a person would stand when cooking. Beneath those worn spots, layers of previous flooring peered through like layers of old paint.

Sharon tugged the back door open and navigated her way out past the heavy aluminum storm door with its damaged screen. An old wringer washer with a rusty galvanized basin and a pair of heavy rubber 'mangling' rollers stood off to the side. Several pairs of muddy farming boots were lined against the wall. For some reason, the sight of those boots brought her to a stop. She could picture Oliver starting nearly every day by stepping into a pair of those boots and wandering out into the misty fields of his farm to see what the day brought. The image filled her with a profound sadness.

The sound of Honey tearing tufts of grass from the high weeds snapped her back to the task at hand. The back porch was only one step high and Oliver had installed a short ramp there to make it easy for her comings and goings. Sharon rolled down the ramp and unclipped the small horse from the leaning post that had once held a clothesline. She clipped the carabiners onto her wheelchair and took up Honey's reins.

She clucked her tongue at the gentle animal. "We need to get moving, girl. This is an emergency."

The pony began walking but there was no *hurry* in its vocabulary. Its urgent pace was the same as its meandering pace and that was just as well. The rigged up wheelchair buggy was functional, but just barely. The tiny front wheels with their solid rubber tires were unforgiving. They jolted with every bump and rock. They had on occasion even dug into soft earth, nearly causing Sharon to turn over and land on her face.

The larger back wheels were more forgiving in handling impacts though not by much. The wheels were of plastic construction with air-filled rubber tires. The plastic spokes flexed if the chair leaned in either direction. Through his friends in the community, Oliver had managed to collect a few more wheelchairs of different types that they'd hoped to assemble into something more durable, but there hadn't been the time. They would have to make time, though. One day this chair would fail from the abuse they were subjecting it to, and if she didn't have a backup, she'd be stuck.

With no choice but to continue up the farm road at a reasonable walking pace, Sharon's mind wandered. She had been so dependent on Oliver's experience, wisdom, and guidance. What was she going to do if he passed away? It wasn't likely to be an "if" at this point, it was more likely to be a "when". She held no illusions that they could keep a stroke victim alive without medical assistance.

She'd nearly died from the accident that injured her spine, but she hadn't. She'd rejoiced in her survival and gone on to live an amazing life. In some ways, her accident gave her an awareness she hadn't had before. From that point forward, she never forgot the fragility of life. She never forgot that death was always lurking out there, waiting to snatch you into the darkness. She never forgot that each day was a gift and she had to make the most of it.

It wouldn't be the same for Oliver. There wasn't going to be any recovery. The odds of a miracle were highly unlikely. The probable outcome was that he'd be trapped in a useless body for the rest of his life, cared for by a group that loved him but could do little for him. She didn't even know at this point if he could eat or drink. Stroke victims sometimes lost the ability to swallow. Without the ability to provide a feeding tube or intravenous fluids he would die if that was the case.

For a moment she wondered if it would be kinder to euthanize him.

She pondered that as she bounced up the road but decided she could not do that. Under different circumstances maybe, such as if he was suffering profoundly and she had the ability to halt that suffering. Otherwise, she couldn't imagine herself doing it. She could not snuff out a life that was not threatening her or the children. She had too much respect for the resilience of the human spirit to do that. She would have to allow nature to take its course.

# 15

B *eartown Mountain*

WHEN THEY REACHED THE TREELINE, the terrain instantly became more difficult to negotiate. Jim's last venture onto the mountain had been in late winter for a variety of reasons. Hunting seasons were over by that point, bears were typically sacked out for the winter, and the leaves had dropped from the underbrush. He still had to hack at rhododendrons with a machete to make any progress, but that wasn't an option from atop a horse. The last thing he needed was to injure himself or his horse with a wild blow from a sharp blade.

"Surely we're not going to ride through this mess," Lloyd complained. "It's like a jungle."

"There's something I want you to see. We'll tie the horses off up ahead and walk. It's not far."

Lloyd looked doubtful. "If you say so."

When they could make no further progress, Jim dismounted, tying his horse and packhorse off to a gnarled, wind-whipped tree.

"Everything up here kind of looks alike but I think it's close." He headed off, carrying his rifle in his hands, and didn't wait on Lloyd.

Lloyd rolled his eyes. "I don't know what your damn hurry is. You could wait two seconds for a man to get situated." Lloyd preferred riding horseback in the open pastures to walking in this rough terrain but felt like he had no choice at the moment. He'd signed up for this ride, for better or worse. He'd assured Jim he was up to the challenge even if that might have been a slight exaggeration. He slung his shotgun over his back and fell in behind Jim.

Both men were soon sweating in the heat. Their arms itched from scratches inflicted by the dense brush. Jim lost sight of Lloyd at some point but could hear him cursing and banging around so he knew he wasn't far behind. Shortly, Jim came across the first piece of wreckage. It was a curved piece of aircraft aluminum laying dirty and without context in a pile of old leaves. From its thickness and numerous sheared bolts, it looked like something structural but Jim wasn't familiar enough with planes to recognize it. It was only the first piece. He remembered from his last hike on the mountain that there would be more.

Soon there were. More pieces of debris appeared, the paint faded by time and extreme weather. Perhaps forty yards from the first debris Jim found the intact fuselage of a small plane. It sat slightly askew, wings and landing gear missing, but surprisingly intact. In the decades since the crash, new growth had emerged around it. Trees locked around it like greedy fingers, clutching and establishing domain over the wreckage.

"Jeez, look at that," Lloyd gasped, leaning against a tree to catch his breath.

"This crash occurred in 1974. It happened on a cold night. People were inside with their windows closed and no one heard it. No one saw a thing. The bodies lay in there for a year and a half before bear hunters found them."

Lloyd straightened up and walked closer to the wreckage. "Weren't they looking for it?"

"The pilot wasn't rated to fly at night so he was supposed to stop along the way and spend the night in Georgia. He didn't. He kept going with his wife and his children until they hit the side of the mountain. No one knew where to start looking."

"That's sad," Lloyd said, approaching the plane. He wrestled a door open and stuck his head inside for a look.

"Sad part is that the crash probably didn't kill them. They were all injured but likely survived the initial crash. They died strapped into their seat belts, probably of hypothermia, blood loss, or dehydration. Can you imagine the hopelessness of that? No idea where you are or if help is coming?"

"I don't want to imagine that," Lloyd said. "I've had enough tragedy in my own life that I got no interest in trying on someone else's for fun."

Jim hadn't gone any closer to the aircraft, hanging back with a reverence that didn't entirely make sense for a man so determined to get there. While he'd had no compunction about going inside the burial cave, this place was different for him. There were memories and feelings associated with it. That was part of why he'd always wanted to come back here—to gauge things, to see if the memory was the same in the light of day.

"About four or five years ago I came up here on a backpacking trip. It was February and I came up from the Tumbling Creek side, which is east of here. There are easier ways to get here but they're all on private land. Sometimes you can get permission and sometimes you can't. The access from Tumbling Creek is brutal. Steep hills, climbing, and fighting for every inch of elevation. It's one of the hardest hikes I've ever taken."

"Then why the hell did you do it?" Lloyd asked. There was a mouse nest in the back seat of the plane made from the gnawed up foam of a seat cushion. He swept it to the ground and took a seat inside, his legs hanging out the door.

Jim shrugged. "I'm a mountain masochist. I've never been in the shape to be good at it, but I love climbing around mountains. I like getting up here and seeing the things not many people have seen. It hurts but the pain shows you that you're earning something."

Lloyd looked doubtful. "Whatever floats your boat, man. Sounds like a lot of work to me."

"It was a lot of work," Jim admitted. "I was worn out when I got here. I had just enough time to watch the sunset and then I set up camp back over that way. There was a clearing big enough for a campsite." He pointed in a southerly direction.

"You camped up here?" Lloyd said it was as if it were the most distasteful thing he could imagine.

"I did."

"That must have been creepy. You're a long way from everything and you're by yourself."

"I didn't think it would be creepy, but it was. It was winter and it got cold that night. It was in the low thirties and there was a strong wind. The wind chill was probably in the teens. I kept a fire for a couple of hours before I crashed out and not for one minute did I feel like I was alone that night."

Lloyd raised an eyebrow. "Excuse me?"

"I didn't see anything crazy," Jim said, "but I definitely didn't feel like I was alone. This isn't the only crash up here. There are several. Civilian and military. Most were fatal. That's a lot of death on an isolated mountaintop."

"That's a lot of ghosts."

"I'm not saying they were ghosts, but there were presences here. There was something. I could feel them."

"What did it feel like?"

"Cold," Jim said without hesitation. "Like the cold you feel when you have a fever. A cold so deep that nothing will ever warm you."

"Fuck that," Lloyd said. "I'd have run down the side of this mountain and all the way home."

"Not a possibility. I was too exhausted from just getting here. I didn't have another mile in me."

"So what did you do?"

"When I started to get sleepy I went to put the fire out. There were pockets of snow up here so I packed snow onto the fire to put it out. The moon was bright that night and I barely needed my headlamp. After I smothered the fire, the world took on that blue tinge of moonlight in the forest. The feeling that I wasn't alone didn't go away. I crawled into my tent, zipped it shut, and I could feel these presences around me."

"Why do you think that was?"

"Trust me, I had a lot of time to think about it that night. At first, I figured it was the fire. Anyone who'd survived a crash up here probably died a cold death. As I lay there in my sleeping bag, I started to wonder if it was my presence that drew them. It wouldn't have just been a cold death up there on that mountain, it would have been a lonely death too."

"You going to tell me that you went outside and hugged them all once you figured that out? You sang campfire songs together and roasted marshmallows?"

"No."

"So you just went to sleep with those creepy ghosts circled up around your tent?"

"No. Didn't sleep a wink. Laid there awake all night."

"Sissy," Lloyd cracked.

Jim chuckled. "You want to try it yourself? I'll come back for you in the morning."

Lloyd promptly exited the plane. "I got no interest in doing that at all. In fact, I've had enough of this place already. Let's get out of here." He started toward Jim.

Jim raised a finger and pointed at the plane. "You might should close that door back."

Lloyd returned to the plane and slammed the door, making sure the latch caught. When he turned away from the plane, Jim was already walking away. "Hey, hold up!"

Jim slowed and waited for him to catch up. "You ready now?"

"Yeah, get me the hell out of here. What was the point of this anyway?"

"I'm not sure," Jim said. "Just wanted to see the place again. Wanted to see if it felt like I remembered it. I imagine it will be the last time I'm ever here. Not sure I've got many climbs like that left in me."

"Not sure I ever *had* one in me."

"Yet, here you are," Jim said, gesturing at the expanse of wilderness around them.

"Don't remind me," Lloyd said. "It's only the first full day of Jim's Morbid Mountain Tour and I'm beginning to wonder if I'm up for this."

Jim grinned. "Too late to back out now, my friend. You're here for the duration."

"What's next? A graveyard? A hanging tree? The site of a murder or suicide? I've never understood these grim obsessions of yours. What is it about the dead that fascinates you?"

"Ain't the dead—it's the history."

"Eh, history is the past. Nothing more. It only has the power you assign to it."

Jim shook his head. "History writes the present."

"Where to next, Mr. Philosopher? You going to plant yourself on a rock and say profound shit all day? Not sure how long I can stomach that."

"Nope. We're going to drop back below the treeline and head north. We'll circle the peak of the mountain and head northeast along the ridge toward Mutter Gap, then ride to Laurel Bed Lake."

"What about this Civil War deserters cave you wanted to find?"

Jim ducked through a gap in the rhododendron, fighting it back with one arm. "I need to think about that some more. I'm wanting a backup location for the family. I need to find a place we can retreat to and hide out if the valley becomes too hot. I'm not sure living in a cave on this mountain is sustainable though. Maybe the lake is a better option."

They reached their horses and found the animals had managed to tangle themselves in the brush. It was unavoidable in this kind of terrain. It took them a moment to set things right. When they had, they mounted their horses and rode out of the shady tunnel of forest.

The midday sun seared away any lingering unease remaining from the crash site.

"You're getting spooky in your old age, Jim. You were always a simmering pot but the contents of that pot are darker than they used to be."

"Well, you're getting uglier in your old age."

Lloyd shifted in his saddle. "Reckon I'd take ugly over spooky any day of the week."

**16**

---

O*liver's House*

GETTING BACK to the camp took Sharon longer than she expected. The mile of road between Oliver's house and the camp got rougher with each rain, exposing rocks and carving troughs into the hard clay soil. She had no choice but to move at a crawl, afraid of damaging her chair or turning it over. When she finally made it back to the camp, Nathan was not yet back from gathering peaches. It took her twenty more minutes to locate him and quietly relay what had taken place.

His immediate reaction was wide-eyed terror. He'd lived a sheltered life, or more accurately a blessed life, up until this point. No one close to him had died or even succumbed to grave illness. Prior to the terror attacks, when he'd been with his family, they'd all been healthy as horses. Because of his inexperience, he was scared by the idea of having to visit Oliver with Sharon. He had no idea of what he'd find there or what he'd have to do.

"It'll be okay," Sharon assured him. "I've dealt with things like this before. I just need you there to help me move him. I can't do it alone."

"Maybe you should take another of the boys. Somebody has to stay here and watch the kids."

Sharon reached out and took him by the hand. "You can do this, Nathan. You're stronger than you think, physically *and* mentally. It's you I need. I'm going to leave Kay in charge here. She can handle things. If we're late, she can help the other kids with lunch. She knows what to do and they'll listen to her."

Seeing there was no way he could easily get out of going, he relented wordlessly, offering a nod of concession.

"You'll be fine," Sharon said. "Let me speak to Kay and then we'll go."

Nathan led the pony to a watering trough, then let it munch on some grass while Sharon talked to Kay. Watching from the corner of his eye, he saw Kay cover her mouth with both hands, a certain indication that Sharon had not sugar-coated the severity of Oliver's situation. As always, she was painfully honest with the children, accurately explaining situations in terms they could understand. She didn't have children of her own but lived a life full of children, all of whom she treated like miniature adults. When they wanted to know the *why* of things, she told them in as plain and honest a fashion as she could.

When she was done with Kay, Sharon waved Nathan over and he led Honey along in her improvised harness. He helped Sharon clip in and they were off, her rolling and him plodding alongside beside her. There was something about traveling the unimproved farm road that harkened back to another time. It demanded patience and laid the stage for introspection. Whether in a car, on foot, or traveling by some other means, it accommodated no hurrying. It took however long it took. Other than the type of fencing that ran alongside the road, most of their surroundings were the same as they would have been a hundred years ago.

"What will happen to Oliver?" Nathan asked.

Sharon was staring ahead, watching the baked road and the

bobbing head of her pony. "It's hard to say. I've known people to have strokes and live twenty more years, their bodies twisted up, having to be waited on hand and foot. I've known others where it was the start of a downhill slope and they died not long afterward. Without doctors and advanced diagnostics, there's no way for us to know what's going on with Oliver."

"Is he...in pain?"

Sharon considered this. "I don't think so. He can't speak, but I don't think he's in pain. I'd guess he's scared and probably confused."

"So what can we do for him?"

"We can try to make him comfortable and see what happens. We can be there for him and hold his hand. The real issue will be whether he can eat and drink. If he can't swallow, it's not likely we'll be able to keep him alive for more than a few days."

Nathan mulled that over as he walked, staring at the ground, and watching rocks fly as he kicked at them. "I don't want to see him die."

"I don't want him to die either but that's not in our hands."

"No, I mean I don't want to *see* it. I don't want to be there when he passes away."

Sharon considered this before replying. "I don't exactly want to watch it either, but you know what bothers me more?"

"What?"

"The idea of him dying alone and scared. Look at what he's done with this camp he built. Look at all the happiness he's given people. Even after the attacks last summer, after things fell apart, he helped keep us alive. He helped us get through the winter and showed us how to plant in spring. Every time our pantry began to look empty he came up with something. After what that man has done for us, I can't turn my back on him. Imagine it was you laying there. What would you want?"

"When you put it that way, it doesn't leave us much choice," Nathan said. "I guess we owe him."

Sharon was pleased to see him arrive at this conclusion on his own, or at least on his own *with* a gentle nudge from her. "That's exactly right. We do owe him. I won't lie. This is going to hurt. It's going to be hard to watch. It's going to make us sad and we're going to want to run away from it, but we won't, will we?"

"No."

"Why not?" Sharon pressed.

"Because we honor our obligations. We take care of the people who take care of us."

She grinned broadly. "That's exactly right, Nathan. You're growing up to be such a smart young man. Your family would be proud of you."

At the mention of his family, Nathan grew quiet. He wasn't sullen exactly, but thoughtful. This often happened with the children who'd been left behind at camp, trying to figure out what had happened to the people who were supposed to come for them. Sharon let each process it in their own way, helping when she was called upon to do so.

With Nathan's silence, her mind traveled. What she hadn't told the boy was that she felt she owed Oliver for more than what he'd done last winter. She owed him for the twenty years he'd allowed her to work at the camp. She was paid a little, as were all the staff who worked there, but she'd have gladly done it for free simply for the privilege of being there.

The camp made her whole. Seeing these children grow, watching them come back year after year until they were no longer children, gave meaning to her life in a way that nothing else did. She knew it wasn't simply what they taught at the camp. It wasn't only about music and becoming a better player. It wasn't about performing and learning new songs. It was the whole atmosphere, the environment. It was the farm and the isolation. It was Oliver and his devotion to what they did there.

When they'd first met, when she'd interviewed for the job, she saw his eyes flicker to the chair. She saw the doubt. He might as well have shaken his head, rubbed his chin, and said, "I don't know about this."

Yet she won him over. She'd never had a doubt in her mind that she wouldn't be able to. It was her smile, her enthusiasm, the glow in her eyes, and her aura of radiance that warmed everyone close to her like a campfire on a cold night. They'd had to make some accommodations, some changes to the facilities to allow her to get where she needed to go. He'd been hesitant about that at first, too. The camp had already been there for more than twenty years and Oliver was kind of attached to the way things looked. He didn't want to go changing things.

They worked it out though. Seeing her determination made Oliver want to remove any barriers to her getting where she wanted to go. After hearing from some of the staff that Sharon had spent four hours trekking to a remote swimming hole so she could watch some kids swim, Oliver bought her a golf cart to make certain that she could get anywhere on the property she wanted to go.

Thinking of the golf cart made her lament the lack of fuel. Before they ran out of gas it had been her primary means of going back and forth between the camp and Oliver's place. It was so much easier. This was the state of things though. There was no point in dwelling upon that which she could not change. She learned that long ago.

**17**

___________

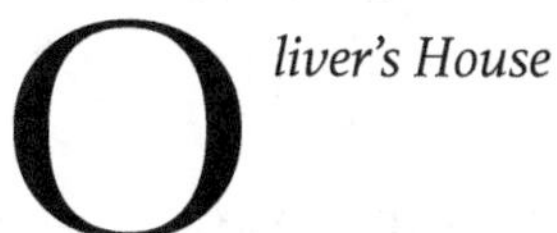



THE TRIP to the camp and back consumed over two hours. Sharon was uncertain of what she'd find at Oliver's house so she was apprehensive as she rolled onto the back porch and opened the door, though her level of apprehension was nowhere in the range of Nathan's. He lingered over tying up Honey, not wanting to cross that threshold.

"C'mon, Nathan. We need to check on Oliver."

He gave the pony a rub between the ears and headed for the house. Sharon went on through the door and Nathan followed, closing it behind them. The house was totally silent, the thick walls shutting out the few sounds of the outside world—roosters, distant dogs barking, the bleat of a goat, and the cawing of crows. The sound of Sharon's wheels on the multiple layers of vinyl flooring made a sound both sticky and hollow at the same time. She thumped over an aluminum transition strip at the doorway and headed down the hall toward Oliver's bedroom.

Natural light flooded the long hallway through tall windows but it did nothing to lighten the mood. The sunlight emphasized the grain in the dark maple floors and revealed the texture in the hand-plastered walls with their thick layers of paint. It filled the dusty gossamer curtains that hung as a remnant of the day a woman had cared about such homey touches. Despite the brightness of the midday sun and the sweltering heat of the outside world, no warmth reached the interior of this house. It was not humid, the air tinged with mildew as one might expect. It was cool, cavernous, and solemn as a church.

The sound of Sharon's wheels echoed from the hard surface of the walls. She neither lingered nor wasted time, as Nathan did behind her. She turned right at the end of the hall and found the door to Oliver's bedroom shut. She paused to try and recall if she'd closed that door. She couldn't imagine she had. There'd be no reason to do so in the empty house.

She turned the old glass knob and the well-worn innards moved with a fluid mechanical efficiency. The bolt retracted and Sharon pushed. The hinges creaked and the door swung. Oliver lay unchanged before her. His eyes were open and he was pitched awkwardly on his side. His large chest moved with the intake of breath, though perhaps faster than ideal. Uncertain if he'd detected her presence, she moved forward and took his hand. It was warm, dry, and rough with callouses.

"I'm back, Oliver. I brought Nathan with me. You haven't moved. You still feeling the same?"

He moved his thumb against the back of her hand, the only digit capable of cooperating with his intentions. He moved his mouth in an awkward contortion that never did produce speech. When the effort failed, Oliver quit trying. He closed his mouth and issued a low groan, a mournful rattle of air over uncooperative pipes.

Oliver's eyes flickered beyond her and she knew he'd caught sight of Nathan. Sharon turned around to offer the boy a supportive smile but he'd not entered the room yet, unable to bring himself to step over the threshold. He stood in the doorway, his hand clutching the jamb as if to anchor himself in place. Perhaps it was all that kept him from fleeing.

"Oliver, I feel like we need to try to make you more comfortable. Maybe if I can get you over on your back we can see if you can take some water. How's that sound?"

The response was a resigned groan.

"Nathan, can you get to the other side of the bed, please? We're going to try and roll him over onto his back."

Nathan hurried to the task, as if the sooner he got to it, the sooner he could be out of there. "How do I...where do I hold him?"

"We're going to be gentle and move slowly," Sharon said. "Sometimes a stroke can make a person's body rigid. He might not roll easily. I'm going to have you put your hands on the shoulder that's sticking up in the air. I'm going to reach for the shoulder that's beneath his body. We're going to slowly pull on him until he starts to turn over onto his back. If it looks like we're hurting him, we'll stop. If it causes him any distress we'll return him to the position he's in now. Got it?"

Nathan let out a long breath, a steeling of the nerves, before answering. "I'm ready."

They put their hands in position and Sharon noted the coolness of Oliver's body. It was exactly the opposite of what she'd expected. They turned him and the dank smell of urine rose in a cloud around them. Oliver was not a slight man. He was over six feet and two inches, over two hundred and fifty pounds. As they rolled his body, his limbs did not yield but protruded in an awkward and insectoid manner.

He moved though, his body turning inch by excruciating inch, and Sharon's mouth curled in a smile of triumph until they got him over on his back. Oliver immediately began choking and coughing.

"Raise him up! Raise him up!" Sharon said urgently.

Terrified, Nathan grasped Oliver by the shoulders and tugged him forward so that Sharon could slide pillows beneath him. Nathan stared at Oliver's face, his deep-set eyes crushed together in an urgent cough that provided no relief.

"Now set him back," Sharon said, struggling to help Nathan lean Oliver back onto the pillows.

When they had him settled back, Oliver's eyes opened wide and his chest expanded in a great wheeze. The coughing began anew, a violent choking hack that made Sharon's heart ache. She felt totally helpless.

Nathan was panicking. "What do we do?"

Sharon's face bore a pained expression. "We're going to have to put him back the way he was when we came in. Lift him up!"

Nathan again tugged Oliver forward while Sharon removed the pillows this time.

"Put him down, then we'll turn him."

Nathan did as instructed, laying Oliver onto his back and then gently rolling him onto his side, back the way they'd found him. Oliver continued to cough and wheeze for a painfully long period but his distress subsided.

"What happened?" Nathan said, his face bright red. He was ready to cry.

"I think that means his throat isn't working right," Sharon admitted. "He can't swallow on his back. His saliva runs into his lungs and causes him to cough."

"What does that mean?" There was a note of fear in his voice, an underlying awareness of what this meant. The boy just didn't want to put it into words. He needed to hear it from someone else. Someone with more experience. Someone with authority.

"It probably means he's going to die, Nathan."

## 18

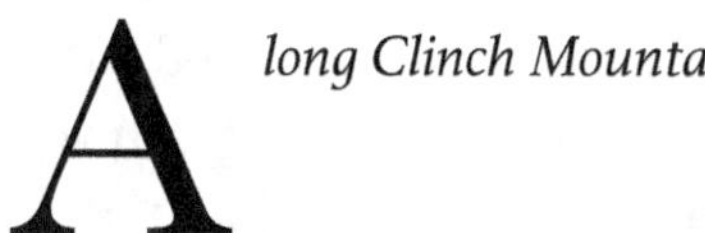

A long Clinch Mountain

Jim and Lloyd spent the afternoon riding a faint hunting trail along the ridge of Clinch Mountain. At times the jungle became impenetrable and they dropped to the north side of the crest, above the communities of Rosedale and Belfast. The sounds of industry and human effort rose from the valleys below them. Those who'd previously used grid power to push electricity through their fences sought other means to keep their cattle contained.

They hammered barbed wire to those same posts that held the now-useless electric fencing. High-tensile electric didn't require nearly as many posts as other means of fencing so farmers found themselves forced to add more posts. They resurrected rusty steel posts, lengths of cedar, old pipe, and anything else capable of standing upright and holding a strand. Young farmers scratched their heads as they tried to rediscover the way in which previous generations had performed this task.

In the search for barbed wire, farmers scoured their barns and outbuildings. They took down old, abandoned fencing and raided the rusting mounds of trash packed in the old sinkholes farmers used as landfills. Those who couldn't find enough resorted to even older methods of fencing, using wedges and sledgehammers to split logs into rail fencing that they either stacked or affixed to posts, depending on the availability of nails. In a throwback to the days of the Great Depression, bent nails were no longer casually discarded. They were laid on a flat surface and tapped back into rightfulness so that they might be used again.

Other farmers struggled to free those pieces of horse-drawn equipment that had served as nothing more than lawn ornaments for the last half-century. Some pieces yielded easily, perhaps eager to find new purpose in the powerless world. Other equipment, grown rusty and arthritic with the passage of time, preferred to sit this one out, perfectly content as the centerpiece of a roadside flowerbed.

The riders saw cattle grazing the steep slopes of high pastures, but saw no one tending them. They spotted no hunters, though they stirred deer of all age and size, from the spotted fawn to the heavy old bucks. They drove rabbits from cover and flushed ruffed grouse that exploded from the brush with a heart-pounding intensity. Several times they heard an indelicate crashing in the deep brush off-trail that they attributed to bear, but only once did they meet one. They ran headlong into an old black bear who shared their trail and had no more interest in surrendering it than the riders did.

Lloyd drew his shotgun and sat ready to shoot.

Jim raised a hand to stop him. "No, I don't want these old farmers to think we're up here poaching cattle. If we have to interact with them, I might be recognized."

"I ain't getting ate up just to keep your secret," Lloyd hissed.

The horses shied and skittered beneath them, nervous at the sight and smell of the predator. Every equine instinct told them to flee.

"Usually bears are more afraid than this," Jim said. He turned his attention back to the distant bear, head raised and sniffing at the air. "Hey bear!"

The common backpacker's chant, the call of "hey bear", had no effect on the animal. Perhaps isolated on this distant and hiker-less peak he'd not gotten the memo. Maybe he'd missed the instruction that other bears got, not understanding he was supposed to flee at those magic words, leaving the relieved hikers with a good story to tell.

"He don't care about all your 'hey bear' bullshit," Lloyd growled. "If you can't get rid of him, I'm shooting him with this shotgun."

With a sigh, Jim dismounted.

Lloyd looked at him in concerned confusion. "You going to go all Daniel Boone on him? Fight him bare-knuckled and kick his ass?"

Jim stared at his friend like he was an idiot, then selected a rock the size of a tangerine from the trail. With a hand on the reins of his horse, he heaved the rock with all his might. It hit the bear broadside with a hollow fur-muffled thump. The bear bellowed and huffed, then twisted, charging away full-speed into the dense forest. To ensure it didn't lose its motivation, Jim retrieved a second rock and chucked it in the general direction of the fleeing bear. They could no longer see the bear and the sound of its escape was growing fainter. It was gone. Jim swung back into the saddle and gave Lloyd a satisfied grin.

Lloyd wasn't impressed. "Yeah, any peckerwood can throw a rock. A real man would have kicked that bear's ass."

"How about you show me on the next one," Jim said. "You want to ride point?"

Lloyd had no interest in that and quickly changed the subject. "We going to sit here until he gets back or are we going to get riding?"

Jim nudged his horse and they resumed their ride. They'd gone about seven or eight miles from the site of the plane crash when they ran into a more heavily-traveled trail crossing their path.

"I think this is the old farm road from Belfast to the lake," Jim said. "The Clinch Mountain Wildlife Management Area used to be part of Rockdell Farms but they sold it off."

The farm road paralleled a utility right-of-way, a swath of cleared land that sliced through the hardwood forest like a scar bereft of pigment, forever a shade lighter than its surroundings. Useless high-tension powerlines hung from galvanized steel towers, no better than a disused clothesline at the moment. The riding was easier here. Though the land had seen no maintenance in this past year, there were signs that someone kept it open prior to that, a dozer or tractor passing through to mow down saplings and clear thorns.

The horses seemed to know their business here, perhaps following some remnant scent of past horses that had traveled this way. It was also possible that they simply preferred the easier traveling of going downhill and would do so until directed to do otherwise. The lay of the land and the dense forest conspired to hide the lake from view as the two riders descended, but Jim knew it was there. Though he'd never come by this route, he'd been to this lake many times over the years—hiking, kayaking, and fishing.

Laurel Bed Lake was a high-altitude lake situated in an almost Alpine setting. It was man-made, created when the state dammed a creek moving through a vast bog. The lake was over three hundred acres and surrounded by forest on all sides. It was beautiful and rarely crowded because there was no easy way to get there. The shortest route to the lake, the one Jim and Lloyd were now traveling, was closed to the public and inaccessible to most vehicles. Every other route was a long haul over winding dirt roads, with the last miles winding up steep hills.

Even as they neared the bottom of the trail and the gravel road that ran along the lake, they only caught glimpses of the water. The tree canopy was too dense at this time of year to offer much in the way of long views.

Lloyd reached the gravel road first and reined his horse to a stop. "I don't know this place. Which way?"

Jim considered. "Let's go right. That will take us to the boat ramp and the dam. There's a trail there that will get us to my favorite campsite, as long as it's not taken."

Lloyd frowned. "I can't imagine it's crowded."

"Maybe not, but we might not be the only folks up here either."

Jim turned his horse in that direction and headed off, gravel crunching beneath the hooves. They didn't go far before they had to skirt the first of several downed trees. Some of these remote wilderness areas required a lot of maintenance. Without constant attention and a supply of fuel, the wilderness quickly retook the ground it had once yielded. Perhaps it had always understood that man's attempt to claim domain over it was both inadequate and impermanent. It had only to wait patiently for men to falter and fail, certain of that inevitability.

The gravel parking lot beside the primitive boat ramp was rarely crowded on the best of days. Many visitors used canoes or kayaks and didn't require a ramp. The riders found a rusty old RV, which they first assumed to be abandoned and vandalized. It was a short 1970s model that had seen better days. The vehicle was surrounded by a circle of what could have been trash, camping gear, or someone's possessions. It was hard to tell. There was a homeless camp vibe about the setting.

"Look at that," Lloyd said, pointing toward a portable toilet left at the ramp for the convenience of boaters.

Jim quickly noticed what had gotten Lloyd's attention. Someone had used an ax to chop a hole in the sewage tank compartment. All of the contents of the bright blue outhouse streamed in a pungent and discolored trail down toward the water.

"Someone must be using it," Jim said. "Think someone lives here?"

"Someone does live here, by damn!" came a voice from inside the camper. "That someone was taking a nap till you come up here with your jawing and judging."

Lloyd looked at Jim with raised eyebrows, but Jim didn't catch his gaze. He was spinning his rifle off his back and leveling it toward the camper. The vehicle rocked on its springs and the door flew open with a creak. The RV disgorged its occupant into the parking lot and the pair found themselves staring at a toothless old man with thick, misshapen gray hair. He was wearing long denim shorts and a grubby blue t-shirt that said "Show Me Your Bobbers and I'll Show

You My Pole". He assessed the situation for a moment before speaking to them.

"You can just put that gun away right now," the old man scolded. "Ain't no call for that."

"Are you alone?" Jim asked.

The old man squinted his eyes and bobbed his head. "Can't say they ain't no one else around but if there is, they ain't with me. I'm alone. Been up here alone since this whole mess started."

Jim lowered his gun and clicked the safety back on. He kept his hand on the grip and the gun laying across the saddle in front of him. He could get it up in a moment if the old man was lying to him, but Jim didn't get that feeling.

"Don't mind my buddy there," Lloyd said to the old man. "He's just that way, a little awkward when it comes to meeting people. I try to tell him that's why he ain't got no friends but he don't listen. You say you been up here the whole time?"

The old man took a step away from his camper, his gait impaired by a limp. "Damn right. I lived in a trailer park there in Richlands. People there'll steal from you on a good day. The last thing I wanted was to get stuck there if times got worse. I saw the writing on the wall and got my ass out of Dodge."

Jim nodded. "Smart man."

"Momma didn't raise no fool," the old man crowed. "My name is Andrew. Andrew Jackson. To whom do I have the pleasure of speaking?"

"I'm Lloyd. My buddy here is—"

"Jay," Jim interrupted. "My name is Jay."

Lloyd squinted at him as if he were being an idiot, but Jim gave him a warning look. He had no idea how far word of the bounty on his head had spread. He had no intention of giving out his real name to anyone he met on the road.

"Why did you come up here?" Lloyd asked. "This is the middle of nowhere."

Andrew gestured at the lake. "Middle of nowhere is where you want to be. Hell, I was up here all the time anyway, fishing or hunting. I couldn't think of a better place to be."

"Get much company?" Jim asked.

Andrew looked at him, then flinched and rubbed the back of his neck. "Look, y'all are welcome to stay and shoot the shit but you're gonna have to get offen them horses. It pains my neck to keep looking up at you."

Lloyd glanced at Jim to see what he wanted to do. Jim gave him a "why not" shrug and the two dismounted.

"We're going to tie our horses off where they can get a drink," Jim said.

"Suit yourself," Andrew said, dragging a camping chair out from beneath his camper and taking a seat.

There were several posts in the ground along the water for tying off boats. The riders tied their horses to them and rejoined the old man.

"Ain't got no more chairs but you're welcome to pull up a bucket," Andrew said, gesturing at a couple of five-gallon buckets with lids on them.

Jim and Lloyd found a couple of buckets and plopped down on them. Jim sat far enough away that he could keep an eye on his surroundings. He kept his rifle on his lap.

Andrew leaned toward Lloyd with a conspiratorial air. "Your buddy there is a little edgy, ain't he? Don't like to let no breathing room get between him and that rifle."

Lloyd sighed as if Jim was a disappointing son. "I've tried to talk to him about it. He ain't a people person like us. He don't act right half the time."

Jim sighed. "When y'all are done talking about me, I'm wanting to hear if you get much company up here."

Lloyd gestured at Jim as if his words were further confirmation of the point they'd just been discussing. "See, he's like that all the time," he told Andrew. "All business. And God forbid you cross him."

"Testy, is he?"

"Lord, you ain't seen nothing to beat it," Lloyd said, his voice animated and musical as if he were about to launch into a song. "He'd just as soon shoot a man as look at him."

"Is that right?" Andrew drawled as if it was the darndest thing he'd ever heard. "Reckon I'm safe even sitting here?"

"You're probably safe if I'm sitting here with you, Andrew. Just don't make any sudden moves."

Andrew winked at Lloyd. "Iffen I go to scratch my ass, I'll do it slowly."

Jim watched the two of them without a hint of amusement. It was bad enough dealing with one lackluster comedian and now he was confronted with two of them. He tried again to get things back on a serious track. "So, you get much company in these parts?"

"Reckon I better answer him this time," Andrew said in an aside to Lloyd. Then, giving Jim a friendly smile, said, "Some but not much. It's a far piece to all but those who live just over the mountain there. Got a few dirt bikes and four-wheelers at the beginning, when people noticed they wasn't no law on duty anywhere. Get a few hunters and every once in a while someone shows up on horseback, like you two. Some of them camps a night or two but nobody stays long. I reckon I'm the only full-time resident. In fact, folks has taken to calling me The Mayor."

"What folks?" Jim asked.

"Why, the folks who pass through," Andrew said. "Ain't many, like I said, but enough that I've become a fixture around the place."

"You get by alright up here by yourself?" Lloyd asked.

"I'm fine on both accounts. I get by alright and I don't mind being by myself."

"I'd get lonely," Lloyd mused.

Andrew shook his head adamantly. "I used to be married and it was an awful time. I swore if I got out of that I'd never complain about being lonely again. That woman was lazy as the day is long and ugly as a look into Hell. If I start to get lonely, I just think about her and the fact she ain't here. Next thing you know, I'm grinning like a possum."

"You got plenty to eat?" Jim asked, casting a sideways glance at the belongings piled around the truck.

"I see you there with your judgey eyeballs," Andrew said, "looking at my rig like it's a piece of crap, but don't let looks fool you. I'm a retired coal miner and I didn't do nothing in my off hours but fish, hunt, and camp. When I saw the writing on the wall, I loaded up all my gear into my camper and strapped my canoe on the top. I stopped by the grocery store and stocked up on a few things. Got rice, beans, and noodles. Lots of canned stuff."

"I'm assuming you hunt too?" Jim asked.

"Oh yeah, since there ain't no game wardens to be concerned about I use a few means the law ain't particularly fond of. I got fishing lines out on old milk jugs and pop bottles. I run a trotline on the trout stream that feeds out of here. I got snares for beaver, rabbit, and deer. For squirrels, I nail them big old rat traps right to the tree and put bait on them. Works like a charm."

Jim smiled. "Sounds like you're working smart. You got traps hunting for you while you're doing other stuff."

Andrew gave him a smug look. "Sorry you gave me them judgey eyes now, aren't you? There you were, thinking I was dumbass, and I had to go and prove you wrong. Smarts a mite, don't it?"

"I never thought you were a dumbass," Jim replied. "I didn't know you well enough to make that call. Usually it takes me a few minutes to figure it out and go to putting labels on stuff."

"What label you gonna give me now?"

Jim considered. "Resourceful."

"*Damn* right," Andrew said. "And you don't even know the half of it. The tailwaters below the dam are full of cattails. I eats the shoots all spring and eats the roots in the fall and winter. I got morels in the spring, chicken-of-the-woods and hen-of-the-woods in the summer. I dry them and eat on them all winter."

"That a bird?" Lloyd asked confused.

"Mushroom," Jim said.

Andrew grinned eagerly. "I cooks up fiddleheads too. Ever eat 'em?"

Jim nodded. Lloyd looked confused.

"It's a fern," Andrew said. "You eat them when they're coming up in the spring. They're curled up like the head of a fiddle. Easy to spot. There's nuts and berries too. Plenty to eat if you know what you're looking for."

"Sounds like you eat well," Lloyd said.

"Grew up poor but never went hungry," Andrew said. "The mountains provide if you know where to look. Say, speaking of fiddleheads, that a banjo I spy on your horse there?"

Lloyd had been waiting for this opportunity. "I been known to pick a banjo."

Andrew grinned. "Did you know there's a perfect weight for a banjo player?"

"No."

"They is. It's about three and a half pounds, including the urn." Andrew burst into laughter, slapping his knee.

Jim joined him. He too was a fan of banjo jokes. "Hey Andrew, you know the difference between a banjo and a trampoline?"

Andrew shook his head.

"You take off your shoes before you jump up and down on a trampoline," Jim said.

Andrew cackled. Jim snickered. Lloyd sat stone-faced.

Andrew reached over and smacked Lloyd on the arm. "Hey, we're just funning you. Wouldn't play a tune for a man, would you?"

Jim stood up before Lloyd could head for his banjo. "Listen, if you all are going to start playing music and swapping lies, I'm going to head around the lake and look for a campsite."

"Whereabouts you thinking of camping?" Andrew asked.

"That cove at the mouth of the lake," Jim said.

"They's bears," Andrew said, pronouncing it *bars*. "You'd be much better off camping right here with me. Strength in numbers and all that."

"I appreciate the offer, but I kind of had my mind set on that other spot. You all can sit a spell. I'm going to go check it out."

"Suit yourself," Andrew said.

**19**

L*aurel Bed Lake*
*Clinch Mountain Wildlife Management Area*

MOST OF LAUREL BED LAKE was visible from the immediate shoreline, with the exception of a small cove at the mouth of the lake. That isolated cove had always been a favorite destination for Jim's family when they kayaked here. They'd park at a gravel lot with no boat ramp and drag their kayaks to the water. When they first started paddling here, they piled into two boats, but soon Pete and Ariel wanted their own. Jim bought them smaller kayaks and carried a rope so he could tow them along behind his own if they got tired.

They'd paddle along the shoreline, sticking to the shallower water. The quiet boats allowed them to creep up on beavers, turtles, and birds. When they spotted something that caught their eye, they'd stop and explore. Sometimes they'd fish, though their destination was always the gravel beach in the sheltered cove. They'd pull their boats onto the shore and throw out a blanket on a carpet of ferns.

Lunch was a cooler of drinks and a backpack of whatever snacks the kids wanted.

Those were magical times. Despite the hassle of getting everyone ready, loading all the gear, and driving the hour to the lake, they were memories everyone treasured. Now, riding along the shoreline on horseback, traversing the lake in a manner he'd never experienced before, Jim couldn't help but be bombarded by those memories. He scanned the water, almost expecting to see their colorful kayaks and his children waving at him. The water was empty though. Not his kayaks, not anyone's kayaks. No boats at all.

The trail he took was mostly used by shore fisherman trying to reach a better spot along the densely wooded lakeshore. The path rode high on the slope above the lake in order to miss the deep coves where feeder creeks notched the shoreline. Not long after leaving Lloyd behind Jim had to climb off his horse and walk. There were too many low branches for horseback.

The wilderness area was over twenty-five thousand acres. The lake was deep in the interior and provided habitat for a lot of wildlife. As Jim walked, he heard critters in the forest reacting to his presence. Deer sprinted for safety. Birds flushed or called out warnings to their fellow birds. Snakes oozed along like ancient evil. Jim kept his eyes open for more bears, fully expecting to run into another.

It took him nearly forty-five minutes of walking to reach the gravel beach he was looking for. He'd never approached the place by foot before so he took a couple of false turns on the last section of trail. When he stepped foot on the carpet of moss and ferns where his family had picnicked so often, he was again hit by memories of the times he'd spent here. In his customary practical manner, he reminded himself that dwelling on the past accomplished nothing. He needed to keep his head in the present. That was where the pressing concerns were.

The beach and campsite had seen better days. There had sometimes been a little trash left there back when he and his family frequented the lake, but the area was cleaned up regularly. Volunteers and employees picked up cans, bottles, and items left over by less considerate campers. Now there was scattered evidence of longer-term camping. Jim tied his horses off and wandered around.

A frame of stripped poplar poles appeared to have been the basis of a large tarp shelter. There was a supply of firewood stacked off to the side. A crude table had been fashioned between standing trees. Deep slices in the surface of the tabletop made Jim think it had been used for processing game. He crouched over the circle of stones they'd been using as a fire pit and raked a twig through the ashes. Most of the fine ash had already been washed away, exposing the unburned wood once buried there. This told him the fire pit hadn't been used recently. The twig unearthed rusting can lids and a slender bone that he suspected belonged to a doe.

Jim took a seat on a log and stared out at the calm water. Strains of banjo music reached his ears. He shouldn't be surprised at the way Lloyd had taken to that old man. It was a sign of how difficult the isolation of valley life had been for him. Lloyd was used to meeting people like that every week. He was used to entertaining strangers and playing for crowds. He missed the energy of having new people in his life, though the same might be said for most of the people in the valley.

Well, everyone except for Jim.

That awareness only furthered his quandary. With everyone already suffering the effects of isolation, of missing their routines, of losing the lives they were used to, how could he consider dragging them off into the woods? He hadn't made up his mind that he was going to do it. He wasn't committed to the idea, but it was a strong enough consideration that he was up here looking at the lake this very moment, wasn't he?

Besides the logistical issues of moving up here and constructing a shelter that would keep his family warm in the winter, what would the isolation do to them? He couldn't imagine that the entire valley would move up here with them. His family would lose the only other people they had in their lives at the moment. And what about Nana and Pops? At their ages, he couldn't expect that they'd want to explore the pioneer homesteading lifestyle.

It was a stupid idea. A flight of fancy brought on by the stress he was dealing with. There were times in everyone's life when escaping and running away seemed like the way to go. Sometimes starting over helped but other times it fixed nothing. Maybe it would have worked for him years ago, as a single man with no one to worry about. He was far from that now. Not only did he have a family to take care of but parents who needed his help. Then there were the friends, who benefited from his assistance.

Yet the issues that drove him here—drove him onto this mountain, into these woods, and to this very campsite on the lakeshore—were real. He'd kicked a hornet's nest in destroying that power plant. He'd never considered the pushback he might take for an action like that. At the time he hadn't cared. He was so offended by the idea that his government would hold them hostage, not releasing power or even aid for those in need, until they had total control. Give us your guns or you get nothing.

Scuttlebutt Hugh heard on the radio had led Jim to believe that it wasn't the entire government behind it. He'd heard as much from Scott and the other East Coast Power Recovery Commission people they met back in the winter. As always, various factions were vying for power and each had a different vision for America. There were competing agendas and at the moment, the folks making the decisions about power and aid were able to further their own agenda. They weren't holding all the cards though. Jim had reason to believe there were people out there who would support the action he'd taken. He just had to find them and ally himself with them.

What did that mean for him in the interim? He had no support and no allies outside of his own people. If he couldn't take his family out of the valley, what did he do? What were his options? Did he continue to hide out in the mountains and leave them to their own devices? He couldn't imagine doing that. He'd found it difficult to go to sleep last night just thinking about them. How much more intense was that feeling going to be in a week? A month? There was no way he could do that. That was no way to live. Not for him and not for his family.

He was reminded of his grandfather whose imagined reminders to *harden the fuck up* had gotten him home from Richmond. His grandfather had never hidden from the deeds he'd done. He'd shot men and slit throats. He'd had gunfights in town and killed men who crossed him in front of restaurants full of customers. If the law wanted him, they knew where to find him and he dared them to come. They never did.

Perhaps Jim needed to adopt a similar philosophy. He wanted to fly under the radar to keep his family safe. He wanted his community to think he was dead so no one would come looking for him with the expectation of obtaining a bounty, or perhaps even in search of vengeance. Maybe it was time to tell the world to kiss his ass.

If he had no way to guarantee his family's safety and nowhere to shelter them, then maybe it wasn't time to hide. Perhaps he should go on with his life as if nothing had happened. He could dare the world to come for him. Let them give it their best shot.

He'd already taken men's lives and popped that cherry. The taboo was broken. He wouldn't lose any sleep over more spilled blood. If there were any out there who imagined they could collect a bounty on him, let them bring it. If there were those who wanted to make him pay because they didn't have power, they could bring it too. If there were those who just didn't like his attitude, he'd be ready for them as well.

Let the world come for him and let them give it their best.

## 20

T*he Big House*

SHARON TRIED her best to keep Oliver hydrated but she simply didn't have the knowledge or equipment to get enough fluids into his body. She considered using a teaspoon to feed him water but was concerned it might run into his lungs and cause more distress. In a technique she'd once used on a kitten, she saturated the corner of a clean towel with water and put it in Oliver's mouth. She'd never get a sufficient quantity of fluids into him that way, though. The best she'd accomplish would be to keep his mouth from completely drying out. She couldn't save him, but maybe she could keep him comfortable. It was all she knew to do.

Nathan assisted as he could, jumping at any task that didn't require him to be in the room with her and Oliver. Sharon understood. At his age it was difficult to see such things. She remembered it vividly. Young people didn't have the experience to know how to handle those situations. They don't know what to do with the emotions that flared up from what they were seeing before them. They hadn't been beaten down and damaged enough by the world, hadn't been hardened and had their more delicate feelings singed away.

Sharon did her best to accommodate Nathan. She wanted him handy. She wanted him close by in case she needed to move Oliver or in case she needed something from outside the house. Since he wasn't comfortable alongside the deathbed, she found tasks for him to do elsewhere in the house as she could. She had him tidying things, checking the animals, and making sure her pony, Honey, was okay.

Oliver's lips didn't cooperate with his brain, but Sharon saw within him the desperate desire to communicate. She tried once to assist him by placing a pen in his hand and a notepad beneath it, but his hand was no more cooperative than his lips. Whatever he so desperately needed to say remained with him. All she could offer him was consolation.

"It's okay, Oliver," she said, stroking his brow with a damp washcloth. "We'll be fine. There's nothing to worry about, my friend. There's nothing here for you to concern yourself with. Whatever is on your mind, just let it go. You don't need to worry about anything anymore. There are people waiting for you on the other side. People you're going to want to see. Don't let us hold you back."

She saw the reaction in his eyes, the understanding, the processing of her words. He was hearing her but it did nothing to calm the desperation in his eyes. Maybe it was fear or confusion, something more basic than a desire to communicate with his friend? Maybe it was the instinct to fight? She'd seen that before in dying animals, the desire to live so strong that they fought even when there was no quality of life worth preserving. She could do no more for her friend Oliver than she'd been able to do for those animals she'd loved so much. Soothing words and a calming touch. Being with them so they understood they were not making the journey alone.

She thought she understood what kept him here. It was the campers. While she ran the day-to-day operations of the music camp, they were all his guests. He felt responsible for them. He'd tried, as much as Sharon would let him, to help care for her and the children. He was having trouble letting that go. Even as the body failed and the other side pulled at him, the sense of obligation to the living was powerful. It persisted even when all was burned away in the heat of death.

There was a tap on the door and the click of the latch echoed in the quiet room. Sharon released Oliver's hand and turned to see Nathan peering through the door opening.

"Can you come here a minute? You're going to want to see this."

Sharon patted Oliver on the hand. "I'll be right back."

She moved toward the bedroom door and Nathan held it wide, closing it behind her. Nathan skirted around her in the wide hallway and walked ahead.

"What is it?" she asked. "Is something wrong?"

"No, but you'll want to see this."

He led her to the front door, one she didn't use because of the high porch. It appeared Oliver hadn't been using it either because Nathan had some difficulty pulling the swollen door open after he unlocked the various latches. When he finally managed to tug it open, he swung it wide and stepped clear.

"What is it?" Sharon asked again, rolling up to the door. Before he could reply, she saw it for herself. The front porch looked off onto the camp road for some distance. Coming toward them, she could see the children from the camp. All of them. They walked in groups, holding hands and swinging them as they walked. Some carried baskets. Others held water bottles.

Sharon understood why they'd come. She was both overwhelmed with the emotion of it and concerned that they'd made the long walk. She rolled out onto the wide porch and stretched her arms wide. The children were too far away to receive the hug but it was a gesture she often extended to them. It was a greeting that meant they were welcome and they were loved.

They didn't see her at first, hidden in the shadow of the covered porch, but soon one of them caught sight of her and cried out. Heads popped up and scanned, seeing her on the porch, her arms wide. Then the children were running toward her. Sharon hadn't realized how hard the situation with Oliver had been on her until she saw those smiling faces and burst into tears.

The children reached the house in no time and clambered up the high steps. The army of little feet was loud on the old boards. They swarmed her like puppies and she hugged them in one all-encompassing embrace.

"I've missed you so much today," she cooed. "You have no idea. You're so brave to walk here from camp. You are all so big and so brave."

It took several minutes for the scene to calm down. The sight of their strong camp director crying made one of the children start crying and it spread like wildfire. Soon all of the children were crying along with Sharon. Nathan even shed a few tears himself, but shrank back into the house to wipe them away. He didn't want to be seen crying. He was too old for that.

When order was eventually restored, Sharon had all the children take a seat on the porch surrounding her. Kay spoke up first, afraid she might be in trouble for bringing the children to the house.

"They were asking where you were. They wanted to know about Nathan. You've always been honest with us, Ms. Sharon, so I was honest with them. I told them that Mr. Oliver was sick and you were helping to take care of him. They wanted to come see you. They wanted to bring him flowers."

The children had indeed brought baskets of wildflowers and perennials they'd cut from around the camp. Seeing their proud faces made Sharon smile. Children weren't always thoughtful but it was incredibly heartwarming when they were.

"Those will make him very happy," Sharon said. "I'll put them in a vase at his bedside."

"Is Mr. Oliver going to be okay?" Tara asked. She was the nervous one, forever fearing the worst.

Sharon took in a long breath and let it out slowly. She forced herself to shake her head. She was always honest with them, even when it was difficult. This would be one of those times. "Honey, I don't think Mr. Oliver is going to be with us much longer. He's very old and very sick."

"He's going to die?" Jenny asked.

"I'm afraid so. There's nothing we can do to help keep him alive. Even if we were able to bring a doctor here, he wouldn't make it. He needs a hospital with electricity and complicated machines to keep him alive. We don't have access to anything like that."

"Can we see him?" Kay asked.

The other children were also interested in that idea, wanting to see if they could make the grandfatherly man feel better.

"I don't think you want to do that," Nathan said, stepping back out onto the porch and sitting down with the children. They hung on his every word. He was the oldest and they all looked up to him like a big brother. "You know how Mr. Oliver looks happy all the time when he sees you?"

The children nodded.

"He always smiles," Tara said.

"That's right," Nathan said. "He always smiles and looks happy. The problem is that what Mr. Oliver has right now makes him look sad. He can't help it and I don't think he'd want you to see him sad. Do you want to remember Mr. Oliver with a sad face or with a happy face?"

"A happy face," one of the children responded and the sentiment rippled throughout all of them.

Nathan smiled at them. "I think that's best. I've seen Mr. Oliver with his sad face. Ms. Sharon has too and it's sad, isn't it?"

Sharon was impressed with the way Nathan was handling the situation.

"How long will he live?" Kay asked.

"I don't know," Sharon replied. "I suspect no more than another day or two. It's hard to say."

"Is there anything we can do?" Stevie asked. He was only ten but always trying to be helpful and take on the biggest jobs he could do.

Sharon looked to Nathan, then back to Stevie. There was something they needed to talk about and it would not be easy. "Where do you think Mr. Oliver would like to be buried?"

Stevie furrowed his brow before shooting a finger up in the air. "The Fairy Circle!"

The Fairy Circle was a spot in the field near the dining hall where the children gathered to hear stories from Oliver, Sharon, or a special guest storyteller. There was a circle of logs and stumps for the children to sit on and a fire pit in the middle. Everyone loved the Fairy Circle.

"That's an excellent idea," Sharon said. "Maybe close by so he can always hear the stories we're telling. He loves that place."

"If you don't need anything more from me, maybe I could go dig the grave," Nathan offered. "The children can help if they want to."

"I want to help," Stevie said. He wanted to do everything Nathan did.

All of the children wanted to help, though Sharon wondered how long that enthusiasm would last once they actually tried heaving a shovel of dirt out of the ground. "That's fine, Nathan. Maybe come back after dinner and check-in with me, if you don't mind. I should be okay until then."

"If you're sure it's okay," Nathan replied. "I'll walk back with everyone else."

Sharon patted him on the back. She'd feel more comfortable with him going along with them anyway. It was only a mile and they hadn't had any trouble, but you never knew. Stories of violence in the community had reached her through Oliver. It sounded like the world outside of their insular little nest was going to hell. "I'll be fine. I have Honey if I need to come back any earlier."

With that agreed upon, the children handed their flowers over to Sharon. They each wanted to tell her where they'd found them. Some wanted her to deliver special messages to Mr. Oliver and she promised each child that she would. When they were done, they carefully descended the steps and set off in the same manner they'd arrived—hands held and swinging.

Sharon couldn't help but smile as she watched them go. She

wasn't a parent and they weren't her children, but she felt they were thriving despite the circumstances. She was proud to know that part of that was her doing. Those children were surviving and they were growing into good little humans. Having met all of their parents, she couldn't help but think they'd be proud if they could see them now. It made her wonder if any of them were still alive out there in the world. If so, they had to be terribly worried. She wished she could get a message to them, even a simple note to let them know that their children were alive and doing well.

She spun and rolled back over the dark wooden threshold into the house. She closed the front door behind her and it took a couple of hard shoves to get it fully closed. She stretched to fasten the various locks and latches that secured it, then went to the kitchen. She found a tall blue Mason jar, the antique kind that used a zinc lid with a rubber gasket to form a seal. The house had a gravity-fed water system so she was able to use the tap to fill the jar halfway with water. She placed the flowers inside, carefully arranged them, then placed the jar in her lap.

She rolled down the hallway, the sound of her wheels echoing off the hard floors and plaster walls. She twisted the knob on Oliver's door and shoved it open. "The children brought you some flowers," she announced, entering the room.

She held the jar up with both hands for him to see. When she looked at his face to see his reaction, she instantly knew. His eyes were closed and the tense facial muscles were relaxed. His grimace was gone.

Oliver was dead.

Sharon closed her eyes and sat there in the utter silence of the room. The only sensation was the cool glass of the water-filled Mason jar beneath her fingertips. She said a prayer for her friend, then opened her eyes. He was unchanged. Part of her hoped that he'd be awake and looking. Another part of her understood that this was the most merciful outcome.

Sharon moved closer and placed the jar of flowers beside his bed. She touched his wrist and felt for a pulse. There was none that she could detect. She held her palm in front of his lips and nose, feeling for the warmth of his exhalation, but felt nothing.

She backed away from the bed and stared at it. "Oh, Oliver, what am I going to do?"

In some ways, she was not surprised it had happened this way. She'd seen it before. When the dying were surrounded by people they cared for, it was harder for them to let go. When their family stepped out for a cup of coffee or to run home for a shower, that's when they passed. Family members felt bad about it, that they hadn't been there at the bedside holding their loved one's hand.

Sharon felt otherwise. She knew that leaving the bedside for a few moments was sometimes the most merciful thing the family could do. It allowed the spirit to leave if it was ready. It gave the loved one the strength to die and the permission to move on.

## 21

*Laurel Bed Lake*
*Clinch Mountain Wildlife Management Area*

JIM'S STOMACH was going off like an alarm clock as he rode back toward the boat landing. The sound of banjo music got louder. He could hear Lloyd and Andrew singing a tune together now, a sound like two animals caught in the same trap, mutually dissatisfied with their state in the world. That impression, however, could not have been further from the truth. The two singers had not a care in the world.

By way of their rising voices, the two broadcast their position with no regard for what ill-intentioned man or beast might be lurking in the woods. Were there men in the area with a predisposition toward violence and theft, they would have no difficulty locating an easy target on that boat ramp. If a hungry bear was seeking to add variety to his diet, he would but have to cock his furry ear to locate a meal of a fragrant old man and a pickled banjo player.

They stopped their caterwauling when Jim arrived, but not immediately. Instead, they marked the finale of the song with a rising crescendo and a flurry of banjo strumming that moved like a cheese grater over Jim's soul. As those final strains of struggling harmony faded, Lloyd and Andrew sat there with their eyes closed and faces raised to the evening sun in utter musical bliss.

Jim could do nothing but shake his head. He and Lloyd had been friends since childhood. This was what you got when you took him places. His inner hillbilly could not be contained any more than the musician that also resided within him. Jim slid off his horse, tying it and his packhorse up by the water. He returned to the old RV and retook a seat on the same dirty bucket he'd perched on earlier.

Andrew gave Jim a wide grin. "Find that campsite, partner?"

Jim let out a long breath. "I did. Looks like some folks stayed there for a while. There's an old hunting camp or something set up there."

Andrew looked off in recollection. "That would have been them Saltville boys. They hiked up in here back in the spring. Took a couple of deer and a bear. Smoked the meat and hauled it out of here on plastic sleds. Hooked them up to their belts and towed them, like there was snow on the ground and they was sled dogs."

"They stay long?" Jim asked.

"Eh, about a week, I reckon. Had good hunting and wanted to get the meat home. That's the way it's been the whole time. A group shows up here or there. Some camp but others just pass through."

"Any trouble out of them?" Lloyd asked, pecking at the muffled strings of his banjo.

"Nary a bit. You'd never know the world outside of here had taken a crap from the way these people acted. It was just like running into hunters in the woods during regular times. You shoot the shit and talk about what you saw that day. If they camped close by, we might swap a few stories and share a meal. They was all good people though. Never had a bit of trouble out of any of them."

"That's good to hear," Jim said. "And a bit surprising. We've seen a lot of violence. I've got friends who had to move out of their neighborhoods and come join up with us because it got too dangerous to live out there on their own. You must have made the right call in coming up here."

Andrew shrugged. "Could have gone either way. I knew that when I came up here. I could just as easily have been set upon by rogues intent on killing me and taking all my worldly goods. Just got lucky."

"You best stay up here, then," Lloyd said. "The lowlands is thick with rogues and criminals. There's been days my fingers was so stiff from digging graves that I couldn't even pick a tune on the banjo."

Andrew jerked his head toward Lloyd as if this were the most appalling thing he'd ever heard. "Don't say!"

"I do!" Lloyd held up his hand, curling it into a gnarled claw. "Like this, it was. Cramped like I was clutching a shovel."

"That's a tragedy," Andrew said.

"A blessing," Jim clarified. "He misses one night on the banjo and the world's a different place. The wild game returns, the flowers open again. The clouds part and the sun shines. A chorus of angels sings from the heavens."

"Yeah, quit being dramatic. If you'd slow up on the killing, we wouldn't have to do as much burying," Lloyd chided.

"I ain't the one being dramatic. Besides, some people need killing," Jim said, repeating a line he used all too often. "It must be true because I've read it in books and heard it in movies all my life."

"It is true," said Andrew. "There are people out there whose existence is a very affront to our Creator. Sometimes it's up to man to correct that."

Lloyd frowned. "If that's the case, then why did the Creator create them in the first place?"

"I've got two theories on that and I've had a long time to arrive at them. One is that bad people exist to serve as lessons to the rest of us."

Lloyd laughed. "My friend here used to have a t-shirt that said 'I'm not useless, I can be used as a bad example.'"

"Exactly." Andrew cackled. "The other possibility is that God creates us but gives us the freedom to choose our path. It's up to us whether we become good folks or evil shithead bastards."

"Which of those do you believe?" Jim asked.

"Both," Andrew replied. "Just depends on when you ask me and who we're talking about at the time."

"You think some people are born bad?" Lloyd asked.

"Nah, that's just in the movies. I have a hard time believing that," Andrew said, "though some do turn dark early because of things beyond their control. Things they've either seen or had done to them."

"Sometimes going from good to bad is a spontaneous thing," Jim said. "Someone makes a half-cocked decision in the heat of the moment that ends up having larger repercussions. It's one impulsive act, like flipping a switch, except you can't un-flip it no matter how bad you'd like to."

"Oh, you'll find no one who believes that more than me," Andrew said. "My whole life I've lived with the consequences of decisions like that."

"What did you do?" Lloyd asked.

Jim shot him a look. "Ever think it wasn't any of your damn business, you nosy bastard?"

Lloyd shrugged. "If it's a secret, why'd he mention it?"

"Ain't a secret. I'll tell *you*," Andrew said. "But only 'cause you and I are hitting it off on such a high note. I'll tell you because you're a musician and since the beginning of time musicians have been men who got out and saw the ways of the world. They've seen the good, the bad, and the ugly."

"That's true," Jim said. "Lloyd has seen the world and thrown up in the bushes of some of the finest establishments in the whole country."

"And I've spent the day riding with the *bad* and *ugly*," Lloyd countered. "It goes without saying, of course, that I'm the *good*."

Andrew ignored their banter. "My daddy was a doctor there outside of Richlands. He was a classic country doctor. You could barter for services and he'd give you credit. Lord, people loved him. He was a well-respected man in the community. One night he'd been out late delivering a baby. On his way home, he run up against a roadblock outside of Raven. Anyone from that area knows that in those days the miners were bad to get drunk on the weekend and block off the road. Sometimes they'd rob people or just give them a bit of a hard time. I mean, you're talking about a town of less than two acres that had seven bars. That's just asking for trouble."

"Did he stop?" Lloyd asked.

"Nope. He suspected it was drunks so he stomped the gas and ran right through it. He had this 1955 Plymouth, two-tone with white and baby blue. What he didn't know was that it was actually the law had the road blocked off."

"Uh-oh," Jim said.

"Damn right," Andrew said. "They wasn't in any mood to be trifled with so they drew their guns and opened fire on him. Of course, he should have known better than to run and they should have known better than to shoot at him. Everyone in those parts knew his car. Wasn't another one like it in that community. They could have figured out who it was by asking around, but it never got to that. Both of them deputies emptied their guns at him, then they jumped in their cars and went after him."

Lloyd reached into his banjo case and removed a jar of moonshine. He passed it to Andrew, who oddly enough had no question as to what was in the jar. Jim figured out then that they'd been drinking the liquor in his absence, but had hidden the jar when he returned. Lloyd knew he'd be in for an ass-chewing over day-drinking in strange territory, but he was motivated by the understanding that all good tales go better with liquor.

"I figure my old daddy was in a panic by that point. Folks found blood in the car later—lots of it—so they knew he'd taken a bullet or two. He headed for the office where he saw patients in town. We guess he must have been looking for something to stop the bleeding, trying to bandage himself up. The law followed him there though. They opened fire on him from outside and shot all the windows out. My daddy always kept a pocket gun on him. Everyone did in those days. He pulled it out and started shooting back. We don't know if he ever figured out it was the law shooting at him or not. In some ways it didn't matter. Whoever it was, they were trying to kill him, so he fought back."

"Didn't anyone in town notice this was going on?" Jim asked.

Andrew paused and took a drink from the jar proffered to him. When he was done, he passed it back to Lloyd. "The bars had closed for the night but there were people out and about. They ran toward the scene. When they saw those cops shooting into the office of their beloved doctor, they didn't take kindly to it."

"What did they do?" Lloyd asked.

"They drew their own guns and opened fire on the deputies," Andrew said. "Those lawmen saw they were outnumbered so they climbed into their cars and took off. Someone called out to my dad to tell him it was safe to come out, but he didn't answer. They went inside to check on him and found him dead. The law had shot him all to hell and he'd bled out right there on the floor."

"I'm sorry," Jim said. "That must have been awful."

"I was just a boy so I don't recall much of it. Barely remember my daddy at all. The story didn't end there. Folks was outraged about what happened. They loaded up in cars and headed for the police station like villagers heading for Frankenstein's castle."

"Were they going to lodge a complaint?" Lloyd asked.

"You better believe it. Complaints was lodged different in those days, though," Andrew mused. "Those two lawmen locked themselves up inside and wouldn't come out to face that angry mob. A couple of men busted out windows, dumped some gas inside, and set the place on fire. It wasn't long before smoke was pouring out the windows and those two deputies came stumbling out the front door, choking and coughing."

"What happened then?" Jim asked.

"They lynched them," Andrew replied. "Someone had some rope in their pickup truck and they strung them up on a maple right there in the yard of the police station. The two must have had time to make a phone call while they were inside because it wasn't long before the sheriff and a state trooper showed up, but it was too late by then. Both of those men were hanging dead, twisting in the firelight like a couple of snared coyotes."

Lloyd laid the banjo down on the case and took a drink from the jar. "That's awful."

"The whole lot of it was awful." Andrew shuddered. "It was awful my daddy was dead and awful the town lost a doctor. It was awful those men hung the two deputies. It was awful what come of it later too. There was a hearing but no one ever got charged. Nearly tore the town apart. People were all taking sides over what happened. Took years for everyone to put it behind them. Some of us were never able to put it behind us. Not me, and not the families of those dead lawmen."

"I see what you mean," Jim said. "That was all a string of impulsive decisions, all of them adding fuel to the fire until it was too big to put out."

"That's exactly it," the old man agreed. "My daddy's decision to stomp the gas instead of stopping at the roadblock. The lawmen's decision to open fire on him instead of trying to track him down later. Their decision to shoot into his office even after they knew who he was. The mob's decision to chase those deputies down and lynch them instead of letting the judge handle it. Every fucking decision was a bad one."

"Sorry you went through that, Andrew," Lloyd said.

"Eh, everyone has their burden to bear. I figured out early on that it wasn't my doing and I wasn't carrying it with me. I can't pay for other men's mistakes. I put it behind me and moved on. Lived a good life and I still am, right up to and including this very moment."

"I've been known to make a spontaneous decision or two in my life," Jim offered. "I'm kind of paying for that right now. I reckon there's others been paying for it too."

"Is it too personal to ask the nature of your problem?" Andrew asked. "I ain't trying to be nosy but I've got a few miles on me. I know I'm a crusty old bastard but I have the occasional insight. I'm smarter than I look."

Jim had to agree with that. The old man was indeed sharper than he looked. He had a way of tying the little things in life to the bigger things in life, which was much the way Jim saw things. He recognized patterns and took lessons where he found them. He was almost tempted to spill his whole story. *Almost.*

"We can't talk about it," Lloyd said. "I was warned to keep my big trap shut."

Andrew winked. "Top secret stuff, huh?"

"Probably stuff you're better off not knowing and we're better off not talking about," Jim said. "I just saw something in the world that really bothered me and I couldn't live with it. I acted on impulse and set my world on fire as a result."

Andrew narrowed his eyes. "You're contradicting yourself there, son. Doesn't sound like you acted on impulse. Sounds like you acted on principles. That's two different things. I see impulse as a poorly thought out and spontaneous action, a man acting without regard for consequence. Did you consider the consequences before you acted?"

"I did. I knew it would get bad, but I still did it."

"Then you got nothing to feel bad about," Andrew said. "Would you do the same thing over again?"

"Probably."

"He's a slow learner," Lloyd commented.

"Or maybe he was right in what he did," Andrew countered.

Lloyd buried his head in his hands. "Lord, don't encourage him. That's the last thing we need."

"I ain't encouraging nothing," said Andrew. "I'm just saying that maybe he was right in what he done, whatever it was. He thought it out and acted on principle. That's all a man's got to go on in this world. Until the good Lord gives us clairvoyance, the ability to see the outcome of things before they happen, we have to go with our gut and our reason. Your buddy did that. He ain't got nothing to feel bad about."

"It's something I'm still coming to terms with," Jim said. "Just being away from home and getting my head clear is doing wonders. Constant worry eats at you. Makes it hard to process things."

"I wouldn't know about that," Andrew said. "I stay pretty relaxed up here."

"I wouldn't know about that either," Lloyd chimed in. "I tend to avoid stress as much as possible."

Jim raised an eyebrow at his buddy. "I've noticed—stress, work, sentry duty, sobriety—all things you tend to avoid."

"Your buddy here can't help it," Andrew said, interceding on Lloyd's behalf. "Musicians are of a certain cut. He can't help how he is any more than you can. I've known a musician or two over the years. Growing up, we used to go to these square dances all the time. Seemed like there was one every weekend. I was drinking with fiddlers and banjo players before I was old enough to drive."

"I've played a few square dances over the years," Lloyd said. "Used to do a lot of them. I think they've about died out now. Only place I ever play them anymore is at that young musician's camp over in Bland County."

Andrew furrowed his brow. "Never heard tell of such a place."

"There's a summer camp over there. It's out in the boonies on this big old family farm. Guy that owns it is a friend of mine, a decent bluegrass player. He wanted to carry on the tradition of kids learning to play Appalachian music so he started this camp. People come from all over the country to take lessons there. They have adult sessions too. It's a nice place. I love playing out there. Been around for nearly fifty years."

"Sounds like a worthwhile thing to do," Andrew said. "Passing on what you know to the younger generations."

"I never knew you did that Lloyd," Jim said with surprise. "How come you never mentioned it?"

Lloyd frowned. "I probably did mention it and you just weren't paying any attention."

Jim held up a hand. "I do listen but you play a lot of places. They all run together."

"Well, this ain't like any other place I play. I play square dances but I also teach sessions out there. Speaking of which, I wonder how the owner is getting along. He's a good guy but he's old as dirt."

"Excuse me but I'm offended by that," Andrew said.

Lloyd looked at him apologetically and mumbled, "Sorry."

Andrew grinned. "Just messing with you. I'm proud to be old as dirt, but still on this side of it."

"We could go check in on him if you wanted," Jim offered. "Bland County isn't that far. We're probably halfway there already."

"I'll think on it," Lloyd said.

Jim winked at Andrew. "You catch that? He mispronounced *drink*."

**22**

———————

SHARON SAT at the foot of the bed staring at Oliver's body for a long time. While her thoughts weren't exactly racing, there was a steady and continual stream of disjointed thinking, pouring through her mind like muddy water through a ditch. There were immediate concerns, like preparing the body for burial and getting it up to the camp to bury, assuming they were even able to dig a proper grave. There was also the matter of getting the word out. Oliver had people he was in contact with in the community and on the surrounding farms. His family had been in this valley so long they had deep roots. People checked in on the old man and they cared about him, just as she and her campers did.

How did she get word to them? Should she send Nathan or try to go herself? Oliver's house wasn't too far from the main road. Maybe another half mile. Could she do it with Honey pulling her?

From those more immediate and pressing concerns, her mind

wandered to the long-term issues they'd face because of his death. Over the past year, Oliver had invited them numerous times to come live with him in the big house, but she'd always declined. They'd been able to keep themselves comfortable and warm at the camp. They had the garden, and the setting was familiar to them. Oliver had insisted they'd be no bother, but she didn't feel right about invading his space like that. He was an old man with a lot of memories in this house. Despite his assurances to the contrary, she worried they'd make him uncomfortable in his own house and she didn't want that.

That would no longer be an issue. She'd seen his will with her own eyes. Upon his death, the house and farm went to the camp. There was to be a board of trustees, local folks, who'd help decide how to best utilize the land so they could maintain enough income to run the camp. Sharon had also sworn to him that she'd move the children into the house if anything happened to him. She would honor that promise but there'd be a lot of work involved in making that happen. They had things they'd need to bring from the camp, lots of them, and she had no idea how they'd do it.

Overwhelmed by her rushing thoughts, Sharon decided she had to do something. She kissed Oliver's forehead and gently pulled the blankets over his face. "I hope you're at peace now, old friend."

She left the room, closing the door behind her. The stark hallway looked different now as she imagined seeing it every day as a resident of the house. For a while, perhaps for the life she had remaining, this would be *her* home. Hers and the children's. If the country never recovered, she too might die in that bed where Oliver had just passed away.

Sharon went to the kitchen, opened the door, and rolled out onto the back porch. She moved into the yard where she sat surrounded by the tall grass. An overgrown rose bush grew against the fence, long, thorny branches hanging dense with lush red blossoms. It was the kind of rose bush you only saw at old country homes, the kind that had grown undisturbed for more than a century, roots as deep as those of the people that lived there.

The sun beat down on her and sweat trickled down her back. She took a deep breath, aware now of how claustrophobic she'd felt in the house, overwhelmed by the responsibility thrust upon her. The humid air hanging in the fertile valley felt like warm water sucked into her lungs. There were so many things to do and she had no idea where to start, but she needed to do something. Only physical activity would calm her mind. She understood that about herself.

The yard wasn't easy to navigate in a wheelchair. There was nothing uniform about it at all. It was irregular and rutted with paths cut by one hundred and fifty years of people walking to the same places every day—the outhouse, the barn, the back gate, or the springhouse. The house was built at a time when people didn't meticulously grade and excavate their yards with powerful machinery. Sharon was strong from regular use of the chair under tough conditions. She wrestled the awkward terrain until she was alongside her pony. "Honey, we're going for a ride."

Although she didn't require Nathan's help to harness herself to the pony, it was easier when he was there to lend a hand. Yet she managed, straightening the leads and clipping the carabiners to the anchor points on her chair. When she had the pony pointed in the right direction and her chair oriented so the pony wouldn't pull her over sideways, she clucked her tongue and snapped the reins. Despite the instability of having the horse pull her wheelchair, it was engaging on all levels. It left her no brain space for worry about the future. She was more concerned with keeping herself upright and not getting hurt.

The house had a rutted gravel drive that led from the farm road to the backyard. It was always how she approached the house since the back entrance had a ramp for her. When she reached the bottom of Oliver's drive, the pony attempted to turn left, toward the camp, out of habit. She reined the gentle animal to the right and it balked, stopping in the road.

"It's okay, Honey. We're going the other way this time."

The pony cocked an ear like it couldn't believe what it was hearing. Horses could operate with reasonable autonomy as long as they were kept to their routine, but throw in something new and they acted like you'd lost your mind. Sharon tugged on the reins again, firmer this time, and the horse conceded.

Sharon hadn't been past Oliver's house in a year now. Much like the rest of the road, it was suffering from a lack of maintenance. Besides the weeds popping up in the center of the road, numerous branches were laying in her path. Most were small enough she could go around them. Not far from the house Sharon encountered a massive oak that had dropped a limb across her path.

The branch was attached to the oak, but stretched across the road at an angle and extended a short distance into the weedy shoulder on the opposite side. Sharon considered turning around at this point, but the prospect of returning to Oliver's house was overwhelming at the moment. She couldn't face it right now. She needed to be out of the house and doing something to occupy herself. It was how she processed things and restored her equilibrium.

"We can make it," she assured the uncertain pony, flicking the reins against its back and urging it onward.

The deep weeds on the shoulder hid the terrain. As the chair began to lean precariously, Sharon second-guessed her decision to keep going but it was too late. The shoulder sloped down to a woven wire fence and Sharon saw no way to turn around in the narrow space between the fence and the branch. She was committed now. Moving forward was her only option.

She weighed urging the horse on faster against slowing down, but both moves had their risks. She opted to continue forward at the same steady pace. She held her breath and shifted her body, leaning uphill like a motorcyclist in a tight corner. Then the chair lurched, the downhill wheel dropping into a rut, and Sharon knew she was going over.

She released the reins and flailed her arms, but there was nothing to grab onto. Dumping on the steep slope, she was slammed to the ground, landing on her shoulder and back. She cried out, small rocks and sticks poking at her, jabbing, tearing. She rolled twice before being caught by the mesh of the rusty old fence. Despite the possibility of broken bones and torn muscles, her first thoughts were of poison ivy and snakes.

"Damn it!" She'd nearly broken herself of cursing in a year of constantly being around children but some situations warranted it. This was one of them.

She was wedged awkwardly between the fence and the steep bank. It reminded her of rolling out of bed as a child, getting stuck in the narrow gap between the bed and the wall. Except her bedroom didn't have snakes and poison ivy. The fact wasn't lost on her that she'd once seen the largest rattlesnake of her life less than a half-mile from here. She watched the big timber rattler crossing the road near Oliver's house, its body as thick as her thigh.

She twisted and wrestled her arms out from beneath her, then grabbed the fence. She pulled until she was sitting upright. The angle was so steep, her body positioned so awkwardly, that she wasn't able to keep herself in that position without the support of the fence. She looked for her pony and was pleased to see that Honey had stopped when Sharon toppled over.

"That's a good girl," Sharon gasped, her breathing labored by the exertion of holding herself up.

She quickly assessed her situation and determined that she needed to get her body oriented into a better position before she tried getting herself up the bank. This required her to pull herself up the woven squares of fencing like it was a ladder while twisting and pulling at her lower body. In the heat and humidity, the effort was exhausting. When she was finally in a comfortable position, she sagged back against the fence to catch her breath.

She could see now that she had eight feet of bank to climb before she'd be back on the road. Both the slope and the distance were manageable, but the bank was strewn with sharp stones. Smooth vines of poison ivy wove across it and occasional shards of old broken glass glinted in the sunlight. Even scarier, she imagined snakes were lining up in the grass, just waiting for the opportunity to sink their fangs into her.

She released a long exhalation and pushed herself over until she was face down on the bank. She figured the longer she laid there, the more opportunity she gave the snakes to organize against her. She needed to get moving. She reached for a sapling the thickness of her thumb and grasped onto it. She pulled herself up onto her elbows and started climbing.

The surface of the embankment was a mix of thick weeds and patches of bare soil. The weeded areas were not too bad but the bare sections ground at the flesh of her elbows and forearms. Several times she had to stop and peel embedded stones from her skin. Gradually she made progress, getting nearly halfway to the top before she had to stop and rest for the first time.

She dropped her face onto her forearm, the sweaty surface slick with mud and streaks of blood. Her heart pounded in her chest and her biceps trembled from the exertion.

"I'll be there in a second, Honey," she whispered. "Don't you go anywhere. You just stand there and wait for me, okay?"

The pony shifted at the mention of its name, shuffling a foot and cocking an ear toward Sharon. She hoped she didn't startle the animal into wandering off. She started climbing again, wrapping her cramping fingers around clumps of grass, exposed roots, and saplings. Soaked in sweat, her shirt didn't offer much in the way of protection, and the ground clawed at her belly. She expected she'd be in rough shape tomorrow, sore and scratched, but this was far from the worst she'd ever endured.

Inch by inch she gained ground, eventually cresting the shoulder like a haggard mountaineer summiting Everest. Her legs dangling down the bank, she rested her head on her forearms again, studying the situation with her horse and chair. The chair had rolled down the embankment too but the harness had caught it. The tangled mess hung about six feet away from her, still tethered to Honey.

Sharon forced herself over the edge and moved toward her horse. There was less grass here on the gravel farm road and it was like climbing over coarse sandpaper. Since the road was relatively flat, she didn't allow herself to pause there, pushing on until she reached the single rein that lay nearest her. She clutched it like a lifeline, wrapping it around her hand several times since she didn't trust her ability to hold onto it.

When she'd recovered sufficiently to sit upright, she knew there was no way she was hauling the heavy chair up to road level. She had nothing left after the exhausting climb. She was drenched in sweat from head to toe and her muscles were spent to the point of failure. She would have to rely on Honey, hoping she could coax the animal into cooperating.

She crawled up alongside the pony and sat there for a moment, patting and soothing it. When the pony seemed calm she pushed past it, getting as far ahead of Honey as the reins would allow.

"I'm going to need you to walk to me," she explained, as if the pony was waiting for her instructions. "We need to get my chair up here so I can turn it over."

Honey shook her furry head, her tack rattling with the movement. Sharon hoped that wasn't an indication that it wasn't going to cooperate.

"Come on now," she urged, tugging the reins.

Honey took a tentative step toward her, pausing as she encountered the tension on the harness. The chair might have been snagged or it could have been friction from how it hung over the bank. Either way, it was going to take some pulling to get it back up. Sharon hoped the effort didn't break the harness. If it did, she faced a long haul back to Oliver's house.

"Pull!" she urged the pony, tugging harder on the reins.

Honey leaned into the harness, moving toward Sharon. Though she couldn't see the chair over the far embankment, she could hear the sound of it bumping along as Honey pulled. It was moving.

Sharon couldn't help but smile at the progress. "C'mon girl, you're doing it. Keep pulling."

Gaining momentum now that the chair was moving, Honey easily tugged it up the hillside. Soon she was alongside Sharon and the chair was cresting the hill. When it finally came to rest on the flat surface of the road, Sharon tugged on the reins and halted the pony. "You did it, girl. You did it!"

Sharon painfully made her way down the length of the harness to where the chair lay in the dusty road. Aside from a few scratches and abrasions to the harness it didn't appear to be damaged. She flipped it upright and tentatively rolled it back and forth a few inches. Everything was moving as it should.

She ducked beneath the nearest harness line and maneuvered herself into the chair. It was never easy getting in there from ground level, especially with spent muscles, but she made it with a fair amount of grunting and swearing. When she was finally settled in, she sagged backward, letting her head hang. She spent a minute catching her breath and resting.

When she felt ready, she took stock of her battered body. The denim shorts and t-shirt she was wearing were filthy, as was her body beneath them. The dust she'd crawled through had mixed with her sweat to form a film of mud that stretched from her face to her ankles. Her legs were skinned, knees raw, and blood seeped from dozens of tiny scratches. Long raised welts striped her legs from the briars she'd pulled herself over. She worried she'd be covered with poison ivy too, though that may not show up for a few days.

Her upper body was no better. Her hands were tough but they were sore. Her elbows were scraped, as were her forearms, from the uphill crawl. Rivulets of blood ran from her raw wounds, mixing with the dirt and the sweat. There was nothing here life-threatening. Nothing a few days of rubbing alcohol, Neosporin, and Band-Aids couldn't fix.

She dropped her hands to the wheels and tentatively rolled back and forth a few times. Aside from a bent brake lever everything was working. She picked up the reins and held them in her lap. Mobile again, she was now faced with the prospect of where to go. She glanced over her shoulder, staring at the section of the embankment that had been her undoing. That was not a possibility. There was no way she was going to risk it. She knew how that movie ended.

Looking down at her bedraggled condition, she didn't look like anyone fit to go visiting at a neighbor's house. She looked more like the kind of vagrant you'd turn away at gunpoint. Yet it was either proceed with her original plan or attempt to find an alternative route back to Oliver's house.

She didn't go backward. That wasn't how Sharon lived life. She wasn't a quitter. She didn't flee and she didn't run. She used the damp tail of her shirt to wipe her face, then attempted to do the same to her grubby arms. When she was done, she flicked the reins and clucked at Honey. "Let's go, girl."

**23**

———————

T*he Farm Road*

AFTER HER SPILL, it wasn't five minutes before Sharon came to the first of the houses along the road. The first thing Sharon noticed was that the folks who lived there had somehow managed to come up with an old reel-type mower that allowed them to keep their lawn cut even without fuel. Sharon hadn't been certain which of the houses she'd stop at. She'd met several of the folks along the road but didn't really *know* any of them.

She ended up stopping at the first house when she spotted two figures on the porch. A man in overalls and a cap was stringing beans with his wife. Both were timeless figures who by dress and demeanor appeared as if they could have stepped from the late 1960s. They were not modern people but faithful recreations of those who'd come before them. Farmer and wife. Rural porch-dwellers who preferred to watch the world over watching the television.

They'd heard her coming, the crunch of gravel beneath wheel

and hoof. They stopped mid-bean to stare at her as if she were some apparition. What Sharon initially took as unfriendliness was instead surprise at both her appearance and her condition. She wasn't just a woman traveling along a dirt road. She was a blood-stained and dirty woman being pulled along in a horse-drawn wheelchair.

The pair on the porch exchanged a few words between themselves without taking their eyes off her. Apparently coming to some conclusion, they stood in tandem and placed their stainless steel bean bowls down on the padded glider from which they worked. The man came down the short set of steps first, hurrying toward Sharon with surprising grace, like a dancer in bibbed overalls. The woman came behind him, moving with the same urgency, apron flapping.

Familiar with the way of horses, the husband reached out and took hold of the pony's bridle before turning his attention to Sharon. By then his wife was already upon on her, bent over with a gentle hand on Sharon's shoulder.

"Honey, are you okay?" she cooed. "What happened?"

Sharon, who'd managed the day's events with grit and stoicism, erupted into tears she couldn't hold back. She wasn't certain what had done it. The sincerity of this couple? The woman's genuine concern? The fact she'd gone through so much today with no adult to share it with?

The woman looked at her husband with concern. The man's brow was furrowed. "Is everything okay? Are those children okay?"

Sharon took several deep breaths, trying to control her sobs. "The children are...fine."

"Let's get you over to the porch," the woman said. "I know who you are but I don't think we've ever been introduced. I'm Freda."

The husband studied Sharon's rig for a moment before unclipping Honey's harness from the chair. He led the pony off into the yard and tied it to a cherry tree. When he was done, he rushed back to the road, where Freda was assisting Sharon toward the porch. Two concrete steps led up to the broad country porch and the pair worked together to get Sharon's chair up.

When they were done, she rolled out of the sun and started

wiping at her eyes. "I'm sorry about the crying. I don't know where this came from."

"Honey, all you're doing is smearing mud around your face," Freda said. "Let me get something to clean you up."

"I don't want to be any bother."

"Nonsense," Freda said with a tone that made it clear it would be the last word on that.

Her husband took a seat beside Sharon. "I don't know if you remember me or not. We've met a time or two. I cut hay off Oliver and graze a few head on his place. Name's Kendall."

"Kendall, I'm Sharon. I run the camp."

Kendall nodded seriously. "I recollect that. Oliver mentioned you often. I told Oliver you all should come by if you needed anything, but he said you all were doing well under the circumstances. He put all the credit for that on you."

Sharon smiled, trying to get her emotions in check. She was saved from having to speak by Freda's appearance on the porch. She handed Sharon a tall glass of water with a concerned smile.

"Thank you," Sharon said, taking a sip of the water. "It's nice and cold."

Kendall smiled. "Got a spring-box up on the hill there. Feeds the house. Never been much pressure but it's the best water you'll ever drink."

Freda disappeared again, then backed through the door with a basin of water and a towel draped over her arm.

"I don't want you to go to any trouble," Sharon protested, resting the glass of water on the arm of her chair.

Freda gave her a stern look. "We're going to clean you up and see if any of those scratches need tending."

Sharon reached for the towel. "I can do that."

Freda pulled it back from her reach. "I never said you *couldn't* do it, but you look to me like someone in need of a little help right now. Why don't you just sit there and let me help you? While I'm scrubbing you off, you can tell us what's going on."

Sharon relaxed, or tried to. She was fiercely independent but she'd triggered Freda's maternal instinct and it was better to give in to it than risk offending her. "On the road between here and Oliver's house there was a limb down in the road and I tried to go around it. My chair turned over and I rolled down the bank. That's why I'm such a mess. I had to climb back up the hill."

"Why would you do a thing like that?" Freda asked. "Why were you coming up the road alone?"

Kendall was a step ahead of his wife. He'd already put together that Sharon wouldn't have made this trip if there wasn't something wrong. "Is Oliver okay?"

Sharon looked him in the eye and shook her head. As much as she tried to fight it back, her eyes filled with tears again. "He died."

Freda's hand moved to her mouth. "Oh my."

Kendall's mouth tightened. "Lord, I hate to hear that. We've been neighbors for better than forty years. What happened?"

Sharon wiped at her eyes, prompting Freda to get on her knees beside the chair and start dabbing at Sharon's face. "I'm pretty sure it was a stroke. I've seen them before. I found him like that this morning. I tried taking care of him but he couldn't swallow or anything. He passed about an hour ago."

"Have you thought about what you intend to do with the...his body?" Kendall asked in as delicate and considerate a manner as he could.

"I told the children he probably wouldn't make it, but they don't know it's already happened. They're back at the camp with the older children looking after them. They suggested we bury him at the camp, at the circle where he used to tell them stories. Some of the kids are already working on digging the grave."

Kendall started shaking his head again. "That's the saddest thing I believe I've ever heard. That ain't no job for children."

"I know," Sharon admitted, "but they wanted to do it and I don't know how else it's going to get done."

"That means you're going to have to get him from his house to the camp," Freda said, moving on to scrubbing the grime off Sharon's arms. "Have you thought about how you're going to do that? That's a mile of bad road."

Sharon shrugged, a wordless concession that she had no clue how they were going to accomplish that.

"That's the kind of thing neighbors are for," Kendall said. "We can help."

"While that would be much appreciated," Sharon said, "I didn't come up here to beg for help. I thought you all might want to know he'd passed and might want to come for the service."

"We'll definitely do that," Kendall said. "Oliver was a might protective of you all. He didn't say much about what was going on up there, other than that some of the kids got stranded. He insisted you all were taking care of it."

Sharon smiled. "That camp was his baby. He was protective."

"Oliver was highly thought of in the community here," Freda said. "We'll pass the word up and down the road. There might be a few folks who want to attend if that's okay with you."

"Oh definitely," Sharon said. "If folks want to pay their respects we'd be glad to have them."

"Are you aware of the arrangements Oliver made for the camp to continue?" Kendall asked. "Did you know about his will?"

"I do," Sharon replied. "I had to go to a lawyer's office with him several years back to sign some papers. Since he didn't have any immediate heirs he left everything to the camp. There's supposed to be a trust formed upon his death. The trustees are supposed to ensure that the farm is operated in a manner that will make the most money for the camp. He envisioned selling some timber each year, some hunting rights in the winter, selling leases for grazing cattle and raising corn. He thought that would be enough to keep the camp going since he set the whole thing up as a tax-exempt organization."

"He told me about it," Kendall said. "I saw the papers. He asked if I'd be willing to serve as a trustee and I told him I would. He sure was proud of the camp. He wanted it to keep going."

Freda was wiping down Sharon's legs now and shaking her head with disapproval as she went. "Lord, look what you gone and done to yourself."

Sharon laughed. "I promise you it wasn't intentional."

"We need to put some alcohol on there and clean that up. It might sting."

Sharon smiled. "Don't worry. I can't feel them."

Freda looked embarrassed. "I'm so sorry. I didn't mean..."

Sharon put a reassuring arm on Freda's shoulder. "Don't worry about it. It's fine. I appreciate the help. I didn't realize how bad I felt until I started sobbing like a baby."

"Now, honey, don't you worry about a thing," Kendall said. "People need neighbors. They need help sometimes. With Oliver gone, we'll do our best to help you in every way we can."

When Freda finished rubbing on the alcohol she stood and stretched. "That's about as good as it's going to get for now. You're going to need to keep an eye on all those scratches."

"I'm going to clear that tree out of the road for Sharon and then I'll let the neighbors know about Oliver," Kendall announced, standing.

Sharon felt tears well up at the warmth she felt for this kind older couple. She hadn't known them even an hour ago and now she felt like she'd known them all her life. This was just what she needed and it came at the exact moment she needed it. She was almost certain that she could feel Oliver out there smiling at her choice to travel up the road.

**24**

———————

L*aurel Bed Lake*
*Clinch Mountain Wildlife Management Area*

BEFORE THEY LOST all light for the evening, Jim walked to the water's edge and gathered his horses. He stretched his headlamp over his sweat-dampened cap and slung his rifle over his back. Mosquitoes swarmed around his face and hummed in his ear.

"Whereabouts you going?" Andrew called.

"Going to find a spot to settle in for the night," Jim said. "I'm beat."

The old man cocked his head at Jim. "I thought you didn't find that old campsite up the lake to your liking?"

"I didn't. There's too many memories there," Jim said. "Don't want to be tripping over them all night. I'll find a clearing in the woods somewhere and stretch out."

"I thought we'd just camp here with Andrew," Lloyd said, looking disappointed. He wasn't anxious to leave the first new friend he'd made in a while. "We've kind of hit it off."

"You're welcome to stay here tonight but I'm not comfortable out in the open with all this racket. Sound travels on the water. Fires reflect. I'll sleep better in the woods."

Lloyd cast a glance at Andrew. "You hear the way he talks about my playing and singing? A racket! He does me that way all the time. No regard for a man's feelings. Ain't sure there's a shred of human decency in him."

Andrew mumbled and nodded, agreeing with the injustice of it all.

"You can come with me or stay here, Lloyd, but I'm headed into the woods and turning in early," Jim said. "It's been a long, hot day and I expect tomorrow will be more of the same."

Lloyd raised one of his quart-sized traveling jars toward Andrew, gesturing at it like some magic potion. "What were you planning for the evening?"

"I got a big old lake trout on a stringer over there. Figured I'd fillet it out and throw it in a skillet with some lard. Y'all are welcome to join me."

Lloyd licked his lips. "Ooh, that sounds good. I might be able to scrape up a can of corn. Maybe a handful of noodles or something."

Getting the hint, Jim dug into the bags on the packhorse and tossed Lloyd a can of corn and a package of ramen noodles. "Here you go. Guess you're staying over here?"

"Ain't decided if I'm staying all night but I ain't leaving yet." Lloyd rubbed his stomach. "Sounds like we got dinner to cook. Might be some picking and singing later."

"That's fine but if you come looking for me later you better announce yourself first. If I hear steps in the woods I'm going to be assuming it's a bear or an unwanted guest."

"I've dealt with some pushy bears, but I ain't had no trouble out of people since I been up here," said Andrew. "People have behaved themselves."

"Then you've been lucky," Jim said. "We've run into every kind of slack-jawed, drug-addled scoundrel walking on two legs. They're everywhere. If you haven't seen them yet, you will."

Andrew rose from his chair. "Well, I hope it ain't tonight because I got fish to fry."

The old man disappeared into his RV. Jim heard pots and pans banging around. Cabinet doors were slammed and drawers yanked open.

"I'm leaving. You guys be careful," Jim warned. "Try not to get so drunk that you can't keep an eye open for trouble. Despite what Andrew says, I ain't letting down my guard. I'll be back first thing in the morning and we'll get a start out toward that music camp if you want."

"Can you have me a couple of cinnamon rolls and a cup of black coffee ready when I get up?" Lloyd asked.

Jim raised an eyebrow. "Yeah, I'll run my horse through the Starbucks drive-through on the way over. Can you at least keep a weapon handy tonight?"

Lloyd looked around confused, trying to remember where he'd left his shotgun.

"It's still on your horse." Jim pointed. "Which you need to unsaddle if you're going to stick around here for the night."

Lloyd laid his banjo on the case and stood up. "Nag, nag, nag."

Jim led his two horses away, listening to Lloyd mumbling complaints behind him. The guy was the best friend he'd ever had, but he wasn't cut out for the current state of things. That was obvious from his joy at having someone new to talk to. It also showed in the fact that no amount of lecturing could force him to remain vigilant. It simply wasn't in his nature to constantly be on guard against trouble.

Lloyd didn't have the ingrained paranoia and distrust that made Jim a natural in this world. In the old world, those personality traits made Jim too intense for some of the people around him. He'd been called everything from an asshole to a crackpot, but he was fine with it. He suspected those folks who called him out years ago might be having a change of heart right about now, wishing they'd been nicer. They were probably wishing they had someone like Jim Powell in their life.

Jim mounted up and rode south across the dam. To his right, far below him, a doe and fawn were wading through the marshy grass along the tailwaters. The gravel road beneath Jim was showing signs of neglect. Weeds poked through, both wildflowers and tall stalks of grass heavy with seed.

Beyond the dam, Jim rejoined the same trail he'd ridden earlier to the old campsite. He didn't have to follow it far until he ran into a flat clearing that would make a decent campsite for the night. There was enough grass for his horses and a thin feeder stream ran alongside the camp, dumping into the lake. He unsaddled the horse and stacked the gear nearby. He didn't anticipate rain so he strung a hammock between two trees and tossed his sleeping bag into it. He was tired and the sight of the hammock was inviting. He was ready to stretch out and call it a night but his stomach had other plans. It was demanding food.

He removed a surplus Gerber entrenching tool from his gear and dug a small pit for a fire. The forest loam was soft, the digging easy. When he was done, he piled a few rocks around it to offer even more protection against the fire being seen from a distance. There was plenty of deadfall around and he soon had a tiny blaze going. He laid out his wire grate across the rocks and filled a pot in the stream, setting it over the heat to boil. He returned to his gear and searched through his supplies, coming up with a freeze-dried tuna casserole that looked tolerable.

When the water had boiled long enough to kill anything of concern, Jim poured the appropriate amount into the freeze-dried meal packet and sealed it back up. He squished the pack between his fingers to thoroughly distribute the water, then set it aside to rehydrate. He dumped the extra water from his cooking pot and pulled his grate off the fire to cool.

While the meal cooked, Jim refilled his water bottles by the light of his headlamp. There was no sediment visible in the clear mountain stream so he didn't use a pump filter. He filled the bottles directly from the stream, then twirled his ultraviolet Steripen in each of them.

Jim took a sip of the cold water and felt it coursing through all the places in his body that needed it. He took a seat on the ground and leaned back against a tree. He clicked his headlamp off, staring at the glow of his fire and listening to the forest around him. It was dark now and the wildlife was changing shifts. The songbirds were clocking out, the owls and whippoorwills clocking in. Somewhere along the dark shore a heron issued its raspy and prehistoric cry. Raccoons, bears, coyotes, and possums would all be moving around out there too. It was a reminder that he'd need to hang his food bags when he was done eating.

When the tuna casserole reached the right amount of *squish*, Jim opened the package and dug into it with a long-handled spork, specially designed for eating from freeze-dried pouches. He kept his fire to twigs, low enough that it wouldn't illuminate the tree canopy overhead. He just needed enough of a fire to provide light for his lonely camp.

Laughter rolled across the water. Jim recognized the sound. It had to be Lloyd laughing at one of his own jokes. It must have been funny enough to amuse Andrew because he was braying along. Despite the fun they were having at the other camp, Jim didn't mind being alone. He'd always been comfortable in his own skin and his own head. However, the laughter made him think of his family. What were they doing tonight?

He imagined their day had been longer with someone else having to perform the chores he usually did. He assumed Hugh and Charlie were helping them out with that. They would be canning tonight, trying to preserve as much of the garden food as possible. Nana was probably helping while Pops read stories to Ariel.

Jim would return to them soon. He knew that now. When he'd left home, it had been with the understanding that he could be gone for months. Yet in the short time he'd been gone he'd come to some conclusions. Bring what it may, he wasn't going to hide anymore. Let the community wonder why he'd survived. Let them wonder why he had the nerve to walk among them after what he'd done. If they dared, they could come for him. He had a lot of shovels and a lot of places to dig holes.

The tuna was okay, but not something he'd ever crave. In his current condition it filled his stomach and would help him sleep. When he was done he tossed the pouch into the fire. He washed his spork in the creek and set it in his cooking pot to dry. He'd pack that and his fire grate in the morning. He clicked his headlamp on then used the toe of his boot to rake dirt into the fire hole, extinguishing the low blaze.

Before laying down, Jim prepared his gear for the night. He didn't ready his gear to bug-out in the middle of the night. That would be difficult with the horses, the amount of gear he had, and with Lloyd sleeping in a separate camp. He did prepare to come up fighting if it came to that. He hung his plate carrier on the tree beside him and propped the rifle against it. He would sleep in his gun belt with the handgun ready to go. He kept his backpack beside the hammock with the top open. Nestled there in the open top was his good nightvision. If he had to get up at night, his hand would fall right on it. He'd pull the rig over his head and be good to go.

He yawned and stretched, then unrolled his sleeping bag onto the hammock. He carefully took a seat, making sure he didn't dump himself out on the ground. He crossed his legs and was preparing to unlace his boots when a rifle shot split the night. The crack of the round rolled over the water like thunder, followed by a scream of terror.

Lloyd's scream.

**25**

———————

L*aurel Bed Lake*
    *Clinch Mountain Wildlife Management Area*

JIM DOUSED his headlamp and yanked it down around his neck, leaving him in the dark. He shot up from his hammock and dropped his plate carrier over his head. He groped for the nightvision he'd left at-hand and pulled the skull-crusher rig onto his head, cranking it tight. He dropped the twin-tube goggles down in front of his eyes and hit the power. Before the white glow even filled his vision, he had his rifle in hand and was tearing down the trail toward the dam.

Running the rough trail in the dark would have been hard enough by headlamp. In the otherworldly glow of nightvision, it was an acquired skill that Jim hadn't yet mastered. He couldn't see his feet and it was hard to see the obstacles that tried to snag them. Several times he slipped or stumbled. The hardest part wasn't regaining his balance, but suppressing the urge to curse out loud.

There was a second gunshot. Perhaps the same high-powered rifle. Lloyd was no longer screaming. In fact, there was no sound at all. Even the creatures of the night had fallen silent at the eruption of violence in their peaceful haven. They knew when to lay low.

Jim listened as he ran, desperate for any information his ears might provide. There had to be someone, maybe several people, out there moving in the night. If there was more than one attacker, they were probably speaking to each other at that very moment, coordinating their movements. All Jim could hear was his heart pounding like a freight train in his ears, his breath rushing in and out of his chest like a bellows.

He hadn't camped too far down the trail so it only took him a few minutes to emerge from the forest near the dam. He hooked a right and could see the glow of Andrew's bonfire in the distance. While part of him wanted to barrel into the scene and find Lloyd, he forced himself to slow down. There was at least one shooter out there in the darkness and getting himself killed helped no one. It was not the time for reckless, stupid moves. He wasn't going to die up here and leave his family not knowing his fate.

Jim cut into the weeds alongside the gravel road that stretched over the dam. It was further from the lakeshore and closer to the steep bank that sloped down to the tailwaters. The weeds there were waist-high, the ground beneath his feet quieter than the crunching gravel. He doubled over, getting as low as he could, and rushed toward Andrew's RV. There was no sound from the camp and that was terrifying. The injured could cry out. The dead were silent.

He dropped to a knee and forced himself to carefully scan the camp. Although the bold campfire, way too bright in his opinion, illuminated the full breadth of the camp, he couldn't see everything. The high weeds prevented him from seeing the ground, presumably where the injured or dead were laying. He moved forward about a dozen more feet and did the same thing again, poking his head up like a gopher checking his surroundings. This time he saw movement in the trees beyond the boat landing.

Jim was perhaps sixty feet from the camp, near the point where the weeds stopped and the gravel parking lot of the boat ramp began. In the ghostly white glow of his nightvision, Jim spotted a thin, bearded man in camouflage creeping into the camp with a hunting rifle raised. He was moving stealthily, like a man approaching a wounded bear to see if it was indeed dead. Jim wanted to throw up his rifle and drop him immediately, but what if he wasn't alone?

Jim dropped his head and crawled toward the end of the grassy stretch. There, trees lined the edge of the parking lot and he took cover behind the base of a thick poplar. He raised his rifle and braced it against the tree. He wouldn't take the shot yet but wanted to ready himself. Sure enough, the camouflaged figure paused in the firelight and waved a beckoning hand toward the darkness.

Not hearing any cries from the camp, Jim had to assume the worst. He tried to not think about it. His best friend was probably dead and the stranger before him was responsible for it. A second man, also dressed in hunting camo, approached the camp. He moved slowly, his rifle at the ready.

The two camouflaged men conferred, then walked closer to the RV. Jim couldn't see the ground, couldn't see what they were looking at. One of the men drew back and kicked at something. Whatever response that provoked made both men jump back. The first snapped his rifle up and was preparing to fire toward the ground when Jim beat him to the punch, squeezing the trigger on his M4.

The man in the crosshairs of his reticle flinched and twisted, dropping his rifle. The second man swung toward the darkness where Jim hid and let a shot fly. He couldn't see what he was shooting at and the shot wasn't even close. The man desperately worked the bolt, his eyes never leaving the darkness as he tried to find his target. Unfortunately, his target found him first, nailing him with a rapid double-tap. The first shot hit his rifle, splintering the stock and sending shards of wood into his face. He jerked and slapped at his bleeding cheek. Jim's second round went high of center mass, punching in just below the man's Adam's apple.

Jim flipped his nightvision up and waded in, trying to keep the RV between him and the men he'd shot. He heard gurgling, moans, and attempts to shout. He couldn't be certain if the men were trying to shout at him, each other, or for help that lurked out there somewhere in the darkness.

Andrew's RV was surrounded by the old man's belongings and Jim had to watch for it as he moved. Old coolers, plastic buckets, a shovel, and a folding chair. A barbecue grill, a canoe paddle, a spare tire, a car jack, and more stuff hidden beneath tarps. Jim popped around the edge of the RV to find one of the men crawling toward his dropped rifle. The other lay on his back, clutching at his throat with both hands as if he could stop the bleeding and survive this. Jim put a round in his temple and the two hands slowly unfurled from his throat. That solved the matter. There would be no surviving.

Jim flipped his rifle to safe and swung it around to his back. He drew his knife and dropped onto the crawling man. He hauled his head back and stuck the point of his knife to the man's throat. He may have been pressing a bit hard because blood was already oozing from where the razor-sharp tip met flesh.

"Why did you do this?" Jim growled.

"Supplies."

"Are there more of you?"

The man hesitated.

Jim wasted no time pressing the knife harder. The tip pierced the skin and buried itself several millimeters deeper into his neck. The man flinched hard and Jim could feel the pain ripple through the body beneath him. "Are there more of you?"

"Our families are camping down the mountain," he croaked. "We came up here alone."

Jim didn't believe a word of it. He shoved the blade through the man's neck and pushed forward, raking it out the front. He choked as his blood ran free, swallowed by the dirty gravel beneath him. Jim crawled off him and launched himself toward the fire, tipping a plastic bucket of water over into the roaring blaze. There was a hiss and a mushroom cloud of steam rose in the warm night. The fire wasn't completely extinguished but reduced to the orange glow of coals.

Sheathing his bloody knife, Jim whipped his rifle to the front of his body and dropped the nightvision goggles over his eyes. Only then did he dare look down at the two bodies on the ground beside the camper. Andrew was toppled over backward in his camping chair, half of his face missing. Lloyd was beside him, eyes wide and mouth open, blindly groping at the ground around him. He was alive but petrified with fear.

"Lloyd! It's me! Are you hit?"

Lloyd's head shook in a violent tremor.

"Are you sure?" Jim demanded. "You're not hurt?"

"I…I was playing dead. I didn't know what was happening. I didn't know what to do."

Jim scanned the ground around his fallen friend and located Lloyd's shotgun. He picked it up, confirmed there was a round chambered, and shoved it into his arms. "You sit right fucking there! Don't move and don't run off. I need to check the woods and make sure there's not more of them. Got it?"

"Got it," Lloyd said, his voice quavering.

As much as Jim hated to leave his friend behind, he raised his rifle and moved away from the RV, walking in the direction from which the men had come. He desperately wished he had a thermal optic at the moment. In the darkness, he'd have had no problem picking up the heat signatures of anyone lurking out there within range. As it was, he had good visibility but there could be someone hiding in the underbrush and he might never see them.

Assuming there might have been a grain of truth in what the man said, Jim stuck to the road. He walked slowly, trying not to dislodge any gravel as he moved. He scanned both sides of the road, watching for anything out of place in the dense vegetation. Leaving the boat ramp behind, he turned a bend in the road and spotted a nervous-looking figure standing in the road about seventy feet ahead of him. He was frantically pacing, likely alarmed by the shots he'd heard and uncertain of what he should do.

Jim moved to the shoulder of the road and took cover behind a tree.

The figured must have heard him or detected his movement. He stopped and raised his gun toward the darkness. "Who's out there? Is that you, Miller?"

"Drop your gun!" Jim bellowed.

The figure did drop his gun but Jim couldn't tell if it was because of his command or out of fear at the loud voice coming from the darkness. Before the gun had even hit the ground, he turned tail and ran. Jim tracked him through his optic, conflicting thoughts battling in his head. He knew the dangers of letting a survivor escape. He could get back to his camp and lead others here. He could also hide and ambush the two of them later.

"Dammit!" Jim hissed. He didn't like being put in this position.

He did a hasty calculation for hold-over and laid his crosshairs on the crown of the fleeing man's head, then pulled the trigger. The gunshot exploded in the darkness and the man's head instantly snapped to the side in response. He hit the ground and tumbled into a pile.

Jim watched him for a moment, his teeth gritted against what he'd been forced to do. The man didn't move. Jim watched the woods for several minutes before he was satisfied there was no one else in the immediate area. He didn't like having to do things like this. He could just as easily have let the last man go, but experience had been a hard and merciless teacher. He'd learned a few bitter lessons over the last year and this was one of them. He didn't leave survivors. To do so would most certainly cost lives later.

Jim hustled back to the boat landing. "Lloyd, it's Jim!" he called before he got close. "Don't shoot! You hear me?"

"I hear you."

Jim could hear a hollowness in Lloyd's voice. He knew that sound. It was the tone of someone disgusted with what the world had thrown at them. Steam from the partially extinguished fire hung over the camp, illuminated by the glow from the embers and from stray flickers of firelight. Jim waded through the otherworldly scene and found Lloyd standing over Andrew's body.

"We were just having a good time," Lloyd said. "Playing some music and cooking some dinner. Having a little drink. He said it was safe. He said everyone he'd run into was friendly and he hadn't had any trouble."

"Any one of those men he talked to could have been scouting out what he had. They could have planned to come back for it later. These men I killed might have been here before and played all nice. Doesn't mean they weren't dangerous. It doesn't mean you can let down your guard."

Lloyd couldn't pull his eyes from his new friend's mangled face. "It's my fault. Too much noise and a big old fire. Not paying attention to what was going on around us."

"It's not your fault. He wasn't taking any precautions before we came along. We didn't bring these men here. This probably would have happened with or without us."

Lloyd shook his head slowly. "You don't know that. The music might have drawn them in. You knew enough to camp away from us, we just didn't want to listen. We thought you were being paranoid."

Jim scanned the darkness behind him again. "Lloyd, we need to get out of here. If there's more of them, the shooting might draw them. We can't stick around."

"What do we do with all his stuff?"

"If it wasn't for the fire risk, I'd burn it all to the ground," Jim said. "If there are more of these folks out there, they don't deserve Andrew's stuff."

"We could go through it? See if there's anything we could use?"

"I don't think that's a good idea. We need to get out of here. We need to put some miles between us and the lake."

"What do I need to do?"

"I'm going to keep watch. You saddle your horse and get your gear together. We'll go to my camp, tear it down, then haul ass out of here."

"I don't want to leave him," Lloyd said. "He deserves better than being left here with the men who killed him."

"You're wanting to bury him?"

"Can we?"

Jim considered. "You pack your shit. When you're done, we'll roll

Andrew up in something and lay him across your saddle. You can't ride on this trail anyway. We'll find a place away from the lake and bury him."

"Sounds right," Lloyd said. First things first, he located his banjo, leaning against the side of Andrew's RV. He placed it in the case and carried it toward his nervous horse.

## 26

Laurel Bed Lake
*Clinch Mountain Wildlife Management Area*

IT TOOK Jim less than five minutes to saddle his horses and get them loaded. The nightvision gear like he had was in limited supply. Half of what his people had were battlefield pickups from skirmishes with better-equipped folks. The other half came from their contact with Scott and his Energy Recovery people. There weren't enough sets for Jim to bring two with him. He didn't want to leave the folks back at home short-handed if they ran into trouble.

As a result, he led the way wearing his nightvision, his rifle hanging across the front of his body. Lloyd wore a headlamp with a red LED. They followed the same trail Jim had followed earlier to the campsite on the backside of the lake. Jim pointed out the side trail that led to the beach, but the two of them continued along the main trail.

The headwaters of the lake was a series of small streams coursing through hundreds of acres of marshland and bogs. The mosquitoes were relentless here and tortured them like minions sent from Hell. Both men pulled on long-sleeved shirts and wrapped bandanas around their necks, trying to limit the amount of vulnerable flesh available for insect dining. Jim had a pair of gloves in his chest rig and soon pulled those on to protect the backs of his hands. He could already feel them swelling from the bites. Lloyd didn't have any gloves, but eventually pulled a pair of spare socks over his hands when the bites became maddening.

The headwaters were secluded from the main body of the lake. Things were quieter and more insular here without every stray sound amplified by the surface of the water. Undisturbed by the distant shooting, the wildlife continued its nocturnal activity. Somewhere a heron cried in distress, likely fighting off a raccoon trying to invade its nest. Coyotes yipped in the excitement and frenzy of the hunt. Somewhere, the calm hooting of an owl seemed the lone voice of reason in the night, unperturbed and omniscient.

When they'd gone a mile or so beyond the lake, the marsh began to transition to thick rhododendron and hardwood forest.

"We should bury him here," Jim said. "This is pretty isolated and the ground is soft. Once we get back into these woods we'll never get a hole dug. Too many roots and rocks."

"Gimme a shovel," was Lloyd's only response.

Jim switched from his nightvision to his headlamp and located the entrenching shovel, or E-tool, in his gear. He tossed it to Lloyd. Unfolding the device, Lloyd grasped the magnitude of digging a man-sized hole with the miniature implement. While he got started, Jim tied the horses off where they could drink from the stream and nibble at the tall grass. He left the gear on them in case he'd been wrong about how isolated the area was.

He built a fire while Lloyd dug. When the blaze cast enough light to work by, both switched off their headlamps and worked by firelight to preserve their batteries. Green limbs tossed into the blaze produced enough smoke to thin the hordes of mosquitoes. In a few minutes they switched off, Lloyd taking a breather while Jim took a turn behind the shovel.

"Digging here in the firelight makes me feel like I'm burying treasure," Jim said.

"Guess you might say that," Lloyd said. "He was a nice old man."

This reminder of what they were doing was sobering. Over the ride through the woods, some of their adrenaline-fueled anxiety dissipated. The deep forest had that kind of relaxing effect, at least until you had to stop and bury a body. Then relaxation fled with the abruptness of a tonearm being swept across a record on a record player.

"Shit like this is the reason I'm the way I am," Jim said. "You haven't seen as much of it. You remember when my friends and I stopped at your apartment when we were coming home from Richmond? That old man shot those English boys and then his own son. You were shocked by that but we weren't. We'd seen that kind of ugliness, that kind of senseless and incomprehensible violence, ever since our first day on the road."

"Seems like I only see it when I'm around you," Lloyd said. It wasn't intended as an accusation. More of an observation.

Jim wasn't certain of how to take the remark. "I don't invite it, I only react to it. I do everything I can to make sure it's not me or someone I care about that's left bleeding out in the end. What do you think would have happened if I hadn't killed those men back there?"

"They'd have killed me," Lloyd said. "When that guy kicked me, I couldn't help but move. He was getting ready to shoot me when you killed him."

"Exactly, and none of that was my doing. I was at my campsite minding my own business. I was just trying to save your ass."

"And I appreciate it," Lloyd said. "I know I give you shit about your body count but I'm only teasing. I know it's not *always* your fault."

"It's a bit of a sensitive topic. You don't get that sometimes. There's a lot of blood on my hands bnd it's not always easy to live with. Back at that boat landing, I shot a man who was running away from me. I shot him in the fucking *back* to protect us. I don't feel good about that, but I'd feel worse about him showing up later with help."

"I'm sorry," Lloyd said. "I'm usually just trying to be funny. To keep things light-hearted. The way you pick on my drinking."

Jim had no response to that. He dug for a while longer, then climbed out, tossing the tool to Lloyd. Lloyd stood up, stretched his stiff back, and went to it. After a while, he stopped and wiped the sweat from his forehead.

"You know, this makes me see why Randi is so hard. It doesn't pay to let your guard down. It's not worth making new friends. You love the people you already love because you don't have any choice, but it's not worth letting anyone new inside. The odds of losing them are too high."

Jim scrounged up a few more lengths of deadfall and tossed them onto the fire. Sparks rose in the heat, fading out against the night sky. "I'm with you, buddy. People have to earn their way into your heart by surviving past a certain point. Like a probationary period at a new job. You can be my friend, but you have to survive six months of knowing me first."

"Surviving six months as your friend can be kind of a challenge," Lloyd acknowledged.

Jim agreed. "Some don't make it."

They let the truth of that hang in the air and didn't speak for some time. They stopped digging at around two feet, neither having the energy for a regulation-depth grave. They laid Andrew's body out, wrapped in a blanket they'd found in his RV. They raked the dirt back into the grave, Jim using a shovel and Lloyd using a forked branch.

When they were done, Lloyd took off his battered felt hat and held it across his chest in a serious manner. The firelight reflected off his sweaty, dirt-smudged face. "Andrew, it was a pleasure to meet you. Sorry you met such an unfortunate end. You were a good man, with fine taste in music and stories. I hope we get a share a fire again one day and pick up where we left off. I'll bring the liquor." When he finished, he looked at Jim expectantly.

"What?"

"You don't have anything to add?" Lloyd asked.

"Hell, I barely knew him," Jim complained. He yanked off his sweaty ballcap and held it over his heart, then cleared his throat. "Andrew, you'll be pleased to know that I killed the sorry sons-of-bitches that did this to you. May they rot in Hell. Amen." He swung his clammy cap back onto his head. Jim looked back at his buddy with satisfaction. "Happy now?"

Lloyd looked appalled. "You don't go to many memorial services, do you?"

Jim shook his head. "No. Can you tell?"

Lloyd raised one eyebrow. "Maybe a little."

They piled rocks atop the grave to discourage all but the most determined scavengers. The coons, coyotes, and birds would give up, but these impediments would hardly slow a hungry bear.

"Can we camp here?" Lloyd asked.

Jim checked his watch. It was after 3 AM. "Let's douse this fire and get further up the valley. If anyone is looking for us, the smell of this smoke might draw them in."

They used the shovel to pitch dirt onto the fire and it was soon extinguished. The weary men mounted their equally-weary horses and set off again. They were too tired to swat at bugs now. Too tired to think. Too tired to feel.

## 27

————

T*he Farm Road*

WHILE FREDA TOPPED off Sharon's scrapes with a bright orange tincture of mercurochrome, Kendall went to one of his sheds, digging out a come-along and a newly-sharpened ax. The hand-cranked winch would be plenty powerful enough to pull the branch from the roadway once he cut it loose from the tree.

"You all still living up there at the camp?" Freda asked.

"We are," Sharon answered.

"I imagine that's tough. That place wasn't set up as a home."

"Oliver wanted us to move into the house with him, but I didn't want to be a bother."

"Wouldn't have been a bother to him," Freda assured her. "Everyone who ever came to that camp was family to him. He'd have taken any of them in."

"We'll probably move in there now. I've been thinking about it ever since I found him."

Freda tightened her lips. "That's a good idea, but that's a big move for someone with nobody but children to help them. Do you even have a way of hauling things back and forth?"

"Not really. I hadn't got that far in my thinking yet."

"Well you strike me as a bit stubborn, but I hope you'll accept help from your neighbors if it's offered."

Sharon had to smile. She was always amused by the way older ladies felt obliged to speak their mind. She didn't have much room to talk though. She was getting there herself. "I will gladly accept help."

"That's more like it," Freda said. "You can be independent without being so stubborn that you make life harder for yourself."

"I wouldn't know," Sharon said. "I've always insisted on being too stubborn."

Freda put a hand on Sharon's chair and used it to push herself to a standing position. Her knees popped and cracked. She screwed the cap back onto her fiery bottle of mercurochrome and set it aside. "I'll help you down the steps and we'll see about getting you hooked back up. I imagine you're a bit anxious to get back to those kids."

"I am."

Freda awkwardly helped Sharon down the two steps to the yard.

"I can get it from here," Sharon said, rolling toward Honey. When she reached her pony, she clipped into the harness and untied from the tree. She flicked the reins and clucked her tongue, and Honey began ambling back toward the road.

Freda walked alongside her, talking about her home and family. They talked about the neighbors and the community in general. Sharon just listened and in no time they were at the downed limb where she had spilled down the embankment.

"I got it cut loose," Kendall said. "I'm fixing to crank it out of the way now." He'd used a short length of chain to attach his come-along to a stout tree, then fastened the braided steel cable of the winch around the far end of the dropped limb.

While the powerful winch easily moved the heavy oak limb, it took a lot of arm power to make it happen. When Kendall paused to wipe his brow and shake some fresh blood back into his arm muscles, Sharon insisted on taking a turn.

"No offense but it takes a little strength," Kendall said.

Sharon raised an eyebrow at him. "And rolling this chair every day doesn't?"

Kendall conceded the point and stepped out of the way. Sharon disconnected from her pony and rolled into position. She began steadily shoving the winch lever, bringing a small bite of cable onto the spool with each movement.

Working up a sweat of her own now, Sharon glanced at Kendall. He gave her a nod of approval. She was glad to see that he was acknowledging her abilities and not dismissing them. That attitude would go a long way toward keeping them on good terms as neighbors. She'd have a hard time trusting anyone who didn't respect what she was capable of.

"That enough?" she asked, once she'd opened enough of a gap for her horse and chair.

"Let's go a hair wider," Kendall said. "In case we need to bring something bigger than your chair through here."

Sharon moved back and let Kendall take over the winch again. When he was done, the branch had been moved entirely clear of the road and lay in the ditch.

"I'll nibble away at that for firewood," Kendall said. "We'll clear it out of there eventually."

"I appreciate the help. I wasn't sure how I was going to get back around it."

"A body shouldn't be too proud to take help when you need it," Freda said in her customarily blunt manner.

"I'll remember that."

Kendall took a seat in the shady fence-line by his winch. He mopped at his brow with a grimy handkerchief. "If you don't mind me asking, how did you get around the camp before all this mess happened? Ain't exactly smooth ground for a wheelchair up there."

"I had a golf cart. Oliver bought it for me. Once the gas ran out, I had to park it and start using the pony."

"I've got one around here somewhere too. Mine was electric. We used to have a camper over at the lake when the kids were young. We'd ride that golf cart between the lake and the camper and back. Eventually, the battery crapped out and I was too cheap to buy another one."

"Not to change the subject," Freda said, "but we need to think about what we're going to do with Oliver. You sure you want to bury him at the camp?"

"I asked the children and that was their idea. I hate to let them make the decision then overrule them."

Freda ignored the comment, likely of the mind that you shouldn't put such decisions in the hands of children to begin with. "Were you going back to the camp tonight or staying at Oliver's house?"

"I'm going to head back to the camp to speak to the children. I need to let them know that he died. He was still alive when they stopped by earlier. To occupy them, I'll let them help plan his service. Maybe they can play some music. That's something Oliver would have enjoyed."

Kendall smiled. "He sure would. Nothing warmed his heart like seeing those children pick up an instrument."

Freda was staring at the ground, rubbing her chin, brow furrowed in thought. Sharon could see that she was a planner. An organizer. She didn't like loose ends, like a dead body with no plan for getting it in the ground. "How about you just stay up there at the camp with them young'uns tonight. Help them figure out their service and whatnot. Kendall and I will tend to the body. You have a watch?"

"I do."

"Then we'll be up there around 3 PM tomorrow. We'll arrange to get the body up there to the camp and make sure that any folks who might want to come knows about it."

"You'd do all that?" Sharon asked.

Freda looked at her in surprise. "I said I would, didn't I?"

"Well, yeah, but that's a lot. I'm grateful, it's just that we've spent an entire year doing nearly everything on our own. I guess I'm just not used to getting a lot of help."

"Weren't our fault," Kendall said. "Oliver was just as proud as you. Didn't want to take any help. Any time we asked about the camp he said you all had it under control."

"I guess we did," Sharon said, "but it wasn't always easy."

Freda was nodding as if this was confirmation of the point she'd been trying to make. "Like I said, take help if you need it. Ain't no sense in being so proud that you cut your nose off to spite your face."

"Guess not," Sharon admitted. "Well, I'm very appreciative. I was pretty overwhelmed when I came upon you folks. Guess you could tell that."

"Like Freda said, folks needs help sometimes. Ain't no shame in taking it."

Sharon smiled at Kendall's delivery. It may have been exactly the same thing Freda was trying to say, but it was certainly delivered in a much gentler manner than the abrupt woman had delivered it. That didn't mean Sharon disliked her. She appreciated people who were honest and direct. She was simply more accustomed to being on the delivery end than the receiving end.

"Thank you folks so much. You'll find Oliver in his bed. The house is open. I guess I'll see you tomorrow."

Freda surprised Sharon by wrapping her in a warm embrace. "Don't you worry about a thing."

When Freda backed away, Kendall gave a friendly wave and Sharon headed off. She let Honey pull at her own pace, aware of the rough road beneath her wheels. She realized she was going to be sore tomorrow. That was okay. Sharon was never one to complain about soreness. It meant you were working toward something. It meant you were *feeling*.

It meant you were alive.

**28**

————————

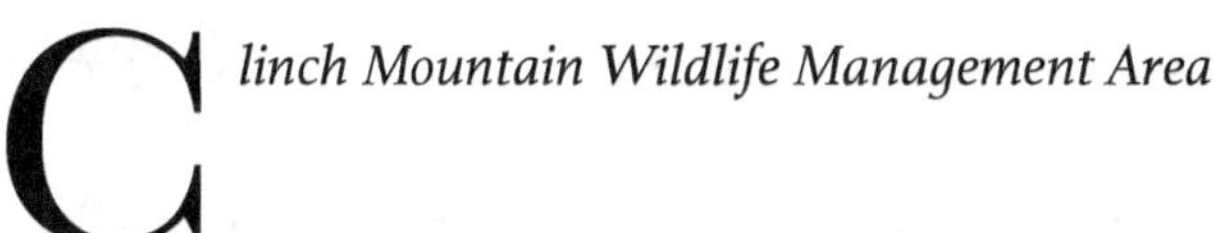

C*linch Mountain Wildlife Management Area*

LLOYD AND JIM worked too late into the night to get any decent sleep. After leaving the burial site they camped at the location of another plane crash, finding an artificial clearing created by a Beechcraft plowing away the vegetation like some aerial bulldozer. Jim didn't remember the story behind this particular crash but it was known to authorities. A bright orange X spray-painted onto the broad aluminum surfaces marked it as discovered, hopefully preventing some pilot from reporting it as a new crash.

It had been there long enough that the woods were attempting to swallow the plane. Still, enough of a clearing remained for the weary travelers to settle there. Jim strung his hammock for the second time that night while Lloyd spread out his sleeping bag on a ground cloth. Neither found a good night's sleep awaiting them. With their sore muscles, itchy bug bites, and being well past the point of exhaustion, it took them a bit to fall asleep.

Two hours after they stretched out the sun began to peek over the horizon. The pair managed only about three or four hours of shut-eye before the heat caught up with the sun. Soon the humid forest was like a sauna and they became too miserable to sleep any longer, sweating beneath their sleeping bags. When they tried tossing them to the side and sleeping uncovered, insects feasted upon them with a maddening fury.

"Fuck," Jim groaned, kicking back his sleeping bag and surrendering to the day. He furiously scratched the red welts covering his arms, neck, and forehead.

They were following the stream and Jim wandered over to its weedy bank. He waded in, splashing himself thoroughly until he felt human again. By the time he was done, Lloyd was sitting up in his sleeping bag, looking like shit. Considering the day they'd had yesterday, the look fit him.

"I can't believe I volunteered for this trip," Lloyd groaned. "I'm an idiot."

"You didn't volunteer because I wasn't *looking* for volunteers. You insisted on coming. You invited yourself."

"Is it too late to change my mind?"

Jim looked at him like he was crazy. "You're committed now. You try to go home on your own and you'll get lost. You'll die in the woods and bears will scatter your bones."

Lloyd glared at him, not impressed with how little faith Jim had in his survival abilities. "Any sane man would know better than to set out on a trip with you. They always turn out the same. One minute I'm having a good time, the next you're killing people."

"We've beat that horse already. Remember that when you're recounting this tale to your drinking buddies. I came to save your ass and that's how I ended up killing people. I could have stayed in my hammock and ignored the whole thing. I could have left you to your own devices but we know how that ends too, don't we?"

"Bears scattering my bones in the woods?"

Jim grinned. "Exactly."

Lloyd ignored him, fighting the urge to lay back down. Jim began refilling water bottles from the stream, using the Steripen to sanitize them. He went ahead and refilled Lloyd's too since he hadn't budged. He was sitting there with the same scowl on his face, hating life. When Jim was done refilling the bottles, he tossed one in Lloyd's direction. The bottle landed on his sleeping bag and thumped off his shin.

"Ouch."

"Drink up."

Lloyd groaned in response, fumbling for the bottle without opening his eyes. Jim dug into his packs and found a couple of energy bars. He tossed one of those at Lloyd too, bouncing it off his chest.

"What the hell is that?" Lloyd asked, eyes closed.

"Breakfast. Tastes like bark, but we're in the woods so it's kind of fitting."

"I can't wake up and I can't sleep," Lloyd moaned. "I'm trapped in limbo."

Jim unwrapped his energy bar and took a bite. He shoved the rest in his pocket and began packing his gear. When his packs were closed up, he saddled his horses and slung the packs onto them. "You better get your ass moving. You wanted to go check in on that camp in Bland County so that's where we're headed."

Lloyd held the bottle of cold water to his head, then twisted the lid off and took a long pull. He tossed back his sleeping bag and staggered to his feet. He spent a moment getting his balance, then set about packing up his sleeping gear. "I used to like camping."

Jim smiled. It wasn't the first time he'd heard a comment like that. "It was different when camping was recreation. When it's your only choice it isn't so fun anymore."

In another twenty minutes or so they finished rehydrating and topped off their water bottles. They finished their breakfast and took care of any business in the woods that needed to be taken care of. When they were done, they saddled up.

"I forgot how sore you can get from riding a horse," Lloyd griped. "I remember now."

Jim grinned. "Toughen up, snowflake. We got a long day ahead of us."

Lloyd didn't toughen up. He continued to complain for most of the morning. The sun was too hot and the woods too buggy. There were too many spider webs and he was tired of riding through them. He couldn't escape the feeling that thousands of baby spiders were crawling up and down his back. He asked Jim to take a look but Jim ignored him. Lloyd complained his horse didn't walk smoothly enough and that his saddle was insufficient in its padding.

After two hours, Jim had all he could take. "Damn, Lloyd, I don't know whether to shoot myself or shoot you. Maybe I should have snuck off while you were sleeping this morning. I don't know how much more of this whining I can take."

"I ain't whining, I'm commiserating."

Jim rolled his eyes. "It ain't commiserating unless I'm sharing my misery too and you'll notice that I haven't said a fucking word. If you're wanting to hear about it, though, my biggest misery right now is your flapping gums."

Lloyd grinned knowingly. "See, I knew you were thinking about being miserable too."

"Then if you're such a psychic, what am I thinking now?" Jim growled, shooting Lloyd a dirty look.

Lloyd frowned. "Ain't a hundred percent sure but I know it's not nice. I suspect it's something unkind about your only friend and traveling companion."

"You'd be right about that."

Lloyd reached back and unzipped the soft banjo case. He extracted the vintage instrument and slung it around his neck. He gave it a hard strum and glared at Jim with a "take that" look. When that had no effect, he launched into a tune, writing it as he went along.


*"MY FRIEND JIM ain't so nice,*

*He feeds me nothing but beans and rice.*

*I just came along for the ride,*
*To watch out for his sorry hide.*
*But it ain't a very easy job,*
*Cause he acts like a total knob."*


"ARE YOU DONE?" Jim asked.

"Oh, not nearly."


"HE AIN'T GOT *no people skills,*
*Most people he meets, he kills.*
*That's why he ain't got no friends,*
*Every word he says offends.*
*I'm pretty sure he got dropped on his head,*
*When his momma got him out of his bed."*


"THAT'S the dumbest song I ever heard," Jim groaned. "Shut up!"

But Lloyd didn't. On and on he went, insulting Jim's lineage all the way back to his earliest cave-dwelling ancestors.

They continued to follow Laurel Bed Creek for most of the morning, Jim trying his best to block the obnoxious musician out of his head. He found only limited success with those attempts, knowing that if he plugged his ears he might miss some critical threat along the way. They eventually encountered the cleared right-of-way for a high-tension power line running perpendicular to the creek. High metal towers stood at intervals to the north and south, looking like a procession of robots frozen in their tracks.

Jim reined his horse to a stop and fished his GPS from his gear. He allowed his horse to drink while the device acquired satellites and located his position on the tiny screen. Waiting for the device to sync, he pulled out his water bottle and took a long pull. Lloyd stood off to the side tuning his banjo. Jim watched him out of the corner of his eye, wondering if he could put a bullet through the instrument without hitting the horse or rider.

When he returned his eyes to the screen of the GPS, he zoomed in and studied the image. If he could travel along the utility clearing it would drop him off the high plateau and connect him with the Cove Road. He'd only been to the section of Tazewell County known as The Cove a few times over the years. It was a remote farming valley surrounded by mountains on three sides. There were some old farms there, a couple owned by the same families for over two hundred years. Sprawling homes were set back from the road amidst massive oaks and overgrown shrubs of long-forgotten varieties, imported from distant lands by prosperous landowners.

It was a beautiful area in better times, but it was hard to predict their current sentiment toward strangers. The more Jim thought about it, the sentiment wasn't hard to predict at all. It was unlikely that any of the residents would be welcoming to their passage. He imagined dogs might be turned upon them and shots loosed in their direction.

"We've got a long day ahead of us," Jim said. "We're headed into farmland and I don't want to cut across some stranger's land. People might not take kindly to it."

Lloyd nodded, more focused on tuning his banjo. Proper tuning did little to minimize how the instrument of torture grated on Jim's nerves. It sawed on him like a dull knife on a nerve.

Jim pointed along the power lines. "If we can follow this clearing to the Cove Road, we can travel through The Cove and Thompson Valley, then pick up the Appalachian Trail at the Chestnut Ridge trailhead on Route 625. It might be as far as thirty miles, but if we get on good roads we could make that in one day. Then we could camp in the woods near the AT, which would be safer than camping along the road." Getting no response, Jim studied his friend. "You got any opinion on any of this?"

"I don't want to die today. Find me a route where I don't get killed and I'll appreciate it."

Jim raised an eyebrow at his old friend. That seemed kind of an obvious request. "Yeah, that's what I'm trying to do here, Lloyd. Find us a route where we both survive. Any more useful input?"

"No, I'm good. You lead and I'll follow. Any idea how far the camp might be?"

Jim studied his GPS. "You said it's in Bland County, right? Off I-77?"

"Yep."

"We might make it tomorrow afternoon if we get a good ride in today."

"Then let's hit it. Talking ain't getting us there."

Jim tucked his GPS away. "I don't know when you suddenly got so focused on the mission. You're the one who usually won't shut up."

"And you're the one still talking," Lloyd said, swinging his banjo onto his back.

Jim let out a sigh and nudged his horse. This was going to be a long day.

**29**

---

T *he Valley*

Pete and Charlie were standing at the garden fence. Inside the enclosure Ellen, Pops, and Hugh were picking tomatoes for another day of canning.

Ellen was shaking her head. "I don't know. Hugh, what do you think?"

"It was pretty calm last time," he replied. "There wasn't any hostility or tension. As long as they go straight there and come straight back they should be fine."

Ellen looked uncertain.

"I brought a lot of useful things back last time," Charlie said. "I've got more to trade. I might be able to get more seeds. There might be different vendors with other stuff we need."

Ellen had been impressed with Charlie's purchases last time. He'd brought candy for the children and several other things they'd been in dire need of. His decision to purchase for the tribe instead of himself had shown maturity.

"I'd rather you have an adult with you," Ellen said.

"All the adults are busy," Pete countered.

"Maybe that's a hint that you should be too," Ellen said pointedly.

"Randi might want to go," Pops said. "Poor thing is kind of missing Lloyd. Might be good for her to get out of here for a while."

"Can we go if Randi goes?" Pete proposed.

"Okay," Ellen conceded, "if Randi will go, you can go. But you have to listen to her. Okay?"

Pete couldn't hold back a grin. He was excited to get into town and see what was going on.

Hugh straightened up and stretched his back. "You guys know how serious things are, right? Always be on guard but don't present yourself as a threat. Don't make people feel like they need to take you out for their own safety. There's a time when being menacing is a good thing and this is not one of them. Stay low key but watchful. Don't let yourself be caught off-guard."

Both boys nodded, then sprinted for their horses.

"Stop by here on your way out," Ellen called out.

"We will!" Pete yelled back.

They found Randi in her garden, fighting the constant and overwhelming battle against weeds. She was wearing shorts and working barefoot, her sweat creating a layer of mud that reached up past her knees. Her face and arms weren't in much better shape.

"I hope you boys came to help," she said, standing splay-legged over a row of carrots.

Pete and Charlie looked at each other, then back at Randi.

"No, we were wanting to take you away from all of this," Charlie said. "Thought you might need a break."

Randi frowned. "Boys, I'm a grandmother. I know bullshit when I hear it. What are you up to?"

"We want to go in to the farmer's market," Pete said. "No one else wants to go and my mom says we have to find an adult to go with us."

"And since you couldn't find an adult you decided to ask me?"

The boys smiled in tandem.

"I look like I've been rolling around in a pigsty. I ain't fit to go into town."

"Ain't like the old days," Charlie said. "You don't stink any worse than anyone else."

Randi narrowed her eyes at him. "I ain't sure that's a compliment, Charlie."

"Please?" Pete pleaded.

Randi swiped at her forehead with the back of a grubby arm. "I tell you what. I'm going to the bathroom and scrub this mud off of me. If you pick weeds until I get back, I'll go."

"You sure you're not going to sit in there and wait on us to finish before you come out?" Pete asked. "Is this a trick?"

Randi shook her head. "Nope. I just need a quick scrub to get the mud off me."

The small farmhouse where they were living had an improvised hot water system, thanks to Jim. The gutters on the back of the house filled a raised water tank. The tank was painted black and the sun kept the water warm for much of the year. When it got cold enough that the house required a fire, the family relied on water they heated on the woodstove instead.

"It's a deal," Pete said.

Before the boys could change their minds, Randi high-stepped her way from the garden and jogged toward the house. "Five minutes," she called back over her shoulder. "Maybe ten."

The boys kept their promise, pulling everything that didn't have a vegetable attached to it. It was hot work that both boys would have complained about a year ago. While they didn't enjoy it, they enjoyed hunger much less. They understood that gardening was a communal effort and a healthy garden benefited everyone.

True to her word, Randi emerged in ten minutes. She was freshly scrubbed and wearing clean clothes. She had her Go Bag on her back and a shotgun slung over her shoulder. Ten minutes ago she looked like a hippie gardener. Now she looked ready for trouble.

Randi had horses that had belonged to her father. That was how she'd originally brought her daughters and grandchildren to the valley after her parents were murdered. She collected a saddle from the shed behind the house and whistled for her horse. In the field near the garden, it pricked up its ears and came trotting in her direction.

"We'll meet you at our house," Pete said. "Charlie has to get a sack of stuff out of my parent's barn and we need to get our gear together."

"Be ready when I get there," Randi said. "I ain't got all day to fool with you knot-heads."

The boys climbed on their horses and galloped off toward Pete's house. Despite Randi's harsh words, both boys knew the truth. As Pops said, she needed the break and there was an undercurrent of excitement in her voice at escaping her routine, even if it was only for a few hours.

**30**

———————

T*he Farmer's Market*

THIS RIDE into town was no different than Charlie's previous trip. They passed a few folks with whom they exchanged little more than nods. People were more accustomed to moving about now but maintained a wariness beneath their casual demeanor. Charlie did most of the talking on the ride, telling the others about the things they'd seen and what he wanted to look for this time. Pete didn't have much to trade so he was just along for the ride. Randi had some baby clothes that her grandchildren had outgrown and were too small to fit Gary's grandchildren. She'd be willing to part with them if she could find something of interest.

While the boys were excited, riding through town made Randi nervous. Despite what they'd been through, the boys were too young to understand her vigilance. She'd seen a lot. Charlie had been through a lot too, but he hadn't walked home from halfway across the state. He'd not seen the way that each town brewed its own particular cocktail of violence and mayhem. Randi would never feel safe in town again. If she had anything to say about it, she'd never live in town again either. She'd stay as far outside the limits as she could.

Near a burned-out fast food restaurant, the trio turned down the road toward the farmer's market. In the distance, people wandered through what looked like a large yard sale. Goods were thrown out on blankets, tarps, or scattered on cobbled-together tables. Some laid their goods out on the hoods of abandoned cars. Others walked among the crowd, selling on the move. They announced their goods like carnival barkers, their cries adding to the festive atmosphere.

To the left of the road, a message was spray-painted on a rotting sheet of plywood:

Corral space available. *We watch your horse while you shop. Prices flexible.*

"That wasn't here last time," Charlie said, pointing to the far corner of the farmer's market.

Someone had seen a need and jumped on it. They'd hauled in steel corral sections and build a portable structure that could hold a dozen horses while the owners shopped at the market.

"What did you do last time?" Randi asked. "Lead them around?"

"No, Hugh watched them from the dentist's office over there."

"That means one of us wouldn't get to shop," Randi said.

"What if we leave the horses at the corral and they steal them?" Pete asked, already demonstrating his father's distrust of strangers.

Randi shrugged. "We kill them."

"Fair enough," Pete said. "Let's go."

They skirted the crowd, their shod horses clopping loudly on the asphalt parking lot. Although theirs weren't the only horses there they were a rare enough commodity that the arrival of anyone on horseback drew attention. The people on foot always wanted to know who had transportation when they didn't. It was part envy and part resentment. Some may have even been taking notes for later, memorizing who had horses they could steal when the opportunity was available.

A fat man chewing tobacco sat in a camping chair with his arms folded across his belly. Two younger versions of the man stood behind him. One was in his twenties, the other in his younger teens. The fat man had a revolver holstered on his belt, but carried it directly below his belly button. A lever-action rifle was propped up against an empty chair. The proprietors offered nothing by way of a greeting as Pete, Charlie, and Randi reined their horses to a stop in front of them.

"How much?" Randi asked.

Pete couldn't help but notice that interactions were much different than they had been over a year ago. There were no friendly greetings, no small talk, nor comments about the weather. It was straight to business with a guarded and almost unfriendly directness.

"I get a .22 shell per horse to watch them while you shop," the man said. "You ain't got .22, tell me what you got and we'll see if we can work out something."

"You keep them safe?" Randi asked.

He tilted his head toward the lever-action rifle, as if that gesture were sufficient to answer her question. Randi wasn't impressed.

"Any son-of-a-bitch can haul a gun around," she said. "What I want to know is if this horse is going to be here when I get back. I'm going to be a mite pissed off if it ain't."

"I ain't lost one yet," the man replied.

"Then mine better not be the first," Randi replied.

He gave her an indifferent look. "We ain't come to an agreement yet. Far as I'm concerned, you're just blowing hot air."

"You take .25 caliber?" Charlie asked.

He shook his head. "Ain't got no call for it. Ain't worth spit."

"What about 16-gauge shotgun shells?" Charlie asked.

The man hesitated and mulled it over. "I'd take three for three horses."

"I bet you would," Randi said. "How about one shell for three horses?"

He scratched his beard. "What load is it?"

"Number four shot," Charlie replied.

"I'll keep your horses for two shells. I water them too."

"I'll give you one of the shotgun shells and two of the .25 caliber shells," Charlie said.

The man mulled it over. "I'll take it, dammit. I'm tired of jawing with you."

The riders dismounted and Charlie paid him while the sons collected the reins. The younger son gave Pete a long look as he took his horse.

"Ain't you Pete?"

Pete looked harder at the boy. "Yeah, why?"

"I'm Duane. We went to school together."

Pete recognized the boy now. He was a lot skinnier than he'd been in school and was starting to grow a beard. Duane was a year older than him but they'd had gym class at the same time. "Oh, hey Duane. Didn't recognize you."

That was the extent of the conversation. The two weren't friends and this wasn't exactly the environment for making new ones. Duane led his horse off and released it into the small corral.

"We'll be back in a few," Randi said, her tone more of a warning than conversational. The unsaid but implied message was that her horse better be there when she got back.

"Suit yourself," the man replied. "Don't rush on our account. We're here all day."

They walked away from the corral, each wearing their packs and carrying their guns. When they were out of earshot, Randi leaned toward Pete. "You know that family?"

"Not really. I went to school with that kid but he's a grade older than me. His dad has a store in town that sells the kind of crap you see on TV commercials. You know that as-seen-on-TV stuff? They live above the store. I think his name is Willie or something."

Randi rolled her eyes. "God, I remember now. I've been in that store before. Willie's What Nots. The guy didn't have a beard at the time."

"Yeah, the son didn't either."

"Listen, it's probably not a big deal but, just to be safe, you should probably avoid any folks you recognize. If you see a kid from school, just go the other way."

"You and Charlie aren't from here, but I know a lot of folks in this town. I grew up here. That's going to be hard."

"We need to maintain a low profile, Pete. I don't think it's dangerous for you to be here with us but there are a lot of people in this town who are not fans of your dad. There were people killed on the 4th of July when we supposedly gave your dad up to the government. There'll be people here with hard feelings about that. We need to do our business and get out of here with minimal interaction."

Pete understood all that in a general sense. He understood they had to be constantly vigilant in the valley because people were trying to kill his dad. He knew that even with his father gone, they had to stay alert. In the excitement of coming to town and visiting the farmer's market, he'd kind of put that to the side.

He felt a surge of anxiety as he suddenly understood that anyone who met his eye might recognize him. They could follow him home. They could attempt to kidnap him to manipulate his family. They could abduct him and torture him for information about whether his father was alive or not. He was suddenly terrified.

Randi must have sensed it, must have seen the flicker in his eye, the racing thoughts. She threw an arm around him. "Relax, Pete. No need to panic. Just be careful. That's all I'm saying."

He took a long breath and let it out. "I'm good. I'll be okay. I guess I just associated all that with being at home and not with being out in the world."

She smiled. "We can talk more about it later but being alert in a crowd takes some getting used to. Do you want to split up or look around together?"

"Let's stick together," Charlie suggested. "I've got a lot to trade and not much I need. I'm more interested in getting things that help us as a group. You might know about more things we can use than Pete and I do."

"Good enough," Randi said.

They started at one end and worked their way through. There were eggs and chickens. One man had piglets while another had a string of goats on leashes. One woman was selling books on farming, survival, and homesteading that were stamped as belonging to the library. Several people were giving her a hard time about selling books that belonged to the community, but others were buying them up, desperate for the information.

When the bookseller grew tired of the harassment, she drew a revolver and pointed it at her critics. That was the state of the world. People who had become accustomed to being badasses on the internet learned it was a lot different to harass people in real life. They could do more than block you on social media. They could pound you into a puddle or put a bullet in your head. Bystanders watched such disagreements with amusement. They knew to mind their own business and stay out of fights that weren't theirs.

The three spent nearly two hours roaming the vast parking lot of the local government offices. It took a while not because of the number of vendors but because of the time required to negotiate each purchase. It had been simpler when all transactions were based on a standardized currency. Bartering took more creativity and more thought when all manner of objects could be used as money.

Among their more interesting purchases, Charlie managed to buy an entire box of DVD movies for a cheap Swiss Army knife he'd gotten for subscribing to a magazine. The DVDs were bulky but he had a nylon duffel bag in his pack and he was convinced they'd fit in it. The movies wouldn't be of use to most folks because of the lack of power, but Pete's house had enough solar power to run a small TV and DVD player.

They'd also managed to trade for more seeds and a broken hoe that Randi was convinced she could put a new handle on. One man had a ziplock baggie packed full of tiny travel-sized shampoos from hotels he'd visited over the years. Charlie got the entire bag for a

Harley Davidson collector knife that had belonged to his dad. Charlie had several of those and they had no value to him, either sentimental or otherwise. They were lousy knives and heavy to carry around. If he could trade them for something useful he was glad to do it.

Their packs were crammed with new acquisitions and their hands were full, but Charlie and Randi weren't done. They were deep in negotiation with a man who had two dozen cloth diapers, which he apparently felt were lined with gold based on his trading demands. Charlie was offering up the remainder of his .25 caliber rounds for the diapers, but the man wasn't even listening until Charlie sweetened the deal with a hatchet. To anyone who knew edged tools, it was probably one of the lousiest hatchets ever made. It was a piece of Chinese garbage that sold for no more than $2.99 when it was new. Charlie's dad had gotten the thing for free at one of those Chinese tool stores for using a coupon that came in the mail. It might be useful to someone who didn't have any other means of cutting wood.

"I'm going to go get the horses while you guys fight this out," Pete offered. They were close but hadn't yet struck a bargain.

"That's fine," Randi said. "We'll meet you in the parking lot over at the dentist's office."

Pete saluted and wandered off with his full pack and the bag of DVDs. None of the items he carried were things he'd bought. It was all Charlie's and he expected it was going to take him a few minutes to get it arranged on his horse. He made his way through the crowd and back to the corral at the back corner of the parking lot. The same assembly greeted him in exactly the same stances as earlier. Willie ran the show from the comfort of a camping chair while his two sons slouched against the corral, their limbs woven through the bars like they were lifers relaxing in a prison cell.

"I need our horses," Pete asked.

Willie gave Pete a sly smile. "I only saw you ride in on one horse, kid. Why should I give you three?"

Pete had dealt with men like this before, dissatisfied and unhappy men who enjoyed giving kids a hard time. He'd had one for a gym teacher last year. The guy was an asshole. "I need *my* horse and *my* friends'* horses. They're busy trading."

The same irritating grin never left Willie's face. "I'm just supposed to take your word for that?"

A year ago Pete might have teared up and left in frustration. He was different now. He had a whole new set of experiences under his belt and with it, a newfound confidence. "Why you got to be an asshole about this, man? You got my horses and I'm taking them."

In tandem, as if operating from a single, slow-functioning mind, Willie's sons began to move in Pete's direction, apparently taking offense at the way he was talking to their dad. In the blink of an eye, Pete dropped his gear and flipped his rifle around on the sling. The metallic click of the safety moving to the fire position reached all ears in that intimate circle. Pete didn't make a scene, didn't raise his rifle high for fear of drawing attention. It was leveled at Willie's belly, though, and at this distance he couldn't miss.

Willie stuck out an arm to arrest the movement of his protective sons. "Get his horses. All of them." His eyes were fixed on Pete's, his face wearing an expression that was both amused and dangerous at the same time.

"All I wanted was my horses," Pete said. "I don't know why you had to act like this. If Randi, the woman who was with us, saw you acting this way she'd kill you on the spot. She ain't one for bullshit."

With his sons in the corral gathering horses, it was just the two of them. Willie kept his voice low. "I tell you what's bullshit, boy. What's bullshit is what your daddy did to this town. Yeah, I know who you are. Duane told me all about it. Said you two went to school together. Your daddy is responsible for a lot of suffering. My family would be living in that comfort camp right now but we're all being punished for what your daddy did. You got a lot of fucking nerve showing your face in town."

Pete's blood ran cold. This was exactly what he'd known could happen and here it was unfolding right in front of him. Pete nodded at Willie's belly. "You don't appear to be starving."

Willie snarled. "Why you little bastard."

His sons led the horses out and stood there looking at Pete. Duane extended the reins but Pete wasn't sure he could take them without putting himself at risk. If he took his gun off Willie, the two brothers would jump him. He was certain of it.

"Take'em over yonder and tie them off to the bumper of that pickup truck," Pete said. "I'm going to stay where I'm at until you're done."

The two brothers looked at each other as if they'd had a plan and Pete had screwed the whole thing up. He'd figured as much.

"I don't suggest you ever come back here, boy," Willie growled. "It ain't right for you to be in here buying up stuff that good folks need. Your family done took enough from people and they don't need to be taking more. I see you back here again and I'll call you out in front of all these folks. I'll tell them who you are and remind them of what your daddy done. What do you think will happen then? Hell, I imagine they'll tear into you like a pack of dogs. There won't be enough left for your momma to bury."

"You'll only get a lot of people killed."

The grin returned to Willie's face. "Maybe, but you'll be one of them. Just like your old daddy. *If* he's even dead."

Willie gave Pete a wink that both chilled and angered the boy. His finger stroked the trigger and he wanted to pull it so badly that his heart ached from the want of it. If he shot Willie, though, he'd have to kill his sons too. Then a lot more people might die, including him.

"There's your horses," Willie said. "Take them and go."

Pete backed away, putting the rifle back on safe. He let it hang but kept his hand wrapped around the grip, ready to swing it back up and fire if he had to. He leaned over and collected his gear, then moved to his horses. Not feeling like this was the time or place to repack his gear, he looped everything around the saddle horn and untied the other horses.

He started to mount up but didn't want to present such a tempting target to Willie or his sons. Instead, he led the horses away and into the crowd, their broad bodies sheltering him against his new enemy.

Before he even reached the dentist's office, Randi and Charlie fell in alongside him, taking the leads of their own horses. Randi studied Pete, picking up on something he was trying hard to hide. She must have sensed the tension, the coiled spring inside him that threatened to break loose at any minute. Maybe she smelled the adrenaline.

"You okay?" she asked.

Pete nodded.

She wasn't convinced. "Something happen with that creepy old bastard?"

"No, it was just weird. That's all. Seeing someone from school. It reminded me of a lot of things, like what I'd be doing right now if this hadn't happened. Made me miss my friend." He couldn't tell if Randi bought it or not, but she let it go.

"Yeah, I get it. We all get in funks over that sometimes. Weird things set it off and then we remember that what's normal now is a lot different than what was normal a couple of years ago."

"I get that too," Charlie said. "Memories hit you sometimes."

Pete forced a smile onto his face. "Let's get these horses packed and get out of here. This place is too crowded for me."

Randi laughed. "You're starting to sound like your dad."

"Really?" Pete asked.

"Yep."

The idea struck Pete as strange for a moment, then he became comfortable with it. It was a reminder that his dad was always with him, even if he wasn't.

## 31

---

T *he Camp*

SHARON WOKE up early in her familiar bed at the camp. Sunlight was already pouring through the window, a sure sign that she'd slept later than usual. Despite the light, the desire for more sleep tried to hold her in the bed. She wasn't certain if it was the soreness in her body or the overwhelming weight of the day ahead that woke her, but she couldn't allow herself to go back to sleep. There was too much to do. She flipped back the sheet and sat up.

Despite the exhaustion she felt when she made it back to camp yesterday, they'd stayed up late. She had to explain to the children that Oliver had passed away and then help them process their emotions. Many of them had been working on digging a grave at the Fairy Circle so they were tired and emotionally frail. There had been a lot of tears and a lot of hugs. She did her best to focus them on the positives of Oliver's life, how he loved music and built this camp so more people could learn how to play it. She went around the group and had everyone share their favorite Oliver memories.

Those who'd been digging were proud of their efforts and took her to see the grave so they could get her approval. They'd worked hard but it was barely over two feet deep. They'd encountered a lot of tree roots that had to be chopped out of the way and it made for slow going. They'd have to go deeper today, though she couldn't imagine they'd be able to reach the customary depth of six feet. They could deal with a few roots but if they hit a rock they were screwed.

As a group, they'd also worked to organize a memorial service for their friend. Thinking it was best to keep it simple, they planned on playing several songs that were special to Oliver. Kay was in charge of helping with that today, making sure the children picked songs they were comfortable with playing, then helping them run through the setlist. Nathan and Stevie were going to have to work on the grave some more and Sharon intended to help them. She wasn't all that good with a shovel but could swing a mean pick.

She hoped Freda and Kendall came through with a means for getting the body up to the camp. Sharon was certain she could come up with something if forced to, but she didn't relish the task. If it came down to her doing it, she'd need the children's help and she was trying to protect them from that. She didn't want them to handle the body or see it heaved around in an undignified manner. It would be too traumatic for them. They might have nightmares or experience lasting trauma from it. She'd managed to insulate and protect them during these trying times and she hoped to continue with that.

Sharon swung out of bed and examined her body. Before doing anything else she needed to tend to the cuts and scrapes from yesterday. There were also deep bruises along her legs from the tumble down the embankment. It was nothing too bad but she treated the scratches to avoid infection. Even a scratch could kill her if infection set in. She had some alcohol and expired antibiotic ointment. She'd observed in treating the children that the ointment still did the job, it just took longer than it had when it was new.

When she was done, she dressed and left her cabin. She saw no other signs of life anywhere else in the camp. The kids were not yet awake, despite the hour. They must have been as exhausted as she was. She went to the kitchen for a cup of the tea she had steeping in a glass jar. She would have preferred it hot instead of room temperature, but that one job, warming her tea, would require a whole lot of effort. She'd drink it like it was.

Sharon went out on the front porch, the wooden screen door clattering shut behind her. Tendrils of fog hung in the valley extending before her. She knew from the hundreds of times she'd surveyed this view that the sun would soon burn that fog away. Dew glistened from spiderwebs draped between tall weeds. Crows called, the most verbal of birds at this hour. Her roosters crowed too, not wanting to be left out.

Sharon knew this place. She knew these sounds and this view as well as she knew herself. She'd sat on this porch for thousands of mornings like this one. It was for this reason that the clatter of stones in the stillness distinguished itself and instantly put her on guard. When it came again, not exactly the same sound but similar, she was struck by how much more alone she felt without Oliver's presence in the valley. He'd been their gatekeeper. Their watchman.

Her second thought was of the pistol Oliver had offered her so many times since the collapse. She'd refused it, not because she was opposed to guns, but because she didn't have any way to properly secure it from the children. She knew Oliver had more guns and she supposed that was something she would soon be dealing with. There would be so much to deal with.

She set her tea down and moved to the edge of the porch. It was a wide affair, spanning the entire front of the dining hall, but she'd moved to the side closest to where she thought the sound had come from. She held her breath and listened hard.

There were voices, a low murmur that sounded like people speaking between themselves. It appeared to be coming from the road. Sharon angled her chair so she could see in that direction but the road was wooded, hidden by thick trees and brush, until that last turn swung it into the camp.

Sharon had no way down to the ground from this porch. There was no ramp on this high side of the building. She opened the screen door, hurried through the dining hall, and emerged onto the much smaller back porch. She rolled down the short ramp and onto the uneven ground facing the road.

The voices were louder now. Clearly people. She had no idea who they were, what they wanted, or what she was going to do when they turned the corner. Then the first of them emerged from concealment and walked toward her. She couldn't make out features at this distance but it didn't appear to be anyone she knew. It was a slight, older man. He was wearing a red cap and a mint green button-down shirt. The shirt was tucked into gray dress pants, which were in turn tucked into black farming boots. He carried a shovel thrown across his shoulder like a rifle.

A second man came behind, then a third. These two were younger, both in t-shirts and jeans. One carried a pick, the other a shovel. Behind those two came a larger cluster of people, a half-dozen more men carrying digging tools.

The lead man spotted Sharon and tossed up a casual wave. When he approached, she could see that he was probably in his sixties. He removed his cap and wiped his forehead with a handkerchief. She noticed he still had a full head of dark, curly hair with only the odd strand of gray.

"You must be Sharon?"

She gave a wary smile. "I am."

"I'm Cecil, a neighbor from up the road. I used to lease pasture off Oliver a few years back and we were buddies. I hated to hear of his passing."

"It looked like a stroke. It was probably merciful that he went pretty fast."

Cecil nodded. "Probably so. You all haven't finished digging the grave, have you?"

Sharon shook her head. "No. The children tried but it's hard work for kids. They're not very experienced at digging and they hit a lot of roots."

Cecil gestured at the folks ganged up behind him. "I figured that'd be the case but we can take care of that. I brought some friends and neighbors with me. Some of us are old hands at running a shovel. We should be able to knock it out for you. It's the least we can do for Oliver."

"I-I don't know what to say," Sharon stammered. "I appreciate your help very much."

"Reckon we just need you to show us the spot and we'll get on with it. Figured we'd get an early start, before the heat of the day."

"Follow me," Sharon said, spinning her chair and starting toward the Fairy Circle.

She led them past the dining hall to a smooth trail through the woods. The children kept the path groomed and free of debris specifically for Sharon. In a few minutes, they were at the Fairy Circle with its log benches and crude seats.

"Seems a right nice spot," Cecil commented.

"Oliver liked it here. This is where he told stories. The children loved it. They like the idea of him always being here with them. They thought he might like it too."

"Reckon he would at that." Cecil gestured toward the shallow grave. "Yonder, boys. Best get to it."

The rest of the men headed in that direction. One with a mattock wasted no time jumping in the hole and slinging the tool with a mechanical efficiency.

"What's that for?" Sharon asked, pointing to a man with a medieval-looking ax in his hand. The handle was not aligned with the head in the normal manner but angled away from it at a thirty-degree bend.

"Grave-digging broad ax," Cecil said. "Folks quit using them when backhoes come along. I had one in the barn. Granddaddy used it for smoothing the walls of a grave. Made it look nice for folks. It's something my family always took pride in, digging a nice grave."

Sharon found herself welling with tears in what she imagined would *not* be the last time that day. The kindness of the neighbors and the attention that they paid in this final gesture of respect to

Oliver was almost too much for her to bear. She'd been to enough funerals in her life to know it wasn't only the loss of a loved one that got to you. It was those hundreds of tiny gestures. Those little things people did and said, the memories they shared. When she'd lost her sister, those were the things that got her. The things she'd never have known about her sister if someone had not made the effort to share them with her. It taught her a lot about how to help people grieve.

Cecil awkwardly patted Sharon on the shoulder. Like many men, he was uncomfortable with offering solace to women he didn't know. "Now, you don't worry about a thing. We'll take care of this. The women are heading up this way later to bring you all some lunch."

Sharon waved a wand. "That's not necessary. People don't have enough to be sharing right now. They don't have to do that."

Cecil wasn't hearing any of that. He held up a hand. "It's tradition. Just 'cause times are hard doesn't mean you turn your back on doing what folks have always done for each other. You take food to the bereaved. It's what you do."

When he put it that way, Sharon understood. It was like the grave digging. There were things the men traditionally did and the women had their own tasks. It wasn't just how the community supported each other, it was the essence of what made them a community in the first place. It was how rural folks, mountain folks, and poor folks had always retained their humanity when they had very little. It was by holding onto their traditions, many of them so ancient that they were brought here from other continents.

She smiled. "That's so kind of you all. We appreciate it very much."

"It's what neighbors do."

"Well, if you don't need anything from me, I'm going to go wake the children. We have some cleaning to do before company comes."

"Don't put yourself out now," Cecil said.

"It's fine. We just have a few things to straighten out before the place is fit for company. If you men need any water, there's a spigot outside the dining hall that's fed from the spring. Help yourself."

"Thank you kindly."

Sharon headed back toward the dining hall. She needed to wake the children and get them moving. Not having to dig the grave was a huge relief but there was work to do. The dining hall looked *very* lived in at the moment. There were toys, blankets, and musical instruments scattered everywhere. She didn't expect the children to work a miracle, but she'd like to be able to offer their guests a place to sit down.

# 32

# The Camp

By afternoon, the camp was bustling with more folks than they'd seen since the attacks. While the grave-diggers labored, their wives and daughters had appeared next. They rode on a hay wagon driven by a man even older than Oliver. A grin stretched across sallow cheeks and toothless gums as he worked his team of horses. It was as if he'd waited his entire life for this very day. Despite the heat, he wore a long checked shirt with a white t-shirt beneath it. Black suspenders held up brown polyester pants that may have once fit but were now too big.

The harness attached to the wagon was old but appeared to have been preserved out of love more than utility. The leather straps and traces had been maintained with a treatment that left them supple and glowing. The yoke and singletrees were varnished as if the entire rig had come straight from a museum wall to the backs of these sweating horses. The metal tongue connecting the wagon to the harness showed that the trailer had recently been used with a tractor, but even this ancient operator understood that adaptability was the greatest attribute of a farmer. It was the ability to forge the broken into the functional. It was the talent of squeezing one more season out of collapsed, broken, and rust-seized equipment.

Females from age eight to eighty scooted off the wagon while the whip-thin driver held the horses steady. Some of the women wore thin scarves to keep their hair in line. They reminded Sharon of the aunts she'd known from her childhood in the 1960s and 1970s, those women at family reunions with their beehive hairdos and long menthol cigarettes.

"See if you can give them a hand," Sharon instructed the campers.

The women on the hay wagon were unloading boxes containing Tupperware and white CorningWare. They had clear casserole dishes and stainless steel bowls, the tops covered with clean linen dishtowels in the absence of foil and plastic wrap. The children went forward with some apprehension but were greeted warmly by the neighbor women. They were hugged, patted, and complimented. By the time everyone made it inside to spread the food on the table, the camp children had overcome their apprehension and were basking in the attention. The women understood what the children had gone through and were supportive.

"I can't believe you all have been back here for a year and we haven't visited," Cordelia said. She was Cecil's wife and the organizer of the group.

"Oliver was very protective," Sharon explained. "He told me he was afraid for people to know we were back here. He thought that was the best way to keep us safe."

Cordelia tilted her head. "He might have been right. There's ugliness out there. We do our best to stay away from it and only socialize with them what lives around us. The good Lord has kept us safe and fed. We ain't well off but we're getting by."

"Same here. We're getting by. Anything we needed and didn't have, Oliver tried to track down for us. He was our connection to the community."

Cordelia stuck out a hand and rested it gently on Sharon's shoulder. "Cecil and I will try to help with that. I know Kendall and Freda are going to check in on you too. You'll need people so don't be afraid to ask."

The sound of shod hooves on gravel reached Sharon's ears and she moved to the window of the dining hall. The old wagon driver had hauled the grave diggers back down to Oliver's house to help Kendall and Freda load the body. Now they were returning, leading the funeral procession. Behind them, a single horse pulled the most elaborate enclosed buggy Sharon had ever seen.

"My God," she mumbled.

"Horse-drawn hearse," Cordelia said. "Belongs to my Uncle Donald. He's the old man driving the hay wagon. He's been collecting those buggies since people quit driving them. He'd find them in fields and bring them home to restore. That hearse is his pride and joy. Keeps it in the barn all covered up. It's in better condition now than when it left the factory. He shows it at fairs and stuff, but that's all it's been good for, until now."

The buggy pulled alongside the dining hall and stopped at the beginning of the path to the Fairy Circle. It was as far as the wagon could go. Beyond that point, the trail got too narrow and there was nowhere to turn a team of horses.

Sharon stared at the buggy in amazement. It seemed almost delicate with its tall, spoked wheels and spare construction. It was flat black and the driver sat high on the front, like a stagecoach or buckboard wagon. Arched glass windows made up each side and the back. There were elaborately carved moldings applied to the flat surfaces. Brass lanterns mounted alongside the driver's seat allowed him to operate at night.

Through the windows, Sharon spotted a newly-made coffin. Oliver was in there. She put her hand to her mouth. "Someone made a coffin," she commented, feeling stupid for stating the obvious. She didn't know what else to say.

"The boys had some boards in the barn. Ain't nothing fancy, but they did what they could. He deserved more than a sheet."

"I should have thought of that," Sharon said.

Cordelia waved her off. "Only so much one woman and a houseful of kids can do. I'm surprised you get anything done beyond caring for these kids."

"Speaking of kids, I reckon I better get them wrangled up," Sharon said, backing away from the window. "We should probably get on up there. No use putting this off any longer."

"Can you get up in those woods alright?" Cordelia asked, ready to offer assistance if it was required.

Sharon smiled. "I've been doing it for twenty years. I'll be fine. But thanks."

Cordelia returned to the kitchen to gather the other women. Sharon went to the center of the dining hall and called to the campers in the same manner she always did. It was part of their routine, part of the structure she maintained.

"Campers!"

The children responded to her voice, gathering around her in a circle.

"It's time for us to go say good-bye to Mr. Oliver. I need you to get your instruments and follow me. We're not going to talk a whole lot because we want to be respectful. Don't strum on your instruments until it's time for you to play. Funerals are a time for being quiet. If you need me, just ask. If you need to cry, that's fine. If you need to hug each other, that's fine too. This is going to be hard on all of us, but we're going to get through it together. Okay?"

The children nodded, their hesitancy belying uncertainty.

"You've got this," Sharon said. "You're going to play for these folks and it's going to be the best you've ever played in your life. Right?"

Sharon brought them in for a hug, as much for herself as for them. When they parted, the bigger kids helped the smaller ones get their instruments ready. Everything had been tuned that morning. The children filed out and Sharon fell in behind them. The women who'd been working in the kitchen were also outside now and they walked together as a group.

Everyone deferred to Sharon and she took the lead, though she was no more anxious than the children to go down that trail. It felt different this time, knowing what lay ahead of them, but she went on. At her movement, everyone else fell in behind her. It was like sand pouring through the hourglass after the first shake sets it in motion.

When she reached the clearing, she moved off to the side to allow the others to pass. She directed the children to line up beside her. Everyone's eyes fell on the crude wooden coffin, sitting on cinderblocks like a broke down car. A gaping hole lay beside it, now at the proper depth. Sharon noticed that the men had done as they said, using the broadaxe to smooth the walls to a uniform finish. It was somehow the most orderly aspect of the entire scene. In this jungle, among this motley gathering, this perfect and exact hole in the soil waited to receive their friend.

When the last person entered the clearing, Sharon found that all eyes were on her. Somehow she hadn't thought this far ahead. When she'd imagined this situation she'd only thought about it being her and the children. She hadn't prepared anything but she understood that this was her show. This was her territory. All of these people had come to help but they were awaiting her words. The ball was now in her court.

She cleared her throat. "I'd like to thank you all for coming. You've helped to make a stressful experience much easier for us. I appreciate it and I know that Oliver would have too. I worked for Oliver every summer for the last twenty years. He was my boss, but he was my friend too. It never felt like work when I was here at the camp. This felt like home and the rest of the year was just the things I had to do to come back here."

Sharon looked around the circle. Some faces smiled back at her while others stared down at their clasped hands. Even for those who weren't grieving Oliver, the presence of the dead affected people. Everyone handled it differently. It made some uncomfortable and others somber.

"The children have prepared some songs for today. They're going to play a number to get things started. They wanted to begin with an old Carter Family tune, *My Dixie Darling*." She gave the children a reassuring smile. "If you're ready."

The children took the cue and raised their instruments. The smaller children, some of them new to performing, stared at their instruments, getting their fingers in just the right places. Nathan looked at each child. When he was certain they were ready, he strummed his guitar and then eased into the tune. Nathan had picked this one and he knew all the words. At the chorus, all of the children joined in, their harmonies beautiful from sheer intent and purity of emotion.

When the song ended, the children looked up and smiled, forgetting for a moment the occasion of their performance. Then when people failed to clap, instead returning their smiles and offering reassuring nods, the children remembered and fell somber again.

"That was excellent. I'm sure Oliver is smiling down on us right now. He loved that song so much," Sharon said. "This next part is purely optional so don't feel like you have to participate. Since we're informal here and many of us had a relationship with Oliver, I'd like to invite anyone who feels moved to do so to tell a story about him. Maybe just share a memory. I'll start."

Sharon looked down at her lap. She'd already picked the story she wanted to tell. As the recollection of the experience filled her, she couldn't hold back a smile. She opened her mouth to begin speaking but noticed that all eyes in the circle were now staring at the trail they'd come in on. It was to Sharon's back and she couldn't see without turning her chair.

When she heard footsteps approaching, she wheeled around to find a woman around her age and a younger man staring at the assembled mourners. Sharon didn't recognize the pair but she understood the look on their faces. It was a bitterness bordering on hatred. She wondered what she or anyone in this group might have done to provoke such a reaction from the woman.

"Excuse me, I'm Sharon, the Program Director at the camp. Can I help you? Are you here for Oliver's service?"

"You'd think folks would notify the next of kin when one of their family dies," the woman spat.

Sharon plastered a smile across her face. "You must be Oliver's niece. Come join us."

"I ain't doing it. I reckon if you wanted me here in the first place I'd have been invited," the woman replied.

"It's Kimberly, right?" Cordelia said. "We didn't know where to find you. There was a lot needed done so we just spread the word among the neighbors. It wasn't like we could run an obituary in the paper or anything."

"No one figured you'd come anyway," Cecil said. "Everyone knows how you felt about your uncle."

Kimberly narrowed her eyes. "That don't mean that you can just knock me out of line to get what's coming to me."

Sharon gave her a confused look. "What exactly do you think is coming to you?"

Kimberly raised her hands and gestured around her as if the answer was obvious. "This."

"The camp?" Sharon asked. "The farm?"

"Every damn bit of it," Kimberly replied.

The boy at her side, likely her son from the resemblance, bobbed his head in agreement. He looked to be in his thirties, a scraggly looking man with homemade tattoos.

Sharon shook her head. "I'm sorry but there's been some kind of misunderstanding. Oliver made arrangements for this years ago. He had a will and it's on file at the courthouse. I was a witness. Upon his death, everything he owned went into a trust to support the camp. There's to be a board of trustees who'll help manage the operation of the farm so that we get optimal yield from the property."

Kimberly pursed her lips and gave Sharon a defiant look. "That's news to me."

"I'm sorry if you felt like you should have been notified but it's only customary to contact the people named in the will. There wouldn't have been any reason to notify you about his decision."

"She's telling the truth, Kimberly," Cecil said. "Oliver told me I'd be on that board of trustees. Kendall is on it too."

Kendall and Freda nodded.

Kimberly erupted. "That ain't fucking right! My momma should have had a piece of this. I'm all that's left of that family and it should be mine. Ain't right that it's going to some outsider and some stupid kids. I'm his blood! Y'all ain't shit!"

Cecil waved a finger at Kimberly. "You can hush that mouth up right now. You ain't talking that way in front of these children."

Kimberly gritted her teeth and practically snarled at the older man. "What are you going to do about it, you old bastard? You all are trying to rob me. You're all in it together. I see what's happening."

Cecil gestured at his sons, the boys who'd helped dig the grave. "You all show her to the gate, please."

Sharon, used to handling matters herself, wasn't done. "And I suggest you don't come back. If you have any questions, you hire a lawyer and take them up with the court."

"The court?" Kimberly snorted. "You going to hide behind a court and lawyer? There ain't no fucking courts right now and there ain't anywhere for you to hide. The best thing for you to do is get your ass out of here and give us what's ours. If you don't, you won't have a minute of peace here. I guaran-damn-tee you that."

Kendall stepped out of the circle and stalked toward Kimberly. "That's it! I heard enough of that nasty mouth in front of these children."

Kimberly turned and hurried down the trail, her son on her heels. Kendall was trotting behind them, Cecil's sons with him. When they were gone, several of the children rushed to Sharon, throwing their arms around her.

"Do we really have to leave?" one of them asked. "We don't have anywhere to go."

Sharon was aggravated. She'd worked hard to make these children feel safe here and would not let anyone threaten that. "No. We're not going anywhere."

## 33

T azewell County, Virginia

THE RIDE through The Cove went exactly as Jim expected. Dogs barked and drew glaring farmers who weren't excited at the sight of unfamiliar interlopers. Some watched from their porches, armed and ready to shoot strangers for the crime of appearing where they were not welcome. Jim fully understood the sentiment. There were times he'd been that man on the porch. He didn't react any better when strangers traveled through his valley.

The ominous sense that this might inevitably lead to a confrontation encouraged him to consult his GPS and find an alternative to the more populated Thompson Valley. If they went that way, closer to town, they were bound to butt heads with someone. Instead, they headed southeast on Route 91, which soon turned into a dirt road. There were farms, farm dogs, and armed farmers, but fewer of them. People here, perhaps less accustomed to travelers, were not so aggressive in their response. Some waved and even spoke. A few asked of any news from the outside world. When prodded for information, Jim relayed what he knew of things, as if the road required a toll and information served as payment for his passage.

The route wound over Clinch Mountain and it was a beautiful ride. Farmers had warned them that trees frequently fell across the road but they'd done their best to keep it open. Many had family or farmland on both sides of the mountain and had an interest in keeping it open. The riders saw plenty of evidence of this. There were rotting piles of sawdust from the days when there had been chainsaw gas in the farmers' barns. As cutting firewood burned through their supply of fuel, they fell back to old bucksaws and axes, cutting only enough clearance to allow a wagon through.

Jim and Lloyd stopped for a meal on the peak of the mountain, tying off their horses and sitting in the middle of the road, although perhaps "meal" was too glamorous a word for it. It was only sustenance to keep their bodies operating, to keep them upright in the saddle until they reached their destination. Jim removed two MREs from the packhorse and tossed one to Lloyd.

"I don't get to pick?" Lloyd complained.

"They're the same."

"Sure they are. You're keeping the best one for yourself. Greedy bastard."

Jim rolled his eyes and showed Lloyd the label, then sat down on the road. He used the heat pack to warm the meal and stared off through the trees while it worked its magic. He found as much sustenance in the view as he expected to derive from the meal. "Beautiful country here."

Lloyd nodded.

Jim studied the package his MRE came in. "You know where these MREs came from?"

"No."

"They came from that chopper that landed in town. The one that hauled us back to the valley. This was supposed to be part of the bounty paid to whoever turned me in. Even though MREs suck, these are more satisfying because of that. I'm eating my own bounty."

Staring off at the valley below them, Lloyd replied, "Yeah, I can imagine." He didn't even seem to be listening.

Jim pulled out his GPS and examined the map. He punched buttons and did some calculations. "I'm not sure if we'll make it all the way to the trailhead today. We're still twenty miles off."

"I don't know much about horses but that seems like a long ride, considering how far we've already come today."

Jim stuck the GPS back in his pack. "It's a couple of more miles to Tannersville. It's nothing more than an old post office, a church, and a few houses. We'll travel the Freestone Valley from there to Route 16. I'd like to make it as far as Route 16 today, at least. This valley is cleared for farming and there aren't many places to camp. Once we get out of this valley and on Route 16 we'll be back in the woods again. I'll be more comfortable setting up camp for the night."

Lloyd looked grim as he tore into his MRE.

"What?" Jim asked.

"We spent our entire childhood dreaming of the day we'd be mobile, of finally being able to drive anywhere we wanted. Now we're back on foot again."

"Ironic, isn't it?"

"Pathetic is more like it. I'll never complain about a road trip again. I'll just appreciate that I'm not walking."

"If we ever get to take another road trip," Jim said. "That remains to be seen."

"You don't think this will pass and get back to normal?"

Jim poked at his turkey chili with beans and pondered how to respond. "What's happening now will pass but who knows what the country will look like. I think normal will be different from here on out. How long will it take to clear and reopen roads? To rebuild gas stations and repair power lines? It can take months to rebuild after a hurricane or tornado and things are never the same in those places after that. Blow that up to a national scale. Some things will be rebuilt and some won't. Things will never look the same again."

"That's depressing."

Jim shrugged. "It is, in some ways. The only way to make peace with it is to be flexible and appreciate the new normal, whatever it looks like. If we base our happiness on getting things back to the way they used to be, we may never be happy again."

Lloyd tightened his mouth into an expression of disgust. "That's just great. I guess we learn to live like we're in the Great Depression again. We're down to appreciating a roof over our heads and a full belly."

The turkey chili wasn't great but it was food. It was too salty and the flavor wasn't what Jim expected. He added some sriracha from a bottle he carried in his food sack and doctored it to the point it wasn't half bad. "You know, Lloyd, our people, our hillbilly ancestors never had anything. They were poor before the Great Depression and they were poor afterward. They found happiness. They found a reason to live life and carry on. That's what we have to do too. It's a time for resilience, not weakness. When you've lived without a roof, with an empty belly, you understand that those things are significant. There *is* reason to celebrate them."

Lloyd ignored him. "What was that shit you dumped in your chili?"

"Sriracha."

Lloyd stared at him like he was speaking Greek. "What the fuck is that?"

"Hot sauce."

"Well, let me have some."

Jim tossed him the bottle and smiled as Lloyd gave himself a generous dose. He'd be complaining about the spiciness next.

"Was it really just yesterday that I was hanging out with that old man and telling stories?" Lloyd asked, stirring the sriracha into his chili.

"Yeah."

Lloyd shook his head in disgust. "Things change fast don't they?"

"Some things do. Some things never change at all."

When they were done eating, Lloyd wandered off to the side of the road to relieve himself. When he returned, he pointed to a tree growing alongside the road. "You see that?"

"What?"

Lloyd pointed again and Jim walked over to see what he was looking at. There were two crude letter Ms carved into the tree with an ax. Jim furrowed his brow.

"What the hell is it?" Jim asked.

"That's what I was just asking you."

"Looks like a cattle brand or something."

"It's at the crest of the mountain. Maybe it was a message for someone. A signal that they'd made it this far."

"Could be." Jim pulled his iPhone from his pocket, hit the button, and waited for it to power up. When the phone booted he took a picture of the symbol.

## 34

T azewell County, Virginia

THE VALLEYS along Clinch Mountain were remote country. The farmers who lived there had long ago chosen isolation and abundant, fertile farmland over convenience. They preferred starlight over streetlights. They preferred walking muddy fields to afternoon strolls along tree-lined sidewalks. In the best of times they'd had unreliable electricity and non-existent internet. A run into town to pick up a tractor part or buy groceries consumed half the day. Any frozen food they bought would be melted before they even got home.

Even the post office at Tannersville was a remnant of a bygone era. It was the epicenter of a scattered community that offered nothing in the way of amenities. The post office was a cinderblock building with a metal roof, looking like a country store from the 1960s, which it might have been at some point. It was a throwback to the day when even the smallest community had a post office crammed into the corner of a feed store, a mercantile, or a pharmacy.

It took the pair a couple of hours to make their way through the Freestone Valley. Jim was anticipating Route 16 and its winding passage over the mountain. It was a paved road with a lot of curves. Before the collapse, it was nothing to see a Porsche club or group of motorcyclists racing at top speed through the countryside. Their vehicles would be bristling with tiny action cameras, trying to catch every nuance of their ride. That would be one hassle Jim wouldn't have to worry about encountering today. No one would be driving in the middle of the road at twice the speed limit.

About a mile before the intersection with Route 16, the road ran parallel to a large farm. Most of the road was tree-lined but there were gaps where Jim and Lloyd had a good view of the fields. While farms in this part of the country were nothing compared to the vast fields of the Midwest, this was a big farm for the area. Part of the fields were in corn and the rest grown up in hay.

The hay fields wove close to the road, then dipped farther away as they followed a meandering creek. When the trees opened up again, the riders caught a glimpse of activity in the field. Jim paused to look and saw a small army of men stacking hay in the same manner they likely used a hundred years ago. They were collecting it from orderly windrows that had been cut and raked using horse-drawn equipment of some type. Those machines sat rusting on nearly every farm in this valley so it wasn't hard to imagine that some industrious folks had found a way to restore one to working order.

While cutting and raking could be done with a horse, Jim knew of no provision for baling without a tractor. Without one, the laborers were using the ancient technique of building haystacks with pitch-forks. Some of the tools they used were of ancient origin, resurrected from the rafters of barns and called into duty. Others were of more recent construction, made from forked tree branches with an extra tine or two added. This was a situation where the modern pitchfork was at a disadvantage; its tines were too short to hold large clumps of hay and the slick finish of the steel tines more easily allowed the hay to slip through. Sometimes the old methods worked best with the old tools.

Despite the steady pace at which the hayers worked, someone noticed the pair of riders on the road. It could have been that the sound of hooves announced them, or perhaps Jim's attention to their work had raised someone's hackles, giving them the feeling that they were being watched. When one worker spotted them, pausing in his labor, the others slowly ground to a stop. Soon, all eyes were focused on Jim and Lloyd. Jim guessed they were deciding if they should get back to work or reach for their guns.

"Guess we should have kept moving," Lloyd mumbled. "Now look at all them people you're going to have to kill."

Jim gave his old friend a sideways glance. "We aren't there yet. Chill out." He probably should have kept moving, but he was interested in what they were doing. It reminded him of old pictures of early farmers, men in misshapen felt hats wearing bibbed overalls held up by a single denim strap. Jim was uncertain as to what to do for a moment, then he held up a hand in greeting. "Y'all need some help?"

A hand was raised to them, first as a wave, then turning into a beckoning gesture.

Jim smiled at Lloyd. "See what I did there? I used my words like a civilized man and didn't have to shoot anyone."

"I can see why you're impressed with yourself since being a gentleman is new territory for you. I don't expect we're out of the woods yet. And why in the hell did you just volunteer us to help those guys?"

Jim grinned. "I want to see what they're doing. I might be able to learn something."

"Maybe you'll *learn* how to keep your mouth shut."

"You think so?"

Lloyd smirked. "I doubt it."

Someone in the field gestured down the road and called, "Come across!"

The pair rode about eighty yards further and found a concrete bridge crossing over to the farm. It was a huge operation by local standards with over a dozen barns and sheds. There was a large old farmhouse near the barns and a newer house stood along the road. They passed through two gates, turning into the stubble of a freshly cut hayfield.

They rode toward the one who'd waved them over. Even if these men weren't wielding guns, they remained wary of the newcomers. Everyone stopped working and stood in a way that they could draw a handgun at any sign of trouble.

"You're late," a man called to them. He appeared to be in his midsixties with the coarse, sun-ravaged skin of a lifelong farmer. He wore a straw cowboy hat, a t-shirt, and jeans.

Jim smiled. "Sorry about that. Thought it was tomorrow."

The farmer approached Jim's horse and stuck out a hand. "Name's Orbin McCall. This is my place. What can I do you for?"

Jim's gut told him that he could trust this man and that these were not people to be wary of. He took the farmer's hand and shook it. "I'm Jim Powell. This is my friend Lloyd. We were passing through from Russell County, going to check on a friend of his in Bland." Jim pointed to the haystacks. "I saw what you were doing here and it made me wonder if this was something I could do in my neighborhood. We have a lot of this old equipment laying around but I've never seen it in use."

"Best way to learn is by doing," Orbin said. "If you're interested in helping, we can talk while we work. We're putting on a feed when we're done so you'll get dinner. Probably got about three more hours before we call it a day."

"I'm in," Jim said, climbing off his horse. He led it over to a hay wagon scattered with tools, a water jug, and discarded layers of clothing. He tied his horse and packhorse off, then gestured at Lloyd. "You coming?"

Lloyd gave him a disgusted look. He couldn't believe that after a day of hard riding he'd been volunteered for one of the hottest, most miserable jobs God had ever seen fit to provide. Jim could see it in his eyes, the accusation, the reminder that there was a reason Lloyd had become a barber. He didn't like having to bust his ass all day.

Jim took up one of the hay forks stacked on the wagon and

jumped in while Lloyd tied off his horse. While the labor felt good after a day of having his spine compressed in the saddle, he also found it to be harder than it looked, especially as the stacks got higher.

Watching discreetly from the side, Orbin handed out some pointers. "One of the secrets is using your arms, shoulders, and legs as much as possible. If you twist your back all day, heaving that rake, you'll be so sore tomorrow you won't be able to get out of bed. You'll be all broke down."

Jim adjusted his technique some, using his legs more and his back less. He watched the others and soon fell into the same rhythm they employed so effortlessly. He would still be sore tomorrow. He could feel the stretch of muscles he hadn't used lately.

As they worked, Jim prodded Orbin with questions about the equipment they'd used to cut the hay and how long they allowed it to dry before stacking. Others in the group of hayers spoke up in response to some of his questions, offering their perspective. They ranged in age from teenagers to some that looked even older than Orbin. There were some in the group who said nothing at all and wouldn't even meet the newcomers' eyes. Jim couldn't be sure if it was distrust or simply the backward nature of folks who spent their lives in isolated communities, only socializing with folks they already knew.

They worked until it was nearly too dark to see, the sound of crows cawing from the hay stubble giving way to katydids and frogs. Though the sounds were the same as those of Jim's valley, this location felt more insulated. There were fewer houses and they were much farther from town. They were far enough from the local communities that people on foot wouldn't wander out just to see what was going on. It wasn't likely they got any foot traffic other than that of neighbors or the occasional traveler.

They piled their hay rakes onto the wagon when they were done. Those who'd not worn gloves picked at fresh blisters. Everyone wiped itchy hay from sweat-dampened collars.

"We're laying out a feed for everyone who helped today," Orbin offered. "Y'all are welcome to join us up at the barn. In fact, you're welcome to spend the night there if you want. I assume you'll be going on your way tomorrow?"

"That's the plan," Jim replied. "But we'll gladly take you up on the offer of food and a place to stay for the night."

"Good," Orbin replied with genuine warmth. "We'll head up to the barn then. You all can corral your horses for the night. There's fresh hay and clean water. You can throw your gear anywhere in the barn. Nobody will mess with it."

## 35

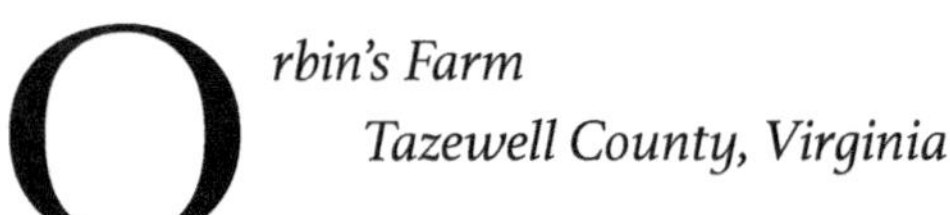

*rbin's Farm*
*Tazewell County, Virginia*

THEY SMELLED the food before they even reached the barn, a rich aroma of grilling meat, sauces, and spices. Orbin led them to the corral. It was too dark to see by this point and everyone was working by headlamp, though the interior of the barn glowed with warm lantern light.

Seeing Jim immediately start unpacking his horse, Orbin said, "I respect a man who tends to his duties before himself. Take good care of that horse and it will take care of you."

Jim was pleased that Orbin made the comment, but not on his own account. It would discourage Lloyd from arguing that they should eat first and unpack later.

"I was never a horseman before this whole mess," Jim admitted. "I'm still not much of one, but I've got a whole new respect for the animal."

Orbin smiled fondly at the horse, stroking its neck. "Horses were the way for a long time. A man can love a truck but that truck will never love you back. It won't look out for you the way a horse will. A truck can't intentionally get you home when you're not capable of doing it yourself. A horse will."

It took them a couple of minutes to remove saddles, weapons, and packs. When they removed the bridles and turned them out, each horse trotted off into the spacious fenced corral and shook off like a wet dog. One dropped to the ground and rolled. Another stepped to the water trough and drank.

Jim and Lloyd hauled their gear into the barn and stacked it in a spot where they could keep an eye on it. It wasn't so much out of concern there might be a thief in the group as out of a desire to keep an eye on their weapons. That gear kept them alive. There were battery and kerosene lanterns scattered around the barn, providing just enough light without being obnoxious. It made for a warm, comforting atmosphere. People stood at a row of plastic folding tables, filling plates with various cuts of roasted meats. There were baked potatoes, roasted carrots, corn, and various casseroles. There were pots of beans and bowls of rich homemade barbecue sauce.

"I've died and gone to heaven," Lloyd said.

Orbin grinned. "We know how to put on a feed."

Outside the expansive rolling doors at the front of the barn, a bonfire was burning, illuminating dipping moths and more smiling faces. Kids were eating hamburgers or roasting tiny sausages over the fire. Some poked at coals with sticks in the way of children, catching them on fire and then blowing them out. It was likely the oldest form of worship, that adulation toward the force that gave light, heat, and cooked food.

Orbin introduced the newcomers to people in line and to others already eating. They nodded with mouths full or raised a few fingers in greeting.

"These are friends, families, and neighbors. We've been doing this up and down the valley all summer," Orbin explained. "Putting up hay and corn for everybody with fields. Thank God for mild winters. Most of us are able to graze our cattle on grass all winter now, but we can't count on that. We need something to fall back on if the snow comes. But y'all aren't here to listen to me flap my lips so get in line."

Jim took a plate and began filling it. There was enough food that he wasn't shy about sampling everything that caught his eye. Lloyd was in front of him and doing the same thing. Jim was certain these people were putting food back, but they also understood the value of celebrating a bountiful harvest with a good meal. It helped with morale and made sore muscles a little less irritating.

"You guys fare all right last winter?" Jim asked. "We had a few bad snowstorms over our way."

"We got them here too, but it wasn't too bad. Most of us got two cuttings of hay in before things fell apart. That gave us something to feed the cattle when the ground was covered. We never got the corn in so we just turned the cattle out into those fields last winter too. They ate well. All their eating, pooping, and stomping around helped plant this year's corn crop."

"Really?" Jim asked.

"Yep," Orbin replied. "Cattle did most of that planting for us. Of course it ain't as high a yield per acre as if we'd done it right but it's better than nothing."

"Most of the farms around us are small cattle farms," Jim said. "The only big operation is the Rockdell Farms bunch and you don't see much activity there. They've got workers tending to bits and pieces of the operation, but I haven't seen any organized farming there in a year."

"The one advantage I had was that my granddaddy farmed this place with no power," Orbin said. "I grew up hearing stories about how they used to do things. The old man would point out pieces of equipment sitting by the barn and show me how they worked. That knowledge is what kept us going. Last winter I pulled all that old equipment into the shop and tinkered with it until I got it going. I repaired the harnesses and had everything working by the time spring came. We've run horse-drawn equipment all summer."

"I'm impressed," Jim said. "I could tell from the road that you all knew what you were doing. It's different than anything I've seen."

"Ain't as good as the Amish over there in Burke's Garden, but we try."

Jim finished filling his plate and stood at the end of the line, waiting until Orbin caught up. Lloyd wasn't waiting for anyone. He took a seat on an empty bench and was tearing into thin strips of steak with his pocket knife. When Orbin had his plate full, he grabbed a small canning jar filled with spring water and directed Jim to do the same. They joined Lloyd on the bench.

"Best meal I've had in forever," Lloyd said. "This is amazing. Thank you so much."

Orbin smiled. "You're welcome, friend. Good to see new faces."

"Ain't always been so good to see new faces where we came from," Jim said. "Most of them just brought trouble."

"You must be too close to town. We don't get much in the way of strangers back in here," Orbin said, forking into some green beans. "Usually it's someone taking a shortcut across the mountain. A couple of times it's been rogues who tried to steal off of us."

"You send them packing?" Jim asked.

Orbin chewed, then spoke. "We dealt with them. We're good Christian people, but there are some things you can't tolerate. A thief is one of them. You turn them back out in the community and they just go back to stealing. It's like rabies or something. Once it's in their blood, they're a blight on the community. You might as well put them down and be done with it."

"We've had our share of that," Jim said. "Lone thieves, groups of thieves, people wanting to run us out and take our lands. We've fought with the government, other counties, and even some of our neighbors."

"The government, you say?" Orbin asked, slicing off a chunk of beef. It was done to perfection—charred on the outside, pink on the inside.

"I ain't sure it's the same government we always had but they were from Washington. They were getting a local power plant up and running, but they were going to send all the power up to the Washington, D.C. and Northern Virginia area. The only power they were going to share locally was to be in one of those special camps where folks could go if they turned in their guns."

"I heard tell of those. Not sure there was one close to here, but I ain't fond of the idea. I'm not a fan of the government coercing people into doing stuff. It was the biggest mistake we ever made in this country, letting the government get big enough that they couldn't keep their nose out of our business and their hands out of our pockets. There's some that will tell you the poor in this country are parasites, living off the working man. The truth of it is that the government is the real leech here. They throw all kinds of blame around because they want you looking everywhere but at them. They like to keep us fighting with each other so we don't throw them out on their butts."

"Don't get him started on politics. You'll never shut him up." The comment came from an older woman in jeans and a flannel shirt. She was smiling warmly. "I'd shake your hand but I know you're busy eating."

"Yeah, you don't want to lose a finger either," Lloyd commented. "Get it close to his mouth and that's what'll happen."

Orbin gestured at the woman with his fork. "This is my wife, Frannie. She's responsible for the spread we're all appreciating at the moment."

"It's amazing," Jim said. "Thanks for having us."

"Definitely," Lloyd chimed in. "I was telling Orbin it's the best food I've had in a while."

Orbin pointed at Lloyd, then Jim, and introduced each of them.

"Whereabouts are you all from?" Frannie asked.

Jim swallowed what was in his mouth. "Russell County."

"Oh, I've got a lot of friends and family over that way." Frannie started rattling off a list of people she knew in Russell County, some of whom Jim knew and some of whom he didn't. When she'd exhausted her list, she addressed Lloyd. "You're from Russell County too?"

"I'm living there now, but before the country fell apart I was living in Wythe County."

Frannie furrowed her brow. "Don't know many folks over there. What are you all doing so far away from home?"

"They said they were headed to Bland County," Orbin offered.

"What for?" Frannie asked. "Ain't nothing over there but woods and maybe a couple of people."

Jim tossed his head in Lloyd's direction. "It's his deal. I'm just along for the ride."

Frannie looked at Lloyd expectantly.

"I'm a musician. I have a barbershop over in Wythe County, but I've played music all over the world. I give lessons too and there's this camp over in Bland County where they focus on Appalachian music. Kids and adults can come and stay there for sessions where they get to play all day, every day. They improve as musicians and learn how to play with other folks. I play square dances over there and teach a few classes over the summer. I just wanted to check on the place and see how the old man that owns it is doing. He's become a friend."

Frannie tapped her lip with a finger and shook her head. "Ain't heard of a camp like that but do you have an instrument with you?"

Jim fought not to roll his eyes. It was the question Lloyd lived for. He was mouthing the words to Lloyd's response even as Lloyd was speaking them.

"I just so happen to have a banjo with me. Would you like to hear a tune?"

"Oh, I surely would," Frannie cooed. "Let's do it outside so there's plenty of room for people to dance."

Lloyd retrieved his banjo from the soft case and tuned it up. While he was tweaking a tuning peg, he gave Jim a look. "You coming?"

Jim shook his head. "Think I'll just hang out here and talk to Orbin for a bit."

Lloyd scowled. "Fine, be that way."

"Reckon I will." Jim noticed Orbin looking at him. His response must have appeared unfriendly to someone not used to their interaction. "It's okay. We grew up together. That's just how we talk to each other."

Orbin smiled. "Yeah, you build a special language with the folks who have known you longest. I've got a few like that in this valley."

"Lloyd and I crossed paths right after the attacks and I invited him to come join up with us if he wanted to. It's a long story but I had to walk home from Richmond. In fact, I passed through Burke's Garden on the way home, not too far from here."

Orbin let out a low whistle. "That's a long haul."

"It was long and ugly. I'm home now, but things are still ugly. To be honest, I've struggled with it a bit. You seem to be the person in charge around here so you probably understand. In my valley, that's me. I'm the one who people come to. It's a lot of responsibility. You have to make hard decisions. People expect things from you."

"And you can't make everybody happy," Orbin inserted. "I know exactly how it is."

Jim nodded. "I try to make the right call, but I have to stay true to myself too. I have to stick by my own values. It may be 'safest' to go along with what the government asks us to do, but is it really? I'm willing to compromise, but I won't give up my freedoms. Not everyone agrees with that. Some are more than willing to give up freedom for comfort. They like being taken care of. That's one of the ways we've changed as a society. Independence no longer seems to be important to some people, but it's everything to others. It's everything to *me*."

Orbin grinned. "You know, I ain't the oldest son-of-a-bitch in this valley but I'm a member of that club. And though I ain't bound to a rocking chair yet, I may not be far from it. If I've learned one thing in my life it's that most people act out of fear. When I look back on every bad decision in my life, that's where it came from. Fear of missing out, fear of losing *someone* or *something*, fear of getting my ass kicked, or even fear of getting my heart hurt. Fear is the worst reason to do anything."

Jim took a bite of cornbread salad, something he hadn't had in years. "Sometimes I struggle with that. I fear I'm doing the wrong thing and I'm going to get people I love killed."

Orbin pondered that for a moment. "I don't consider that to be fear exactly. I consider that to be the mark of a responsible person. You're acting out of concern for others. To me, acting out of fear is acting from weakness. It's action based on the assumption that you don't have what it takes to get control of the situation. It's action based on your shortcomings rather than your strengths."

"You think so?"

"Yeah, I do. For example, when we saw you on the road this evening, some of those young ones thought we should take a shot at you to run you off. To keep you moving along."

Jim laughed. "I halfway expected that."

"They were speaking out of fear. They didn't recognize you. My position is that you have to give a man a chance to prove he's bad before you go that far. You can always shoot him later if it comes to that." The look in Orbin's eyes showed he wasn't joking. He was deadly serious. "That's why you always have to fear the old, experienced man. By the time he decides to kill you, there ain't no changing his mind. The matter is settled."

Jim smiled at that. "There was an older man in the valley where I lived who was a big influence on me. His name was Buddy and he was a good man. He got killed for his horse. I miss having him around. It was helpful to be able to talk things out with him. He kept me pointed in the right direction."

"I'm sure it's a long ride, but you're welcome to swing by and jaw a spell whenever you feel like it, although I might put you to work when you're here."

Jim laughed. "I wouldn't expect any different."

"Seriously though, that's something I miss about the time I grew up in. A man had older men around to help guide him. I assume women had the same thing but I never paid no mind to that. I had grandpas around. There were uncles and great-uncles. There were old men who lived in the valley here. You saw those old men all the time and they asked you questions about your life. They helped keep you pointed in the right direction."

"I didn't have much of that growing up," Jim admitted. "Don't have any of it now."

Orbin nodded as if this proved his point. "Makes things harder, doesn't it? If you go it alone, all you have is the school of hard knocks to keep you straight and that's a rough ride."

"Tell me about it. I know all about learning from mistakes."

"At least you're learning, son, and you care about learning. That's important. Many folks these days are more concerned with being right than becoming better people. They don't grow and change. They get some crazy idea in their head and then find something on the internet that validates it for them. Then they never have to grow, you see? They never have to get better. The truth is that you're never perfect just the way you are, no matter what the internet says. You should always be working toward being better. By the time you're old, like me, you'll be damn near perfect." Orbin let out a huge laugh and patted Jim on the back.

"Hey, Orbin!" Frannie was in the barn door, beckoning her husband. "Honey, you got to see this. Lloyd has all these kids out here flat-footing."

Orbin pushed up from the bench. "Let's go see the show."

Jim came along politely, not wanting to admit he'd seen enough banjo playing to last him a lifetime. Outside, the music was in full swing. Lloyd was in his element, his felt hat pulled down to his ears. He was dancing and pounding out *The Banjo Am The Instrument For Me*. The children were clogging, flat-footing, and square dancing all at the same time, feet and legs flying. There were smiles around the fire and as much happiness as Jim had seen in some time. He was glad to see it. Glad to know it still existed out there in the world.

When the song came to an end, Lloyd doffed his hat and bowed as clapping hands and cheers filled the night. This was what Lloyd needed more than the food and a roof over his head. This was what was important to him. Without pause, he launched into *Little Liza Jane*.

Jim stepped away from the fire and stared out into the dark valley around him. The sound of insects and frogs was like the clapping of hands. The outlines of the high ridges were visible against the night sky. Music echoed in the vast spaces. From nowhere, Jim felt the cold hand of loneliness plunge into his chest and twist at his heart.

Whatever his family was doing tonight, he couldn't imagine they were smiling as widely and laughing as freely. They would likely be feeling his absence as strongly as he felt theirs. Talking with Orbin tonight had only reaffirmed the conclusions he'd already come to. He needed to get home to his family. His absence was not the way to keep them safer. He knew that now with a certainty as powerful as the stars above him.

**36**

———————

# J im's Valley



"WHAT'S WRONG WITH YOU, DUDE?"

Pete had been quiet all evening and Charlie knew something was up. The two hung out every day and were fairly tuned-in to the other's moods. Pete wasn't his normal laid-back self. Something had to be bothering him.

Pete shook his head and kept walking. "Nothing."

Charlie wasn't having it. "You were quiet all the way home and you haven't said shit since we got back. I might as well be working by myself."

As soon as they'd come back from the farmer's market they'd distributed the goodies they bought, then set out to check their fishing lines. They'd been setting out branch lines in the river that ran through the valley and had good luck with them. The technique involved tying a short length of baited fishing line to a tree branch and dropping it into the river. They had dozens of lines out and had been catching fish every day without having to waste time standing on the bank. This method of fishing usually didn't kill the fish either, so they could unhook it and toss it back if it wasn't something they wanted.

They were each carrying a five-gallon bucket about half full of water. It was enough to keep the fish alive until they could get home with them. So far they had a few rainbow trout and a rock bass, known locally as a "redeye". They'd tossed back two suckers and an overgrown goldfish that must have started out in someone's decorative pond.

They wouldn't eat the fish immediately. They'd converted an old watering trough into a holding tank for fish. Cold creek water constantly ran through the tank, keeping the fish alive until someone was ready to eat them. The tank was a recent project, something Jim had put together before he left on his trip.

"Did something happen in town?" Charlie asked. "Is that why you're not talking?"

"Man, you were with me the whole time? What could have happened?"

"Not when you went to pick up the horses. You did that alone."

Pete hesitated just a second too long and Charlie caught it. The two knew each other pretty well by this point. Hiding anything from each other was about impossible.

"Was it that punk, Duane?" Charlie asked. "Was he being an asshole? He seems like the type."

"No one *did* anything."

"Did he *say* something?"

"No," Pete finally admitted. "Not Duane, anyway."

"Someone else? Who?"

Pete stopped and set down his bucket. He faced Charlie. He might as well tell him what happened or he'd never shut up. "Duane's dad, Willie, said that Duane told him who I was. Who my *father* was. When I went back to get the horses, he was a jerk. He started giving me a bunch of shit about us being at the market. He said all these people were suffering because of my dad and if I came back there again he'd tell everyone who I was. He said they'd probably kill me right there on the spot. Then he started going on about whether my dad was even dead or not."

"Damn, I knew something happened." Charlie opened his arms in a gesture of incredulity. "Why the hell didn't you say something? Randi would have taken him apart."

"Dude, if he told that crowd who we were they might have turned on us. He was probably right about that. They might have rushed us and we wouldn't have had a chance."

"We *would* have had a chance. We have guns and we know how to use them. We'd have been outnumbered, but we'd have still had a chance."

"They'd have killed us. The whole town hates my dad. They hate all of us."

Charlie waved off his concerns. "I think you're worried about nothing."

Pete didn't see it that way. His voice rose higher and the words came faster. He was anxious, scared. "You don't know what it's like, man. When my dad was here, my mom was constantly worried that someone was going to figure out he was still alive. Now he's gone and she's terrified he's never coming back. There's no peace for us, no way this is ever going to get better. And when I was finally having a good day, when it was finally out of my head for one minute, I run into some stupid asshole like Willie who threatens to make things worse. That's the last thing we need."

Charlie gave him a serious look. "You're right, Pete. I don't know what that's like anymore because I lost everyone. My entire family is dead."

Pete instantly felt like crap. "Man, I'm sorry. I didn't mean it like that. I know it's not the same, but you have a new family now. We're your family. You and I are brothers." Pete picked up his bucket and started walking again. He felt like shit now. His best friend had tried to help him and he'd said the wrong thing. Now Charlie probably hated him too.

Charlie hurried for a few steps and fell in alongside his friend, throwing his arm over his shoulder. "Don't worry about this, Pete. We *are* family and I'll do everything I can to help protect you guys. That's what family does."

"I'm sorry I said that you didn't know what it was like," Pete said. "I wasn't thinking."

"It's no big deal, buddy. That was my old life. The past. I have a new life now. We all do."

Pete couldn't respond. Words failed him. He focused on the ground as he walked, his face red and his eyes filling with tears. He couldn't be certain if it was anxiety, sadness, or anger. Perhaps it was just the onrush of all those confusing emotions overloading his circuitry.

Charlie's mind was elsewhere. These people were his family. They'd taken him in when he'd had nothing, when he'd thought all was lost. Now he was part of something. Whether you wanted to call it a community, a tribe, or a family, he was part of it. They respected him and treated him like he was one of them. Like he was their blood. He'd do anything he could to protect them.

Anything.

## 37

J *im's Valley*

SOME NIGHTS PETE and Charlie camped out, sleeping in the barn, the woods, or one of the outposts. The two were perhaps the most well-adapted to current conditions, almost enjoying the return to a simpler bygone era. They liked living closer to the land and providing for their families. They enjoyed the time spent outdoors, even when the conditions were less than pleasant. They'd done a lot of camping out this summer, but some nights they stayed in homes with their families. Although everyone was concerned they might be getting too feral, neither boy was concerned about that. It was a badge of honor to them. They cherished their wildness.

With Jim gone, Pete's mom wanted him around more. Even with Hugh keeping an eye on things, Ellen liked the comfort of having her son there. She needed his presence. Randi often felt the same way about Charlie. With Lloyd gone, she'd been moody. Having Charlie there was a break in the routine and it pulled her out of her shell. Her daughters were also very appreciative of Charlie's presence since it meant they didn't have to deal with their mother's funk. Randi was the epitome of *If Mama ain't happy, nobody's happy.*

After dumping their buckets of fish into the holding tank, the boys said their goodbyes and split up for the evening. Pete stayed at his own house to help Pops with their garden, while Nana, Ellen, and Ariel were canning. Charlie went to Randi's, certain she had something for him to do around the house. Pete would sleep at home with his family that night, while Charlie would sleep on his familiar cot at Randi's house. They made plans to get together after breakfast the next day and spend the morning cutting firewood.

That night at Randi's house they all played a board game by lantern light until everyone's eyelids were drooping. The long days of working in the garden had everyone exhausted by sundown. Most folks were on a dawn-to-dusk workday now and fell asleep shortly after the sunset. They had to maximize daylight while they had it and get everything done that they could. They had no promise of food for the winter beyond what they grew and stored now. There were no conveniences in their lives anymore. Everything came by the sweat of their brow, by blisters and aching muscles.

Randi's daughters wandered off to get the children to sleep. Randi was already yawning and sinking deeper into the couch.

"You might as well go to bed," Charlie said. "I won't be far behind you."

Randi gave a weary smile. "I was just enjoying the company."

Charlie laughed. "I don't know who you think you're fooling. I ain't no company at all. I'm barely even awake."

Randi rolled forward on the couch, resting her elbows on her knees. She pushed herself to her feet, moaning and groaning as sore muscles protested. "I'll be glad when these gardens are done."

"Don't get too excited," Charlie said. "Something else will come along to take all your time. That's how it works. You'll be sewing or making Christmas presents or something."

Randi gave him a wry look. "You're full of positive energy. Remind me of why I like having you around?"

"No idea," Charlie laughed. "Been wondering that myself."

Randi leaned over and hugged him. She tried to do it every time the opportunity presented itself. She'd made a promise after Alice's death that she'd care for the boy and show him love. She'd try to hug him every day since his mother couldn't.

Charlie hugged her back, then headed toward the old laundry room, which he'd adopted as a bedroom. Randi turned off the lantern in the living room as he closed the laundry room door behind him. They'd moved the appliances out onto the back porch to give him more room since they didn't work anyway. He took a seat on his cot and listened as Randi walked to her room. He heard her shut the door softly so she wouldn't disturb her grandchildren.

He sat there in the dark for a long time. In the time he'd spent in this house, Charlie had learned the habits of this family. He knew that the young children exhausted Randi's daughters. They would fall asleep quickly. Randi would lay there in bed for a few minutes and then she'd be asleep too. Being exhausted when you went to bed was a good thing, helping to counteract the lack of air conditioning in the houses.

When he was certain they were asleep, Charlie slipped off his boots and stood. He slung his pack onto his back and crept out onto the back porch. He carried his boots in one hand and his rifle in the other. He closed the door but left it unlocked. He hoped to get back in time to catch a few hours of sleep, otherwise it was going to be a long day tomorrow.

Their old black dog sniffed at the air and thumped its tail on the floorboards of the porch.

"It's just me," Charlie whispered. "Good dog."

The dog settled back onto the old couch cushion that served as a bed. Charlie sat down on the steps and pulled his boots back on. The moon wasn't full but it was bright enough to help a man familiar with where he was going. He headed out into the fields, staying to the back of the house. He didn't want to walk by Randi's open window in case she was awake. The last thing he needed was someone screaming or taking a shot at him.

A safe distance away, he turned and intersected the trail to Jim's house. He didn't dare take a horse this time of night. It would make too much noise, both here and where he was going. He had to make this trip on foot. Because of that, he was going to take the shortest route, which was the old farm road that crossed the river. It was the only way they had into town until the Wimmers rebuilt the bridge.

Near Jim's place, Charlie cut away from the trail to avoid getting too close to the house. There were too many people there to take a chance on waking someone up. Plus Hugh was staying there now, sleeping in Jim's shop, and he kept odd hours. He was probably still awake and sitting out there in the dark somewhere like an owl. Charlie idolized the guy but no one ever knew where he was going to pop up. He was spooky like that, always skulking around in the darkness, keeping an eye on things.

Once past Jim's house, Charlie picked up the pace and began jogging. He was wound up and the activity might help burn off some nervous energy. This part of the valley, the trail to the river, had no houses anywhere close by. He didn't feel like he had to be on guard here. The chances of running into anyone were pretty slim.

He'd worked up a good sweat by the time he reached the river. On the grassy bank, he pulled his boots and socks off as he'd done many times and waded into the river. The moon reflected off the dark water, the image rippling with the current. The cold felt good on his hot feet. This time of year the river was low, less than a foot deep at this crossing.

On the far side, Charlie sat down and used a bandana to dry his feet, then put his socks and boots back on. When he stood, he was facing the cornfield where his mother had died. He thought he could feel her out there and wouldn't have been surprised if she'd walked right up to him. He didn't know what he'd do if that happened.

Would he run? Scream?

He knew what she'd say; she'd tell him to go home. She'd tell him to be careful and not do stupid things.

"I love you, Mom," he whispered.

He was not comfortable running in the dark here. As far as Charlie was concerned, he was in enemy territory now. The super-store wasn't far off and there could be people staying there. He hadn't been there at night but he'd heard stories. He gave the place a wide berth, walking slowly along the access road and stopping frequently to listen.

Then, on one of those pauses, he heard voices.

He scanned the parking lot and spotted a low fire at a far corner of the parking lot, near the storefronts. Men were talking there, laughing at some story a man was telling. A year ago he'd have assumed these men were drunk but alcohol was in short supply these days. It was more likely they'd been smoking marijuana because it was a lot more common than a bottle of liquor.

Charlie used the moonlight to watch his path, careful not to step on any garbage. Crunching an aluminum can or kicking a glass bottle would certainly catch these men's attention. He didn't relax again until he'd lost sight of their fire. When he was safely past the super-store, Charlie cut across the four-lane highway. It was odd to stand there in the center of the road without a car or electric light in sight. It truly felt like the end of the world.

He stood there for a moment and took it in, listening to the sounds of the small town in the darkness. It was easy to think the place was empty and abandoned, but it wasn't. There was life and there were sounds. Somewhere in the distance a bottle broke and a guitar played, loud voices struggling to harmonize. A woman yelled but it was unclear if she needed help, wanted to fight, or was just crying out against the injustice of her circumstance. A dog barked, calling upon his brethren, and soon more joined in. The sounds didn't come from any single place within the town, but were the collective utterances of a dark and broken community.

Charlie got moving again, hurrying beneath the powerless stop-light, and crossing the guardrail at the far side of the road. He cut around an old cornfield that someone had spent the last two decades trying to sell as "prime commercial real estate". Neighbors had spent the summer planting gardens there, though Charlie couldn't imagine how well that worked with so many desperate, hungry mouths around. Thievery had to be rampant. You'd need a live, armed scarecrow to keep a garden here.

He skirted the field with plenty of room to spare just in case there was a sentry on duty. He didn't want to be mistaken for a corn thief or catch a bullet over a cucumber. Once past the field, he entered a neighborhood he'd never been in before. It was only a few streets deep and he understood the general layout. He hurried along in case anyone noticed him. Again, he didn't want to be mistaken for a thief.

Although it only took him five minutes to pass through the neighborhood it felt much longer. When he was finally through, he paused at a wall of hedges and sat down. It wasn't so much to catch his breath as to calm himself for a moment and collect his thoughts. He tried to relax and slow down his pounding heartbeat. That anxiety wasn't just because of what he'd come through but because of what lay ahead of him. This had been the easy part. The worst was yet to come.

Charlie dug into his pack and came out with a cheap pair of binoculars. They'd only been around fifteen bucks in the best of times and weren't anything fancy, but they did collect light better than the human eye. He scooted away from the hedge to look down Main Street.

He was far from the center of town, on the eastern side. Directly across from Charlie was the cemetery where Buddy had been killed while visiting his daughter's grave. He wondered if that old man was watching out for him tonight, same as his mom. Most of the structures along the street were businesses with a few old homes scattered between them. He saw a tire shop, a couple of fast food places, and a bank. There was a hotel with a Chinese restaurant that had been empty long before the collapse. Stuck in the middle of it all was an older two-story storefront with an apartment upstairs, Willie's What-Nots. Charlie had never been in that store but he'd passed it when he'd driven through town with his mom and dad.

There were no lights inside that Charlie could see. No candles or lanterns. A green canvas awning imprinted with the store name stretched across the front. In the shadowy recess below the awning, Charlie thought he could see that the front windows were boarded up with plywood. He stashed the binoculars in his pack and headed toward the store.

As he walked, he stoked the fires of hatred and anger within himself. He took long, determined steps. He'd lost everything in the world that meant something to him. His grandmother, his dad, his mom—they were all gone now. Then strangers had taken him in, making a place for him in their lives. Now, it was all threatened because of people like Willie. He couldn't allow that to happen. He couldn't lose everything for a second time.

There was no hesitation in Charlie's steps. He approached the store with razor focus, his head on a swivel. Exposed metal stairs ran up the side of the building to the apartment above. Aware that everyone was sleeping with their windows open right now, Charlie went slowly on the steps. He placed his feet carefully and made certain nothing banged against the railing.

He listened as he climbed. There was no talking inside. No sound at all. Charlie's mind raced as he covered those final steps, trying to come up with a plan for how to do this. In his mind, he'd only got this far and no further. He didn't know what happened next.

When he reached the top landing, he knocked firmly on the door because it was all that he could think to do. It wasn't an aggressive cop knock. It sounded more like a neighbor. Like someone needing something. It took a couple of knocks before he heard movement inside the apartment. As soon as he did, Charlie ran down a couple of steps, turned, and flattened himself out. He was angled upward, his rifle aimed at the door, waiting for it to open.

The footsteps paused at the door and Charlie imagined someone inside trying to stare out the peephole. They wouldn't be able to see anything, though. Only blackness. He heard the sound of a chain, then a deadbolt, and the door cracked open just enough for someone to peer out. Unable to see anything, they opened it wider

Charlie triggered the weapon light on his AR. Willie was caught in the harsh glare of the light, standing there in stained boxers and nothing else. Willie slapped a hand up across his face, trying to block the powerful light from his eyes. That hand held a revolver. Charlie didn't hesitate. This was the man he was here to kill. He pulled the trigger and the shot boomed in the night, the round penetrating up through Willie's chin.

There was a scream from inside the house. Willie dropped his revolver and wrapped both hands around his face, trying to hold it together. Blood sprayed everywhere. Willie was choking and his legs went. He slumped in the doorway, spluttering and gagging.

Charlie started to put another in him but there was no use. Willie couldn't speak and he'd bleed out in minutes. Hell, the bullet was probably lodged in his brain. This was done. It was over and it was time to get out of there. Charlie started backing down the stairs on wobbly legs. He heard the voices of people coming to life in the neighborhood around him so he killed his light, not wanting to present himself as a target, not wanting someone out there in the darkness to start firing at him.

He reached the first landing, halfway to the ground, and glanced back over his shoulder. He spotted a light shining out the door of the apartment. A figure raced out and wrapped a towel around Willie's neck, trying to staunch the flow of blood. A second figure came out behind the first, this one holding the flashlight. He aimed it down the steps, trying to find who'd shot his father, and caught Charlie in its beam.

"You!" Duane screamed.

He didn't get the opportunity to say anything more. Charlie silenced him with a gunshot to the chest. Duane dropped his light and tumbled down the steps, rolling right into Charlie's legs. Charlie couldn't see him since his weapon light was off, but a desperate hand clutched at his leg. Charlie dropped the barrel of his rifle and shot blindly into the body at his feet. There was a wheeze and the grip loosened.

There must have been more people in the apartment because there were more cries from the top of the stairs. A female voice was screaming for help. Charlie threw his rifle back up in that direction.

He didn't dare turn his weapon light on but loosed a handful of rounds at the top landing. There was splintering wood as the rounds hit the doorjamb and more screams. Charlie scrambled down the remaining steps, leaping when his momentum outpaced his ability to keep his feet on the steps.

There was a sharp pain in his ankle when he landed and he gritted his teeth. The screaming at the top of the steps was louder now. Neighbors were calling out, their voices getting closer. People wanted to see what was going on. They wanted to help. Charlie knew some of them would have guns. They would want to kill him for what he'd done. They would tear at his flesh with the same fury as his clan would if someone violated the sanctity of their valley.

He wouldn't give them the satisfaction. He ran behind the store and blindly scrambled up a weedy bank. At the top, he ran as hard as he could, making no attempt to keep a low profile. He was more interested in speed than stealth at this point in his operation. Cutting across a yard, he was knocked flat on his ass when he ran headlong into the guy-wire supporting a power pole. Although rattled and seeing stars, he was back on his feet before his vision had even cleared, charging headlong into the darkness.

He didn't travel the same route he'd used on his way into town and had to pause several times to get his bearings. He was soon on the four-lane again and ran full-tilt down the northbound lane. At the familiar superstore stoplight, he slowed, hoping the sound of his steps wouldn't carry to the men he'd seen around the fire earlier.

Charlie focused on calming his breathing. As he walked, the loudest thing reaching his ears was his own heart, pounding like a train in his ears. He stayed on grass when he could, sticking to the concrete-wrapped medians with their decorative trees. It seemed to take forever to get past the superstore, but he was soon beyond it, speeding up to a run. If anyone heard him now, they'd never catch him in this darkness.

At the river, he didn't stop to remove his boots this time. He charged in, slowing only enough so that he wouldn't fall on the slippery rocks and soak all his gear. When he emerged on the far side of the river, he ran again. Out of breath, he slowed to a walk at the river outpost, the log structure his people used to keep a watch on this trail into town. No one had been stationed here since they faked Jim's death.

Charlie was in home territory here. He felt safer and stopped for a moment. His rapid breathing had dried his mouth until it felt like it was lined with flannel so he fished his water bottle from his pack. When he tipped his head back to drink, a hand came from nowhere and wrapped around his neck.

Charlie hadn't heard a thing.

## 38

J*im's Valley*

BEFORE HE EVEN KNEW WHAT was happening to him, Charlie was flat on the ground and a bright light was in his face. He squeezed his eyes shut against the blinding light, unable to throw a hand up to shield them because of the person sitting on his chest.

"What have you been up to, boy?" a voice growled.

Only then did Charlie know he wasn't going to die. It was Hugh.

The hands released him and the light shut off. Hugh got off him. Charlie's ability to see in the dark was shot now and he couldn't make out anything but tiny starbursts in his vision.

"You nearly scared me to death," Charlie muttered, sitting up. "I didn't know who you were."

"I knew exactly who *you* were," Hugh said. "I could see you in my nightvision goggles, but I wanted to teach you a lesson."

"Consider it taught. I think I might have pissed in my pants."

"Serves you right. What the hell were you doing in town this time of night? Did you meet a gal when you were in town the other day?"

"No."

"Then what?" Hugh pressed.

Charlie avoided the question. "I dropped my rifle and I can't see it."

Hugh found the weapon and stuck it in Charlie's hands. "Better clean it before you use it. There might be a plug of mud in that barrel from when I took you down. But back to my question..."

"I had some business in town."

Hugh plucked a hand-rolled cigarette from a metal tin in his pocket and lit it with a zippo. "At this hour?"

Charlie's vision was returning after the blast of light to the face. He could see the glowing cherry at the tip of Hugh's cigarette as he inhaled, the pale red glow of Hugh's face above it. "It ain't nothing I can talk about."

Hugh was silent for a moment, smoking and thinking. "You know, I'm not asking as an adult. I don't intend to tell anyone. You're not in trouble, but I need to make sure you don't *get* yourself in trouble. It's not safe in town. None of us ever go there alone, especially not at this time of night."

"I know," Charlie admitted.

"Then why did you go?"

"Like I said, I had business in town. It's nothing I want to talk about."

Hugh took another draw off his smoke. "And it wasn't a girl?"

"No."

"That doesn't leave much, Charlie. I could almost understand if it was a girl. Anything else it might be is probably something you best stay out of. I'm not sure how people would handle it if something happened to you. Randi loves you like a son. You and Pete are best friends. Hell, even Jim likes you and he probably doesn't like ten people in the whole damn world."

Charlie smiled at that. "There's nothing for you to be concerned with."

"That all you're going to tell me?"

"Reckon so."

Hugh stood. "I can't make you talk, Charlie, but I'm here for you if you need me. Just be careful. I don't want to have to bury you." He extended a hand and helped Charlie up.

"I'm going to be fine," Charlie groaned, tiring of the interrogation.

"Can you promise me you won't go into town again on your own?"

Charlie considered his response. "I can't promise you that but I will say I don't have any immediate plans to go back. I'm done there."

They walked back to the valley in silence, guided only by the moonlight and their familiarity with the terrain. They were each in their own heads, Hugh wondering what it meant that Charlie "was done" there.

Charlie was wondering if his work in town was indeed done. Were those killings enough to keep his tribe safe? What if it was only the beginning? Maybe it was only the first of many mouths that would have to be shut in order to preserve the life they had. He wasn't sure how he felt about that.

He had no revulsion or guilt over what he'd done tonight. His conscience would not plague him later as he tried to sleep. Indeed, he felt an odd sense of satisfaction. He done what was required of him. In the end, how was keeping his friends safe any different than gardening or hunting? Safety was as critical to survival as food.

If there was a part of him that was supposed to be experiencing remorse it was gone. His emotions had been so battered by loss that they probably didn't work like they were supposed to. He felt love and a sense of duty to those who loved him. He understood those emotions. Remorse and guilt he had more trouble with.

This awareness of his emotional shortcomings wasn't something he was going to lose sleep over. He was a product of this new world and there were going to be many more like him. Possibly millions. They felt different. Their values were different. He hoped the world was ready for it.

## 39

———————

T*he Camp*

WHEN SHARON WOKE at the camp, in the cabin she'd stayed in for so many years, she wondered if she'd ever spend the night there again. She had no way of knowing what the future held for her and these children, or even for the nation itself. She knew her mind went to these dark places because she'd not slept well. That was unfortunate because this was to be the big day. They were moving. She'd need all the energy she could muster and she had no means of artificially boosting it with caffeine.

Her rough night was entirely due to the confrontation at the funeral service. Oliver's niece had been a bit of unexpected nastiness at the ceremony and Sharon knew it wasn't over. They hadn't heard the last of Kimberly.

When the last Oliver story had been told and the children had played their last song, the mourners retreated to the dining hall to enjoy the food everyone had prepared. It was amazing to have such variety, considering the things that everyone had run out of after a year of deprivation. There were missing spices and sauces since a lot of the staples had disappeared from kitchens. People were improvising with substitutions, some of which were effective and some of which were questionable.

Out of their favorite spices, some used the odd ones from the back of the cabinet that never seemed to run out. Others were using the fancy spice mixes they'd received in gift baskets and never opened. The cayenne sprinkled on the deviled eggs may have looked like paprika but it wasn't even close. Same with the Italian spice mix in the Southern yellow potato salad. Yet everyone ate heartily and enjoyed the socializing despite the circumstance.

The guests stuck around for a long time, getting to know Sharon and the children. That went a long way toward making Sharon feel more comfortable about their new situation. These were good people, apparently willing to do anything they could to help them get by. Sharon couldn't have asked for anything more. While Oliver's death was a tremendous blow, his absence had created the avenue by which these relationships were being created. It was the best possible outcome of a tragedy.

Aware that it might be the last time she performed this routine in the familiar setting of the camp, Sharon got dressed and went to the dining hall. The sky was already light but the sun not yet up. She drank her lukewarm herbal tea and sat on the front porch watching the sun climb over the horizon. Even with the fear, deprivation, and challenges the last year had brought, there was nowhere she'd have rather spent this time. This was her place. It was the place she was whole. Even without her friends, family, and possessions, this was home in her heart.

When their guests had left last night, Sharon explained to the children that they'd be moving today. She did her best to present it as an exciting adventure, though the children were understandably apprehensive about leaving the familiar camp. Sharon extolled the virtues of Oliver's house and how he'd want them to take advantage of this opportunity. She mentioned the benefits of being close to the neighbors and how that might help them in the future. While no one complained, there was an undercurrent of uncertainty on their faces and she didn't like it.

All she could do was try to soothe them through this transition. There was no escaping pain in life. It came with the territory, with being alive and human. The best she could do was to help them cope and find the strength within themselves to deal with the challenge. It was what a teacher did, or a parent. You didn't help people by removing the obstacle. You helped them by showing them how to overcome it.

After everyone understood the plan, she sent them to their cabins to begin packing.

"You don't have to take everything," she explained. "We'll be back here almost every day. We'll be taking care of the gardens and moving things slowly over time. We can't take it all at once so pack what's important to you. We'll get the rest later."

She had no idea how they were going to make the move down the mile of camp road, other than with wheelbarrows and wagons. The children could wear backpacks. They'd do it one step at a time and they'd be fine. She did not doubt their abilities.

When she finished her tea, Sharon returned to the kitchen and began packing items she expected they'd need at Oliver's house. She didn't bother with the institutional-size pots and pans, or the two-foot long serving spoons. She began with spices and the packaged food they had remaining. Some of it was on high pantry shelves and she'd have to get Nathan to get it down for her. As she thought about all the things that needed to be done, she decided to go ahead and get the children up. It was going to be a long day and there was no use delaying it.

Sharon went to the back porch and tugged the white cotton rope hanging at the edge. Above her head, the cast iron bell rang and could be heard even at the farthest reaches of the camp. Traditionally it was how they called people to meals or signaled that it was time to attend a session. They hadn't used it often in the last year but it was somehow fitting to use it now, on what might be the last day of camp.

The sound of crunching gravel on the road caught her attention for the second day in a row. For some reason, her first thought was that the gravediggers might be returning for some reason. Then, in a surge of panic, she imagined Kimberly and her son returning to continue yesterday's argument.

She moved further down the porch to where she could better see the road and was surprised by the appearance of a horse. It wore a more conventional harness and was towing a golf cart behind it. Kendall waved eagerly from the driver's seat. Freda followed along behind him on her horse. She waved when she saw Sharon on the porch.

Sharon shot down the ramp and headed toward the small parking lot. Kendall reined the horse to a stop and set the parking brake on the cart. He stiffly maneuvered out of the seat, straightening the Levi Garrett Chewing Tobacco cap that got knocked askew in the process.

"You like it?" he asked, gesturing at the vehicle.

She smiled. "That's cool! Reminds me of the way I used to get around here before we ran out of gas." She pointed to the tall weeds beside her cabin. "Mine is setting over there."

"I'll trade you."

Sharon looked at him, eyes wide. "Are you serious?"

He grinned. "It's only one horsepower but it'll go." He cackled at his joke.

"I don't want to take your cart. You might need it."

"He made it just for you," Freda said from the back of her horse. "He was out there half the night banging and tinkering."

Sharon rolled forward and opened her arms wide. Kendall leaned over and she gave him a powerful hug. "It's amazing. I can't thank you enough."

"I yanked the battery out and everything else it didn't need. That got the weight down. I used some old pipes to make the shafts that connect to the harness. I mounted them to the bumper and it seems to work all right. That horse doesn't have any trouble pulling it. You should be able to load this cart up and go all day."

"I don't know what to say."

"You done said it," Kendall said. "You thanked me."

"But don't you need your horse?"

"Honey, I got more of them. And even though folks need them for riding right now, there's a lot of them being given away. People ain't got no way to care for them so some are free for the asking."

"You want to try it?" Freda asked. "Kendall can ride with you and make sure you got the hang of it."

"I'd love to!"

Kendall looked at her chair. "You need...help?"

Sharon shook her head and smiled, trying to dispel his awkwardness. "I've been doing this a while. I've got it."

By the time Kendall circled to the passenger side, Sharon was already in. "You need help?" she teased.

He laughed. "I might." He ducked and slid in beside her.

"What do I do?"

"Steering will be about the same. The brake pedal barely works so you don't have to worry about that. Reining in the horse is how you slow and stop it."

"That's perfect since my other cart had hand brakes," Sharon said.

"Now you still have a hand brake for parking," Kendall said. "That'll keep the horse from wandering off with your cart if he sees some juicy grass somewhere or takes a notion to get him a drink."

"It's a he?"

Kendall nodded. "Nice old gentle horse. I've had him for years. I let my grandchildren ride him if that tells you anything. He's got a good disposition."

"What about the harness?"

"I didn't have a harness with a collar so this relies on straps across his breast when he's pulling. It's a basic buggy harness. You can probably put it on by yourself with some practice, but it may take two of you in the beginning. He don't mind being harnessed so he's not going to fight it. He'll just stand there and let you do it, pretty as you please."

"Can I go?"

Kendall latched a hand onto the roll cage. "Let's do it."

Sharon released the parking brake and the cart rolled a tiny bit as it took up the slack in the harness. Same as she'd done with Honey, she clucked her tongue and snapped the reins. The horse started walking and they moved through the pastures below the dining hall, Kendall giving a few pointers along the way.

"He might be able to turn the cart without you steering, but it's going to be a lot easier for him if you help him out with the steering wheel. Given enough time I might have been able to integrate the harness shafts into the steering of the cart, but it wasn't going to be easy without a welder."

Sharon was beaming. "You did an amazing job. I'm so excited about this. You don't know how much this is going to help with our move." She glanced in his direction, expecting to see him smiling too, but instead she found his face clouded, a frown crinkling his brow. "What's the matter?"

"I should have expected this but we found Kimberly at Oliver's house when we took out of here yesterday. She and that son of hers were going through the place, trying to find anything of value."

"I figured we hadn't seen the last of her," Sharon said.

"They didn't trash things too bad, but they left a bit of a mess. Emptied some drawers and shelves. Don't know what they expected to find, probably searching for a stash of money or something."

"If Oliver had any money laying around he probably spent it on this camp."

"I know that and you know that, but Kimberly won't believe it. She's probably going to continue being a thorn in your side until she gives up on this and goes away."

"What happened when you found her?"

"She gave us the same garbage she said at the funeral, about how all this should have been hers. She accused you of trying to weasel your way in and steal it off her."

"I never—"

"I know," Kendall said, throwing a hand up. "None of us believe that. We got her to leave. Reckon we shamed her out of there. She had a few things in a pillowcase and wouldn't show them to us. The younger fellers were ready to take it from her and dump it out, but we didn't want to go there. Didn't know if she might have a gun or something."

"Oliver offered me one before. I know he has some."

"Any idea where he kept them?" Kendall asked.

"Not really."

"She might have found them." He shrugged. "It's hard to say."

"I'll do some looking once we get into the house."

"You'll need to keep an eye out for that woman. She was raised with the idea that all this should be hers. That's a long time to let hate fester. You think on something that long, you aren't going to let it go overnight. Not without a fight."

"I'll remember that," Sharon said. "We'll be careful."

"The wife and I will keep an eye on the road but that don't mean anything. She could slip right by us. You might want to think about a dog or something. You'll need some way to keep an eye on things."

"A dog is an excellent idea. The children would love that, but I'd like to start it as a puppy. Something that can grow up around them and they'll be comfortable with."

"I'll keep my eyes open."

They circled back to the parking lot and found several of the children standing there with Freda. They were petting her horse. One sat in the saddle, grinning broadly. They watched in amazement as Sharon came riding through the tall grass in her new golf cart.

"Look what Mr. Kendall brought me," she announced.

Kendall climbed out and the children swarmed the cart. They climbed on the back and into the seat with Sharon. One of them tried to honk the horn, disappointed that it wouldn't make a sound.

Kendall ducked back down to where he could see beneath the canopy and waved at Sharon. "I'll get out of your hair. I know y'all have a big day ahead of you. If you have any trouble with the cart...or any trouble at all...just give us a holler."

Sharon grinned widely. "Thanks again. I appreciate you guys very much."

Kendall climbed into the saddle and steered his horse over

toward the dining hall porch where Freda was already waiting for him. The porch had her at the same level as the horse's back and it was a simple transition to climb on. As they rode off, they waved at the children.

Sharon waited for a break in the chatter and got the children's attention. "Okay, someone bring me my chair. We've got a lot to do but I need to get some breakfast in you guys first."

**40**

———————

# T*he Camp*

IT FELT strange going into Oliver's house for the first time. It wasn't *really* the first time, but it was the first time since several significant things had happened. It was Sharon's first visit with Oliver not there, either living or dead. It was her first time visiting the house since Kimberly and her son had ransacked it. It was also her first time visiting the house with the idea that, at least for the short term, it would provide a home for her and the children.

It was only her and Nathan on the first trip. The children had collected all of their sleeping gear—pillows, blankets, sleeping bags —and it was strapped onto the golf cart. Kay was in charge back at the camp. She was supposed to help the kids pack up the personal items they wanted to bring with them. Within reason, they were encouraged to bring anything that would help them feel at home in their new surroundings.

"You unload the golf cart onto the porch," Sharon said. "I want to take a look around before we start moving things in."

Sharon opened the back door and entered the kitchen. The unlocked door was a stark reminder that this would have to be one of the first things she addressed. She had to find some way to secure the house. She couldn't trust the existing locks even if she found the keys because Kimberly might have found a set while she was going through the house. She could use slide-bolts or even bar the door while they were inside but there would be times they went back to the camp to work in the garden and she wanted to be able to lock the house behind her.

There were clear signs that someone had been in the house since she'd left. She knew Kendall and Freda had been there because they'd helped with Oliver's body, but they wouldn't have done anything like this. There were some cardboard boxes and plastic shopping bags on the table. Sharon moved closer and saw that they contained food from Oliver's cabinets. That explained why all of the cabinet doors were open.

Sharon resisted the instinct to close all the cabinets and drawers, to return everything to the way it had been. There would be time for that later. She made a circuit through the house. In every room, she found drawers pulled out and closet doors swung wide open. There were items on the beds in the unused bedrooms, like this was where they'd sorted through what they found or where they piled items they intended to take.

She saved Oliver's room for last. It wasn't a shrine but it provoked intense feelings in her. When she'd last been in there his body had been stretched out on the bed. It was where she'd said her last goodbye to the friend who'd given her the opportunity to run the camp. When there was nowhere left to go, no excuses remaining for not checking his room, she rolled up to that door and paused. She almost felt like she should knock.

Sharon turned the handle, heard the polished latch work its smooth magic. She swung the door wide and regarded the room before entering. The curtains were open, allowing the light of the day into the room. That was a small blessing, dispelling some of the gloom from the empty chamber. Then it occurred to her that the curtains had probably been opened by Kimberly to better see what she was doing. The idea of that woman despoiling the sanctity of this room angered her.

While the space felt almost sacred to Sharon because of what she'd experienced there, it meant nothing to Kimberly. To her it was just another room. The closet door stood agape. Drawers hung open, clothes draped from them. Sharon spotted several guns on the bed and moved closer. Her dad had served in the army and she'd been raised around guns. She even owned a few but had to wonder if they were still at her home. Someone might have broken in and stolen them. She tried not to think about that.

There were a couple of shotguns. They were in good condition but well-used, the bluing worn down to the polished metal beneath. There were a couple of hunting rifles too. Several boxes of ammunition and shotgun shells were scattered on the bed. There were no handguns, though.

Sharon had no idea how many pistols Oliver might have but figured there had to be at least one since he'd offered to let her borrow it. That meant it was either hidden in the house or Kimberly had taken it. Sharon would have to give the children some instruction on not plundering around until she'd had time to thoroughly search the house. She'd also have to ask them to let her know if they saw any guns.

The guns on the bed would be safe for now. She assumed the children would naturally shy away from Oliver's room because of what had happened there. They would be superstitious. Looking around at the mess, she experienced the same desire that she felt in the kitchen, the urge to right things, to return the room to the way Oliver had kept it. But not now. They needed to return to the camp for the next load. She closed Oliver's door behind her and hurried down the hall.

Nathan was done unloading and sitting on the edge of the porch, awaiting further instruction.

"Things are a bit of a mess," she said. "There were some visitors yesterday during the funeral…"

"That woman? Mr. Oliver's niece?"

Sharon nodded.

"Is it safe for us to live here?"

Sharon let out a long sigh. "As safe as anywhere else. That's nothing for you to worry about. How about you start carrying sleeping bags to the bedrooms? For now, let's do a girls' room and a boys' room. Just use the downstairs rooms for now. We can spread out more once we get settled into the house."

Nathan hopped up from his seat and gathered some items from the porch. While he was ferrying loads to the bedrooms, Sharon began unpacking the items Kimberly had collected on the kitchen table. She put everything into the cabinets she could reach, closing all the doors as she worked and sliding all the drawers closed. By the time Nathan had all the sleeping gear stowed, she had the kitchen back in order. It wasn't perfect but she preferred it over seeing that reminder of Kimberly's intrusion every time she entered the house. That was like a slap in the face.

"All done," he announced. "What's next?"

"Are you comfortable operating the cart?" she asked.

"Yeah. It's pretty simple."

"Then I want you to go back without me and get the stuff I left on the porch of my cabin. That's all the gear I'll need for now. If the other kids ask when they're coming, tell them it probably won't be for a couple of hours. After you bring my stuff, we'll start bringing the children's stuff. We'll haul the packed items from the dining hall and camp kitchen, then we'll bring the instruments. The children will be able to walk from the camp to here and they can lead the goats with them while they walk. It'll take longer to get the chickens because we need to make sure we have a place for them. That might take a couple of days."

Nathan smiled. "Some of the kids will gripe."

"That's okay," Sharon said. "It won't hurt them. Try to play up the idea that they're getting to take the goats for a walk. Maybe that will make it more entertaining."

"Will you be okay here?"

"Are you serious?"

He nodded.

"Yeah, I'll be fine. I want to get a few things squared away before the children get here." Sharon was so independent that she was almost offended by his question until she considered what motivated it. It was his maturity and sense of responsibility. He was starting to think like an adult. "And thanks for asking."

"Then I'll be going. I'll be back in a few."

"Be careful!"

He raised a hand, waving in response to her comment. He reminded her of a teenager heading out in the family car, except he wasn't old enough yet and the family car was a horse. She remained in the open doorway, watching as he settled into the golf cart, snapped his reins, and headed off down the driveway.

When he was gone, Sharon backed through the door and sat there thinking. After a moment's hesitation, she closed the door and locked it. She was uncertain of what to do next, so suddenly confronted with the enormity of what lay ahead of her. She was no stranger to managing big jobs so her reaction surprised her at first. Then she understood that she wasn't just overwhelmed by the size of the physical task, but also by all the other things that came along with it. There was the loss of Oliver to deal with and the sense of aloneness that brought. She also felt the burden of being the only adult. Then there was the looming conflict with Kimberly that was bound to rear its ugly head again.

Sharon headed toward the hallway, deciding she should at least move the guns from the bed to the closet. She was fairly certain the kids wouldn't venture into the room, especially if she asked them not to, but she'd feel more comfortable with the weapons stowed. As she headed in that direction she regarded the old family photos on the walls of the hallway. It was tragic in some ways that this once large farming family had dwindled, but that was the way of things. Empires rose and fell. Even large and prosperous families could die out.

In some of those pictures, the large family stood in the yard of this very house, faces somber. Others were taken around the property. Men were farming with teams of horses, men posing by logs they harvested from the forest, and men standing alongside kilns they used to bake bricks. There were men posing by cars, trucks, and tractors. Some photos were only men, others only women.

One that caught her eye showed three men dressed in patched bibbed overalls but sporting rakish felt hats that would have been more suited to an evening in town. There was nothing in the photograph to indicate the occasion or where the men might be headed but the hats were not the only distinctive feature of the photos. Each man held a shiny black revolver and they were pointing them at each other in a manner that was definitely unsafe.

She understood that times were different then. People were more tolerant of risk. Perhaps it was because they were more responsible and had more common sense than the people of today, so obsessed with doing things that would gain them visibility on social media.

In those bibbed overalls, the men would have nowhere to carry those guns but their pockets. They wore no belts and had no holsters on display. She remembered that was how her grandfather had carried one at the store he operated, just shoved into his pocket like it was nothing more than a ring of keys.

She screwed her mouth up in thought. That gave her an idea and she hurried to Oliver's room. She opened the door and went to the foot of his bed, scanning the room. When she spotted what she was looking for—Oliver's clothes, piled exactly where he'd left them when he last took them off.

Everyone had their own rituals, especially an old man who'd been living on his own for a number of years. His clothes were draped across a very feminine dressing bench with pink padding that was probably a remnant of his late wife. She approached the pile and studied it. There were bibbed overalls and a stained white t-shirt. She could smell the clothes and they smelled like Oliver. It wasn't a comment on his hygiene in general but more of a reflection of the state of things. No one was as clean as they wanted to be. Deodorant had disappeared as a concern in the early days of the event.

She picked up his t-shirt and folded it neatly before placing it on his dresser. While she was there, she tucked everything back into the drawers so that they closed neatly. She returned to the bibbed overalls and picked them up from the bench. They were a heavy item of clothing anyway, requiring a significant amount of denim to make, but these were heavier than normal. It made sense in some ways. Why bother to empty your pockets if you're going to be putting the exact same thing back on tomorrow?

She started with the chest pocket. She slid a finger in there and found a stub of a pencil, along with a worn notepad. She flipped it open and found lists, notes Oliver had written to himself about things he wanted to do. She set those items aside to review later. In his back pocket, she found a wallet so worn that the leather was scarcely thicker than the paper in the notepad.

She couldn't bring herself to open the billfold. It was too personal. She expected there would be family photographs, a driver's license, and some paper money worn smooth as silk from the carrying. She set that aside also.

In the left front pocket she discovered a ring of keys. It reminded her of a ring of keys she'd found after her father died. Despite the durability and strength of metal, nothing polished keys and a keychain like carrying it in a pocket every day. The ring would eventually wear thin. The keys would become polished until the teeth disappeared and the edges wore smooth.

She tucked those keys into her pocket, hoping they went to some of the doors she planned on securing. Returning her hand to the pocket, she found an elastic capo, a device for changing the key of a stringed instrument. There were probably a dozen loose picks for guitars and banjos. Some were flat plastic, others metal and designed to fit over the fingertips. There was also an Old Timer pocketknife, the bone scales worn nearly flat, the original blade profile long ago lost to countless sharpenings.

In the front right pocket she found exactly what she was looking for. She was expecting it the closer she got, from the way the garment hung in her hand, but she intentionally left that pocket for last. When her hand slipped into the pocket it touched the cool steel of a pistol frame. She closed her hand around the grip and extracted the gun, holding it up in front of her.

It was a .38 Colt revolver. She'd handled one before but it had been a while. It took her a moment to remember how to open the chamber, but she figured it out. She dumped the rounds into her hand and confirmed that they were all good. No spent shells. She hoped there was a box of them somewhere because this wasn't many.

She tucked the revolver into the pouch that hung from the right side of her chair, then proceeded to carefully fold the overalls. She placed them on the dresser, then stacked the t-shirt on top of it. That was one small mystery solved.

Oliver's closet door was still open from Kimberly's explorations. Sharon stared inside. She was surprised to find that it wasn't like modern closets at all. It was shallow, perhaps only a foot deep. People of the era when this house was built wouldn't have owned hundreds of items of clothing. They might have owned a half-dozen if they were lucky. Those would be hung on nails inside the closet. No need for hangers, bars, or elaborate custom closets. Anyone of sufficient wealth to have more clothes would store them in a wardrobe.

The closet only contained a few sets of bibbed overalls similar to what Oliver always wore. She knew he had nicer clothes because she'd seen him wearing them. They must be folded into the dresser drawers or stored in another closet elsewhere in the house. This one must have been strictly for overalls and guns. Sharon carefully leaned all the rifles and shotguns in the closet and closed the door.

She decided she'd try to find a hasp and padlock at some point so she could lock it. If she could find a couple of them that might give her a way to lock the house when they were gone to the camp. It was kind of a redneck approach to locking a house but she had to work with what she had.

She straightened the bed and made certain everything was in order. She backed out of the room and closed the door behind her. Nathan would be back with another load soon and she needed to figure out which room she was staying in.

**41**

---

T*azewell County, Virginia*

THE STAY at Orbin's farm had been good for both Lloyd and Jim. After the experience at Laurel Bed Lake, it was nice to have a social experience that didn't end in bloodshed. Jim also felt good about his talk with Orbin. It reaffirmed a lot of the things spinning around in his head since he'd left home. It confirmed that going home after they were done at the camp in Bland County was the right thing. He'd take his chances with his family. He'd stay put there in his valley until there was absolutely no other option.

His head was in the right place now. Sometimes it took putting some space between yourself and those you loved to gain that perspective. It was hard to see the totality of your surroundings, of your life, when you were immersed in it. Maybe it wasn't that way for everyone, but it was certainly that way for Jim. In the past, he'd gotten that experience when traveling on a work trip or back-packing in the mountains. There were fewer opportunities for that perspective now since everyone was so engrossed in struggling to survive.

Jim had planned on getting up early and hitting the road. He'd made Lloyd aware of his plans before the two settled into sleeping bags the previous night but Lloyd had been noncommittal. Jim knew what that meant. He'd have to shake Lloyd out of his bag to get him moving.

Instead, Orbin and his family took care of that. The people working the hayfield started early and they started with a hearty breakfast. Jim was already awake and packing his gear when Orbin strolled into the barn.

"You staying for breakfast?"

Jim stuffed his sleeping bag into its sack. "I'd love to but we need to hit the road. I'd feel bad about taking your food when I can't give you a day's work."

"I got ham, eggs, and bacon," Orbin threw out, fully aware that he was using one of the most powerful lures in the tackle box.

"Bacon?" Lloyd groaned.

"He's alive!" Orbin said.

"He's alive. Just lazy," Jim confirmed. "But like I said, we can't give you a day of work."

"Ain't asking for it," Orbin said. "Every family in this valley has been raising hogs and chickens. Ain't no shortage of eggs and pig meat around here."

"We'll take you up on it," Lloyd said, suddenly energized and sliding out of his bag.

"It's a miracle," Jim said.

"It'll be ready in about fifteen minutes," Orbin said. "Come on over."

Jim gave him an appreciative nod. "We'll be there then. Thank you."

"Bacon. Bacon." Lloyd was reciting it like a mantra as he hurriedly dealt with his gear.

"Didn't know you were so partial to bacon. You have a spring in your step and you aren't even stepping yet."

Lloyd looked around for the stuff sack for his sleeping bag. "Ain't just that. It was nice to play music for folks again. You have no idea how much I miss that."

"You play for folks in the valley."

"Yeah, but it's the same old people and half the time I just feel like they're humoring me. They're sitting there to be nice but don't really care about the music."

"I didn't know that was such a big deal to you," Jim said honestly.

"That's because you're not a musician. If you were, you'd understand."

"You could try playing in town."

Lloyd shuddered. "Are you kidding? I'm halfway afraid to even set foot in that town the way they treat you folks. If people figure out I'm from your valley, I'm liable to get killed."

Jim didn't respond to that. There was an element of truth there and it was his fault. There was no escaping the fact that his choices about the power plant had alienated him from much of the community.

"Then there's the whole teaching thing. I miss that too. I had dozens of students back before this whole thing happened."

"I didn't realize."

Lloyd found his stuff sack and hurriedly shoved the bag inside. "Because individual aspirations aren't acknowledged in your community, Jim. Every day turns into some dramatic life or death struggle. There's very little discussion as to how people feel or how they're dealing with it. You've built a strong group but there's not much emotional support."

"I can't even believe we're having this conversation," Jim said. "Emotional support? You think I'm a fucking social worker?"

Lloyd pointed a finger at his old friend as if he'd hit the nail on the head. "That's exactly it, Jim. You set the tone for the whole thing. Every person in your community, everyone you've brought together, has emotional needs. They have things they want out of life and things that bring them joy. You've got the basic needs taken care of. You can feed your people and kill anyone who threatens you, but do you ever wonder if your friends are happy? I can answer that question. No, you don't. Those kinds of things aren't even on your radar."

Jim didn't answer. Of course he didn't worry about that kind of crap. In the scheme of things, in the face of keeping everyone alive, he didn't think things like that mattered. People needed to eat. They needed to be safe. Someone had to take the lead and make those things happen.

He hadn't wanted to be that person in the beginning. He'd resisted it. He wanted to be left alone, but it didn't work that way. He became the default leader of his tribe. The minute he owned that, the minute he started taking the lead in the decision-making, they ended up destroying the power plant. Now they were paying for that and the struggle for survival was even more intense. That was the kind of thing he had to worry about, not *feelings*.

Lloyd tightened the drawstring on his stuff sack, then worked the bag into his pack. He didn't meet Jim's eye or offer anything else. Jim figured his old friend was afraid he'd made him angry with his honest admissions of how he felt. Maybe Lloyd was afraid Jim would see this as a sign of weakness and he might be right. Perhaps he did.

Then Jim had one of those revelations that hit him like a bolt of lightning. He felt so stupid that it almost made him sick. Why was he so blind? Why didn't he have more self-awareness? How could he not see the things that seemed so obvious to others?

Lloyd was *right*.

Reeling, Jim grabbed his bridles and headed for the corral to catch his two horses. He felt anxious, his heart racing as he turned his friend's words over in his head. He was so bad at this, so inadequate at taking care of the needs of his clan. There was never a moment when he felt that he was doing them justice. While he'd managed to keep them safe, he did just as many things that put them at risk. Though he'd helped organize his group through a summer of growing food that just might sustain them through a long winter, his best friend had just pointed out that he was an inconsiderate asshole who was unconcerned about the feelings of those around him.

At least, that's what it felt like Lloyd had said to him.

The degree of truth there was why it stung so badly. He did believe that emotions were tied to weakness. He did believe that what people *felt* was secondary to nearly everything else in their lives right now. If they had time to dwell on emotions, they weren't working hard enough. It was one of his core beliefs and it could quite possibly be alienating him from everyone he cared about. He felt like an idiot.

He had no treats with which to bribe his horses but they stood calmly and allowed him to bridle them. He led them back to the barn and tied them off to posts. He passed Lloyd heading out into the corral to gather his horse. It was an awkward passing, the two neither speaking nor meeting the other's eye. Jim efficiently saddled his horses and loaded his gear. He was done and headed off for breakfast before Lloyd made it back.

**42**

———————

J *im's Valley*

HUGH WAS no psychologist but he knew a bit about human nature. He'd been around the block a few times and he'd been a young man once. He knew there had to be some reason why Charlie had ventured into town last night. Compounding the strangeness of it was the fact he hadn't taken Pete with him. What would he have been doing that he wouldn't have involved his best friend in it? Maybe the place to start was with Pete.

Since Pete had stayed at home last night, Hugh wanted to get to him before he and Charlie had a chance to talk. Breakfast was a big meal in the valley, fuel for a long day of physical labor. Folks usually had a good dinner at the end of the day, a reward for their efforts. Lunch was whatever you could scratch up in between.

Hugh usually took his breakfast at his place, but he'd been eating with Jim's family since he'd been staying in Jim's shop. He caught Pete when he went inside that morning. "Pete, when you fill your plate, come meet me at the fire pit. I want to talk to you about some projects."

"Sure, Hugh." There was nothing usual about the request. There was no shortage of projects either in the planning stage or the *doing* phase.

Hugh helped himself to a ham biscuit and found a seat outside around Jim's backyard fire circle. The grass was dew-soaked, the air so humid and still the entire valley felt like a terrarium. Pete joined him a few minutes later with a heaping plate. No one ate like teenage boys. They burned calories just sitting still.

Seeing no reason to interrogate Pete in an artful and elaborate manner, Hugh just came out with it. "Anything unusual happen in town yesterday, Pete?"

Unaccustomed to deception, the guileless and good-natured young man gave himself away immediately. The change in the tension of his cheek muscles and the flicker of his eyes away from Hugh's told the story. "What makes you think something happened in town?"

"I'd prefer that your mom and Randi not hear about this, but I caught Charlie sneaking back into the valley last night. He'd been to town for some reason."

"Town?"

Again, Pete gave himself away. Hugh could tell that Pete wasn't aware of his friend's late-night foray into town and was trying to process that information.

"Yeah, I wondered if he might have been going to see a girl or if he had some business that, for some reason, had to be conducted in the middle of the night. He doesn't strike me as the type who'd go there to steal so I'm at a bit of a loss."

Pete shook his head adamantly. "Charlie wouldn't steal. He's not like that. Did you ask him why he went into town?"

Hugh took another bite of his biscuit, chewed a while, and let Pete simmer. "Yeah, I asked. He said he couldn't tell me but it was nothing to be concerned about. Not sure I believe that. Town isn't safe, especially at night, and I can't imagine he'd go for no reason."

"I can't believe he went without me," Pete said. "Not that I'd have gone, but I'm surprised he didn't even ask."

"Yeah, that surprised me too. So back to my original question, did anything happen in town yesterday that might have made him want to go into town last night?"

Pete couldn't lie to Hugh, wouldn't lie to him even if he could find the words. He looked around to make sure no one was nearby. "I didn't want to say anything when it happened because I didn't want Randi to flip out, but the guy running the corral was a real asshole."

Hugh looked confused. "A corral? That wasn't there last time I was at the market."

"The guy must have seen the need and acted on it. He set up a corral at the farmer's market and charges people to watch their horses. Turns out he's the dad of a guy I knew from school. He has a business in town, one of those variety stores that sell discount junk."

"How was he an asshole?"

"We left the horses at the corral so we could all look around. When we were ready to go, I went back to pick the horses up by myself because Randi and Charlie were still trading with some guy. The kid I knew from the corral had told his dad who I was and the guy started giving me shit. He said we didn't have any business being in town after what Dad had done. He threatened to tell everyone at the market who we were, and he said they'd kill us. Then he started questioning whether Dad was even dead or not."

"How did you leave it?"

"His sons started coming at me," Pete said. "I didn't know what they were up to so I had to turn my rifle on them. I had the safety off and my finger on the trigger. They knew I was serious. He didn't hand my horses over until I turned a gun on him. That's when he started mouthing off."

"Sounds like you did what you had to do. You handled yourself well. Now, you said Charlie wasn't there when this happened. Did you tell him about it later?"

"Not at first but he kept badgering me. Said he could tell something was wrong. I eventually told him."

"You don't have much of a poker-face, Pete. Just saying."

Pete frowned. "I'm going to have to work on that."

"But you don't have any idea where he might have gone last night?"

"No, honest. I told him what happened and he didn't say much about it, just said he knew something had been bothering me. I have no idea what he did but I intend to ask him this morning."

"Well, Pete, I hope you have better luck than me. He wouldn't tell me a damn thing last night."

"How did you even catch him?"

"I was just out wandering around, walking a patrol, and spotted him coming across the river with my nightvision. I waited on him to come back and ambushed him."

"You probably scared the crap out of him," Pete said.

Hugh grinned. "Probably."

Hugh let the topic die and they discussed other things. After a while, he patted Pete on the shoulder and got up. "I've got things to do. I'll catch up with you later."

With his mouth full, Pete could only nod in response.

Hugh made his way to the kitchen and thanked Ellen for the breakfast.

"You're welcome, Hugh. Anytime."

"I'm going to ride a patrol around the perimeter of the valley and check on things. I might be out of range at times, but if you need me try the radio."

Ellen waved him off. "We'll be fine. Do what you need to do."

Hugh headed off to Jim's shop and got his gear together for the day. In a well-worn plastic baggie, he collected some deer jerky, a couple of fat carrots, and a handful of cherry tomatoes. That should tide him over until dinner. He collected his horse from Jim's pasture and saddled him, double-checked his gear to make certain he had everything he might need, then headed out.

He rode down the driveway and picked up the road through the valley, headed for the house where Lloyd had been staying. Randi had been keeping an eye on the place in Lloyd's absence. She and Charlie had both been staying there on occasion just to keep the place looking lived in. With the sheriff gone from the valley, having moved back to his place on the other side of the county, Mack Bird's home was the only consistently occupied dwelling between the Wimmers and Jim's farm.

Hugh stopped at Lloyd's place and took a look around. He saw nothing out of order so he took a shortcut through a back pasture and intersected the farm road from Jim's house to the river. It was humid, but a beautiful day. Shortly, he was passing the outpost where he'd nabbed Charlie last night, then he headed into the river.

His horse paused in the water, enjoying the swirl of the cold river around its legs. It lowered its head to drink and Hugh let it. His attention was on the superstore complex in the distance. The place had memories for nearly everyone in the valley. Jim had been taken prisoner there. Alice, Charlie's mother, had been killed there. Gary's family had become involved in a gun battle there. Hugh's memories were different.

He'd been living there when he and Jim had crossed paths for the first time in quite a few years. The cops who'd chosen to live there, a rogue group by most standards, had secured a trailer of radio equipment belonging to the county. They needed someone to operate it and that's where Hugh had come in. He'd been living at the superstore for several weeks, trying to find any news of the outside world, when some of the cops had taken Jim prisoner. Fortunately, Jim escaped and offered Hugh the opportunity to come join them. When the threat at the superstore was neutralized, Hugh took the radio equipment and moved to Jim's valley.

When his horse had drunk its fill, Hugh nudged it on across and it clambered up the bank. Hugh switched his rifle from his back to laying across the saddle in front of him. There was a round in the pipe and his hand was wrapped around the grip, thumb on the safety.

He steered his horse up the approach road and examined the scene as he moved by. It was all cars, chaos, and destruction. There was garbage everywhere. Some folks, likely residents of the empty stores, were selling goods beneath the canopy of the fuel pumps. There had been a market scene growing here until the farmer's market in town got going. There were fewer vendors and fewer customers than Hugh had seen here in the past.

The vendors watched him warily as he rode by them. Hugh offered a nod but it wasn't returned, which was fine with him. He wasn't there to make friends. He simply wanted to do some snooping and not get killed in the process. Once past the superstore he crossed the highway and took the southbound lane to the next exit. The stretch of road was empty except for a mangy coyote that boldly trotted across his path, a limp orange housecat in its mouth. Hugh descended the off-ramp into town and in twenty minutes was closing in on the farmer's market.

The place appeared even more bustling than last time. As he neared the crowd, he dismounted his horse and led it into the vast parking lot. There were vendors selling produce, eggs, and baked goods. Homemade cages held rabbits, chickens, and piglets. The smell of roasted meat hung in the smoky air.

Looking for the source, Hugh found a booth where a man and his daughter were selling strips of cooked meat on thin skewers. A hand-written sign listed prices for chicken, goat, raccoon, and groundhog kabobs. Squirt bottles at their table allowed you to apply a sauce to your treat before you left. One held homemade ketchup, another a jalapeno and honey concoction. They also offered jerky made from the same animals. Many of the people around Hugh would have turned their nose up at such dishes a year ago. Now, with the tantalizing aroma filling the air, he expected these folks would have no trouble selling out.

Another vendor sold hard-boiled eggs, the multi-colored bounty laid out on a towel like they were precious gems. Dozens of other sellers displayed a variety of merchandise at the post-apocalyptic flea market. There was clothing, batteries, and spices. One man had been buying up his neighbors' old medicines and was operating a pharmacy of sorts.

A young couple in their twenties sold marijuana and homemade pipes. You could also buy a pinch and smoke it there if you preferred, using their pipes. One man sold improvised weapons, offering several varieties of bludgeons, cudgels, and clubs. Hugh raised an eyebrow and headed in that direction, intrigued to see what the man had to offer.

Around him, transactions were being negotiated. Without a standard currency, every sale was an adventure. Offers were made, a little of this and a little of that. Terms were volleyed back and forth until a consensus was reached. Some transactions resulted in handshakes and smiles. Others disintegrated into threats, raised middle fingers, and curses when an agreement couldn't be reached.

Hugh led his horse through the crowd and stopped at the improvised weapons booth. A stocky man with a beard and long ponytail sat on a milk crate filing on a piece of steel. Behind him was a bicycle with a trailer for carrying children. The trailer had been repurposed to hold the inventory not out on display. The man wore homemade leather wristbands and a grubby top hat. He had rings on both hands and a variety of piercings. He seemed like one of those people who'd been waiting all his life for this moment and now he was relishing it.

He caught Hugh's eye and nodded a greeting. "Morning."

Hugh returned the gesture. "Just checking out your wares."

"Make them all myself," the man said, paying attention to Hugh's gear. "You appear to have your weapons game on-point, but a lot of folks don't. That's my typical customer. The guy who's late to the game and has to settle for what he can get."

Hugh extended a hand. "My name's Hugh. I'm a big fan of the homemade stuff. Always have been. What you got?"

He stopped filing and shook Hugh's hand. "I'm Ian. Good to meet you. I've got a forge and I make knives, but they take too long. I can't turn them out fast enough. Most folks are just looking for something cheap and stabby."

Hugh grinned. "Cheap and stabby. I like it."

"What's not to love about it, right? Icepick type weapons are one of my specialties. That whole stack of icepicks there is made out of welding rods I pounded the flux off of. I cut up wooden closet rods and stair balusters to make the handles. A little glue, a little sanding, and they're pretty comfortable in the hand. I sharpen them with a file and make the sheath out of a piece of rubber tubing. They're cheap and easy. I sell the hell out of them."

"Impressive. What's that?" Hugh pointed to a selection of longer items.

Ian smiled. "Not everything is for stabbing. Some things are for beating. I got a bunch of heavy nuts from a construction site. They go on the big bolts that hold the steel structure together. They just so happen to have approximately the same inside diameter as a closet rod. I cut off about two feet of closet rod and thread it into that heavy nut with a pipe wrench."

"Can I take a look?"

Ian gave his blessing so Hugh leaned over and picked up the club. He tapped it against his palm a few times, unable to control his grin. That heavy steel nut would crack a skull with a single blow. It was an impressive weapon but would suck against a gun or knife.

Hugh laid it back down. "That's vicious."

"Part of my home-defense line." He grinned. "For that bump in the night."

Hugh recognized some of the other items. There was a baseball bat with nails driven in the end. There were a couple of slingshots made from tree branches and surgical tubing. Then something caught Hugh's eye. "Knucks?"

He crouched down and tried on a set of brass knuckles, relishing the comfortable fit. He made a fist and they felt like they belonged on his hand.

Ian nodded. "I make those knuckles by hand, like the knives. Takes a while because there's a hell of a lot of drilling and filing involved in making a good set. I make them out of aluminum and brass that I cast myself. The two knuckle kind are cheaper. The ones that cover four fingers, like that set in your hand, are more expensive."

"How expensive?"

"Dunno. What you got on you?"

"How about 9mm rounds?"

"I'll take ten rounds for that big set of aluminum knucks you're holding."

"How about four?" Hugh countered.

Ian pondered, scratching his chin. "I can do four. I'll take it."

Hugh figured he would. Ammunition was in short supply for most folks. The people in the valley were sitting on a good supply thanks to their own preparedness, a delivery from Scott and the energy people they'd met last summer, and their battlefield pickups. Hugh pulled a spare mag from his battle belt and thumbed out four rounds. He replaced the mag on his belt and extended the four rounds to the seller, dropping them into his open palm.

While Hugh stashed the aluminum knuckles in his pocket, the seller tipped his hat. "Thank you and come again. Tell your friends. I've got new shit every week, depending on what I can scrounge up."

"I'll definitely do that." Before leaving Ian's booth, Hugh scanned the area. He crinkled his brow. "Someone told me there was a place here to corral your horse. I was hoping I could do that so I wouldn't have to lead him around the whole time. You know where that is?"

Ian gave a regretful shake of his head. "Rumor is that fucker got killed last night. Not surprised really. He was kind of an asshole."

"You know what happened?"

"I heard someone went to his house and shot him. Killed one of his sons too. Might have been a robbery or he might have run his mouth to the wrong guy."

Hugh nodded, the pieces falling into place. "Dangerous times. A man has to be careful."

He waved at Ian and wandered off. He was so lost in thought that he had no interest in any of the other booths. He mounted his horse and started home. He had a lot to think about.

## 43

 liver's House

SHARON WAS EXHAUSTED. Had she thought this through, she would have had the children come to the house earlier so they could help her put things away. As it was, Nathan brought each load from the camp to the back porch and unloaded it. Sharon immediately sent him back, determined to haul the loads in herself to save time.

Nathan made her promise to leave the big stuff for him, but that went totally against her nature. She didn't leave things for other people unless there was no other option. It required a lot of effort and ingenuity, but she got nearly everything. Unpacking and stowing it away in the house was an entirely different story. She would save that for when she had the children's help.

Several times Sharon emerged onto the pack porch only to feel like she was being watched. The hair stood up on the back of her neck and a creepy sensation settled over her. She scanned her surroundings but it would be difficult to spot a person in this setting.

There was a barn and several outbuildings surrounding the house, their dark recesses offering no shortage of hiding places. Despite the cattle and horses, much of the grass around the house and barn was high too. A person could be laying on their belly in that thicket and staring right at her. To her right and up a slight hill, the forest began and a person in plain sight would be difficult to pick out of that greenery.

She'd always been aware that being in a wheelchair put her at a disadvantage if a confrontation got physical. She understood she couldn't let that happen so she carried a gun when she traveled. At least she had back in her other life. She never traveled with one when coming to the camp because it seemed like the last place in the world she'd need one.

While that may have been true under the previous circumstances, it wasn't any longer. Now, the presence of the gun in the side pocket of her chair was natural and necessary. It was reassuring. She reached in to touch it, to confirm that it was there, and it provided her with a level of comfort. If there was someone out there, she could do nothing about it now. If they showed themselves, if they insisted on being unpleasant, she would "do unto others" and be unpleasant right back.

When she had everything she could budge off the back porch, she locked the kitchen door. It felt silly but she didn't want to take any chances. She didn't want to be somewhere else in the house and have someone slip in without announcing themselves.

She retrieved a plastic cup from the dish drainer and filled it from the faucet at the kitchen sink. Even the simple luxury of having water emerge from a faucet was a miracle in these days of deprivation. Maybe she should have taken Oliver up on his offer to move into the house earlier. This was so much nicer than the camp. It was too late to quibble over it now, but she knew part of it had been her stubbornness. She wanted to do it on her own. She wanted to survive the winter in the camp with those children, just to show she could do it. She understood now how selfish that had been.

Sharon tucked the glass between her thighs and headed for the front porch. She unbolted the door, swung it open, and moved out onto the porch. It was different from the camp porch. The view wasn't as expansive, but it was still nice. It was also covered, which would allow her to sit out there in the rain.

She lost herself in her thoughts, her mental list-making running rampant. There was so much to do to get ready for another winter. They needed to get the garden in, preserve what they could, and start rounding up firewood for winter. That made her think about the chimneys in this house. When were they last cleaned? With that high metal roof and its steep pitch, how could she ever check? There was no way she was sending one of the children up there and she wasn't about to try it herself. She wondered if she could enlist someone from the community to help with that.

As often happened, one thought ran into the next and she lost track of time. The next thing she knew, the golf cart was coming into sight followed by the children. She smiled, thrilled to see them. It was exactly what she needed after this draining day. Still, it was hard not to notice that they resembled a group of refugees straggling through the apocalypse. They were sweaty and bedraggled, their faces smudged with dust as they led the herd of goats on leashes. Some wore backpacks or walked with pillows tucked under their arms. They trudged along at a weary pace as if they'd been walking for days. If the novelty of bringing the goats along had lifted their spirits, the effect had long since worn off.

"Hey!" Sharon called to them, waving her arms.

It was just what the children needed. They perked up at her voice, some of them eagerly waving back to her, others breaking into a run. Sharon moved toward the porch rail and leaned forward. She folded her arms, resting them on the rails, and dropping her chin onto her forearms. This was the silver-lining behind the tragedy of losing Oliver. This would be their new home and they would be happy here. They would make it work.

The first to reach the porch carefully negotiated the high steps, one hand on the old wooden railing. The rest tied their goats off to the fence and climbed onto the shaded porch. Each hugged her in turn, then collapsed onto the floor as if they'd completed a marathon. They detailed their woes and ailments to her—exhaustion, blisters, cramps, bug bites, and sunburn. Some even told her they already missed camp and wanted to go home.

It wasn't lost on Sharon that they now considered camp to be their home, rather than whatever home they'd been part of before coming to camp. It was a statement to the adaptability of children. "This is our new home for now," she said. "It's a regular home, not a cabin or dining hall. We can do all the things we did at the camp, but we'll probably be more comfortable here. There are nice big rooms and comfortable furniture and running water."

"Will we have our own rooms?" Tara asked.

Sharon smiled at her. "There are not enough rooms for everyone to have their own. For now, until we get things settled, we're going to do a girl's room and a boy's room. Once we get things figured out, we'll spread out a little."

No one had any complaints about that. It was the way they were sleeping now and it was familiar to them.

Sharon spotted Nathan turning into the driveway. He'd be at the back porch shortly. She headed for the door and rallied the troops. "C'mon guys. We need to put the goats in the pen and unload the cart, then everyone can take a rest break. Okay?"

The kids who weren't leading goats followed Sharon through the unfamiliar house, taking in their surroundings. They were subdued, sensing the gravity of the situation, understanding in their own way what had happened to make this possible. In the kitchen, Sharon unlocked the back door and headed out onto the porch just as Nathan was setting the parking brake on the cart.

"That it?" Sharon asked. "Are you glad to be done?"

Nathan wiped his face with the tail of his shirt and shook his head. "We couldn't get it all on this load. Kay stayed back with the last of it. After we unload this, I'll go get the last load and she'll ride back with me."

Sharon nodded. "At least it's close. What's left?"

"Musical instruments. Everyone is exhausted but Kay thought the children would be happier if they had their instruments. We'll go ahead and get them tonight instead of waiting until tomorrow."

"That's very thoughtful," Sharon said. "I'm sure the children will appreciate having their stuff here with them. I can't tell you how proud I am. You've done an amazing job today."

She caught Nathan grinning at the compliment as he untangled the miles of rope holding everything onto the golf cart. Sharon looked around, searching for that sensation of being watched again, but things felt better now. She wasn't sure it was the presence of the children that made her feel more comfortable, or if whoever was watching her had gone. Pleased to no longer feel that she was being spied upon, Sharon failed to ask herself an important question.

If her watcher had left, where had they gone?

## 44

T*he Camp*

Kay was comfortable with being alone at the camp. She'd been attending since she was seven years old. She was twelve now and wanted to be a counselor there one day but you had to be fifteen before you could be considered. Even though she wasn't old enough to be a counselor yet, Sharon had let her come to her session a day early this year. She'd arrived on a day when the camp was empty and the staff were preparing for the next session. She'd gotten to help out with all of the things that went into preparing for a camp session.

She'd enjoyed the experience and hoped to do it again when she returned the following summer. What she hadn't expected was that she'd never get to go home from her session last summer. It was already the "following summer" and she still hadn't made it home yet. Becoming a camp counselor now seemed a very distant goal.

She tried not to think about why her parents hadn't picked her up. There was the underlying fear that something bad had happened to them, but she tried not to look at it that way. They lived in Colorado and maybe they simply couldn't make it out there to pick her up with no gas available. That had to be it. Most of the kids who'd been able to leave and head home were from the East Coast. That was a lot different than coming in from the Rockies.

As she'd watched the last of the stranded children leave for Oliver's house, waving at her before hurrying to catch up with Nathan, she noticed how different the camp felt without people. It still felt like a magical place. There was a special feeling that came from everything around her but she was uncertain if it came from her personal memories or instead from the energy that the place absorbed from those who came here.

Sensing that she'd become depressed if she dwelt too hard upon the empty camp, she put herself to work. All of the instruments were stored in a special section of the dining hall. This was where some of the jam sessions took place, though they certainly weren't limited to the dining hall. They had a nice stage in the woods, an informal amphitheater, and several other places where music happened.

Kay grabbed a big old suitcase that contained spare strings, picks, and straps. She carried it out onto the broad front porch, down the steps, and placed it in the grass. She went back inside and grabbed two banjos in hard cases. She hauled those out and placed them beside the suitcase of strings. Over several more trips she ferried out the last of the instruments. It was a big pile, but she thought they could tie it onto the golf cart.

Her work done, Kay climbed back onto the porch and reclined on a wooden bench. Her back ached and her arms felt limp as noodles. She didn't believe she'd ever worked as hard in her life as she'd worked today. All the carrying and packing. Helping children carry and pack. It had been a lot and she was ready for a break.

She closed her eyes against the sun and draped a forearm across her forehead. She was enjoying the feeling of the sun on her skin when the sound of shattering glass caused her to bolt upright. For a moment, she wondered if something had fallen in the kitchen or dining hall. A bottle? A glass bowl?

She stood and peered through the window screen. The dining hall was empty and she didn't see anything out of place. She angled her head, looking toward the pass-through into the kitchen. A figure stepped into view and stood there for a moment, a look of disgust on her face. Kay recognized her immediately as the woman who'd disrupted Oliver's funeral.

Kay ducked, flattening herself against the porch wall. Terror constricted her chest.

"Any of this shit we can use?" a voice asked. It was male. Probably the son she'd had with her yesterday.

"I don't see any food," the woman said. "This is all cooking stuff. Pots, pans, and spoons. Plastic cups and cafeteria trays. Doesn't do us any damn good at all."

Kay's mind raced. They were there to rob the camp. Had they been waiting out there for everyone to leave? They must think the camp was empty. They needed to continue thinking that. She had no idea what they'd do to her if they caught her.

A door clattered shut inside. Kay recognized it as the swinging door between the kitchen and the dining hall. They could show up outside at any moment. On her hands and knees, she scrambled across the weathered porch boards. She couldn't take the steps. Getting to them would require passing by a full-length screen door that would expose her to anyone inside the dining hall. Instead, she crawled toward the opposite end, rolling beneath the rail and nimbly dropping the six feet to the ground. With no steps on that end of the porch, it was a shortcut all the kids used.

She huddled beneath the high porch, trying to figure out her next move. Should she disappear into the woods? The tall grass? Should she head for the farm road and run to Oliver's house as fast as she could? Then she spotted the pile of instruments sitting in the grass and was hit with a wave of indecision. She couldn't leave those instruments behind to these people. The music was all they had to keep them going over the long, dark winter. It was what kept them occupied so they didn't miss their families every waking moment. Above all, it was the reason they were here in the first place and they couldn't lose that. Those instruments tied them to this place and each other.

She listened carefully. She heard steps moving around the dining hall and kitchen but they were still inside. She crouched and ran the length of the porch, coming out from underneath it near the steps. Without even a look back, she bolted for the stack of instruments. She swooped up two cases and ran for the high weeds near the garden, a distance of nearly seventy yards. She dropped the cases there and ran back for the rest of them.

It took several trips. Her heart was pounding from fear and the exertion of lugging the heavy cases. She told herself that if she was spotted she'd drop the cases and run for the woods. She'd have a head start and there was no way they'd catch her, but somehow she managed to go undiscovered. The intruders must have been too busy scouring the building for things to steal.

When she had the last of the cases hidden in the weeds, Kay took cover behind the garden shed and watched. Through the open windows she heard more crashing, the sound of things being over-turned and broken. Kay hated these people for trashing her camp but she knew it could be cleaned up. With a few hours of cleaning it would be good as new. She'd already gotten all the important stuff out. This would be okay.

As her breathing started to calm, she kept repeating that message to herself. *This will be okay. This will all be okay.*

Then, just as she began to believe it, a massive *whoompf* filled the air. Two of the kitchen windows blew out from the pressure. There was a cry from the rear of the dining hall and two figures, Kimberly and her son, came running around the corner, coughing and rubbing their eyes. Whatever they'd done, they'd not allowed themselves sufficient time to escape.

"We gonna burn the rest of it?" the boy gasped.

Kimberly was shaking her head and coughing, still unable to speak. Spittle strung from her mouth to the ground.

"Momma, you okay?"

She straightened and choked out, "We better go. They'll see the smoke."

The boy took her by the arm and led her off into the woods. Kay's eyes flickered between the fleeing figures and the burning building. Flames were now licking at the windows. The exposed framing and wooden interior was a tinderbox, the crackling fire quickly engulfing the interior.

When she lost sight of the arsonists, Kay ran for the garden hose and dragged it toward the dining hall. It was gravity-fed from a spring near the road. When she squeezed the sprayer nozzle, a pencil-thin stream arced for about ten feet before hitting the ground. It was enough to water a plant but would be pointless against a structure fire. Kay threw the hose to the ground in frustration and began crying.

Arms wrapped around her from behind. Kay didn't even scream. Every combative instinct in her body came to life and she was instantly fighting, scratching, and clawing. She tried to break away but the arms only held her tighter.

"Kay!" a voice said. "Kay, it's me!"

Then she recognized the voice. It was Nathan. She quit fighting but her crying intensified. "You have to help me! We've got to put it out!"

"We have to get back," he said. "It's not safe. What happened?"

"We have to put it out!"

"Kay, we can't put it out. The fire's too big. It's too late." He backed away, leading the sobbing Kay by the wrist.

"It was those people," she sobbed.

"What people?"

As she said it, she was hit with a wave of paranoia. They could still be out there in the woods watching her. They could be coming for her and Nathan. "It was those people that came to Oliver's funeral. His niece and her son."

Nathan quit pulling on her wrist and turned to face her. "They did this? They started the fire?"

Kay bobbed her head. "I was on the front porch and I heard them break a window. I hid and watched them. There was the boom and then everything was on fire."

"How long ago did this happen?"

Kay swiped at the tears on her face. Her eyes were stinging from the smoke. "Just a few minutes. They just left. They couldn't have gotten far."

Nathan scanned the woods. "They could still be out there. They could be watching us. We need to go!"

She yanked away from him. "Bring the cart to the garden. I need to load the instruments."

Nathan looked confused. "What are they doing at the garden?"

Kay looked at him as if the answer was obvious. "I hid them. I wasn't going to let them destroy the instruments."

Nathan shook his head as if he were having difficulty processing this.

She pointed toward the horse-drawn cart. "Go! Get it so we can get out of here."

Nathan sprinted for the cart, tied to the fence a good distance from the fire. He was back in less than a minute and they stacked all of the instrument cases in the cart's cargo rack. While they secured the load, Nathan continued to shake his head. "I can't believe you risked your life for these instruments."

Kay didn't answer, focusing on tying knots. Perhaps she couldn't believe it either.

**45**

—————

*liver's House*

THE EXHAUSTED CREW at Oliver's house was trying to put together a simple meal. It wasn't easy because the children were distracted by their new surroundings and couldn't focus. Sharon had to sit them down as soon as they came in the house and establish some ground rules.

"For now, don't open any closed doors. Don't touch any of Oliver's personal items. You can look but don't touch. You can go outside on the porches, but I don't want you running around the yards or exploring any of the outbuildings until I have a chance to make sure they're safe. Everyone understand?"

There were scattered hesitant agreements. Sharon knew she was taking away all of the things they most wanted to do. They wanted to explore buildings and peer behind closed doors. For now, they'd just have to wait.

"Stay together," Sharon added. "You can break into groups but no one goes anywhere alone. Okay?"

More reluctant nods.

"I'm going to try to put together dinner. Anyone want to help?"

For a change, not a single hand went up. Everyone was more interested in exploring their surroundings than assisting her. Sharon wasn't surprised.

"Okay then. Dinner may be something simple if I'm doing it myself. We'll probably just have vegetables, hard boiled eggs, and leftover flatbread."

When that menu didn't produce any volunteers or complaints, Sharon dismissed them and they scurried away like rowdy kittens. This was a meal that wouldn't require any cooking, only some slicing and prep work. After the long day, that was about all she had in her.

The laughs, shouts, and shrieks of the children made it easy for Sharon to forget their circumstances. They were kids exploring and having fun. Even the kids themselves were lost in play, adventuring into the only new place they'd experienced in a year.

Sharon was just laying out the dinner ingredients when Stevie wandered in, a concerned look on his face.

"What is it?" she asked, immediately thinking that he or one of the other children had broken something.

"Something is on fire."

Panic raced through Sharon. "Here in the house?"

"No, outside."

"Where?"

Stevie walked off, beckoning Sharon to follow him. He headed for the front porch, holding the screen door open for her to follow him. He walked to the rail and pointed off toward a rising column of black smoke in the distance. Sharon knew exactly where that smoke came from. It had to be coming from the camp.

Her mind raced in a thousand different directions. Should she harness her pony and hurry back to the camp? No, that would be too slow. Without Nathan's help, she'd be thirty minutes harnessing the horse and at least that long again getting back to the camp. If she tried to hurry, she'd end up turning over and dumping out, which wouldn't help anyone.

Knowing there were people who didn't want her in this house, it also crossed her mind that it could be a trap. She couldn't run off blindly and leave the children behind. They'd be unprotected if someone tried to get in. She couldn't go investigate the fire no matter how badly she wanted to. It was as simple as that.

As much as she hated asking for help, she saw no choice but to enlist the help of a neighbor. She could possibly get to Kendall's house without the assistance of her horse, though she knew there was no way she'd make it back up this driveway with just her muscles. It was too steep. Making the trip to Kendall's would be at least a thirty-minute effort, there and back. Thirty minutes that the children would be alone and unprotected. She was going to have to do something she never imagined she would.

"Stevie, I need you to be a big boy and do something very brave. Can you do that?"

Stevie beamed with pride. "You bet!"

"Do you remember Mr. Kendall, the neighbor who came to Mr. Oliver's funeral?"

"Yeah, he lives that way," Stevie said, pointing down the farm road, away from camp.

"That's right. He does. He lives in the house right next to us. Can you run really fast?"

"I'm the fastest runner at the camp. Even faster than Nathan."

"You can run there in just a few minutes. Much faster than I can get there. I need you to go tell Mr. Kendall that there's a fire at the camp and I was hoping he could ride up there on his horse and check it out. Tell him Nathan and Kay are still up there. Can you do that?"

Stevie nodded eagerly.

"Then go!"

Stevie bolted away from her like he'd been shot from a launcher. His feet pounded down the steps and he leapt when he was halfway to the bottom, hitting the ground running. She watched him go, fighting the instinct to shout warnings that he be careful. They'd go unheeded. He was only concerned with speed now and maybe that was the way it needed to be.

Sharon went back into the house and called to the children. "I need everyone in the living room!"

It took a few minutes for everyone to straggle in. They were at the far corners of the boundaries she'd set for them and everyone immediately wanted to share stories of what they'd found. Sharon held a hand up.

"I need everyone to listen for a moment. We're going to lock all the doors except for the front door and I need you to all go in the living room for now. If you want games or books, you can go get them but I need everyone in here where I can see them."

Tara, always the most serious of the children, crinkled her tiny forehead. "What's wrong, Miss Sharon?"

Sharon took a deep breath, trying to calm herself. "There's smoke coming from the direction of the camp. I sent Stevie to get help. I just need all of you to stay close until everyone gets back here."

"But what about Kay and Nathan?" Tara asked.

"I don't know anything about them yet, but Mr. Kendall is going to go check on them for us."

"Are they hurt?" Tara persisted.

Sharon sucked in a breath but held her tongue. If there was ever a moment she felt like snapping at the children, this was it. She was terrified for Nathan and Kay, terrified for Stevie, and she had no answers for all the expectant faces looking at her.

"We don't know anything yet. I need to you do what I asked, though. Find something to keep you busy. Books, drawing, games, whatever. Just something you can do in this room until we know it's safe. I'll give you three minutes to get what you need, then I want you back here. Go!"

The children rushed off in all directions, looking for their backpacks of personal items or the packed boxes that held their games. They rushed back to the living room, dumping them on the floor, and then scurrying off for more like it was a treasure hunt.

While they gathered their things, Sharon returned to the porch.

She turned her body so that the children couldn't see her and removed the gun from the pouch hanging off her chair. She confirmed that the cylinder was completely loaded, then tucked it out of sight. In the living room, the children were settling in now, talking amongst themselves as they figured out who was doing what.

The sound of hooves on gravel drew Sharon's attention to the road. They were coming too fast to be Nathan with the cart. Kendall galloped into sight, a shotgun in his hand, and Stevie's small body on the saddle in front of him. Kendall stopped at the road and lowered Stevie to the ground. Noticing Sharon on the porch, Kendall gave her a hasty wave and kicked his horse into a gallop.

Stevie ran to the porch and scrambled back up the steps, his breath rapid and his eyes flickering with a satisfied excitement. "I did it! I got Mr. Kendall!"

Sharon pulled him into a tight hug. "You did. You were such a big boy. I'm very proud of you."

## 46

B *land County*

IT HAD BEEN a long day in the saddle. Jim and Lloyd were both tired and getting short-tempered. Jokes were no longer funny. They simply wanted to get where they were going and get off their horses. Lloyd had written a half-dozen more songs about Jim, each of them worse than the one before it. They all exaggerated his exploits and inflated his body count with one goal in mind — pissing Jim off.

"You know what a *narcocorrido* is?" Jim asked, interrupting Lloyd's latest improvisation.

Lloyd quit his strumming and muffled the strings with a hand. "Nope, never heard of it."

"It's a form of music. A Mexican ballad. They're extremely popular. The lyrics are all about the exploits and adventures of drug smugglers and cartel members. Who they killed and how they killed them. That kind of thing."

Lloyd smiled as awareness dawned on him. "Oh, kind of like I'm doing for you."

"Yeah, exactly. Sometimes the *narcotrafficante*, the smuggler, might not like the way he's portrayed in a song. Maybe he's embarrassed about some detail. Maybe he doesn't feel like it was respectful or did him justice. You know what happens then?"

"No."

"The balladeer ends up dying a gruesome death. You see, writing the *narcocorrido* is not without risk. Keep that in mind while you keep writing those bullshit songs about me."

Lloyd scowled and slung his banjo around to his back. They didn't talk for some time, other than discussing routes, landmarks, and directions. Jim would have been fine with camping for the night somewhere along the Appalachian Trail, which they'd traveled for about half the day. He suggested it repeatedly, pointing out nice camping spots along the way.

Lloyd kept insisting that they were close to the camp and should keep going. Jim only continued on because he didn't want to have to listen to Lloyd complaining all night about how close they were. It was too late now though. They were off the AT and following a paved road through a wide river valley with heavily forested slopes to either side. The land was fertile and some of the residents were taking advantage of it, their farms bristling with crops. Other farms sat idle, overgrown with weeds, their fields unplanted for reasons Jim cared not to speculate on. Surely death, misery, and suffering were at the root.

"It's starting to look like home," Jim said, grinning as he pointed at a column of smoke rising in the distance.

Lloyd studied the smoke with a grim expression on his face. "Don't get so excited, Rambo. That's where we're headed."

"Maybe not. Could be something else."

"Not much out there," Lloyd said. "There's a few houses along this main road but not in that direction. There's only the camp."

"So we're headed toward that smoke?"

"Affirmative."

Jim clucked at his horse and nudged it into a trot. "Best get moving then. Something's going on."

Lloyd sat there for a moment, shaking his head in disgust before kicking his horse into gear. He fell in alongside Jim. "I don't like the way you get so excited when you smell trouble."

"That smoke up ahead doesn't have to mean trouble. Might just be someone burning brush or something."

"You don't believe that any more than I do," Lloyd griped. "If you did, you wouldn't have speeded up."

Jim ignored that comment. "How far do you think it is from here?"

"Eh, not far."

They rode through a four-way rural intersection in the middle of nowhere. An abandoned car sat in one lane, pulled up to a stop sign like it had sat there for a year waiting for traffic to clear. They circled around it and turned right. Passing the car, they peered through the grimy windows, almost surprised that no skeleton sat patiently in the driver's seat, clutching the wheel in its bony fingers.

"You see that stop sign?" Lloyd asked.

"I saw the sign but didn't pay any attention to it."

"It was marked with that same double-M mark, like the one carved into that tree on the mountain."

"I meant to ask Orbin about that but I forgot."

Lloyd pointed ahead, to a gravel road branching off the main road. "We turn at the next right. There's two or three houses along the way before you get to Oliver's place. Once you pass his house it's another mile up a rough farm road to reach the camp."

"That's isolated."

Lloyd smiled. "That's the beauty of it, my friend."

Jim swung his rifle off his shoulder and hung it across the front of his body. The paved road turned to gravel immediately after they swung onto the farm road. They trotted past a small house with chalky aluminum siding and green metal awnings over each window. A cast-iron eagle, claws outstretched, hung over the garage door. A short distance further, they passed a big farmhouse. A sturdy country-woman stood in the yard, glaring at them with her hands on her hips. She looked both startled and angry at the appearance of the riders, as if she might attack them had she been given more notice.

Jim paid her no mind once he saw that she didn't have a weapon. He was more interested in the source of the smoke. Lloyd studied her, trying to recall if he'd met her in the years he'd been associated with the camp. They rode past a split tree, a large limb having broken off so recently that its leaves were still green, just beginning to wilt. A thick canopy of trees made a tunnel of the road, blocking the sky and preventing them from seeing the column of smoke.

They could smell it though, the acrid odor hanging in the valley on the hot, windless afternoon. Within the smoke they could distinguish the various odors that made up a burning building—insulation from wiring, shingles, and PVC plumbing pipes. This was not a brushfire. It was a structure fire. Jim had suspected that from the moment he saw the smoke.

"It's not much farther," Lloyd said.

They pushed through a long section of tunneled road, the angular evening light creating striated shadows on the dirt road ahead of them. It would be beautiful, almost hypnotic, under better circumstances. Rusty fences ran along both sides of the road, stretched between leaning posts of locust and split oak. Ahead, a circle of brilliant sunlight revealed the end of the tree-lined tunnel. It was a portal into a world lush and verdant.

The transition into the light was so harsh as to be disorienting. Jim squinted against the light, nearly blinded. As his eyes adjusted, he found himself staring at a group of people gathered in the road ahead of them. An old man stood alongside a saddled horse, a shotgun aimed directly at Jim. There was a horse-drawn golf cart with two kids standing beside it, one of them sobbing hysterically. The child was hugging a woman in a wheelchair and that woman had a revolver aimed in Jim's direction. To the left of the road, standing in the high grass of an unkempt yard, an assortment of wide-eyed children stared at the riders with a mixture of fascination and fear.

Jim reined his horse and it came to a stop like a toy winding down. He kept his hands on the reins, afraid to make any sudden moves. He didn't know any of these people and they didn't know him.

As usual, Lloyd was behind. He came barreling up behind Jim, then tugged at the reins of his horse. He took a glance at the guy with the shotgun, then turned his attention to the woman in the wheelchair. "Sharon!"

"Don't either of you fellers move a muscle," the man with the shotgun announced. He had the gun aimed between Jim and Lloyd. At that distance, he might hit both riders with a single blast from the scattergun.

Sharon released the tearful girl from her arms and studied the riders. "Lloyd?"

An uneasy smile crossed Lloyd's face. "What the hell are you still doing here at camp? Why are these kids still here?"

"What are *you* doing here?"

"It's a long, long story," Lloyd replied.

Sharon agreed. "Same here."

"You know these people?" Kendall asked.

Sharon nodded. "You can lower the gun. I know one of them. That's Lloyd. He was a friend of Oliver's who taught here at the camp every summer. Used to play the square dances."

Kendall squinted at Lloyd for a moment. "I thought you looked a tad familiar." He lowered the shotgun.

"I thought the same thing." Lloyd pointed at Jim. "This here is my buddy Jim. He's part of the reason we're here."

"I'm assuming you all know something is on fire, right?" Jim asked.

There were nods around the group.

"Those young'uns were just up there," Kendall offered. "They're lucky they weren't hurt."

Lloyd slid from his horse and handed the reins over to Jim. He approached Sharon and wrapped her up in a big hug. "I came to check in on Oliver. I never expected you or any of the kids would be here."

Sharon's face grew taut. "Oliver passed away a few days ago from a stroke. As for me and the kids, not all the parents were able to pick their children up before the fuel ran out. I couldn't leave the children behind so I stayed. Now none of us can leave."

"How have you fared?" Jim asked.

"Pretty well until recently," Sharon admitted. "Since camp ended early, we had enough leftover bulk food to carry us through the winter. Oliver helped too. He was always coming up with meat or some canning for us."

"Wasn't it cold?" Lloyd asked.

"The dining hall has a wood stove because the hunting clubs use it sometimes. We all moved in there for the winter and we got by. Had a lot of time to play games and practice."

"I practiced a lot, Mr. Lloyd," Tara said.

Lloyd smiled at the girl. "That's good, honey. Maybe I can hear you play later."

"After Oliver passed, his niece came up here and made a stink," Sharon said. "She said she was entitled to this place and wanted us out of here."

"There's always been bad blood there," Kendall added. "Her side of the family felt like they were slighted. Goes back generations."

"Oliver always told me he was leaving this farm to the camp, to help keep it running," Lloyd said.

Sharon was bobbing her head in agreement. "He did. I saw the will. I had to sign papers at a lawyer's office. I told his niece that but she didn't care."

"Is there a connection between what you're telling us and that fire there?" Jim asked, pointing toward the distant smoke.

"We were just getting the story on that from these two," Sharon said. "We're moving into Oliver's house now that he's gone and Nathan here has been hauling loads all day. He was going back to the camp to pick up Kay and the last load of the day when he spotted the smoke."

"It was those people," Kay said, wiping at her eyes. "I saw them. They were breaking stuff and then they set a fire in the kitchen."

"I found her trying to put out the fire," Nathan said. "It was too far gone though. A fire truck couldn't have saved it at that point."

Kendall nodded in acknowledgment. "Old building. Dry as kindling."

Kay wiped her eyes. "They used something to make the fire because I heard it catch. They nearly blew themselves up. They were coughing when they came out."

"Too bad they didn't blow up," Jim said. "That would have solved your problem for you."

Lloyd, Sharon, and Kendall stared at Jim. They understood the question implied by his statement. Since the fire hadn't solved their problem, what were they going to do about it?

"This would be a topic best discussed in private," Sharon said. "Maybe we should all go inside now. I still need to feed the children."

"I'll put the golf cart away and turn the horse out," Nathan offered.

"I'll give you a hand with that, son," Kendall said.

Jim asked, "Got a place I can keep these horses tonight?"

"Just follow along," said Kendall. "We'll take care of you."

**47**

J*im's Valley*



"HUGH SAYS he caught you coming from town last night?"

Pete and Charlie were on garden duty with Randi, picking some carrots, onions, and more tomatoes. It was the first opportunity for Pete to interrogate his friend over his late-night activities. Pete could tell his buddy was dragging. Charlie wasn't saying a lot and he was sluggish. Randi noticed it too, though she dealt with it in a more aggressive manner than Pete did. She zinged clods of dirt in Charlie's direction when she felt he wasn't pulling his weight.

When Randi was done with them, they told her they needed to check their fishing lines.

"Might as well. You're worthless in a garden anyway. More trouble than you're worth." Of course she was grinning. She enjoyed working with them because they laughed at her jokes.

It wasn't until they were walking away from the garden that Pete could start trying to ply answers from Charlie.

"Guess you've been talking to Hugh," Charlie said. "He's the only one who knows."

"Yeah, he caught me at breakfast this morning. I told him I didn't know anything about it, but I'd ask you when I saw you. So what were you up to?"

"I'm too tired to talk about it."

"Bullshit," Pete said. It was one of his new favorite words, picked up from Randi, and he only felt comfortable using it freely in the presence of a few trusted folks.

"It's not bullshit," Charlie said. "I was up half the night."

"What I want to know is *why*? There some reason you can't tell me?"

"Maybe it's none of your business."

Pete laughed. "Dude, everything that happens to us here is everyone's business. There hasn't been any privacy at all since we started living like cavemen. It's like you pestering me about what was bothering me after we came back from the market yesterday."

"Doesn't that piss you off sometimes? All this closeness? People in your business?"

Pete nodded. "Definitely, but I don't know what we're supposed to do about it. That's just the way it is right now. Little things that used to be private now affect everybody. It may be that way for a long time."

They walked a weedy cattle trail along the river, headed for a wooded section that always held more fish. The pools were deeper and the water cooler. With every flood, stocked rainbow trout fled public fishing areas to come upstream. They settled in the deep pools where there was less fishing pressure. Those were the fish the two had been targeting with their branch lines.

"So you're seriously not going to tell me?" Pete continued.

Charlie stopped in his tracks and turned around to face Pete. "I killed him. Now you know. Happy?"

Pete frowned. "Killed who?"

"That Willie guy. The one who was running his mouth at the farmer's market."

Pete laughed. "Yeah, right."

Charlie didn't laugh. He was staring him in the eye, stone-cold serious. "I'm telling you the truth."

Pete didn't know what to say. "What? Why?"

"Because he threatened you and that threatens all of us. We can't let assholes treat us like that. Your dad wouldn't allow it. He didn't put up with shit from anybody. Just because he's gone doesn't mean we have to start taking it either. I'm not going to. If someone threatens us, I threaten back. That's how it's going to work."

"You didn't exactly *threaten*, Charlie. You say you killed him."

Charlie nodded. He was sweating from exhaustion, his tanned face unusually pale. He looked around for a place to sit, finding a downed sycamore that extended out into the river. "I did kill him."

Pete followed Charlie to the log, taking a seat by his friend. "How? How did you do it?"

"You said something about him living above the store so I went there. I banged on the apartment door upstairs and he came out. I shot him."

"You killed him?"

"I'm pretty sure he's dead. I got him in the neck and there was blood everywhere. Then I had to kill one of his sons too. He got a look at me and I was afraid he recognized me from the market."

"Duane?"

"That's the one. You said you went to school with him."

Pete looked off toward the river. "That's him. You killed Duane. You killed a kid I went to high school with." Pete said it as if he couldn't believe the words coming out of his mouth.

Charlie got offended, feeling that Pete's tone was accusatory. "Look man, you killed people too. It's not like this is a couple of years ago and we're some fucked-up teenage psychos. This is what you have to do now. How many folks have our people killed? I couldn't even begin to count them."

"Dude, I'm not saying you did anything wrong. It's just a lot to take in. We've all killed people in self-defense and in fights. I'm just having a hard time picturing you going into town like an assassin and killing Willie."

Charlie raised his voice. "He needed to be killed. Maybe if the people in town were more scared of the people in this valley, my mom wouldn't be dead and your dad would be home instead of hiding in the mountains."

"My dad isn't hiding," Pete said. "He's worried that he may get one of us hurt."

"Which is exactly why I killed Willie. And it's exactly why I'll kill anyone else who threatens us. I'm not going to end up dead like the rest of my family. I'm not going to be run out of my home again."

The good-natured Pete was silent as he struggled with this. He'd killed people too. He'd been forced to. It had bothered him the first time, but not as much as it bothered his parents. They struggled with the fact that their son had been forced to kill someone. Pete wasn't sure if he'd do what Charlie did. If he could seek someone out like that and put a bullet in them. He'd have to hate them a lot more than he hated anyone right now.

"Are you going to tell?" Charlie asked.

"Tell who?"

"I don't know," said Charlie. "Your mom? Hugh? Randi?"

"No way, man. The stuff we talk about stays between us."

"Even if Hugh comes back and asks again?"

Pete hesitated. "You could talk to Hugh about this."

"I don't think so. He'll tell your dad. Those two are tight. They'll probably tell Randi and then everyone will know. They'll start treating me differently."

Pete thought about that. It was probably true. He'd heard his dad say as much, feeling like people looked at him differently because of the things he did. "I won't say anything, Charlie. If Hugh asks me if we talked, I'll tell him that he needs to come talk to you. Then it's up to you what you tell him."

Charlie got to his feet. "Good enough. Now let's get this done. I'm exhausted."

**48**

———————

 *liver's House*

LLOYD ENJOYED HAVING a new audience and he tried to distract the children from the upsetting events of the day. He'd taught many of them the previous summer and they bubbled at the appearance of a familiar face, just as excited by his arrival as he was. Lloyd loved teaching music to children. Jim pointed out that it was probably because they were at the same level of maturity.

The sun had retreated below the horizon and the light was fading quickly. The late summer heat barely relented at night, leaving a blanket of oppressive humidity that made it difficult to sit inside. After dinner they built a campfire, hoping it would dispel some of the gloom. Sharon was apprehensive about sitting outside, concerned that Kimberly and her son might be lurking out there in the darkness.

"Surely they won't try anything with us around," Lloyd said.

Jim agreed. "They might be afraid to come back around after setting that fire. At least for today."

The children, sheltered from the world for the past year, were unused to the presence of firearms. Sharon took a moment and explained to them that most folks outside of their camp had to carry guns for their safety these days. With Sharon's blessing, Jim explained that they could ask questions about them but they should never touch them without permission.

"If you don't mind, I need to talk with Mr. Jim and Mr. Lloyd a minute," Sharon told the children. "You can play your instruments or play in the yard. Just don't leave the yard or go anywhere without asking. If you need to go to the restroom, you have to take a buddy."

The children groaned at this. They wanted to stay and listen to what the new people had to say.

"If you guys give us a few minutes, I'll play a few songs with you," Lloyd promised. "I might even know a few stories I can tell you."

There was a round of cheers.

"That would be amazing," Sharon said. "Oliver always told them stories and I suck at it."

At the promise of music and stories, the children went about occupying themselves while the adults spoke.

"I can't believe Oliver is dead," Lloyd said when they had some privacy. "I used to run into him at music festivals thirty years ago when I first started playing. That's how come I ended up playing here at his camp. We got to be friends."

"It was a stroke," Sharon said. "He lived for a couple of hours afterward but he was paralyzed and had trouble swallowing. I'm glad he went quickly instead of lying there starving to death. I couldn't bear to watch that."

"Did you all give him a service?" Jim asked, taking a sip from a water bottle he'd refilled inside the house. He felt like he was a quart low.

"The neighbors really stepped up to help. One of them even had this fancy horse-drawn hearse. They moved his body to the camp for us and we buried him at the Fairy Circle."

"He'd like that," Lloyd said with a sad smile.

"The children picked the spot. They played some songs for him. It was a good service until his niece, Kimberly, and her son showed up. They ruined everything."

"Will the neighbors be any help in dealing with her?" Jim asked.

Sharon shrugged. "I don't know them very well. Oliver kept us sheltered, like the camp was his secret. Until Oliver died, I hadn't even met most of them. They stepped up to help though. Kendall especially."

"There's a reason for that and you may not be aware of it," Lloyd said. "Oliver told me that when he first opened this camp, not everyone was excited about the idea. In the seventies, a lot of the folks playing this kind of music were what you might call hippies. Bunch of long-haired folks that dressed differently from everyone else around here. Because of that, he did his best to keep the camp insulated from the community. Because of Manson and drugs, hippies had a bad reputation."

"People don't seem to hold those resentments anymore," Sharon said. "My interactions with the community were always positive."

Lloyd nodded. "That's because of Oliver's efforts. He always shopped locally for the camp's food, fuel, and building materials, which built some goodwill. For a while he even had an open house and the community could come in for a concert and a barbecue."

Sharon smiled and pointed at Lloyd. "I remember those. They did them when I first started here but then they quit. There was a problem with people bringing in alcohol and Oliver didn't want that around the children."

"Hellooooo," a voice called from the darkness.

It startled Sharon until she recognized Kendall and Freda stepping into the circle of firelight. She waved a hand at them. "C'mon over!"

"Got room for two more?" Freda asked.

Sharon pointed toward a couple of lawn chairs leaning against the porch. "Sure, pull up a chair."

Freda took a seat beside Sharon and laid a concerned hand on her forearm. "I'm sorry about what happened. That's just awful. That must have terrified those poor babies."

"Yes, we're all a little shook up."

"I don't know Kimberly well, but her people have always been hotheaded. They stay in trouble with the law. They feud with people. Back when we had a newspaper, I used to see her son's booking photo in there all the time. Always getting hauled in for drugs or stealing."

"Sounds like a bad enemy to have." Jim shook his head. "Even when there is a law, people like that don't have any respect for it. At times like this, when there is no law, those people think they can do whatever they want. We've had a lot of trouble with them."

"How did you handle it?" Kendall asked, giving Jim a serious look.

Jim thought he was joking at first. He figured the answer should have been obvious.

"He killed them," Lloyd answered after a long pause. "But I guess all of us helped to some extent."

Freda covered her mouth with her hand. "Killed?"

"When this whole mess happened I was away from home, in Richmond," said Jim. "I had to walk home with some friends. I ran into trouble the whole way home. When I got there it wasn't any better. We've run into a lot of violence. People who were bad before have become downright scary without the threat of jail hanging over them."

Lloyd held a hand up. "And before you go thinking we're a couple of outlaws, it's not just us. I give Jim a lot of crap for the way he solves problems, but the truth is that it's this way everywhere. People are stealing and murdering people every day. If you don't fight back, you don't stand a chance. You'll get robbed or killed."

"I'm pleased to say that we've been sheltered from all that," Kendall said. "I've heard stories but I figured they were exaggerated."

Jim shook his head regretfully. "No one's exaggerating. If anything, they're minimizing it because no one wants to admit how bad it's really gotten. No one wants to talk about the horrors they've seen or the things they've had to do."

Freda leaned forward and spoke in a low voice, trying to keep the children from hearing. "Surely you aren't suggesting that we might have to deal with Kimberly in some violent fashion?"

"Probably the only way," Jim said. He looked at Lloyd for support but Lloyd gave no indication of whether he stood by this conclusion or not.

Kendall waved them off. "It ain't gonna come to that."

"Surely not," Freda piped up.

"It's not my fight." Jim glanced around at them. "I'm just offering my opinion based on what I've seen in other places, on what I've seen of human nature out there."

"I ain't exactly a fan of Kimberly and that boy of hers but I can't see myself killing them," Kendall said.

"I could," Sharon said, drawing all eyes to her face. It glowed in the firelight, the flames reflected in her eyes.

Freda looked shocked. "You could really kill her?"

"If she presented a threat to me or one of these children."

Freda conceded the point. "I reckon I could in *that* case but not in cold blood."

"Like I said, it's not my fight," Jim repeated. "But these issues don't go away. You can fight her now or fight her later."

"We should try talking to her first," Kendall said. "Maybe I'll get some folks to go with me. We'll explain the situation to her and point out that we're simply not going to allow this to continue."

"We already tried talking to her." Sharon sighed. "We tried at Oliver's service and she still came back to burn down the dining hall." Simply making that statement hit her like a gut punch. She still couldn't believe it was gone. She'd have to go up there and take a look tomorrow. Imagining the loss of that building, where she'd had so many good experiences, was devastating.

"So are you good with us talking to her?" Kendall asked Sharon.

"Fine. But warn her that she isn't welcome here. If she comes back, it won't end well for her, I can promise you that."

"Hey, I got a question for you," Lloyd said, twisting in his chair to face Kendall and Freda. "Several times on our trip over we saw this symbol carved into trees and written on road signs. It was two of the letter M with the legs of each letter kind of crossed over each other. What is it? That some kind of gang or something?"

Freda's eyes brightened with excitement. She enjoyed having the scoop on a juicy topic. "Oh, honey, that's not from a gang. That's the mark of the Mad Mick."

Jim looked confused. "Who?"

"The Mad Mick," Kendall said, waving a hand dismissively. "He's supposed to be some kind of folk hero in these parts. I don't even know if he's real or not but they say he's been fighting off people who come to the area with bad intentions, though I don't know how one man could do much."

Freda was still bubbling. "They say he has a daughter who's just as dangerous as him. I hear no one can stand against the two of them."

"Never heard of him," Jim said.

"Me neither," Lloyd agreed. "But I got enough mad killers in my life already." He cut his eyes at Jim.

"So what are the marks about?" Jim asked.

"They supposedly mean he protects this territory," Kendall said, his expression still revealing that he put no credence in the stories.

Jim's brow furrowed in thought. "I haven't seen those back where we live."

Lloyd grinned. "Maybe he's scared of you."

"The Mad Mick is scared of no one," Freda cooed.

## 49

Oliver's House

DESPITE THE CHILDREN'S long day, Lloyd kept them up late with stories and songs. Sharon was tempted to corral them off to bed but decided that the distraction provided by the activity was more therapeutic than sleep would be. Lloyd's presence was a throwback to more normal times. It was a reminder of why they'd come to camp in the first place.

When Lloyd laid down his banjo for the night and glided into storytelling, it was the reemergence of something the children had lost with Oliver's death. They sat mesmerized around the campfire, glued to every word Lloyd spoke. Sensitive to the tough day the children had experienced, and to the night that lay ahead of them in their unfamiliar surroundings, he didn't tell ghost stories. He told funny stories and old folk tales about how Appalachian people believed things had come to be. They were known as Jack tales and Lloyd knew hundreds of them.

In fact, he probably would have told hundreds of them that very night had Kendall and Freda not stood to leave. As their movement broke the magic of the storytelling circle, Sharon too became aware of the late hour.

"We all probably need to head off to bed," Sharon admitted. "We've got another day of work ahead of us tomorrow."

There were groans from the children. They were exhausted but having the best time they'd had in a while. They begged Lloyd to stay another night.

"If Sharon will put up with us, I'll be here another night," Lloyd promised.

Sharon winked. "I'll put up with you, for the children's sake."

The children cheered and Lloyd waved his arms in victory.

Kendall had a working flashlight and headed off into the dark with his wife. They waved goodbye to the children and the children politely waved back.

When they were gone, Sharon got the children's attention. "Kay has a flashlight and will lead the girls to their room. Nathan will be in charge of the boys. The bathrooms in the house work because the water is tied into the spring. There's also water at the kitchen sink. If you need a drink, fill your water bottle as you go in and drink from that."

She hugged each child. The children shook hands with Jim and Lloyd because they'd been taught to do so as part of their music training at the camp. That was how musicians greeted each other. When they were done, they stepped onto the back porch and headed for their rooms.

"There's a couple of couches in the house," Sharon said. "I've not tried them out but they look nice and soft. You're welcome to stretch out wherever you can find a spot."

"Thank God," Lloyd groaned. "Feels like we've been on the road for months. My back is killing me."

"It's not been a month," Jim said. "It's not even been a week."

Lloyd was up and placing his banjo into the case. "Feels longer. I'm beat."

"You need to be beat," Jim cracked.

Sharon smiled. "Tomorrow I'd like to hear about the experiences you two have had, from walking home to where you live now. What you saw on the way over here. We've been fortunate but I feel like I'm behind the curve. I have no idea what's out there."

"If we start talking now I'll be here all night," Jim said. "There's a lot to tell."

Lloyd headed into the house with a load of gear. It was going to take him a couple of trips.

Sharon yawned, covering her mouth. "You heading in?"

Jim shook his head. "If it's all the same to you, I'll hang my hammock in the barn and spend the night there. The night air feels good after a long day."

"Well, I'm headed in. You have a good night," Sharon said.

"Make sure you lock that door," Jim said. "I won't be needing inside."

Lloyd came back for his second load of gear and noticed Jim still beside the fire. "You waiting for an engraved invitation?"

"No, I'm going to stay outside."

Lloyd rolled his eyes. "Suit yourself. I'm going to bed. Inside and on a soft couch."

Jim waved. Sharon and Lloyd headed inside, locking the door behind them. Jim stirred the campfire ashes with a stick, spreading the coals. When he was done, he gathered his gear from the porch and ferried it to the barn. He didn't want to leave any of it out in case they had company tonight. It took him a couple of trips to get everything.

He'd gone inside the barn when they turned the horses out earlier but he'd not paid any attention to the interior. It turned out to be a sturdy structure of pegged beams three-stories high on the inside. There was over a century of cast-off and accumulated farming equipment stored there.

Tack and harness material hung from hooks on the wall, the leather grayed with mildew and cracked from age. There were antique cans of oil and rusty tins of obsolete chemicals. Cloudy glass bottles with peeling paper labels held veterinary potions evaporated to a resinous syrup. There were broken hoes and busted shovels, snapped chains, and handle-less axes. Nails embedded in the wall held obscure tools and spare fittings to long-gone machines. A blue Ford tractor sat in the center of things, idled by a lack of fuel.

There was a stall of oak boards, the pipe gate laying asunder and so rust-coated as to render the original color lost to history. Jim attached one end of his hammock to a hand-forged iron ring embedded in the wall, likely placed there to hold an animal still while it was tended to. The other end he looped around a gate hinge sunk deep into a support post.

He set his headlamp on his bed and propped his rifle against the stall siding. He kept his boots on and sank into his hammock, pulling the open sleeping bag across his body. It wasn't for warmth but for comfort. He started replaying the day in his head and found reliving it a second time to be just as exhausting. He was asleep within minutes.

**50**

———————

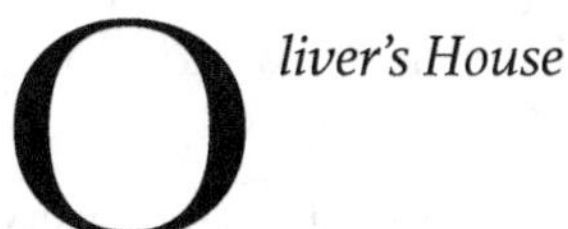 *liver's House*

A SCREAM PLUNGED through the night like a rusty blade arcing toward a bare chest. Sprawled on an antique couch in the living room, Lloyd didn't process the sound at first. He snapped awake but was uncertain of what caused him to do so. He was in a stupor of exhausted sleep and started to drop his head back toward the pillow when the scream came again, the same shrill cry of terror.

Lloyd rolled off the couch, his aching knees hitting the floor hard, and pawed the ground for his fedora. Out of habit, he always laid it beside where he slept, his light and handgun inside. He snatched his headlamp from the cap and tugged it onto his head, flicking it on in the process. Now able to see, he grabbed the 1911, chambered a round, and bolted from the room barefoot, smacking his shoulder against the doorway as he ran.

Now other children were screaming too and Lloyd heard Sharon's voice in the mix.

"What's going on?" she called. "I'm coming. What's wrong?"

There was another scream. Less than a dozen steps down the hallway, Lloyd could tell it was coming from the kitchen and turned right. He was on automatic pilot, driven by the sound of terror, and moved without thinking. He burst into the room and his light hit one of the children. Tara stood in the middle of the kitchen, her back to him, and a water bottle in her hand.

"Tara, what's wrong?"

She spun toward Lloyd, pointing at the window in the kitchen door. She was unable to form words, her eyes wide and filled with tears. Lloyd scooped her up and backed from the room.

"It's okay," he whispered. "What did you see? What happened?"

Tara sucked in a breath and words came in sobs. "A woman...looking...in the window at me."

Sharon came barreling down the hallway, headlamp washing the walls in a bright glare. She sent her chair rolling and extended her arms. "Tara, honey, are you okay?"

Lloyd eased the child to the floor and she sprinted for the safety of Sharon's arms. He headed back into the kitchen, throwing open the back door, and played his light around the porch. He didn't spot anything but that didn't mean there wasn't anyone out there. There were plenty of things to hide behind. Stacks of firewood, old farm machinery, cars, and overgrown brush. A person could be hiding anywhere.

From the safety of the porch, Lloyd called, "Jim! Can you hear me?"

When there was no answer, he repeated himself, yelling this time. "Jim!"

"What's wrong?" Jim called, emerging from the barn fully dressed, rifle held across his chest. His weapon light was blazing and he was struggling to pull his headlamp on.

"One of the kids was up. She saw a woman staring through the kitchen window at her. The woman must be out here somewhere."

At the mention of an unwanted guest, Jim doused his light and retreated into the concealment of the barn. Noting his friend's actions, Lloyd realized that standing on the porch with a glaring beacon on his head might not be the best tactical move. He clicked off his headlamp and crouched down on the porch.

Lloyd wasn't a fighter. He could shoot a gun but he'd never claim to be good at it. For him, it was only about staying alive. He didn't care if he was the most skilled fighter or not. He only needed to be good enough. He listened, trying to pick out anyone moving around in the darkness. All he could hear was the wailing of the terrified children in the house and Sharon's consoling voice escaping through the open kitchen door. He needed to silence that so he crept toward the door and gently pulled it shut. As he turned back around a low voice came from the darkness.

"It's Jim. Don't fucking shoot."

Startled, Lloyd about did that and more, his bowels loosening at the sudden arrival of an unexpected guest. He hadn't heard a sound. "What the hell are you doing?" Lloyd had no idea what else to say. Fright had discombobulated him.

"I got my nightvision gear. I'm going to prowl around. I wish to God we had thermal. I'd be able to pick them out of the darkness if they're out there, even if they were in the woods."

"Be careful. I'm going back inside with Sharon and the kids. When you come back, knock on the door so we don't blast you."

"Yeah, I'll do that."

Lloyd stepped back into the house, announcing himself as he went, and found Sharon had corralled all of the children into a single room. They were gathered around a flickering stub of a candle in the bedroom the girls shared. They looked at him expectantly.

"Jim is out looking around. He's got some nightvision gear that makes it easier to find the bad guys."

"I've used that in video games," Nathan said. "That's badass!"

Sharon cut him a sharp look.

Nathan looked sheepish. "Sorry. I meant to say that's *cool*."

"That's better," Sharon said. "Where did you all come up with gear like that, Lloyd?"

Lloyd let out a long breath and leaned against the wall by the doorway. "It's a complicated story. My friend out there is a prepper. You know what a prepper is?"

"Like a survivalist, right?" Sharon asked.

Lloyd wavered his hand in the air. "Eh, kind of. Let's just say he was prepared for something like this. Or at least he thought he was. I guess no one is ever really as prepared as they think they are."

"He had all this stuff stored at his place?" she continued. "That's why you've been living there?"

"He had a lot of gear, but we've also come by a lot of other stuff through..." He paused to consider his words. "Other means."

"What other means?"

"There's no easy way to say it. We've been in constant fights since this happened. We've fought military folks, we've fought cops, and we've fought neighbors. Winner takes the spoils. Some of the gear we ended up with came to us that way. Because the people who brought it into the fight were too dead to need it any longer."

"You fought cops?" Nathan asked. "Are you outlaws?" He sounded kind of excited about that possibility.

Sharon and Lloyd exchanged a look, both of them understanding that this was probably not the optimal circumstance under which to have such a conversation. It was too late now. It was out there.

"It's a lot harder to know who's a bad guy and who's a good guy now," Lloyd explained. "There are good cops and there are bad cops. There are good soldiers and there are soldiers who are letting bad things happen. Some of them are American soldiers and some are from other places. You can't just look at a uniform now and know who's on your side. It's a complicated time."

"I never pictured you being part of something like that," Sharon said. "You were always the mild-mannered banjo-playing barber."

Lloyd shrugged. "I never could have imagined it either. Could you have seen yourself living at the camp with a group of children through something like this?"

"I'm not a *children*," Nathan said.

Kay piped in, "Neither am I."

"I'm sorry," Lloyd said. "A group of young people. That better?"

They smiled in agreement.

"Yeah, that's the last thing I would have imagined too," Sharon admitted. "If I'd known it was coming, I'd have packed a lot better."

Lloyd smiled. "I bet. How are you guys doing it?" Another bad question to ask in front of the children. Lloyd knew it as soon as he asked it, but tact had never been his strong suit.

There was a flicker of concern in Sharon's eyes, then a forced smile. The children needed her to be strong. "It's tough and it gets tougher every day. What's happening now, what's happened over the last week, has been the toughest yet. We'll get through it though. Why did you end up joining up with your friend instead of staying at your place?"

"I originally went over that way to check on my parents. They live near Jim's place. At least they did."

Sensing the foreboding in his voice, she didn't ask what had happened to them. She could figure it out. "Do you like living over there?"

Lloyd hesitated before answering. "Not really. I've made some good friends there, including a woman that I've been seeing, but I'd much rather be someplace quieter. I'd rather be hanging with musicians than warriors."

"I'd imagine it's quite different than the life you're used to."

Lloyd raised his eyebrows at that. "I think we could all say that of our current circumstances. But yeah, you can't imagine how different. It's stressful."

"You should come live with us, Mr. Lloyd," Tara offered.

Lloyd laughed and automatically rattled off all the reasons he couldn't do that. Sharon helped him out, stroking Tara's hair and explaining that Lloyd had his own life to get back to. Yet the more he talked, the more he wondered who he was really trying to convince. Could it work? Could this be what he needed?

"Besides, I'm not sure Sharon would want me around," he concluded.

"Sharon doesn't have any problem with you being around," Sharon countered. "I make these kids practice and do lessons but I can't teach them anything. They're not covering any new material."

That comment started Lloyd's mind going again, but the thought was interrupted by a sharp knock at the door. The children jumped and Lloyd's hand dropped to his handgun.

"It's me," Jim's voice called from the kitchen.

Lloyd backed out of the room and met him in the hallway. "Anything?"

Jim flipped his nightvision gear up out of the way. "There was a trail of crushed grass from the porch, leading into the woods. One person, best I could tell. I tracked them into the woods but they must have caught a game trail. There wasn't any more sign to follow after that and I couldn't hear anyone moving."

"But there was someone there?" Sharon asked from the other room.

Jim and Lloyd joined Sharon in the bedroom.

"Definitely," Jim said. "It's easy to spot in that high grass. Someone flattened a trail from the woods to the back porch."

"I told you," Tara said.

Sharon leaned over and hugged Tara. "I didn't doubt you, sweetie. We just had to make sure."

"And I found this." Jim extended his hand.

Lloyd clicked on his headlamp to better see what he was holding. "A key?"

"To this house," Jim said. "It was still in the kitchen door. I'm guessing that if she hadn't been caught, that woman would have gotten inside."

Sharon went pale, shaking her head in disbelief.

Lloyd had a look of disgust on his face. "Where does this end? Everywhere we go, we walk into something like this."

Jim pulled the heavy nightvision off his head and replaced it with his headlamp. "You've been living with me for almost a year now. You know where it ends. You know what has to be done here."

Lloyd had nothing to say to that. He and his best friend were different people. This wasn't even Jim's fight. He'd only been along for the ride, accompanying Lloyd on this little side-jaunt to visit Oliver. Neither had counted on something like this. Yet there was no way to back out now. They were in the thick of it.

**51**

———

J *im's Valley*

AFTER RETURNING from the farmer's market yesterday Hugh never found an opportunity to catch up with Charlie. Most days they ran into each at some point unless it was an especially busy day. Hugh assumed Charlie was probably avoiding him. He expected that Pete had asked Charlie about his trip into town, as he said he would. Charlie had already indicated that he didn't want to talk to Hugh about it, but Hugh had more information now. This hadn't been a trip into town to see a girl or take advantage of some obscure resources that others had missed. It was a trip to murder a man he saw as a threat.

It was an assassination.

Hugh didn't want to force the conversation with Charlie. He didn't want to give Charlie the impression he was pursuing him or that he was in trouble. Despite what Charlie might think, Hugh had nothing but respect for the tough, resilient kid. He wanted him to succeed and feel like he was a part of the community. At the same time, he couldn't exactly turn a blind eye to the kid assassinating someone. Even with the state of the world, something like that at least merited a conversation. Since he hadn't run into Charlie yesterday, he would make a point of it today. After waking up in Jim's shop, it was the first thing on his mind.

Some nights the boys chose to stay in the barn, but they hadn't done so last night and Hugh's suspicious nature told him that was probably intentional. Although the boys didn't want to take a chance on encountering Hugh, they couldn't just hide. It was important that everyone know where everyone else was at night so they had to check-in. Around dark last night, Hugh caught a radio transmission between Pete and his mother. The boys were going to be staying at Outpost Pete last night, the observation post located on the highest point of Jim's property.

Hugh set out at first light. Despite the tall grass, prone to swishing against pants and crackling underfoot, Hugh made it to the outpost without anyone inside noticing his arrival. He ignited the tiny stove he'd brought along, an ultralight piece of aluminum gear that burned denatured alcohol, and heated water in a canteen cup. When it was near boiling, he dumped in two instant coffee pouches and stirred the coffee with the tip of his knife. He was enjoying the sunrise with a steaming cup when the first confused face jutted from the outpost.

It was Pete and he muttered some indecipherable comment. Hugh wasn't sure if it was a greeting or merely an exclamation of surprise.

"What is it?" Charlie asked from inside the structure.

"It's Hugh," Pete said.

Hugh raised his cup of coffee to Pete in a toast and offered a wide grin. He could hear Charlie inside, though his words were not loud enough for Hugh to hear. "C'mon out, Charlie. We need to talk a little bit."

"Shoes," Pete said, apparently as much of a sentence as he could fabricate this early. He ducked back into the outpost.

In a moment, both boys came crawling out the entrance, one after the other.

"You shouldn't sneak up on people," Charlie complained.

"It's only dangerous if the people you're sneaking up on are awake and paying attention," Hugh replied.

"You could at least have brought breakfast," Pete said, rubbing the sleep from his eyes.

"You could have had breakfast ready for me," Hugh said. "I guess we're both disappointed."

Charlie had pulled all his gear out and was tucking his sleeping bag and ground cloth into his pack. "You have more questions about town?"

Pete hopped up. "I don't need to be part of this. I'm heading to the house and grab some breakfast."

"You can sit back down," Charlie said.

"You want to have this conversation in front of Pete?" Hugh asked.

"No," Pete said.

"Yes," Charlie said. "Whatever you got to say, he can hear it."

Pete sat back down, looking uncomfortable. "I'd just as soon not hear it."

"I think I know what you were up to in town the other night," Hugh said, taking a sip of his coffee and staring at Charlie over the steaming cup.

Charlie didn't flinch from Hugh's stare. "You *think* you know or you know?"

"I know."

Charlie nodded his head and looked away. He was still nodding, tight-lipped. Pete was looking increasingly uncomfortable.

Pete looked Hugh. "I didn't know when we talked yesterday. Honest. I wasn't lying to you."

"I know," Hugh said. "You're pretty transparent. I figure you found out after we talked."

Whatever was going through Charlie's mind had run its course. He turned his eyes back to Hugh. "You here to give me shit? To run me off? To tell me you're going to rat me out to everyone?"

"Charlie, I'm not here for anything like that. You really expect that from me?"

Charlie pointed toward Pete. "All I know is that you're tight with his dad. With his dad gone, you're kind of running the show. I'm guessing you don't care why I did it. You just want me out."

"I don't want you out and I doubt there's anyone in this group of ours that wants that. You're one of us. You're family."

"My family is dead," Charlie spat.

"Son, you don't really believe that. I know part of your family is dead, but I believe with all my heart that you've found a new family with this group. Am I wrong about that?"

Pete seemed as interested in the answer as Hugh, watching for Charlie's response.

"You're not wrong," Charlie admitted. "You all *are* my family. That's why I did what I did."

"You killed the guy who ran the corral, didn't you?"

"Yeah."

"And his son?"

"Yeah."

"Are you okay with it?" Hugh asked.

"I did what had to be done."

"I mean are you handling it okay?"

Charlie looked confused. "I've killed people before. This isn't the first time."

Hugh narrowed his eyes at Charlie. "This was different. You know it and I know it."

Charlie looked off into the fields. The sun rising through the morning fog gave his tanned face an orange cast. "I'm fine with it. Seriously. I might as well be, right? I don't expect this is the last time I'm going to have to do this."

"You can't think like that, man. You can't just kill everyone you butt heads with."

"Can't I?" Charlie asked, his tone accusatory.

"No, you can't," Hugh replied.

Charlie wasn't buying it. "Listen, I've seen a lot in a year. I've seen that when we kill the threats to our community, everything goes well. When we let those threats grow and continue to be a thorn in our side, everything goes to hell. People get hurt. We get attacked. Pete's dad has to run off to the mountains. I'm not a genius, Hugh, but I can figure this one out. The best option is to deal with threats when they show their face. Don't give them a second chance. When people are scared of us, they leave us alone and that's what I want. That's what we all want."

"I'm hearing what you're saying," Hugh said, "but it's not that simple."

Charlie made an exasperated sweep with his hand. "It's exactly that easy. I watch what you guys do. Every kid in this valley does. We've all seen the same thing. You kill the threat and we're rewarded. You leave the threat, we all suffer. It's pretty fucking simple if you ask me."

Pete's eyes grew wide. He'd never heard Charlie so fired up, especially when talking with Hugh. People figured Hugh was probably the most dangerous man in this entire valley and Pete hadn't ever heard anyone talk to him this way.

Hugh didn't react to Charlie's fury. He didn't say anything at all. He took a sip of his coffee, leaned back against a log, and regarded the view down the valley.

Figuring he may have overplayed his hand, Charlie apologized. "I'm sorry. I'm not pissed at you."

"I know you're not," Hugh replied. "No one is mad at you either."

Charlie let out a long breath, trying to release the tension in his body. "It feels that way."

"That's because you're holding a lot of anger inside of you. That's why we're having this conversation, Charlie."

Charlie looked confused. "You're going to have to explain that one to me."

"You're angry over what happened to your mom and dad. You're angry over having to leave your home. That's a lot to carry inside you and the last year has been kind of crazy. I'm sure it's been a hard time to process those feelings."

"I've dealt with it."

"I know you have. I just want to make sure that when you pull the trigger on someone you can live with what you've done. It should never be casual. It should never be easy. It shouldn't be something you do because you're mad at the world."

Charlie nodded in understanding. "So you think I killed this guy because I'm mad over my parents dying?"

"I'm not accusing you of that, Charlie. All I'm saying is that your life, the experiences you've had, put an extra burden on you. Those experiences could make anyone who'd lived through them carry a little hate inside them. For your own good, for your own peace, you need to keep that in mind. Every time you pull the trigger you need to ask yourself if your head is in the right place."

"Sometimes there's no time for that," Pete said. "Sometimes it happens fast."

"That's combat and it's different," Hugh said. "I understand there's no time for it then. There's damn sure time when you're walking into town in the middle of the night."

Charlie got the point. "Are you going to tell Jim about this?"

"What do you want me to do?" Hugh asked.

Charlie looked surprised. "Are you seriously asking me?"

"Yes, I'm seriously asking you. Do you want me to tell Jim?"

Charlie sat back and considered this. He looked to Pete for support but Pete just shrugged uncertainly. When Charlie looked back at Hugh, he nodded. "Tell him. I don't care if he knows. I want him to understand what I'm willing to do for my friends. For my family."

"I get that. Just so you know, I'm here if you ever need anything. If you need to talk, if you have questions, just hit me up."

"I'm good," Charlie said. "I got this."

Hugh took another sip of his coffee and found that what was left had already gotten cold. He drained it in a single long drink, unwilling to toss good caffeine onto the ground. When he was done, he stood up and shook the cup out. He tipped his boonie hat to the boys. "I'll see you all shortly."

He strode off through the high, dewy grass thinking about what he'd say to Jim when he returned. He was glad the boy agreed to him telling Jim what had taken place. He preferred not to have to go behind people's backs. He wasn't certain Charlie was fully under control though. He still saw the rage seething in that young man even if Charlie didn't see it within himself. He suspected more people would die before those demons were purged.

**52**

———————

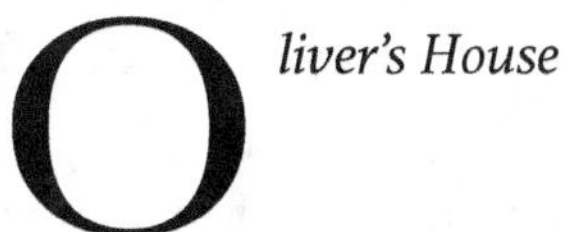 *liver's House*

NOT LONG PAST SUNUP, Kendall and his wife were tapping on the kitchen door. The kitchen was already packed with kids eating breakfast. Homemade yogurt with nuts and peaches had been the normal breakfast for the past few weeks. Jim, leaning against the countertop closest to the door, swung it open and gestured for them to come inside.

Freda accepted his invitation but Kendall hung back. "Reckon I might talk to Sharon outside for a second? Y'all can come along if you want."

Sharon wiped her hands on a dishtowel and headed for the door. Freda took a seat at the table and started talking to the kids like they were her own grandchildren. When Jim, Lloyd, and Sharon were on the back porch, Kendall pulled the door shut.

"I was thinking we might should run up to the camp this morning and take a look at things. There might be stuff you can salvage if we get to it before the rain comes."

Sharon looked uncertain. "Part of me doesn't want to see it, but I know I need to."

"Freda came along to stay with the children. She's good with young'uns."

Sharon smiled. "I can tell and I appreciate that. The kids need other people in their lives."

Jim cleared his throat. "We're thinking the same woman that set that fire was here at the house last night."

Kendall's eyes grew wide and his jaw went slack. "Here?"

Sharon nodded. "One of the children got up in the night to get a drink of water and found her outside the back door. She apparently had a key and was trying to get in."

Kendall winced as if the news caused him physical pain. "She might have found a key when she was here during the funeral service. I doubt anyone ever gave her a key."

"These locks are old," said Jim. "They've probably used the same keys since the house was built."

"I wonder what she wanted," Kendall mused. "What could she hope to accomplish by coming into the house in the middle of the night?"

"She wants to terrorize us into leaving," Sharon spat. "And that's not going to happen."

"It might be time to send a message," Jim suggested, unable to keep quiet on the matter.

Kendall looked at him suspiciously. "What kind of message are you talking about?"

"I'd let her know that you're not going to tolerate this. I'd send a very clear message that you'll put a bullet in her fucking head if she shows her face again."

Kendall frowned. "Now listen, that may be the way that you're used to handling things over in your neck of the woods, but that's not how we do things here. We're good people. We're country folks and we like things quiet. We don't go around killing our neighbors."

"She must not have got the memo," Sharon said. "She's not being good or quiet."

"She ain't hurt anyone though," Kendall pointed out. "She's just riled up because she thinks she's owed something. She's more hurt and confused than anything else."

Sharon's face flushed with anger. "I'm supposed to wait until she hurts someone? I'm supposed to let one of these children get hurt because she feels slighted?"

Kendall held up his hands in a calming gesture. "I ain't saying that either."

"Then what exactly are you saying?" Jim asked.

Kendall gave Jim a look intended to remind him that he wasn't from here. This wasn't his fight. Yet Jim found himself in the middle of it and didn't know what else to do. He couldn't ignore the mess unfolding before his eyes.

"Let us talk to her," Kendall offered.

Sharon appeared unconvinced. "Who's *us*?"

He tilted his head toward the kitchen. "Freda and me. Some of the other folks who came to the service. I believe she'll listen to us."

Sharon, Jim, and Lloyd volleyed raised eyebrows and looks of disbelief between themselves.

Kendall couldn't miss the general sentiment. "You have to let us try. It's how things are done."

There was a lot Jim could have said to that, but he was a guest here. Even with his poor boundaries, his impulsive behavior, and his general lack of social skills, he understood there were times to keep your mouth shut. He'd been raised right, despite what he'd become. He simply nodded at Kendall and smiled because he didn't have a clue what else to do.

## 53

# T *he Camp*

THERE'S a smell at campgrounds some mornings. It's a mixture of morning campfires, along with the ash smell of burned-out fires from the previous night. That was the smell that hung in the valley as the riders approached the camp. Sharon rode in the lead, alone in her golf cart. Kendall was at her side, the two speaking occasionally as they followed the rough camp road. Jim and Lloyd hung back, almost feeling like interlopers, like voyeurs to the suffering of this group they'd dropped into.

"This farm is huge," Jim said, keeping his voice low. "I'd love to have a place this size."

"Thousands of acres," Lloyd said. "It's like a world unto itself. This camp was an amazing place to play music. I don't know if it was the setting, the people, or what. I enjoyed it."

Jim could tell that his friend missed experiences like that. His life had been about playing music. It was all day, every day for him, with rarely a break. He didn't want breaks. Playing for the children at Orbin's place was the most alive Jim had seen him since he'd shown up at his place last year. He'd seen that spark in him again last night when he'd played for the children at Oliver's house. If Lloyd had a purpose in life, that was it. Jim understood that about him but didn't know how to help him. A man who could wield a gun was more likely to survive this world than a man who could wield a banjo. Both might kill you but the banjo took longer.

They were all silent, reverent as they came within sight of the camp. It happened quickly. One moment they were on the tree-lined road, the next they were turning a bend into the camp. Lloyd paused in surprise and Jim reined his horse to a stop alongside him. Kendall came to a halt as well, only Sharon continuing on toward the remnants of the camp's most popular structure.

The building had been made entirely of wood with no masonry or drywall. A support post made from a peeled log was the tallest remaining point. It stretched from the rubble like a charred finger, smoke still rolling off it and disappearing into the morning sky. There were other pockets of smoke and glowing coals. Occasionally there was a pop from the thick bed of ashes.

Jim could make out a stub of pipe extending from a toppled woodstove. There were pieces of charred kitchen equipment partially buried in the debris—a gas stove, refrigerators and freezers. Runs of blackened electrical wiring rose in lopsided arches. A stub of galvanized steel pipe burbled spring water into the ashes, a stream of black effluent running off into the weeds. The fire had been hot enough to char a wide circle. The trees nearest the building had half a canopy of green leaves, while the other half was cooked to a pale gray, already curling in death.

It was an otherwise beautiful morning. Birds sang with no regard for the mourning of men. Goldfinches fluttered from thistle to thistle. Butterflies explored zinnias. Hummingbirds targeted sunflowers, the buzz of their wings loud and insectile. Then a choked sob broke that peace, Sharon breaking down at the sight of the destroyed building.

Kendall climbed off his horse and wrapped her in a tight hug.

"This camp was the best thing that ever happened to me. Losing Oliver, this fire, is almost too much to bear!" she cried.

"It was just a building," Kendall assured her. "You and the kids are safe. That's all that matters. When the country gets on its feet again, we can rebuild all this. There's money for it. You can fix all the things that needed fixing over the years and it will be better than it ever was before."

Sharon pulled away from the hug. "I know. You're right. It's just hard."

He gave her a sympathetic smile. "I know, sweetie."

"For how long?" Jim asked.

Sharon wiped at her tears, twisting in the cart seat to face Jim.

Kendall looked at him confused. "For how long what?"

"You said all that matters is that she and the children are safe. How long are they going to be safe with the people who did this still running loose out there?"

Kendall shook his head in frustration, the same gesture you'd use for a dog that peed in the house despite your best efforts. "I told you back at the house that we were going to talk to Kimberly. We ain't had a chance to do it yet. You're just going to have to be patient."

Jim's eyes bored into Kendall. Since the beginning of this national disaster, he'd had no patience for people who didn't see the world as he did. He felt that he understood human nature a little better than some folks. This situation was nothing he hadn't seen before. He knew how it would end. "Talk won't accomplish a damn thing."

Kendall grew red in the face and waved a finger at Jim. "I'm a Christian man but you're about to make me lose my religion. Maybe you ought to mind your own damn business and leave this to the folks who actually have a dog in the fight."

Jim raised both hands in surrender. "Fine." He spun his horse and wandered off to check out other areas of the camp.

Lloyd followed, catching up with Jim a short distance from the wreckage of the burned dining hall. "This isn't our fight, Jim. We have to let them solve this their own way."

"This was probably a bad idea coming here. As much as I *knew* that it was the right thing to leave the valley when I did, I've had a lot of time to think about it. I'm ready to go back and fight. I'm not going to hide from the community any longer. I'm going to show my face wherever I want and dare people to say anything about it."

"Then maybe you're just itching for a fight," Lloyd suggested. "The folks who set this fire are the only ones around to take that rage out on so you're ready to go after them. You're just looking for someone to pay the price for everything you've been through."

"That may be true, but so what? You can't let people do shit like this. You can't let them run over you and burn your stuff down. You have to fight back. You have to eliminate the threat before it eliminates you!"

"Not your community and not your rules," Lloyd said calmly. "These people might do things differently. They have to live here. They have to live with the outcome of their actions."

"Then we probably need to leave. Let's get our shit and get out of here, because if we stick around, you know how this is going to end."

"You're going to solve it?"

Jim continued riding the shady trails through the interior of the camp looking for signs of damage. "I'm not going to stand around and watch that woman terrorize children."

"Not every problem is yours to solve," Lloyd said.

"I know that! You think I don't get tired of feeling that way? I never wanted to be in charge of our group. I never wanted the responsibility of other people's lives hanging over me. I never wanted my actions to speak for a group. I just want to be left the fuck alone. That's all I want."

As well as he knew him, Lloyd had never fully understood the toll that leadership took on Jim. His friend didn't want the mantle of responsibility. He didn't want other people paying for his choices. "Maybe you should just go on back."

"If I'm going to be here, I'd rather stay busy," Jim said. "What am I going to do back at that house with all those kids?"

Lloyd shook his head. "No, I meant that you should start on back to the valley. You should go home."

Jim stared at Lloyd in confusion. "It's safer for us to travel together. You'd get yourself killed out there alone. You'd get lost or eaten by a bear."

"I'm thinking about staying, Jim. I'm thinking about living here and helping Sharon with the camp."

Jim got off his horse and faced him. "You've got to be kidding me. You're wanting to stay here?"

"You guys don't need me at your place, Jim. I'm a joke. I'm comic relief. There's nothing for me to do but drink and play music. It's not even appreciated."

"We appreciate it."

"Not the way these kids would," Lloyd said. "Can't you see it? Did you see the way they enjoyed the music and stories last night? That's what they came to camp for. Music is what they need to keep their souls alive."

"What about Sharon? Can't she do that for them?"

"Sharon is the camp director. She can play some but she's more of a student than a teacher. Her role was structuring the kids' day, making sure there were activities, and supervising the counselors. They need more than that."

Jim could see a fire burning in his friend's eyes. He could sense his passion. It was something he'd not seen in him in some time. Not since the days he was performing regular shows. This was what Lloyd needed. Maybe he *was* right. Perhaps this was where he needed to be.

"What about Randi?" Jim asked. "I'm supposed to go back there and face her without you? She'll eat me alive."

Lloyd laughed. "I care about Randi and I'll see her again. Hell, I'd be thrilled if she'd come join me but I can't imagine her leaving her grandchildren."

"Maybe she'd bring them. They could all move over here."

Lloyd shook his head, the slightest tinge of sadness in his smile. "Nah, man, she's one of you all. She loves you and Gary like you were family. She loves Charlie. She may never leave that valley, even if life goes back to normal. You're stuck with her forever."

Jim took a seat on a trailside bench and stared off into the woods. "Well shit."

"What?"

"This was unexpected," Jim said. "I think you're serious."

"I'm completely serious."

"What about this mess? What about the people who burned this building down?"

Lloyd shrugged. "That's just hillbillies being hillbillies. If Kendall says he can talk her down, I believe him. Maybe burning the building got it out of her system. This could be the end of it."

"If that was the case, why did she show up at the house last night?"

Lloyd had no answer for that.

Jim didn't believe for a minute this was over. He'd done his best to try and convince everyone of it, but his opinions weren't welcome. As had been pointed out to him, this wasn't his fight. He was done here. It was time to pack his toys and go home.

## 54

T*he Camp*

JIM DIDN'T LEAVE IMMEDIATELY, sticking around the camp to help Sharon, Lloyd, and Kendall salvage a few items from the charred rubble of the dining hall. It didn't amount to much. They found some utensils, cookware, and a few hammer heads with only the burnt stubs of handles remaining.

"Those can be fixed," Sharon said. "We can make handles."

Despite such optimism, there was a lot of tension in the air. Neither Jim nor Kendall had much patience for each other at this point. Sharon was trying to push her feelings of loss aside by burying herself in the work. She grieved for her friend Oliver, for her damaged camp, and for the harsh end to the sheltered existence she and the children had experienced for the last year.

Lloyd was trying to mediate and act as if nothing was out of the ordinary. He made several inane comments, most of which got no response from anyone. It was not a comfortable feeling for any of them.

Jim wandered off to the garden and filled a few old buckets with items that were ready to pick. He preferred the calm of the garden over the tension of those combing the ruins. He found some tomatoes and some green peppers that had ripened to a sweet red. He plucked up some carrots and onions. He filled a bucket with thick ears of corn, aware that corn on the cob was a favorite of children everywhere. It took two trips but he hauled it up to Sharon's cart and found a place for it in the utility bed.

Lloyd, Kendall, and Sharon had scrubbed the soot from their hands in a rain barrel and were now ferrying a few items from Sharon's cabin.

"I assumed I could always come back and get this stuff later," she said. "Now I'm afraid to leave anything." She didn't voice the worry that anything she left behind might be destroyed or stolen if Kimberly decided to come back and wreak more havoc, but everyone understood that.

No one talked much beyond basic instructions. The work they did left a bad taste in everyone's' mouths. This place, sacred to so many, had been violated. It didn't just anger those who loved the place, it left them with a sickening lump in their gut. If Jim had understood that, he might better have been able to process the emotions of this group and their hesitancy toward revenge might have made more sense to him. It wasn't that they didn't want someone to pay for what happened, they were just in shock, unable to determine the best course of action. They were stunned and needed time to collect themselves.

When Sharon's golf cart was full, they strapped everything down and departed for Oliver's house. The procession of riders returned to the same order they'd had on their way to the camp. Kendall and Sharon rode together, occasionally speaking between themselves. Lloyd and Jim rode along together, bringing up the rear.

"You sure about this?" Jim asked. "You really want to stay here?"

Lloyd didn't hesitate with his answer. "It's hard to describe, but you ever just *know* that a decision is the right one?"

"Yeah, I rely on my gut all the time. Sometimes I pay the price for following it, though."

"My gut is telling me that this is what I need to do. I've felt a sense of dread for a long time. All last winter, this anxiety chewed at my gut all the time. I thought it would go away when spring came but it didn't. It wasn't the weather, it was life in your valley. Don't get me wrong. I love the folks there—all of you guys—but it's not a peaceful place. I need someplace quieter. Calmer. Once I figured out that I wanted to stay here at the camp, all that anxiety was gone. What better sign could someone ask for?"

Jim couldn't argue with that. He knew both sensations—the gnawing anxiety of indecision and the sudden relief that came from the awareness of a solution. What could he tell him? Jim was a lot of things but he wasn't selfish. He knew that to try and talk Lloyd into staying was selfish. He couldn't do that. He needed to support him.

"We'll keep an eye on your house and hold onto all your stuff. It'll be safe. I can't promise I won't go up there on occasion and sip from your liquor. I might even play some of the instruments because I know it would piss you off."

Lloyd shuddered. "I could handle the idea of you drinking my liquor, but I don't know about you playing one of my banjos. I can make more liquor."

"Don't disappear out here in the world, Lloyd. If this ain't the place, come back and see us. Even if it ain't permanent, stop by and let us know what you're doing. I don't want to lose track of you. It's not like we can text or anything. You've always got a place with us. You're always welcome."

Despite the seriousness of the moment and the nature of their conversation, there was no sadness. They were old friends—the oldest of friends—and they'd come to many crossroads in their lives. Many times they'd parted with a wave, not knowing the next time they'd cross paths. Life had always come back around to them and Jim expected it would again. This wasn't an end. It was just friends doing what friends inevitably have to do because there are larger forces in the world than friendship. Like it or not, that was the truth of things.

When they reached Oliver's house, Jim pitched in with the rest to unload the items they'd hauled back. With the assistance of the children it took very little time at all. They were done in less than ten minutes, leaving Jim standing there with his hands in his pockets.

"I'm going to help the children get lunch together," Sharon announced, heading for the kitchen.

That left Kendall, Lloyd, and Jim standing together in an awkward huddle around the empty golf cart.

"Reckon I'll unhook this horse," Kendall said.

"I need to see how you do that," Lloyd said. "I might need to do it sometime."

Kendall looked at Lloyd curiously.

"I'm thinking of sticking around a bit," Lloyd told him. "These kids came here to learn music. I intend to make sure they do."

Kendall cast a wary glance at Jim, making Jim and Lloyd both burst into laughter. There was nothing subtle about the gesture at all.

"Don't worry," Jim said. "I've got to get on home. I'm leaving him behind."

With the addition of that new piece of information, that Jim wasn't staying, Kendall was suddenly grinning. "I think that's a dandy idea. That's just what they need around, another set of adult hands to help out. Sharon has had a lot on her plate. I don't know how she's done it."

Lloyd nodded. "She had Oliver's help and she doesn't have that anymore. I bet she's feeling a bit overwhelmed. Even if he wasn't a lot of physical help, he provided emotional support. He was another adult to talk to."

Kendall leaned closer. "Since you're going to be sticking around, how about you come by my place after lunch. My wife and I are going to go talk to Oliver's niece later. We're going to try to get some of the other neighbors to go with us."

"I'll do that," Lloyd said.

"I'm going to get my shit together and get out of here," Jim announced. "I got miles to cover."

"You're not staying for lunch?" Lloyd asked.

"No, I got food. I'll be fine."

"Do you need my horse back?"

Jim shook his head. "You keep it. You're going to need it. Besides, it's enough trouble leading a packhorse. Leading another would be a pain in the ass."

"I appreciate that."

"It's nothing. Maybe you'll be more likely to visit us if I leave you a horse."

"I'm hoping you might convince Randi to come over."

Jim raised an eyebrow. "Maybe if you want Randi to come over you need to ask her yourself. I'm going to get an earful as it is for coming home without you."

Lloyd winced in sympathy. He knew it was true. "Better you than me."

Kendall drove the golf cart toward the barn. They unharnessed the horse and turned it out in the pasture. The three of them shoved the golf cart into the barn, where Kendall gave Lloyd a quick lesson on the vehicle.

While they spoke, Jim prepared his packhorse and loaded his gear. He was anxious to get home but planned on enjoying his trip too. In a world with no vacations, it was amazing how invigorating it was just to get away for a few days. He was enough of a workaholic though that he couldn't escape the feeling he'd been shirking his duties. He'd make up for that when he got home.

Maybe after everything was harvested, he could take the whole family on a trip somewhere. It wasn't like they could go to the beach, but maybe they could ride to the burial cave he and Lloyd had visited. Maybe they could ride to a lake and go fishing. He'd try to think of something. He knew that was the guilt talking.

"Wish we'd brought you more ammo," Jim said, climbing into the saddle. "Didn't expect you'd be staying and nothing I brought will help you."

"I'll be fine. Hopefully, this isn't the kind of place where I'll be burning through it at the rate you do."

Jim conceded the point with a tip of his head. "Eh, I hope it ain't either. I'd appreciate you all telling Sharon goodbye for me. Thank her for the hospitality. I'm just going to ride on out."

Kendall approached Jim and extended a hand. "Sorry about getting pissy earlier. No hard feelings."

Jim took the hand and shook it without a word. He gave Lloyd a wave, their customary manner of departure, and nudged his horse into a walk. He tugged the lead and the packhorse lifted its head from the grass to follow. Jim headed down the driveway and was gone.

"Reckon I'll be heading home for a bite to eat," Kendall said. "Don't forget to head down to my place after lunch."

"I won't forget."

Kendall mounted his horse and rode off. Lloyd headed toward the house and found Sharon on the back porch, staring at him in confusion.

"Where's everyone going?"

"Kendall went home for lunch. Jim's heading back to his place."

Her look of confusion only deepened. "Without you?"

"I was wondering if there might be an opening for an instructor here at the camp. I teach guitar, banjo, and fiddle. I can do a little bit on a mandolin and I can wreak pure havoc with an accordion."

Sharon smiled. "Your friend has already left and you're just now springing this on me? What if I say no?"

Lloyd shrugged. "Last night you kind of made it sound like you'd be okay with the idea. There wasn't much opportunity to talk about it this morning, but I suppose I could go catch up with Jim if you want shed of me."

"I don't want rid of you. We'd be glad to have you. All of us."

Lloyd grinned. "I'm happy to hear that. You don't know how much I need this in my life right now."

"I would have made a formal invitation if I'd sensed this opportunity. I just assumed you had entanglements and obligations in your friend's community."

"I do have a few. One of them is a woman named Randi and I fully expect her to ride over here just for the pleasure of kicking my ass."

Sharon laughed loudly. "Oh, she sounds like my kind of girl. I do hope I get to meet her."

## 55

K*endall's House*

TRUE TO HIS WORD, Lloyd showed up at Kendall's place not long after lunch. He carried his shotgun across the saddle and the 1911 pistol concealed beneath the tail of his shirt. Despite the premise that visiting Kimberly was intended to be a social call, Lloyd had learned a thing or two while living with Jim. He understood that things could go sideways with blinding speed. It was best to be prepared for that possibility and stay ready to shoot back.

Kendall and Freda had just finished lunch and met Lloyd on the porch. In the manner of Southern men of a certain generation, Kendall dropped his pants to his knees before reassembling himself with his shirt neatly tucked in. Freda paid him no mind. When he was done, Kendall mounted his horse, steered it alongside the porch, and Freda stepped from the porch onto the horse's back.

"Used to be that every house had some means for a lady to mount a horse," Freda said. "This keeps up, we might have to go back to that."

"I've seen those," said Lloyd. "Old houses with concrete steps in the yard that seemed out of place."

"Yep, for mounting horses or buggies," Kendall said, steering his horse onto the dirt road. "Used to be something like that at Oliver's place but they used a tractor to pull it off. Rolled it into a sinkhole as I recollect."

Lloyd fell in alongside them. "How far is it to Kimberly's house?"

"A couple of miles," Kendall said. "She lives closer to town. I'm hoping by the time we get there we'll have wrangled up a few neighbors to join us. Things like this carry more weight if you have several folks along with you."

"Strength in numbers," Freda said.

In Lloyd's mind, a larger force increased the chances of intimidating Kimberly into stopping her rampage. He didn't mention that though. Kendall and Freda seemed more intent on this being a social call than a threat. Lloyd didn't care how Kimberly interpreted it as long as she stayed away.

They made small talk along the way. Always interested in history, Lloyd listened eagerly as Kendall and his wife talked about the past of this community. As good southerners, they weren't simply aware of what took place there in their lifetime, but of all things that had taken place locally for the last two centuries. They were a wealth of information on old families, old farms, and the gossip that accompanies such places.

They knew about civil war battles and star-crossed lovers. They knew of horrific accidents, murders, family tragedies, and where ghosts abide. They knew who had money and hid it well, and who gave the appearance of being rich while their pockets were empty. The highly-entertaining and wide-ranging dialogue was interrupted by occasional recruiting stops at houses along the way.

"Hellooooooo!" Kendall would call from the road.

As residents of the house flocked to the door, Kendall patiently explained their mission to each family. While he talked, Freda whispered to Lloyd that all the folks they were visiting had attended the funeral service for Oliver and were aware of the tension with Kimberly. Kendall had to update each group on the latest developments, including the fire at the camp and the appearance of a woman outside of Oliver's kitchen door in the middle of the night.

They were batting about half. Some folks agreed it was the duty of the community to head this off before it got out of control. They were of the same mindset as Kendall and Freda, that a stern talking to from neighbors would bring Kimberly and her son into line. It certainly wouldn't make up for what had been done but should keep things from escalating. That was the way things had always been done in the past and it seemed to work.

While half of the folks they visited came along with them, riding horses or sitting on a horse-drawn hay wagon that had joined them, others had no interest in being part of the mission.

"I don't want to get involved," some replied.

Reading between the lines, Lloyd saw fear in their eyes. They didn't want to put themselves on Kimberly or her son's radar. They didn't want their own houses burned down, or her showing up on their porches at night. They were of the belief that this was what happened to folks who meddled in the affairs of others.

Because of the number of times Kendall had to tell and retell the story, the trip took hours. Then when someone new decided to come along, the rest of the group had to wait for them to get dressed, grab a gun, and maybe saddle a horse. The business of organizing a community activity like this was much more complicated than it had been when electronics were working. There were no group texts, no Facebook posts, nor phone calls.

By the time they reached Kimberly's place, hours had passed. They'd been following the same paved road for the last three miles, the clatter of their hooves loud in the still afternoon. Lloyd's stomach was beginning to complain, suggesting it might be time for an afternoon snack. He had a flat slab of cake from an MRE in one of his pockets, but he'd feel like a bum eating it in front of all these people and there wasn't enough to share. Splitting it this many ways would barely give each person a pinch and that was hardly worth it.

"Yonder," Kendall announced, pointing to a weedy driveway ahead of them.

A drainpipe clogged with trash passed beneath the drive. Muddy ruts in the entrance resembled miniature canyons, created by water and neglect. The entourage steered up the drive with Kendall in the lead. They passed between leaning gateposts, a rusty blue gate hanging open by a single hinge. They topped an embankment and Kimberly's place was less than a hundred feet ahead of them.

It was an old sharecropper's property, a few acres sliced off the larger farm that stretched out behind it. The original house was constructed of sawmill lumber covered in a tarpaper that resembled a fawn-colored brick. In places, it peeled away to reveal the silvery tone of aged poplar. There was no insulation. Lloyd imagined that somewhere inside there was a tall Warm Morning stove that had once heated the house.

When their families couldn't afford coal, children in these parts walked the railroad tracks with burlap sacks, picking up the chunks of coal that had fallen from rail cars on their way to the steel mills of the north. When they couldn't find coal they'd burn slab wood from the sawmill. Only children who grew up in houses like this knew that sensation of standing in their living room with their face flushed from heat while their back was freezing from the cold.

At some point, the family had pulled a mobile home into the yard of the old tarpaper house and that was where they lived now. It had likely happened in the 1980s, based on the age of the trailer. Lloyd seemed to recall that around that time the government came through and tried to get people out of these old, unsafe homes. They offered loans and grants, but despite all those incentives, not everyone was interested in the nearly free mobile homes. They tended to be rightly suspicious of the government and understanding of the old saying that nothing in this world was free. As the old and stubborn died out, the younger generations accepted those offers of government assistance and tarpaper shacks became a thing of the past. Many were burned or flattened in an attempt to erase the memory of poverty.

The residents of the mobile home had done their best to make it feel like home. They threw trash off the front porch when the mood struck them, making the high weeds a minefield of beer bottles and soft drink cans. There were broken-down cars in the yard, mirroring the 1950s vehicles rusting around the original shack. In the same manner that the original inhabitants of the tarpaper shack would have gathered on their front porch to socialize each evening, the residents of this mobile home did the same, and Kendall's party found themselves face-to-face with the people they were seeking.

Kimberly and her son were kicked back in sturdy kitchen chairs, their feet resting on the single bowed rail of the porch. They passed a pipe between them, the smell of marijuana hitting Lloyd's nose even from a distance. At the sight of the large entourage appearing in their driveway, Kimberly had no reaction and made no move to stop what she was doing. She and her son continued to pass the pipe, waiting for the visitors to make the first move.

Kendall cleared his throat and shifted in his saddle as if his back hurt. "Afternoon, Kimberly."

She exhaled the smoke she'd been holding. "Afternoon." She only gave Kendall the most cursory of glances. She was more interested in her pipe, holding it up to the light to see if anything remained in the bowl. Deciding that it was empty, she tapped the pipe against the deck rail to clear the ash.

"Afternoon, Jaybird," Kendall continued, addressing Kimberly's son.

Jaybird gave Kendall a contemptuous look. He didn't speak, but leaned over and picked up a rubber devil's mask from the porch floor. He pulled it over his head and stared at Kendall, the leering red face intimidating and unsettling.

Kendall glanced around at the folks backing him, trying to gather strength for what he needed to say. Lloyd had not seen the man this uncomfortable since he'd met him. To have been so certain that talking would fix everything, he suddenly seemed very intimidated by these people.

Kendall let out a long breath and faced Kimberly. "We need to talk to you about some things that have happened out there at the camp. At Oliver's place."

"Then talk."

Kimberly's son didn't remove the mask, continuing to make eye contact with each of the individual visitors.

"There was a fire at the camp yesterday. Their dining hall was burned to the ground."

Kimberly stared flatly. "Well that's a fucking shame, now ain't it?"

Lloyd heard mumbles behind him. Her attitude and coarse language met with disapproval.

"There was a child at the camp when it happened. They said they saw you and Jaybird there. Said you started the fire."

"Whoever said that is a damn liar."

That response flustered Kendall. "Now, Kimberly, I've known you since you were a kid. I know you're a little hot-headed sometimes. We all saw the way you acted when you showed up at Oliver's funeral."

"I can act any damn way I want to act. Don't mean that I burnt nothing down."

"You know good and well you started that fire. I know it, and all these folks here know it. Then there's the matter of you showing up at Oliver's place in the middle of the night. You scared one of those poor children nearly to death."

Kimberly shrugged. "What if it was me? So what if I built that fire? So what if I showed up at the house? I done told you that I'm the last kin Oliver had. All that is rightly mine."

Kendall shook his head in frustration. "I told you that I saw the will and—"

"I don't care about no fucking will. I care about *right*. What's happening here ain't right. My family was entitled to a piece of that farm a long time ago and I intend to see that we get what we're owed."

"That ain't happening, Kimberly. We might not have courts and we might not be able to call the police, but we're all here to let you know that we're not going to let that happen. You're not going to keep bothering that woman and those children."

Kimberly stood and leaned over the railing. She looked at the serious faces gathered in her yard. She met each face and studied the resolve in their eyes. "And all of you feel this way?"

Kendall nodded and slowly the other heads began to bob too. It was mutual. This was why they'd come. This was where they registered their vote.

Kimberly's mouth tightened. "Fine. I'm done with that place and I'm done with all of y'all. Don't never ask me for nothing again. Now get your ass outta here."

Jaybird removed a hunting knife from his belt and started picking at his nails, still wearing the devil mask.

"We have your word on this?" Kendall asked. "You ain't going to come back there and cause no more trouble?"

"Yes, you have my word," Kimberly spat, bobbing her head with each word.

"Good. Thank you, Kimberly. Y'all have a good day."

Kendall turned his horse and the rest followed him. The hay wagon made a wide loop, crushing several beer bottles beneath its tires as it turned.

Lloyd braced himself for taunts or catcalls as they rode off. He expected Kimberly to gather her bravado and hurl threats but she was silent. Kendall pulled alongside him, grinning with relief.

"That went well, don't you think?"

Lloyd couldn't even make himself answer. He didn't believe a word of what she'd said. That wasn't a woman surrendering. That was a woman choosing her battles. He had no doubt she'd return to fight another day.

## 56

J *im's Valley*

JIM'S FAMILY was eating dinner in the backyard. Pete and Charlie had a good haul of fish that day so they'd decided to have a fish fry, harvesting a few more from the holding tank Jim had constructed. Randi's family had joined in and Hugh was also there. Gary's family declined because it was one of his grandchildren's birthday and she'd requested a spaghetti dinner.

Ariel and Pops contributed by catching dozens of crawfish, though neither would eat them. Pete, Charlie, and Hugh were fond of them and, had he been there, Jim would have eaten them too. They boiled them in the traditional manner, in a pot with corn, potatoes, and spices. Ellen had butchered two young roosters that she didn't want to keep through the winter and fried them into chicken nuggets, breading them with cornmeal she'd ground herself.

Everyone had filled their plates and was beginning to eat when a man and woman they'd never seen before walked around the corner of the house. They appeared to be in their late twenties and were talking between themselves when they appeared. They were both wearing small daypacks which they dropped against the house.

Hugh gave Ellen a questioning look and she shook her head. She had no idea who these people were. He looked at Randi, Pops, Pete, and Charlie, getting the same response from everyone. The pair walked up to the folding table with the food and picked up two plates. The woman grabbed a set of tongs and was using them to lift a corncob onto her plate when Hugh stood.

He approached the table and stood directly across the table from them. "Excuse me, but can I ask who you are and what you're doing?"

The woman placed the corn on her plate, ignoring Hugh. She was going for another ear when his hands closed around the tongs.

"I asked you a question."

She tried to wrench the tongs from his hand, but his grip was tight. Her companion set his plate down angrily.

"Hey, buddy! Get your hands off her!"

He started around the table toward Hugh but didn't get far. Charlie had gone for his rifle the minute he'd seen the strangers. Now he snapped it up and leveled it on the man.

"Stop right there!"

Everyone froze.

Hugh held up a calming hand to Charlie. "I got this."

"Back away from that table," Charlie ordered the couple.

Despite Hugh's assurance that he had this, the newcomers took no chances. Charlie was the one with a gun on them. He was the one who sounded menacing. The woman released the tongs and placed her plate on the table. She stepped back, tugging her friend with her. They stood glowering at Hugh.

"Charlie," Hugh said, his voice firm. "Lower your gun."

Charlie hesitated but eventually complied. Hugh returned his gaze from Charlie to the couple now backed against the house.

"I suggest you answer my questions before this young man loses his patience," Hugh said. "Who are you?"

The woman gave Hugh a defiant look. "We live in town. We're running low on food and we've heard the rumors. We thought we'd come out here and see if they were true."

"What rumors?" Ellen asked.

The woman shifted her arrogant expression to Ellen. "That the reason we're not getting government aid is because the people in this valley sabotaged the power plant. Yet somehow you all are still eating well when the rest of us are fighting to survive."

"We're eating well because we work our asses off," Randi said, unable to keep quiet. "We're out working every day to put food on our tables."

"Looks like you're doing a good job of it," the man spat. It wasn't a compliment or even a statement. It was an *accusation*.

"Just doesn't seem right to me," the woman continued. "That's all I'm saying. Ain't fair that the people who kept us from getting an aid camp are doing so well for themselves. I'm surprised the rest of the town isn't out here lined up at your table. They should be. They should be out here taking this food for the people of the town."

Maybe it was the stress of her husband being gone. Perhaps it was the suggestion that people should try to steal the food her family had worked so hard to grow. Whatever the reason, Ellen lost her cool in a way that no one had ever seen before. She threw her plate to the ground and charged across the yard.

Before Hugh could put himself between them, Ellen grabbed the other woman by the hair and yanked her away from the table. She delivered a roundhouse punch so hard that everyone heard the woman's open mouth snap closed. As everyone stared in shock, Ellen continued to punch, raining wild blows onto the screaming woman. The man lunged for Ellen but Hugh intercepted him, getting an arm around his neck and locking him into a chokehold.

It was Randi who intervened. It wasn't out of any concern for the woman getting a beat down that she clearly deserved. Randi simply didn't want her grandchildren to witness someone being brutally beaten to death at dinner. She forced herself between the two women, something she'd done numerous times over the course of her life. "Ellen! It's done! Let her go!"

Eventually, Randi wedged herself in far enough that Ellen came to her senses. She quit swinging but continued to hold a fistful of the woman's hair. Ellen's chest heaved from the exertion, from the pure, unbridled rage. After a moment she released the handful of hair like it was something vile and stalked away. She made no eye contact with anyone, walking off into the yard, trying to exorcise the demons rearing their heads within her.

Hugh released the man and he staggered to his partner's side. She defiantly brushed him off, wiping at the blood that poured from her nose and mouth.

"You should probably go," Hugh suggested.

Gaining a second wind of rage, Ellen stalked back toward the table of food. As she passed Hugh's seat, she snatched up his rifle and turned it on the strangers. Everyone at the gathering heard the selector flicked to the Fire position. Hugh backed out of the line of fire. He was done.

"If I ever see you in this valley again, I'll kill you," Ellen hissed.

"It's a free—" the woman began.

Ellen raised the muzzle of the rifle and fired into the air over her head, silencing the woman. Though the round didn't hit her, the proximity to the firing weapon terrified her. She covered her mouth and didn't say another word.

"Go!" Hugh repeated. "Now!"

The couple hurried back the way they'd come, snagging their packs from the ground as they ran.

Hugh extended a hand to Ellen. "May I?"

Realizing he meant the rifle, she returned it to Safe and passed it over. Hugh hurried off, trailing the couple to make sure they did as they were told. Ellen turned to face her friends and family. The looks she saw on their faces—fear, worry, concern—made her miss her husband even more. He'd been on the receiving end of looks like this so many times and she hadn't understood what it felt like until now. It was horrible. The feeling that you'd done what needed to be done to keep your family safe, but at the same time your actions had scared them. The sensation sickened her.

How did one reconcile that? No wonder Jim struggled with doing the right thing. There was no emotional reward for it. There was no sense of accomplishment. It left you feeling dirty and weak.

Not everyone who observed these events struggled to process them. Charlie understood very clearly what had to be done. That night, after everyone went to bed, he set fire to the new bridge the Wimmers had built, severing the valley's connection with town once again.

# 57

Oliver's House

IT WAS near sunset when Kendall, Freda, and Lloyd returned home from their mission to talk some sense into Kimberly. Upon reaching Oliver's house, they found a fire in the backyard with vegetables roasting over a metal grate. A couple of the children were using long pieces of wire to shift them around from time to time, making sure nothing burned.

Freda went to the fire to talk to the children. Kendall pulled Sharon to the side and could barely restrain his glee.

"You'll have no more problems with Kimberly," he reported proudly. "She gave it up in front of all of us. Said she was done." He rested his hands on his hips and leaned back with satisfaction.

"That's such a relief," Sharon said. "I was worried about you all. I didn't know how she'd respond."

Kendall waved off her concerns. "I knew we could take care of this without anyone getting hurt. When she saw how many of us there were, she knew she couldn't keep this up. This is the way they used to do things in my grandfather's time. Community pressure. Peer pressure. People didn't run to the law over every little thing. They settled matters personally."

Lloyd had a lump in his stomach. He didn't share Kendall's glee but couldn't bring himself to say anything. Several times he caught Sharon's eyes boring into him but he looked away. Kendall reminded him of old men he'd met before who so desperately wanted to believe everything a woman told them. He was probably a sucker for every drug-addicted young woman wanting money for a bus ticket, a power bill, or food. Wanting to believe the best about people wasn't necessarily a bad thing, but neither was being naive a good thing. A fair degree of skepticism could keep you alive these days.

Kendall couldn't wipe the grin off his face. "Well, I just wanted to share the good news. We need to get on home because I've got chores to do. Freda! You ready?"

She stood from the fire and hugged the nearest children. Those not close enough for a hug got a wave and a warm smile. She gave the horse an uncertain look. "How about we just walk, Kendall? I don't think my backside can handle another minute on that horse."

Her husband agreed. "That's fine with me. Maybe we can walk off some of this soreness." He hugged Sharon and gave Lloyd a firm handshake. When he was done, he untied his horse from the fence and limped off into the evening with his wife.

Lloyd started toward the barn. He needed to deal with his horse.

Sharon shot out a hand and latched onto Lloyd's arm. When he stopped in his tracks she let go. "I take it you're not convinced?"

Lloyd shook his head. "That woman wasn't even a good liar. Those people just heard what they wanted to hear."

"So you think we'll see her again?"

"Yeah. I'm certain of it."

Sharon's face darkened with worry. She turned and headed toward the house.

"Sharon?"

She paused. "What?"

"It'll be worse next time. Whatever it is, whatever she comes up with, it will be worse."

**58**

———

# J*im's Valley*

ELLEN'S CLAN was preparing breakfast when a metallic clanging sound reached them through the open windows. For a moment Ellen flashed back to the initial days of the collapse when a hostile neighbor insisted on banging on the gate to get their attention. That hadn't ended well.

"Can we not get through a single meal without being interrupted?" Ellen complained.

She grabbed a rifle and headed for the porch, Pete on her heels with his own weapon. Hugh was already in the yard. He'd been saddling a horse in the barn when he heard the same noise. He had binoculars pressed to his face, studying the figures at the gate.

"Looks like Mrs. Wimmer and one of her sons. There's a woman with her but I can't tell who it is," Hugh said, passing the binoculars over to Ellen.

"That's her daughter," Ellen confirmed. "Only girl in the family."

The Wimmers had initially been friendly with Jim and his family, agreeing that folks in the valley should stick together to better their chances of survival. They should keep an eye out for each other in the way good neighbors did decades earlier. Over time, however, their goals began to diverge. The Wimmers were not as paranoid and security-minded as Jim was. They hadn't read the same books and didn't understand the risks.

They didn't really agree with Jim isolating the valley from the town by blowing up bridges. They didn't care for his willingness to kill. When there was a bounty placed on Jim's head for destroying the power plant, one of the Wimmer sons abducted one of Gary's grandchildren. It had cost the kidnapper his life. Mrs. Wimmer understood why it had happened but it still left a bad taste in her mouth. She'd never forget that "those people" had killed her baby.

"This can't be good," Ellen said, starting for the gate. "I wonder what she's wanting."

Hugh slung his rifle onto his shoulder and fell in alongside her. Pete did the same but Ellen sent him back, advising him to watch from the porch. He grumbled but didn't question her orders.

It was a long walk, but neither cared. Walking was the way of things these days. If the Wimmers got a bit aggravated at having to wait, it served them right for coming at such an early hour. When they reached the gate, Ellen stopped a good distance from it. Her rifle was at the six o'clock position but she was locked in. Her hands were in position, her grip was firm, and her safety off. The stock was locked into her armpit, ready to pivot the rifle into place at the slightest provocation. These people had been her neighbors for years but those bonds felt strained as of late. If they wanted a fight, she'd give them one.

Mrs. Wimmer had her hands on her hips like an angry woman complaining to the manager. "So, what do you have to say for yourself?"

Ellen was confused, trying to recall all the things Mrs. Wimmer might be mad about. "Is there something in particular that you're talking about?"

"I'm talking about the bridge?"

Ellen nodded slowly. They had to be talking about the bridge the Wimmers had just constructed, reconnecting the valley to town. "We know you built a bridge. We may not agree with it but we kept our mouths shut. We understood your reasons."

"If you understood our reasons, why did you burn the damn thing down?"

Ellen was floored. "We didn't burn your bridge down. I have no idea what you're talking about."

Mrs. Wimmer looked skeptical. "Can't you smell the smoke in the air?"

Ellen took a whiff and did indeed smell smoke. "It always smells like smoke anymore. That's how most people cook. I didn't pay it any mind."

"It smells stronger up at our place," Mrs. Wimmer said. "My boy there was headed into town this morning with a wagon full of corn. When he got to the bridge he didn't find nothing but ashes."

"There are farm roads that ford the river," Hugh said. "You can still get your corn to town."

"That ain't the point! The point is we spent a month of our summer, no help from y'all, building that bridge. All that effort was wasted."

Ellen was getting angry. "I told you we didn't burn your stupid bridge."

"You're a damn liar!" Mrs. Wimmer spat.

Ellen couldn't believe her ears. She'd never heard this sweet old lady utter a harsh word in all the years she'd known her. Was this what things had come to? "I've said all I have to say about it. There's nothing we can do for you. It was probably kids from town. You know they've been burning down empty houses just for the heck of it."

"Could have been kids," the son said. "Or it could have been y'all."

"I think we're done here," Hugh said. "You all are pissed off and we're getting that way. We aren't going to solve this matter here so we best just go home and go on about our day."

"I think you should rebuild that bridge!" Mrs. Wimmer called as Ellen and Hugh backed away from the gate.

"And I think you should kiss my ass," Ellen growled, having reached the point where civility and neighborliness went out the window.

"You bitch!" the Wimmer daughter said, the first time she'd opened her mouth throughout the entire exchange. She rushed the gate and started over.

Hugh and Ellen aimed their rifles at her but the gesture had no impact on her. She kept coming until her brother lashed out and grabbed her by her belt, tugging her off the gate.

"You're going to get your ass killed," he warned.

The daughter was spitting and fuming.

"Good fences make good neighbors," Ellen said. "Just stay on your side and you'll live longer."

"This the way it's going to be?" Mrs. Wimmer asked.

"That's up to you," said Ellen. "I told you we didn't burn the bridge. I suggest you ask your questions elsewhere."

The Wimmers didn't look like they were done but Ellen was done with them. She gestured at Hugh and the two of them continued to back away from the gate, unwilling to turn their backs on the angry neighbors. Seeing they weren't going to get anything else from Ellen, the Wimmers left the gate and headed home.

"You didn't burn that bridge down, did you?" Ellen asked. Her tone wasn't angry or accusing, just curious.

"No. I was up late last night but I stayed around the property. After the dust-up at dinner, I wanted to make sure the couple from town didn't come back."

"Maybe it was them that burned down the bridge," Ellen suggested.

"Maybe."

When they neared the house, Ellen told Hugh that breakfast was nearly ready.

"I appreciate the offer but I've already had some jerky. I'm going to hit the road. Maybe go see this burned bridge for myself."

"Be careful," Ellen warned.

"Always."

Hugh didn't head immediately head for the bridge; he headed for Randi's house. She was already up and working in her garden. She waved as he rode up to the house and dismounted his horse.

"Charlie up?"

"No, I think he was out late last night. I didn't hear him come in but he was there this morning."

"Mind if I speak with him a second?"

"Knock yourself out," Randi said. "If you can wake him up."

Hugh crept into the house, not wanting to wake up the rest of the family. He crept to Charlie's room and opened the unlocked door. Charlie was sprawled out on top of his sleeping bag.

The light coming through the blinds revealed Charlie's boots and clothing on the floor beside the bed. Hugh picked up a shirt and took a whiff, noting the powerful scent of smoke. He examined one of the boots and found black, sandy grit packed into the deep lugs. It was the soil of the riverbank. The type of dirt you'd be standing in if you were at the base of that bridge, perhaps building a fire.

"Find what you were looking for?"

Hugh snapped around to find Charlie's eyes open and looking up at him. "You burn that bridge, Charlie?"

The boy stretched and yawned, the gesture morphing into a nod. "Yeah, I did."

Hugh shoved Charlie over to make room, then sat down beside him on the cot. "I was hoping you'd talk to me before making any more big moves on your own."

"I didn't see nothing to talk about."

"So suddenly you're the one making decisions here? No one in this group acts alone, Charlie. Every decision we make is discussed first. We might not always agree but it's good to get other perspectives. Someone else might see sides to an issue that you don't see."

"Jim never asks," Charlie said. "He does what he wants."

Hugh took in a long breath and released it slowly, trying to keep his voice calm. "If that's what you think, you're not paying attention. He always discusses the implications of his actions with others in the group. He may not be discussing them with you because of your age, but he's discussing them with me, Gary, Lloyd, Ellen, and other folks. He always gets advice before he acts."

"Is there a problem?"

"Yes, there's a fucking problem, Charlie," Hugh hissed, struggling to keep his voice low. "The Wimmers were at the gate this morning accusing us of burning the bridge. Things have been tense with those folks for a while but not openly hostile. Now they're ready to go to war with us, all because of this damn bridge."

Charlie's face clouded. "I didn't figure they could trace it back to us."

"They didn't trace it back to us. We're the most obvious choice. They probably thought of us as soon as they found it."

"I never thought about that."

Hugh reached out and flicked a finger into Charlie's forehead. There was a hollow thump, like tapping a watermelon. Charlie winced and rubbed his head.

"That's why we talk about these things. Other people may see aspects you didn't see. I get your motivation here, man. I understand that you're wanting to help people, but you don't want to make things worse for everyone."

"Like Jim?"

Hugh stared at Charlie. "What do you mean?"

"Like him trying to help everyone by flooding the power plant, but only managing to make life worse for everyone."

"Exactly like that, Charlie. You don't want this kind of responsibility. You don't want to bring pain to the very people you love and are trying to protect. Jim doesn't want it either, but he doesn't always have a choice. That level of responsibility comes with being a leader. You have a choice. You need to man up and stop being a lone wolf. That's not the kind of operation we run here."

Charlie looked at the wall, tracing a finger down the rough groove in the paneling. "I guess I fucked up. What do I need to do about it?"

"You need to keep your mouth shut is what you need to do. Don't tell anyone about this. Not Pete, not anyone. I'm going to try to spread some propaganda. I'm going to mention the trouble we had at dinner last night and try to convince people it might have been that couple that burned the bridge."

"How are you going to do that?"

"Don't you worry about it," Hugh said. "Just promise me you won't do anything else without talking to me first."

"I promise."

"You swear on it?"

Charlie nodded.

"Say it," Hugh demanded.

"I swear."

**59**

———

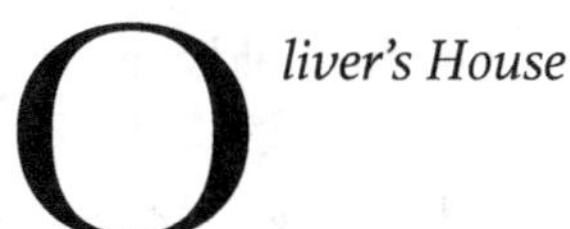

O*liver's House*



"WE'RE PICKING CORN TODAY," Sharon announced at breakfast.

"All of us?" Nathan asked.

"Yep."

Tara giggled. "Even Mr. Lloyd?"

"Yes, even Mr. Lloyd."

Tara cackled, finding it hilarious that Sharon was putting Lloyd to work.

"Corn day!" Stevie sang. "It's corn day!"

Oliver had a massive cornfield below his house. He raised corn for cattle and deer, as well as a few varieties for human consumption. The field was around seventy acres but within that space there were individual blocks that separated the different varieties. He had everything planted to maximum yield last year but had not been able to harvest it because the fuel ran out. The fields sat all winter, the standing corn drawing game into the valley.

This spring Oliver had planted as much as he could using hand tools and hiring labor when he could. The result wasn't attractive. It wasn't the beautiful rows of neat corn that farmers and neighbors admire from a distance. It was a jumbled thicket of year-old stalks and new growth. Still, it was an edible resource and Sharon couldn't let it go to waste. There was corn they could eat as ears, corn they could dry for their animals, and corn they could attempt to grind into meal.

When everyone had eaten and was thoroughly hydrated, Sharon had them fill more water bottles to drink over the hot morning. They scoured the barn for plastic bins, five-gallon buckets, and milk crates for hauling corn. The plan was that they'd all work together to strip ears from the plants while Sharon used her cart to haul them back to the house. Nathan would ride with her and unload the corn onto the porch. Sharon had originally wanted to let Nathan operate the cart while she picked corn but they'd determined that the field was too rough for her to negotiate in the chair.

They loaded their containers into the cargo bed on the rear of the golf cart and Sharon drove it down to the field. Some of the smaller children chose to ride with her, while Nathan and Kay walked with Lloyd. It was a beautiful morning. The grass was damp with dew, the air was still, and wisps of fog hung in the distant hills.

They walked the road for a short distance, then turned onto a weedy access road that separated two blocks of high corn, where a herd of deer picked at the stubble. Startled by the appearance of the humans, they bolted in all directions. Some plunged into the corn with agile bounds, while others ran a short distance and paused warily. Two spotted fawns seemed unsure of what to do but eventually followed their companions. Though they saw deer nearly every day, the children never tired of it. They were part of the magic of the place, the manifestation of wildness.

"How do we do this?" Lloyd asked. "I'm a banjo picker, not a corn picker."

Tara laughed, nearly as amused with Lloyd as he was with himself.

"What about you, Tara? Are you a corn picker or a guitar picker?" Lloyd asked.

She grinned. "I'm a corn picker."

Sharon rolled her eyes. "Everyone is a corn picker today. Everyone takes a container. If we have more containers than we need, dump them out on the ground here. Everyone goes off into the corn and fills their containers. When we have a load, Nathan and I will haul it back to the house and dump the containers. We keep picking, filling, and hauling until we're too tired to do it any longer."

Lloyd decided to dive right in, picking up two five-gallon buckets and stalking off into the corn, singing at the top of his lungs. *"She walked through the corn leading down to the river. Her hair shone like gold in the hot morning sun."*

*Fox On The Run* was a bluegrass standard and most of the kids knew it. Though they dispersed in different directions, each wanting their own territory, they joined in singing with Lloyd. Soon the cornfield was filled with the high harmonies of voices singing along.

Before he disappeared from sight, Lloyd winked at Sharon. He knew what he was doing. It was something cotton pickers, the gandy dancers, and the chain gangs had learned a long time ago. Singing made the day go faster, made you forget the inescapable drudgery of your toils. By the time they were done today every child would know the lyrics to this song and possibly a few others.

The work went fast initially. They picked close to the edge of the access road, filling their containers quickly and hauling them back to the golf cart. When it was full, Nathan and Sharon headed to the house to empty them. By the time they got back, another load was ready and waiting.

They continued at this pace for nearly two hours. When Sharon and Nathan returned from their latest trip, they brought a bucket of peaches so everyone could have a snack. As Sharon was handing them out, she noticed they were missing a child.

"Tara!" she called. "Snack time."

No answer.

"Tara!" Sharon called louder.

"I'll find her," Nathan said. "Where was she picking?"

Lloyd pointed in a direction. "She was just over there. She just brought this bucket up and went back with another." He tapped a full bucket with the toe of his boot.

"Tara!" Nathan called.

"Let's find her," Sharon told everyone, a tinge of worry in her voice. "She might have gotten turned around in the corn and you know she gets scared easily."

"We'll find her," Lloyd assured her, heading off after Nathan.

The children fanned out in the corn, calling Tara's name. Sharon called too, her voice shrill with worry.

"Taraaaaa!"

**60**

———————

liver's House

WHEN TARA SPOTTED the fawn curled in the dirt like a sleeping puppy, she had to go after it. It couldn't have been more than a couple of days old, barely larger than a cocker spaniel and dappled with white spots. She crouched and jabbed her hand through the rattling stalks of dry corn that stood between them. She managed to touch the baby deer and squealed in delight. She grew frustrated when it immediately shot to its feet and moved further away. The fawn settled down a few feet beyond its previous bed, likely assuming it was hidden by the high corn.

Tara could hear people calling her name. It sounded like they were looking for her. She knew she should answer them, but if she did she'd scare the deer. She'd never catch it then. On her hands and knees, Tara pushed between two dead stalks in pursuit of the fawn. It heard her coming and cast her a weary glance.

Tara smiled at it. "Hi, baby deer."

It rose unsteadily and tottered away from her. Tara's tongue stuck from the side of her mouth, the gesture of a determined child. She crawled faster. In response to the sounds of pursuit, the deer sped up. Tara reacted accordingly, hitting her internal throttle and crawling faster. The fawn was running now, increasing the distance between them. Determined that she was going to catch the fawn and make a pet of it, Tara got to her feet and broke into a run.

She made it two steps before she barreled into someone, a figure she hadn't noticed standing in the dense corn. Bare arms wrapped tightly around her. She assumed it was one of the older girls or maybe Lloyd sent to find her. She giggled and looked up. The face she found staring down at her was not smiling. In fact, it was not even human. It was the red rubber face of a devil, an evil grin curling its mouth and the stub of horns protruding from its head.

Tara sucked in a breath, preparing to scream, and a hand clamped over her mouth. The face lowered to hers and a warm, foul breath burned her eyes. Beneath the slit in the mask, she could see pink lips with dirt collected at the corners of the mouth.

"You shut the hell up or I'll hurt you. You hear me?"

When Tara didn't respond, too petrified to attempt to speak, the devil shook her hard. The move snapped Tara from her spell and she nodded frantically. The devil raised up, hand still over Tara's mouth, and scanned their surroundings. Reaching into a pocket, the devil extracted a sheet of paper and unfolded it, then tossed it to the ground. They moved deeper into the corn, the devil holding Tara tight to its side, a filthy hand held over her mouth. The hand reeked. Held just below Tara's nose, it made her want to vomit.

The devil moved faster and faster. With one arm, it batted away corn stalks like they were swarming insects, charging wildly. It was as if they were in a corn maze with no paths and no escape. It was sheer bedlam. The devil soon found it couldn't make any speed with Tara clutched so tightly to its side. They were bulldozing through the corn stalks rather than slipping between them.

The devil came to a stop and leaned down, whispering into Tara's ear. "I'm letting go of your mouth but you better not make a peep. I'm warning you."

Then the devil was running, jerking Tara along behind him. They sliced through the cornfield at a faster pace, and Tara looked behind her, imagining all the things she'd never see again. Sharon, Lloyd, and the other children. The peach tree and the Fairy Circle. The baby deer. She hadn't even had a chance to snoop around the new house. She didn't want to leave. She didn't want to go with this masked devil.

She promised not to do it but she did. She opened her mouth and put everything she had into the loudest scream she'd ever made.

**61**

―――――

O*liver's House*

SHARON HAD JUST LEFT the field, returning to the house in her golf cart, thinking Tara might have wandered back to go to the restroom. She'd done that before at the camp, embarrassed to announce that she needed to go. Lloyd and the other children were still combing the field, calling Tara's name. They assumed it was possible she was just hiding, thinking it was a fun game to make them all look for her. She'd also been known to pull that stunt before, despite stern lectures from Sharon about scaring everyone.

Then they heard the scream in the cornfield.

Lloyd reacted immediately, sprinting through the corn, plowing through it like a human combine. He heard steps behind him and glanced back to find Nathan on his heels.

"Tara!" Lloyd yelled, whipping his head from side to side, looking down the aisles as he ran. Spotting something ahead of him, he stopped in his tracks so abruptly Nathan barreled into him.

"What?" Nathan asked.

Gasping for breath, Lloyd pointed to a white rectangle in the dirt. Nathan grabbed it and held it so Lloyd could read it over his shoulder. A message was scrawled on the grimy paper in blue ink.

*Get out by tonight or I kill the kid.*

Lloyd shoved Nathan in the direction of the other children. "Go! Show that to Sharon. Get all the kids together and take them to the house."

Nathan opened his mouth to protest but Lloyd took off running into the corn. Lloyd lowered his head, bringing his arms to a point in front of him like the prow of a ship. The corn thrashed at him, bits of dead leaves and desiccated corn silk sticking to the back of his sweaty neck.

"Tara!"

Based on the note, he had to assume someone was preventing her from answering. Whoever left that note, Kimberly or her son he assumed, had come here to kidnap a child. Somewhere in this vast sea of green and brown they were dragging Tara away from her family. If he lost her, they might never see her again. They would have no choice but to do as the note ordered them. They would have to give up the camp.

Lloyd wished for a tree or a stump, anything he might climb to better see the entirety of that field. There wasn't anything. It was a sea of flatness, a plane of grown-over sameness and uniformity that made it difficult to see anything. Then it occurred to him that he might be able to hear something even if he couldn't see.

He stopped in his tracks and listened. When he played music, his finely-tuned ears could pick out the dissonant tone of a poorly-tuned instrument. Surely he could hear someone dragging a child through a cornfield. It took him a moment to pick it out. He turned his head, scanning like his ear was an antenna, and then he found it. A rhythmic crunch like someone chewing cereal. It was the breaking of cornstalks in the distance.

Lloyd started running again but it wasn't his superpower. He was made for a slower, more pensive pace. He could play music all day but physical exertion was not his thing. Yet he'd put himself in this situation. He'd come to check on his friend Oliver and found something entirely different. The discovery was unexpected but miraculous at the same time. When he'd seen all of those children trapped here by their desire to play his kind of music, a switch had flipped inside him. He knew he had to stay and be part of it.

In his fantasy, he imagined his stay at the camp would consist of long evenings playing music around a fire. He understood now that it meant more than that. It meant keeping the children safe. It meant doing things like this. For as much as he shunned the violent experiences he'd had over this last year, they were now a part of him. He was a musician *and* a killer. He was an instructor and a fighter. Both the music and the violence lived within him. As much as Lloyd wanted to leave the violence behind, that might not be an option. There was a reason he ended up at the camp and it might be to bring music, but he had to accept that it might also be for those darker skills he was loath to recall and hesitant to employ.

Several times he paused to listen and get his bearings. The steady brushing of bodies through the corn was closer now. He was gaining on them. He surged ahead. Without warning, he burst from the confinement of the corn and into an open field. The transition was so sudden and disorienting that he stumbled, the feeling similar to that of leaning against a door that is suddenly opened.

He stopped and peered around, spotting a figure running in the distance, tugging a much slower Tara along behind him. Lloyd's chest was tight from panic and exertion but he ran after them with all he had. The figure heard him coming, twisting his body, and looking back at Lloyd. Lloyd saw the devil mask and was momentarily taken aback, but he knew that mask. He'd seen it before and knew who was likely wearing it. It was Kimberly's son, the man they called Jaybird.

Slow as Lloyd was, the man was not going to get away while dragging the girl behind him. He screamed at her, shouting for her to go faster, but she couldn't. Tara was an anchor, dragging him down.

All the while, Lloyd was gaining ground with each passing second. He was close enough now that he could see the man's struggle, could sense his indecision. Did he release the child? He might escape but he'd have to go home and face his mother empty-handed. Did he make a stand and see if he could negotiate?

Still running, Lloyd dropped a hand to his waistband and slid his fingers beneath the soft leather flap on Buddy's old GI-style holster. He had the .45 drawn, in his hand, when the man in front of him made his decision. He spun on Lloyd, stopping in his tracks, and pulling Tara tight against him. The blade of a skinning knife flashed in his hand as he laid it across Tara's throat.

The child froze in fear, her eyes wide. Lloyd suspected the man was scared too, staring down the barrel of a gun, but he couldn't see anything beneath the ghoulish red mask.

This devil hadn't anticipated the appearance of a gun. He hadn't taken steps to raise Tara as a shield between him and Lloyd. The top of Tara's head reached the bottom of the man's ribcage. Lloyd had an unobstructed shot at everything above that point.

He knew it wouldn't stay that way. At any moment, the kidnapper's slow mind would catch up with the reality of the moment and he would tuck himself behind the child.

Lloyd had one chance and he took it, praying his aim was true as he squeezed the trigger with the slow pressure that Jim had drilled into his head. The hammer fell and the round fired. Birds exploded from the cornfield, startled by the sound. The seventy-year-old handgun bucked in Lloyd's hand and the man in front of him spun as the round slammed into his face, parting the devil's left eyebrow in a devastating and irreparable manner.

Tara screamed, the knife dropped, and Lloyd rushed forward, gun still on the fallen man. Tara tried to twist her body, unable to resist the drive to see her attacker, to make certain she was truly safe, but Lloyd got an arm around her head and pulled her to him. He shielded her eyes with his body. She did not see the man's awkward writhing or the way his movement suddenly ceased with the impact of a second round from Lloyd's gun.

Lloyd scanned the area around him but saw no sign of Kimberly. If she'd been present for this, for the killing of her son, surely she'd have shown herself. She must have stayed home and sent her son to do the dirty work. The sound of crying against Lloyd's chest snapped him back to the here and now. They needed to get out of here.

"It's okay, Tara. I got you. You're safe."

When she didn't reply, Lloyd gathered her in his arms and they headed back toward the cornfield. He shifted Tara to his left side and carried the .45 in his right hand. He couldn't believe what he'd done, nor how instinctually he'd done it. He'd never killed anyone that close. Even behind the mask, he'd looked that man in the eye as he pulled the trigger. He felt nauseous, sickened by what he'd had to do, but he had not hesitated. He'd killed when he had to and saved a child's life.

It was not lost on him that this was the thing for which he most criticized Jim. They were more alike than he imagined. Perhaps they'd *become* more alike over the past year, though Lloyd couldn't say if it was the circumstances or his friend's influence that had marshaled this change.

"No! Not the corn!" Tara shrieked as they neared the boundary of high stalks.

She tried to wiggle out of Lloyd's arms but he wouldn't let her go. It took him a moment to process that she was terrified of reentering the cornfield. They would have to go around. He looked in both directions, spotting one end of the access road that divided the blocks.

"Okay, sweetie. No corn."

Not wanting to keep Sharon and the other children in suspense for any longer than necessary, Lloyd trotted the fifty or so yards to the cleared gap. He swung a right but didn't make it very far before his arm was cramping and his heart pounding. This level of physical activity was not something he did *ever*. He leaned over and gently set Tara on her feet.

"Can you run with me?" he asked. "I don't think I can carry you any farther."

She nodded, her lip quivering. "I'm fast. I'm really fast."

"Well don't run so fast that you get ahead of me. I'm old and broke down. Let's stay together."

"Then you better hurry," Tara said, shooting down the weedy lane like an arrow speeding from a bow.

Lloyd grimaced. Maybe this hadn't been such a good idea after all. He charged after her and found that he did better now that he wasn't carrying her. Tara was fast and tireless but he managed to stay close enough that she didn't have to stop to wait on him. In a few minutes, they'd crossed the span of the fields and were nearing the farm road. Lloyd holstered the Colt 1911.

"Hold up," he gasped. "Let's do this together."

Tara stopped, her rapid breathing exaggerated. She held a hand out to Lloyd and he took it. They ran together, emerging from the fields and hitting the farm road. In the distance they could see Oliver's house, the front porch crowded with the other children. Lloyd was certain Sharon was there too but the shadows made all of the figures blend together.

A cheer went up when the other children saw Lloyd coming with Tara at his side. He couldn't help but grin, even as his body ached and his lungs burned. He'd done it. He'd saved her.

**62**

———

O*liver's House*

TARA WRAPPED her arms around Sharon's neck and squeezed merci-
lessly. Sharon hugged her back just as hard. Sharon's eyes were not
closed in the fervor of the reunion. They were wide open, glued on
Lloyd, and full of questions.

"I need you to stay here with the other children," Sharon said
when Tara broke away. "Mr. Lloyd and I are going to speak in the
other room. I want you *all* to stay in here together. Okay?"

There were murmurs of agreement. With their cooperation
secured, Sharon led the way down the hall to Oliver's room. When
Lloyd was inside with her, Sharon swung the door shut with a solid
thud.

"What were the gunshots?" Her voice was not accusatory but she
needed answers.

Lloyd frowned at her, assuming the answer was obvious. "We

should have just stayed in the other room. I'm sure Tara is telling the other children all about it right now."

"Who was it? Who took her?"

"The son," Lloyd said. "I saw him on the porch with Kimberly when we paid her a visit. He was wearing the same stupid devil mask he had on that day. I think he was alone. I never saw anyone else out there with him. He stuck a knife to Tara's throat and I didn't know what else to do."

Sharon's eyes widened. "You felt safe taking a shot while he had a knife to Tara's throat?"

"Under the circumstances, yes. If I hadn't killed him, he'd have taken her. You saw the note. We'd have been at their mercy. *She'd* have been at their mercy. I couldn't let that happen."

"I understand. I probably would have done the same thing." Shifting to more practical matters, she asked, "What are we going to do about the body?"

Lloyd shrugged. "Leave it. In this heat, nature will take care of it in no time. Crows and coyotes will strip it and scatter the bones. Insects will eat the rest. It'll be gone in a few weeks."

"We don't have a few weeks," Sharon spat. "What are we going to do when his mother comes down here looking for him?"

The words that came out of Lloyd's mouth almost surprised him. He didn't even realize he had a plan until he was stating it to Sharon. Then he couldn't believe what he was saying. The words were more suited to have come out of Jim's mouth than his. "I'm not giving her the opportunity to come here and ask questions. She's probably sitting at home waiting for her son right now, expecting him to come back with a child. I'm going to visit her."

Sharon looked doubtful. "You really think she's going to listen to reason? It didn't work the first time. Why would it work now?"

Lloyd spoke slowly, choosing his words with utmost caution. "No, I don't think she'll listen. She's made that abundantly clear."

"Then what do you expect to do? You just going to waltz in there and tell her you killed her son? Tell her it should be a warning to her to leave us the hell alone?"

"Nope."

"Then what?" Sharon demanded. As soon as the words left her mouth, realization dawned on her and she began to understand. She suddenly knew exactly what Lloyd was planning. She raised both hands to her face, cradling it, mouth open in shock.

"I'd rather not talk about it, Sharon. I've never done anything like this before, but I don't see any choice. In the year I lived with Jim and his people, I saw this time and time again. Some people can't be reasoned with. The only way you stop them is to kill them. What do you think she'll do next? Burn this house down with you and the children in it? Murder one of the children to avenge her son's death?"

"I couldn't live with that," Sharon said, lowering her hands from her face.

"I know you couldn't and I couldn't either. That's the only reason I'm willing to do it. This isn't why I came here. This is what I came here to escape. Yet here I am." Lloyd was staring at the ground, his voice hollow and emotionless.

It was only then that Sharon understood how difficult this was for Lloyd. She'd seen Jim's willingness to settle the matter with violence, but Lloyd had been the pacifist of the pair, the voice of reason. He'd imagined the camp would be a respite from the violence of the outside world, yet he'd walked into more of the very thing he was trying to escape. She couldn't help but feel guilty about that. Through no fault of their own, they'd put him in this place. This was not his fight but it was something he was willing to do for them. It was a sacrifice.

"When are you going?"

"I need to go now. She'll be waiting. And I understand if you want me to keep riding and not come back here. If you don't want me around the children, I get it."

She saw the sincerity in his eyes, the acceptance that this thing he was about to do might make her banish him from their insular world. That wasn't what she wanted at all. They needed him as much as he needed them. "We want you back here. Be safe."

Lloyd nodded, lost in his thoughts, processing what lay before him. He left the room, his heavy shoes loud on the wooden floors, echoing through the quiet house. Sharon was still sitting in Oliver's room when she heard the back door close.

"Thank you for hiding us, Oliver," she whispered. "Thank you for pushing the world away."

# 63

B *land County*

Lloyd mounted his horse carrying only his weapons. He didn't want to raise any questions so he didn't ride past Kendall's house, instead cutting through the cornfield and taking a direct cross-country route toward Kimberly's trailer. He knew some of the land he crossed was Oliver's. At some point he likely crossed onto other people's land, but trespassing was the least of his concerns.

He intersected the paved road after twenty minutes of riding, turning left and accelerating to a gallop. His mind was laser-focused on the task ahead of him. He wasn't wary of the homes he passed, nor the people observing from the shaded recesses of their covered porches. He ignored those laboring in their fields or searching for stray vegetables among the browning jungles of their gardens. His mind only had room for one thing and that was the act of violence he imagined lay ahead of him. It expanded to fill all the space within him.

When he neared Kimberly's home, Lloyd steered his horse off the road and onto an overgrown patch of vacant land. He hopped off the horse and led it deep enough into the underbrush that it was concealed from the road. He tied it out with a short length of rope and confirmed that his shotgun had a round chambered.

Lloyd figured he was still a half-mile from Kimberly's place but wanted to stop early enough that she wouldn't hear the sound of his horse on the pavement. The place he'd stopped was typical of over-grown farms in this part of the country. High grass clumped together in dense knots. Briars, wild roses, and raspberry bushes tore at him from all directions. Virginia Creeper encircled and choked the older trees, the leaves forming a thick carpet along the bark. Rabbits and groundhogs had cut trails through the field, evidence of their daily travels. Rotting fenceposts sagged earthward, only held aloft by a tether of rusting barbed wire.

Lloyd jogged through the high grass, aware that this was probably the most he'd run in a long time. He tried not to think ahead. Tried not to think about what he had to do. He didn't slow until he saw the chimney from the old sharecropper house on Kimberly's property. He took cover behind a dense ornamental bush gone wild from neglect.

Shifting his body and shading his eyes, he spotted the trailer. Kimberly sat on the porch smoking a hand-rolled cigarette. Lloyd couldn't smell it at this distance but figured it was more likely to be pot than tobacco. Lloyd knew she was waiting for the son who would never return and the hostage who'd never arrive. Though Kimberly didn't know it yet, her opportunity was lost. The farm would never be hers.

He was afraid to approach from the front or the side. If she saw him, she might retreat into the house. She'd either lock the door, which would make everything more difficult, or she'd retrieve a weapon and fight back. He didn't want that either. A protracted gunfight might bring curious neighbors. Lloyd crept toward the back of the property, wading his way through more briars, pokeberries, and high grass.

He soon found himself in a graveyard of agricultural castoffs.

There were old horse-drawn machines that more industrious people might have put to use. Other pieces of equipment were more modern, but still over a half-century old. There was an Oliver tractor on four rotted tires and with only a hint of its original green showing through the patina of rust. A broken-down John Deere track loader sat with old sheets of roofing tin covering its exposed engine, the farmer who last turned a wrench on it long dead and gone.

An ancient Dodge flatbed glowered forlornly from a barn. While the barn may have originally provided some shelter to the truck, the vehicle was now the sole means of support for the collapsing structure. It was a symbiotic relationship, the fallen roof laying across the vehicle like a blanket stretched across a sleeping dog. Lloyd ran up on a blacksnake and they startled each other, both recoiling from the other like mirror images. Lloyd kicked at the snake and it slithered off beneath the back porch of the old tarpaper house.

Lloyd eased around the corner and approached the mobile home from behind. The back porch was as bad as the front. A filthy rug hung over the railing, having laid there so long it was decomposing from the sunlight. There were bags of trash piled in the corner, gnawed open by animals and disintegrating from the elements.

He crept up the steps, taking them slowly to avoid noise. They'd once been painted red but it peeled away in fist-sized shards now, revealing the rotten wood beneath. Once he was on the porch Lloyd found an aluminum storm door missing both the glass and screen panels. It was simply a frame with a latch, left in place as if the mere inference of a door might somehow confuse the insects and keep them from going inside.

After studying the situation for a moment, Lloyd ducked his head and stepped through the empty frame. The space in which he found himself was between the living room and kitchen areas of an old and neglected mobile home. The carpet was crimson and the air smelled of mildew. The walls were dark paneling, the curtains made of mismatched bath towels. The sofa was stained and disgusting in a way that made Lloyd feel as if taking a seat on a razor blade would be preferable to settling onto that couch.

The front door was open and there was no screen door there. Lloyd raised the shotgun and pressed the black button mounted near the trigger guard. There was a tiny *click*. Lloyd kept moving. He heard Kimberly humming some tune he didn't know. It sounded like country. When he spotted a bare shoulder, he side-stepped in the dark interior of the house until she was fully visible to him. He aimed the shotgun at the back of her head.

She somehow sensed his presence. Perhaps it was smell, intuition, or some instinctual revenant from the more animalistic regions of the brain. She suddenly twisted her head around, as if she'd caught movement in her peripheral vision. She'd already turned back to the road, dismissing the sensation, before it hit her that she'd actually seen someone there in the recesses of her home. She twisted again, so hard this time that she fell out of her chair and lay before Lloyd, staring up at him with confused anger.

He stared back. She was missing most of her teeth but had her tongue pierced, likely some drunken impulse intended to make her seem cooler. Her arms and legs were covered in bad tattoos. They looked like notes written in ballpoint pen and left out in the rain, the lines bloated and washed out.

"Who the fuck are you?"

Lloyd focused on his breathing. He didn't want his voice to telegraph his fear. "I was here the other day with those friends of Oliver's. They tried to persuade you to leave well enough alone, but you didn't listen."

"That place should have been mine. It ain't right. It's still going to be mine. You watch and see."

"You talking about your son? The one you sent to kidnap a child from the camp?"

Kimberly looked surprised at that. Surprised he knew. Her smug expression faded with the realization of what that meant. "He get caught?"

"He got *killed*."

She unleashed a scream and tried to get to her feet. Lloyd squeezed his eyes shut and pulled the trigger. There was a *boom* and the sound of choking. Lloyd opened his eyes, aware that he might just screw this up if he couldn't see what he was doing. He wished he hadn't. Kimberly was sagged back against the deck rail, one leg fully-extended, the other bent beneath her. Her eyes were wide open and a choking sound burbled from the missing lower half of her face.

Lloyd tried to shoot again but he'd failed to rack the slide. He hastily corrected that and pulled the trigger again. The shot punched a hole in the center of her chest. She arched backward and the rotted deck rail broke behind her. She tumbled to the ground, hitting like a sack of feed dropped off a loading dock. Lloyd stepped to the edge and peered over at her. She was a bloody mess he wanted no part of, but he understood he couldn't leave her there.

Without a body, they could deny any knowledge of what had happened to Kimberly and her son. If the pair turned up dead, though, there'd be questions. Even if his actions were justifiable because of the kidnapped child, his willingness to resort to violence might lose them support in the community. He didn't want to take that chance.

He slung the shotgun around to his back, scrambled down the steps, and dragged Kimberly to the sharecropper's house. He left a trail of blood, brains, and gore that should disappear with a good rain. He tugged the concrete lid from a buried cistern he'd spotted on his way in. The gutters from the old sharecropper house once drained into it, allowing the family to pump water inside. Peering down into the hole, Lloyd spotted a dead crow floating in oily black water.

He rolled Kimberly into the cistern, trying not to look at her. When he was done he replaced the lid and kicked dirt onto the bloodstains. He didn't want to leave anything that might encourage folks to look into the cistern. He resisted the urge to burn the place to the ground, not wanting the attention that would bring. Instead, he hurried back through the woods to his horse and set out for the camp.

As he rode, he wondered what Jim was doing that very moment.

He'd like to have the opportunity to talk to him about what he'd done. Was this how Jim felt when he killed someone to protect his community? How long would this bitter emptiness last? Did it ever go away once you'd taken such a step?

**64**

———

# Jim's Valley

WHEN PETE TOLD Charlie about the Wimmers showing up at the gate and accusing them of burning the bridge, Charlie pretended like he knew nothing about it. When Pete bought his story, Charlie realized that Hugh must not have told him that he suspected Charlie had done it. The fact that the Wimmers had immediately accused Jim's family solidified some of the things that had been running through Charlie's head lately. It was dumb of them to allow people to live in their valley who didn't share their same values.

Jim was more tolerant of those things than Charlie. He allowed a lot that Charlie might not have allowed if he was in charge. Charlie didn't want to be in charge though. He liked Jim and he liked Jim making the decisions. However, Jim wasn't there and someone had to make the hard calls. Someone had to keep them safe.

He'd been trying. Killing Willie and burning the bridge weren't done for mischief. They were moves intended to make life safer for the people in the valley. Just because Jim was gone didn't mean they could get lazy. They couldn't be seen as weak. They needed to take bold, decisive actions, and that was exactly what Charlie was investigating at the moment.

In between jobs, when he could slip away from Randi and Pete, he'd been watching the Wimmer house. He'd been doing it for three days now, collecting information on who was there and their patterns of movement. What were their routines? Who did what chores? Who ventured out regularly and who stuck close to home? Those were all things he needed to know.

He wasn't entirely certain *why* yet. He believed if he watched them long enough an idea, or opportunity, might present itself. Meanwhile, he wrote down everything he observed in a notepad Hugh had given him. The paper was made out of something special so that it didn't become soggy when he carried it around in his pocket. Pete had one too and they carried them everywhere they went.

The Wimmers hadn't begun rebuilding the burned bridge yet, though they'd been there twice to survey the scene. The obvious problem was that they'd already cut down the most readily accessible trees for use on the bridge. Rebuilding it again would require a greater effort because they'd have to cut trees from a little farther off and drag them to the site. It wasn't a tremendous distance but such efforts were monumental without the assistance of dozers, cranes, and excavators. Unable to hear their conversations, Charlie was uncertain if they were making plans for a new bridge or discussing some alternate plans.

Charlie considered bringing Hugh in on his operation. He looked up to the guy nearly as much as he did to Jim, but something prevented him from doing so. It was a simple formula. If Jim was here, Charlie wouldn't have to be taking these measures. Jim would take care of things and Charlie would fall in line like a good soldier. Without Jim around, Hugh was in a position to pull the plug on Charlie's efforts and he wasn't ready to let that happen yet. In fact, he felt like he had to do everything within his power to *keep* that from happening.

After he'd watched the Wimmers for an hour, Charlie checked his watch and saw he'd spent all the time there he could. He'd claimed that he was going off to take a quick nap at lunchtime. If he didn't show up when work resumed, someone would come looking for him. Then he'd have explaining to do and he wasn't ready for that. For now this was his secret.

Charlie shoved the notebook and pen into his pack. On his hands and knees, he began crawling backward from his observation post, dragging his pack with one hand and his rifle with the other. He'd made it less than three feet before a boot landed on his butt and shoved him face down in the dirt.

Charlie was stunned for a moment, then flipped over onto his back to defend himself. He dropped a hand to his belt, going for his handgun before it clicked in his brain that it was Hugh who'd shoved him to the ground. "What the fuck?"

Hugh dropped to a knee and snatched Charlie's pack. He dug inside it, then extracted the notebook Charlie had been writing in. Charlie made a move to snatch it but Hugh raised a warning eyebrow at him.

"I should be asking you the same question," Hugh whispered. "What the fuck *indeed*?"

Charlie was instantly on the defensive. "I wasn't doing anything. I was just collecting intelligence. That's what you always say you're doing, right? After what happened the other day at the gate, I thought we might need to keep an eye on them. We need to make sure everyone is safe."

Hugh cut his eyes from the open notebook to Charlie. "What were you going to do? Launch an attack on them in the middle of the night? Snipe them from this hill? Burn their house to the ground?"

Charlie shook his head. "I wasn't going to do anything. I was just watching. We can't let these people run over us."

"We can't just run people out of the valley because we don't agree with them, either. This family was here first. These people have roots."

Charlie shrugged. "Things change. Maybe it's time for them to change."

Hugh shoved the notebook into his own pocket. "And maybe it's time for you to grow up and be a team player. We need to be working together here, Charlie. I've got my own shit to do but I can't get to it because I'm afraid to let you out of my sight. I've kept an eye on you for days because I felt like you were up to something. Now I know what it is."

Hugh tugged Charlie to his feet. "Get your shit and let's get out of here."

Charlie grabbed his pack and his rifle. He hurried after Hugh, who was already walking off into the woods.

"You going to ask me what happens next?" Hugh asked. "That's what you always want to know. What I'm going to do with what I figured out."

Charlie shook his head coolly. "Nah, I'm not asking that anymore. I don't give a shit what you do."

Hugh spun in a flash and slammed both his open palms against Charlie's chest, shoving him to the ground. "You don't give a shit what I do? What is this? Suddenly we're enemies? Is that what you're saying?"

Charlie held up his hands in a defensive gesture. "No, that's not what I'm saying. I'm just trying to tell you that I'm doing what I think is right. I can't control what you do. If you have to tell people, then tell them."

"I don't give a damn about telling people, Charlie. I'm trying to keep you from making matters worse. I'm trying to keep you from getting yourself or someone else killed." He heaved an exasperated sigh and helped Charlie up.

Charlie picked up his gear for a second time and fell in behind Hugh.

As he walked, Hugh spoke without turning. "I'm going to call a meeting of the minds tonight, Charlie. I'm bringing the families together. Gary's folks, Randi's, and Jim's family. We're going to talk about this. I don't know what else to do."

"Dude, that's such a dick move," Charlie complained.

"If it keeps us safe, then I'm willing to be a dick," Hugh said. "Comes with the territory."

Charlie was simmering. Though a part of him wanted to respond with anger, he had no choice but to take part in whatever Hugh had planned for him. Not showing up would put a rift between him and the people he cared about more than anything in the world. Everything he did was intended to help them and to secure his place among them. He had to make them see that.

**65**

———

J *im's Valley*

WITH PETE'S HELP, Hugh spread the word to the families that they needed to have a meeting after dinner that night. There would be a bonfire. Children were welcome but their attendance wasn't required. Hugh did express his hopes that any adults not having to babysit could attend.

Everyone wanted to know what the meeting was about but Hugh said it was better they all learn at the same time. He expected Charlie to be angry with him, pouting and glaring, but he wasn't. He went on about his chores and did all the things he was asked to do. Hugh really couldn't figure him out.

He'd never dealt with anyone like that before. It had to be a consequence of the experiences the boy had gone through in the last year. Was this the kind of person that the event was creating? Children who would be violently decisive as adults? Children who would grow up to be wary and suspicious-natured?

Hugh wasn't a psychologist but he'd seen kids in war zones and he knew they were changed by the experience. Charlie's set of circumstances was unique and the result was a unique kid that he couldn't get a handle on. Hopefully, the group could work together to reel him back in.

Ariel built the fire that night under Pete's tutelage. She'd expressed an interest in learning how to do some more "adult" things and they'd all been involving her more. Ellen felt like it was an attempt to find things that would get her out of the kitchen because Ariel hated canning with a passion.

At around 7 PM people began showing up. Randi came with all her clan. Her daughters delivered the grandchildren inside to play with Ariel, then came back to sit by the fire. Gary did the same, his entire brood hiking through the field to arrive at Jim's backyard. Everyone was pleased to see each other. Though they worked together all day, every day, these social moments felt different. There was an easiness to them that was different than the shared labor.

"So what's this all about?" Pops demanded, a grin on his face. "I'm missing *Gunsmoke*."

All heads turned in his direction.

"It's a joke. I'm not senile yet."

When he had everyone's attention, Hugh began. "I need to talk to you all about Charlie." He turned and looked at the young man.

Charlie looked directly back at Hugh without a trace of malice or anger on his face. He was ready to have this conversation.

"Charlie?" Randi asked. "There's something going on with Charlie I don't know about?" She looked from Hugh to Charlie, then around the circle.

"I think Charlie should tell us about it in his own words," Hugh said. "It's his story to tell. Charlie?" Hugh gestured to the position where he stood, the spot where Jim normally stood when he was addressing folks around this circle, then he went to take a seat.

Charlie got to his feet and took Hugh's position. He was silent for a moment, looking at the expectant faces of his friends and family. It was a beautiful late summer evening. The heat of the day was beginning to fade with the evening light now and nights were comfortable. There was the sound of crickets tuning up for the evening and the murmur of the river in the field below them. Charlie cleared his throat.

"After the things that happened to me—that happened to my family—you all took me in with no questions. There was never a time that I felt unwelcome or unloved. I feel so lucky to be with you people because I feel like I'm part of every family here. I don't have just one family, I have several families, and I love each of them in their own way."

The faces around the circle began to darken with concern. Did Charlie have some devastating news? Was he sick? Was he leaving?

"I know Jim being gone has been hard on some of you. We all look up to him and we probably didn't realize how much we depended on him until he was gone. Maybe that's when I started to realize that I could do more to pull my weight around here. I felt like there were things I could do to cover for Jim while he was gone, so I did them."

Charlie caught a flash of movement. He squinted and stared off into the field as a figure on horseback materialized with the haziness of a mirage.

"Well, what is it, Charlie?" Pete demanded.

"Yeah," Gary added, "we're dying here."

"Must be a dramatic pause," Randi said. "He's building tension."

The figure on horseback, a packhorse behind him, was closing on the gate, the sound of hooves muffled by the high grass. Charlie knew who it was now and he took off running.

"What the hell?" Randi said.

Hugh was on his feet, his first thought being that Charlie had chickened-out, deciding he was unable to face his clan. Then he saw where Charlie was headed—not to flee through the gate, but to open it.

Hugh pointed toward the approaching rider but it was too late.

Everyone had already turned, their eyes following Charlie, and some were getting on their feet.

It was Ellen who broke the silence. She screamed, an expression of overwhelming exuberance that turned into his name. "Jim!"

One of Gary's daughters rose to run inside and tell Ariel her father was home, then watch the children so Ariel wouldn't miss the reunion.

At the gate, Charlie gathered the leads and held the horses while Jim took his wife into his arms. Pete joined them, unable to hold back tears of his own. He hadn't expected his father back so soon.

In seconds, Ariel too was tearing across the yard at a dead run. "Dadddeeeee!"

Spotting Charlie shifting uneasily from foot-to-foot, uncertain of what to do with himself, Jim wrapped an arm around him and pulled him into the hug. Charlie grinned broadly, caught up in the excitement of the moment.

"What the hell is everyone doing here?" Jim asked. "I was getting worried. I passed Gary's place and it was empty. Then I got to Randi's place and it was empty too."

He looked at Randi with a grin on his face and realized where her mind had gone when she saw him. He was alone. Lloyd wasn't here and in this environment that could only mean one thing—Lloyd must be dead. Jim pulled away from his family and walked toward her, arms outstretched.

Randi recoiled, backing away from Jim's approach, tears already streaming down her cheeks. "No. No. No."

Jim approached her slowly, speaking in a soothing tone. "No, Randi. It's okay. He's fine. Lloyd is alive."

Randi stopped in her tracks. "Excuse me?"

"He's fine," Jim assured her. "It's kind of a long story but we took a side trip to this music camp where he used to teach. We found out that a bunch of kids had been stranded there and his friend who owned the camp just died. Lloyd decided to stay over there and help them out."

Randi's hands flew to her hips. "For how long?"

"I don't know. Maybe forever."

"That son-of-a-bitch!" Randi spat. "How dare him. Is there a woman there?"

Jim hesitated.

"Is there?" she demanded.

"Well, there is." Jim held up a hand. "But that wasn't why he stayed. He wanted me to tell you that you were welcome to come stay with him. He'd love to have you there."

Randi bobbed her head while she spoke. "I bet he would. That bastard! Make me think he's dead and get all sad for his ass, only to find out he didn't even care enough to come home to me. I might go over there just to kick his ass."

Jim cringed. "We discussed that possibility. I don't think he'd be surprised."

Randi stalked off, fuming. She took a seat some distance from the group, crossing her legs and bobbing her foot as she lit a cigarette.

"What are you doing home so soon?" Ellen asked. "We expected you to be gone for months."

"Oh, you want me to leave?"

Ellen wrapped her arms around Jim. "No!"

Ariel pitched in to help her mother restrain Jim, wrapping her arms around his waist. "No!"

Jim could see that the entire clan was interested in his response, everyone waiting expectantly. "Let's go over here and sit down. We'll talk about it."

His family released him and Jim took a seat by the fire, his family at his side.

"I'm going to put the horses up," Charlie said. "I'll stack your gear in the barn."

"Thanks, Charlie," Jim said.

"Glad you're back," Nana said, trotting over to her son and kissing him on the cheek. Pops didn't rise from his chair but gave Jim a thumbs-up to signal his agreement.

Jim couldn't help but smile, his gaze sweeping around the circle of people he'd missed. "It's amazing how difficult it is to think clearly when you're buried in your life. You get so consumed by day-to-day tasks that you can't always see your situation clearly. It's like that old saying about not being able to see the forest for the trees. When I left here, I sincerely thought it was the best move. I'd just disappear for a while and give the community time to forget about me."

"Something changed?" Ellen asked.

"I spent a lot of time in my head. At some point, it hit me that this was not the right way to handle it. I'm not going to hide from the community, I'm not going to hide from the government, and I'm not even going to hide from the damn neighbors. I'm going to be out there in their faces, doing the things I need to be doing. If that causes problems, I'll deal with them as they come."

"Meaning people leave us alone or we beat on them until they do?" Gary confirmed.

Jim smiled. "That's the good thing about friends. They speak your language. They get you."

"It's not always easy," Ellen admitted.

"Then here it is in plain language. I'm home to stay. The world can suck it. I'm ready to be easygoing with those who are easygoing with me. If there are people out there who can't put the whole 'flooding the power plant' thing behind them, then that will have to be addressed. I'm no longer hiding and I'm no longer taking their shit."

Randi rejoined the group in time to catch that last statement. "Oh shit, someone needs to call the undertaker and tell him to build more boxes."

"I'm hoping it won't come to that," said Jim. "Maybe people are ready to chill out and settle down. They should be focusing on the things they can control instead of the things they can't. I'm one of those things they can't control."

"So, not to interrupt this reunion, Hugh, but why are we up here again?" Gary asked.

"I was wondering the same thing." Jim looked around. "Why is everyone in my yard?"

"Something to do with Charlie," Ellen told Jim. "We were just getting to it when you rode up."

"You want me to leave?" Jim asked.

"We've been through this, Daddy!" Ariel exclaimed. "The answer is no!"

"I'm sorry I brought you all up here for nothing," Hugh said. "The things we needed to talk about were all relevant to Jim being gone. Now that he's back, it changes things significantly. I hate to leave you hanging but that's all I feel comfortable saying right now."

Jim's brow furrowed. It was good to be needed, but he'd hoped for a moment to settle back in before there were demands placed upon him. Perhaps that was too much to hope for. Had he walked into the middle of another crisis?

"Then we're going to gather our kids and head back home," Gary said. "Glad you're back in one piece, Jim."

There were more hugs and handshakes. Everyone except for Randi seemed to be in a good mood. Jim knew he needed to spend more time with her tomorrow and explain the situation in greater detail. He'd been around her long enough to know that if Randi wasn't happy, no one was happy.

"Have you eaten?" Ellen asked.

"I snacked while I was riding but I'm hungry. Got anything easy to put together?"

"I'll find something." Ellen gave Jim another kiss and headed for the house.

"I'm going to head to the barn and get my gear. Pete, will you give me a hand?"

Hugh fell in alongside them. "I'll join you."

They got to the barn and found Charlie patiently brushing the horses. The saddles were sitting on racks mounted to the wall. The bridles and leads hung from hooks on the rough-sawn beams.

Jim stood in the door and sighed. "It's good to be home. I'd like to drop my ass in a chair but I've sat in a saddle for three days so I'll just stand. Now, why don't you all tell me what the hell is going on around here."

There were a lot of glances shooting between Pete, Hugh, and Charlie. Jim watched them with curiosity, his eyes bobbing between them like he was watching a ping-pong game.

Jim took off his hat and rubbed a hand across his sweat-soaked head. "Seriously? It was important enough to hold this big meeting tonight and no one can think of what to say?"

"Maybe Charlie should tell his own story," Hugh suggested.

Charlie sighed. "You're going to need a seat."

Jim raised an eyebrow. "That bad?"

"I guess."

Jim found an old kitchen chair and settled into it. "I've been gone less than two weeks. How much could I have missed?" The expressions on all the faces in the barn told him he'd missed quite a bit.

"It started with the farmer's market in town..." Charlie began.

**66**

———————

# J im's Valley

JIM SLEPT the sleep of the dead. It came from the accumulated exhaustion of his travels and the calories expended by his overworked brain. It came from being in his own bed, in his own house, and among the people he loved. There was nothing like it.

Back at home, he wondered why he'd ever left. How could he have been so stupid to think that it would have helped anything? But sometimes you don't know and you do stupid things in an effort to make life better. Sometimes it even works.

Jim likened it to the structure of the human eye. There were photoreceptors there called rods and cones. The cone-shaped receptors are in the middle of the retina and help with vision during the bright light of the day. The rod-shaped receptors lie on the boundary of the retina and assist with vision in lower light. For that reason, you can often see better in the darkness by turning your head slightly to the side and forcing the eye to use the rods instead of the cones.

By comparison, sometimes you can't clearly see the thing you're looking directly at. You can't always process your life while you're in the midst of it. That was one of the things Jim had learned about hiking, backpacking, fishing, and other solitary activities years ago. Getting that time away, looking at his life indirectly instead of staring right at it, could better help him understand it. That was exactly what had happened to him over the last week.

Charlie's story had taken a long time last night. Since Ellen had prepared a meal for him, he took a break to eat it, then they returned to the barn to pick up where they'd left off. It was a lot to take in. Parts of what he heard provoked a reaction from him, but he withheld comment. In his exhausted state he wanted a night to process what he'd heard. He wanted time to overlay this new information on top of what he'd figured out while he was gone.

Thinking about it overnight had worked. In the light of morning, Jim had a plan. He was in the kitchen drinking a cup of bitter MRE coffee when Pete told him that Hugh and Charlie were outside.

"I'll be right out, Pete."

Jim drained the last of his coffee and rinsed out his cup. He pulled on his gear, grabbed his rifle, and stepped out onto the porch. "Morning, gentlemen."

Like three stooges, the trio looked around curiously for any *gentlemen* who might have approached.

"Ha ha," Jim said flatly. "Let's take a walk."

"Where we going?" Pete asked.

"Lloyd's place. We're going to check on it and we can talk on the way."

"Road or woods?" Hugh asked.

"Woods."

They exited the yard, went through a few gates, and got on the old logging road that would eventually deliver them into the woods behind Lloyd's place.

"The way we're living is not sustainable," Jim said, talking as he walked. "I'm not hiding anymore. If people think they can find a way to collect a bounty on me, they can bring it. If they have a grudge, if they think I kept them from getting to live in an aid camp, they're welcome to come discuss it. Word will soon get around that the topic is closed."

Hugh grinned. "I like where this is going."

"The Wimmers might be our first problem," Charlie said. "They have a grudge."

Jim nodded. "Tell me something, Charlie. Honestly. Were you going to move on the Wimmers? Burn them out or kill them?"

It took Charlie a while to answer. Jim could sense him trying to find the words. "I hadn't decided yet. I felt like something had to happen but I wasn't sure what to do. I was just trying to keep everyone safe."

"I understand that," Jim said. "If you want a more active role in the security of this valley, Hugh and I can make that happen. You're young and hot-headed. You have a lot to learn. It will be a slow process but we can move in that direction."

"What exactly does that mean?" Charlie asked. "Pete and I already do sentry duty. We ride patrols."

"The first thing it means is that I'm thinking you and Pete should move into Lloyd's house. I don't like it sitting empty because it's the first house we control in the valley. It's close to the Wimmers and allows us to keep an eye on their activities. Controlling that position lets us know who's coming and who's going."

Pete and Charlie looked at each other in shock.

"Really?" Pete asked. "You think Mom will go for that?"

"I think I can make it happen. You both have to keep quiet about this for now. Let me talk to Randi and Ellen first. Okay?"

"Sure!" Pete said.

"Okay," Charlie agreed.

"What are we going to do about the Wimmers?" Hugh asked. "I was there at the gate. They're pretty pissed."

"We're going to help them rebuild that bridge."

Everyone stopped in their tracks. Noticing that he was now

walking alone, Jim stopped and turned. Everyone was looking at him like he'd lost his mind. "What?"

"Are you serious?" Pete asked.

"I'm completely serious. They may not want our help, but I'm going to make the offer. I'm going to tell them *we're* going to rebuild the bridge and they're welcome to help if they want."

Charlie looked worried. "Are you going to tell them I burned it down?"

"No. They don't need to know that. Let them think it was people from town. I believe this is the quickest way to build goodwill with those people. There's a lot of bad blood but we're not going to get rid of them. We might as well see if we can win them over."

"Good luck with that," Hugh snickered.

Jim smiled. "Oh, you're coming with me. I'm going to do the talking but I need someone along to take my body home if it goes south."

"Dad!" Pete said.

Jim waved him off. "I'm joking."

Pete scowled. "Not much of a joke."

Jim shrugged. "Your father has a weird sense of humor. You'll realize that more and more as you get older. Let's keep moving."

They started walking again and Jim went on. "We also need to improve our intelligence gathering. Hugh, you've been doing an excellent job on the radios. I know you've been expanding your network over time."

"As time permits," Hugh said. "Gardening has cut into my efforts. In the winter I could sit around all day and fool with my radios."

"We also need more local intelligence. The only way we'll get that is by having eyes and ears in town. We need to have someone at that farmer's market. That's the hub of the community right now. That's the one place where information is coming together."

"What do you mean by having someone there?" Pete asked.

"Customers are on the outside. They're not there long enough to hear anything, but they bring information in. Vendors talk amongst themselves and share the best information they hear. They aggregate intelligence. We need to have a table at that market so we have access to the best intel."

"We've got enough to stock one," Hugh said. "This is a good time. We could sell the extra produce we can't preserve. We've got gear from the skirmishes that we can't use. There's a market for the crappy stuff too. People with nothing are glad to get it."

"I've still got a lot to trade off," Charlie said. "Things I can never use."

"The question is who to send," Jim said. "I'm burned in town. It can't be me."

"I'd like to do it," Charlie said. "I'm not from here so no one should be able to connect me with your family. I've also got a lot to trade off."

Jim frowned. "I'd be glad to send you but you're young to do it alone. People will try to bully and take advantage of you."

"I won't take any bullshit," Charlie argued.

"But you also have to be able to keep a cool head and you're not there yet," Jim said. "No offense."

"How about Gary's wife? Debra? She's been the one pushing to go since the beginning," Hugh suggested.

Jim considered. "We can ask her."

"I'd still like to be part of it," Charlie said. "Maybe she and I could work a table together?"

They discussed a few other items that had come to Jim while he was gone. Eventually, they reached Buddy's old house—Lloyd's new house—and Jim produced a key. They checked it inside and out, finding nothing disturbed.

"Can you picture it?" Charlie asked Pete. "Us living here?"

Pete grinned. "Parties. Chicks."

Jim laughed. "Don't get ahead of yourselves. This is an experiment. Don't blow it."

Pete was undeterred. "When can we move in?"

"*If* I survive the Wimmers, your mother, and Randi, we'll figure that out."

"That's a big *if*," Hugh added.

"You and Charlie can hang out here on the porch and start planning your party," Jim said. "Hugh and I are going over to the Wimmers' house."

Hugh's eyes widened. "Now?"

"No time like the present."

"It's your funeral."

"I don't like these jokes," Pete groaned.

Jim hugged his son. "We'll be back. It'll be fine."

**67**

—————

# J*im's Valley*

THERE WAS no one outside the Wimmer house when Jim and Hugh approached. It was an old farmhouse that had once aspired to be something more. There were details stolen from Greek Revival and Colonial homes, but nothing to tie it all together into a singular style. More than anything it was a vast wooden space where one could raise a large family and a couple of generations of their offspring.

Jim and Hugh let themselves through the gate and walked up the dirt road to the crumbling concrete sidewalk. At the end of the sidewalk was a set of concrete steps that led to nothing, originally designed to aid ladies in climbing aboard wagons. Hugh took a seat on those steps, wary and uncomfortable with the exposed position. Jim approached the house, climbed onto the porch, and knocked politely on the door.

As he waited, he noticed some damage to the door and frame.

Someone had been shot before while standing exactly where he was standing. Jim decided it might be wise to move so he took two steps to the side and waited there instead. To his left he noticed a curtain flutter. Footsteps approached the door, the knob twisted, then Mrs. Wimmer was standing there glaring at him.

"Well if it ain't the devil hisself done come to pay me a visit," she said. Her voice was low and gravely with age. Her white hair had grown long and hung wild around her shoulders. She'd lost weight but had the same harsh features, the same dark, penetrating eyes. "Where you been, Old Scratch? Thought you left us for good?"

She had to be referring to the trip Jim had taken on the helicopter, when most of the locals assumed he was being hauled off to pay for his crimes at the power plant.

"I went on a trip but," Jim ran a hand through his hair, "as you can see, I'm back now. Good as ever. They decided it was all a big misunderstanding and they let me go."

She seemed displeased with that revelation. "I figured they took you back to Hell, where you belong for all the trouble you caused."

Jim smiled. "If this is Hell, I hoped for more entertaining neighbors."

Mrs. Wimmer raised an eyebrow and frowned. Jim felt slighted. It was a rather weak response to what he thought was a funny remark.

"What you doing here darkening my doorstep? I ain't got time to stand here and chew cabbage with you."

"I heard you all built a bridge into town to replace the one that got...*blown up*. I also heard that someone came along and burned your new bridge to the ground shortly after it was completed."

She nodded. "That's a fact. I assume it was them people of yours. They don't take kindly to strangers coming into the valley. They tend toward selfishness and wickedness. I assume they get that from you."

"They're protective and they *did* get that from me. Either way, I'm not here to argue about who burned down your bridge. If you think it was my people, I'm fairly certain I can't convince you otherwise. I am here to offer to rebuild the bridge though. We'll start tomorrow. If you want to help, we'll be there first thing in the morning."

Rather than being surprised or pleased, she looked wary. "You're going to rebuild the bridge your people didn't want? What's the catch?"

"Consider it an effort to make up for some of the bad blood between us. I'd rather we be working with each other than against each other."

Mrs. Wimmer glared at him with cold eyes. "You got a hell of a long way to go before we're friendly again, Mr. Powell."

Jim winked at her. "Same on this end, Mrs. Wimmer. But if you don't mind, please pass that information on to your men. Hopefully, we can have the bridge back open in a week or so."

"I'll tell them." She backed into the house and closed the door in his face.

Jim spun on his heel, descended the steps, and approached Hugh with a grin on his face.

"I couldn't hear the words but the body language was interesting," Hugh remarked. "She looked like a sour old bitch. You looked like honey was pouring from your mouth."

"Our game has to be a lot smarter from here on out, old friend. It's politics. It's building a support network in the community and intel networks on all levels. We need to know everything that's happening and everything that's going to happen."

Hugh fell in alongside Jim. Every couple of steps he turned around to check the Wimmers' house, making sure no one was drawing a bead on their backs. "We've got a good group, Jim. They're tough and scrappy. They're mean enough and resourceful enough to survive, but I know exactly what you mean. We need to take this to the next level."

They left the Wimmers' property and closed the gate behind them. The walk back down to Lloyd's house took only a few minutes. They found Charlie and Pete sitting on the porch.

"We'll need some help going through Buddy's stuff," Pete said. "Lloyd never dealt with any of that. There's stuff everywhere."

"We can help with that. We'll get it figured out. I told Lloyd we'd store his stuff for him. Hugh, you take a seat with the boys. I need to find something inside. I'll be right back."

Jim stepped through the front door and went to the kitchen. He dug into the pantry and shuffled around a few things until he found what he was looking for, then returned to the front porch with it. He held the jar of blackberry moonshine up for everyone to see.

Hugh looked at Jim, then at the boys. The boys looked at each other, then back at Jim with grins on their faces.

"Is that Lloyd's liquor?" Pete asked.

"Yes, but it's my favorite of Lloyd's liquor stash so technically it's as good as mine. Besides, when he said he wasn't coming back, I told him there were no guarantees as far as the blackberry moonshine was concerned."

"Ellen is going to kick your ass if she finds out about this," said Hugh.

"No one is getting drunk." Jim unscrewed the lid from the jar. "I'm simply proposing a toast to returning home and to our new game plan."

Jim took a sip and relished the fruity burn of the liquor. When he was done, he passed the jar to Hugh.

"When do the rest of the folks find out about our plan?" Hugh asked, tilting the jar up and taking a sip.

"That's my plan for the rest of the day," Jim said. "I'm going to visit Gary and then Randi. If I survive them, I'm going to talk to Ellen. I'll update everyone on the new plan and on the boys moving into Lloyd's house."

"We're really going to rebuild the bridge?" Pete asked, sounding a little intimidated by the scope of that project.

"I don't think we'll rebuild it the same way the Wimmers did," Jim replied. "There's a flatbed semi-trailer parked at the superstore. With a few horses and a homemade tow dolly, we could stretch that thing across the gap easier than we could build another bridge. Once we get it in place, we'll ramp up to it on each side. Beats the hell out of dropping trees, limbing them, and dragging them into place. It's a lot safer too."

Hugh rested the lid back on the jar and gestured at the boys, asking Jim with his eyes if he was certain he wanted to do this. Jim gave him the go-ahead. Hugh stretched toward Pete and handed him the jar.

Pete lifted the lid and took a whiff. Despite his initial excitement, he was hesitant now that the moment was upon him. "It smells good but it smells strong."

Jim grinned. "It's both those things. Take a small sip and then pass it to Charlie."

Pete sipped, winced at the bite, and passed it to his friend. Charlie's reaction was nearly identical. When he was done, he passed it back to Jim. The jar made one more circle and then Jim shoved it into his pack.

"Don't you boys breathe on your mother or Randi for a couple of hours," Jim advised. "Don't do anything stupid either."

"Like drive?" Pete asked.

"Or operate heavy machinery?" Charlie added.

The two looked at each other and laughed.

"Don't whoop it up too much, boys," Hugh said. "You didn't have enough to start slurring and staggering."

They looked disappointed.

"Let's get out of here." Jim stood. "We have a lot to do."

While everyone got their gear together, Jim went inside one more time to make sure all the doors were locked. Seeing Lloyd's possessions scattered about the house made him think of his old friend. He hoped Lloyd was doing okay. He hoped he'd made the right call. Maybe if Jim hadn't heard anything from him by winter, he could head over there and pay him a visit. He could take Randi if she'd calmed down by then.

He looked around at the guitars, banjos, and other instruments. Before leaving, he pulled the jar out of his pack and held it aloft.

"To Buddy. To Lloyd. To friends."

He took a long sip, then resealed the jar and stashed it in his pack. He backed out the door and closed it behind him.

## 68

*liver's House*

WITH LLOYD'S HELP, they cleaned the chimneys in the big house. Using a trick he'd learned from his grandfather, he crumpled a section of rat-wire into a ball and fastened it to the end of a rope. Getting on the roof was sketchy but they managed to do it. He dropped the rope down the chimneys and drew the ball of wire down through them. The wire acted like a chimney brush, scraping the chimneys clean with a little effort. The next day they used levers and rollers to move a rusty old cookstove from the barn to the kitchen, reconnecting it to the abandoned thimble hidden beneath a decorative trim cap.

Lloyd was adjusting, both to being in a new place, among new people, and to feeling like he was responsible for their safety. Somehow that detail had not entered his mind when he decided to move here. He imagined carefree days playing music and helping out, much as he'd done in Jim's valley.

Now he was seeing the ugly side of keeping the peace in a small community. Someone had to be willing to make the hard calls. Someone had to be willing to pull the trigger. He was reminded of that every time he looked to the north and saw buzzards circling beyond the cornfield. He knew they were circling that young man's body. He wished they'd just eat him and be done with it.

That afternoon Kendall and Freda showed up. They were out for an evening stroll after dinner. Lloyd was outside heating water in a cast-iron cauldron for washing dishes. It was the same vessel that Oliver's family would have used for scalding a hog before they scraped the fur from the hide. Now that they had a working stove they could have heated the water inside but it was too hot for a fire in the house.

Nathan was demonstrating his fire-building skills to Lloyd when Kendall joined them. Freda went straight for the house, wanting to visit with Sharon and the smaller children.

"Any trouble out of that bunch up the road?" he asked.

Lloyd knew he meant Kimberly, but he seemed hesitant to even use the name, as if speaking it might invoke her presence. "Nah, it's been quiet."

Nathan gave Lloyd a nervous glance, then smiled at Kendall. "Yeah, things have been great. The new house is a big improvement."

"Yeah, I think that whole mess is over with," Lloyd agreed.

Kendall took a seat on a log and slapped his leg enthusiastically. "Dang it, I knew we could make her listen to reason. That girl might be hot-headed but she knows to respect her elders. She knows when to listen to reason."

When Kendall looked away, Lloyd gave Nathan a wink. The boy had been convincing. He felt a twinge of guilt at asking them to lie. Neither he nor Sharon had felt good about coaching the children to do it, but they'd assured them it was a necessary evil. Sometimes you had to do things to protect the people you loved because people outside of the family wouldn't understand. This was one of those things.

They'd discussed it as a group when he got home from killing Kimberly.

"You all know that Mr. Lloyd did what he did to help us, right? To save Tara?" Sharon had asked the children around the fire that night.

They'd all agreed, every little face nodding in the firelight.

"He did it for us," Sharon said. "He'll do it again if he has to. I'll do it if I have to. Nathan, would you do it if you had to?"

"I would."

"Kay, would you?"

Kay nodded.

Everyone around the fire was asked the same question and they all agreed. If they'd been in Lloyd's situation, facing a man holding a knife on Tara, they'd have done exactly the same thing.

"Then I want each of you to pick up a handful of grass," Sharon said.

Each of the children reached down beside their seats and plucked a large handful of grass.

"Now cup it in your hands and I want you to whisper to it. I want you to tell it what you remember of today. Tell it the story—the true story—and this will be the last time you ever speak of it."

She allowed each child as long as they needed. Some, like Tara, had a lot to say and spent several minutes whispering into their cupped hands.

When everyone was done, Sharon confirmed it. "That everyone?"

They all nodded.

"Then stand up and throw your grass into the fire. Let the truth burn away. The old story is gone and the new story is now the truth. We forget everything that happened today and we let it go."

Each child did as they were told, throwing their clumps of grass into the circle of fire. The green strands curled and burned, going from green to red to black, then disappearing into the greater ash of the fire.

The next day they'd practiced the story several times but it wasn't until now, until Kendall and Freda's visit, that they'd had the opportunity to practice it on outsiders. Lloyd couldn't be certain how it was going inside, but Nathan had passed with flying colors.

"Wonder what them danged old buzzards is circling," Kendall remarked, noticing the birds. "Couldn't see them from my place."

"It's a coyote," Lloyd said, afraid that if he didn't have an answer, Kendall might go investigate on his own. "I shot him in the yard then hauled him off to the cornfield. It's too hot to stand out there burying a varmint."

"Yeah, I thought I heard someone shooting at something the other day. No big deal. You'll hear some shooting around here. Folks killing a deer or slaughtering livestock. That kind of thing."

"Yeah, I didn't want it scaring the children," Lloyd offered.

"Everything else going okay?" Kendall asked.

"Sure is. I'm helping them get settled in," Lloyd replied. "I think they'll be a lot more comfortable here."

"I'll like having you around too," Kendall said. "Good to have another man you can depend on. That friend of yours, Jim, seemed like a good guy but he was wound a little too tight for me. We're better off having a banjo player in the neighborhood than someone like that. Most musicians I know are peaceful folk. Wouldn't hurt a fly."

Lloyd grinned. "I don't know, Kendall. Reckon there could be some dangerous banjo players out there."

Kendall's laugh started as a chuckle, then turned into a deep belly laugh. His face turned red as his laughter filled the valley. "A dangerous banjo player. That's a good one."

Lloyd winked at Nathan. "Get your guitar, boy. Let's play some *Little Liza Jane*."

**The End**

www.ingramcontent.com/pod-product-compliance
Lightning Source LLC
Chambersburg PA
CBHW070305310726
48976CB00005B/1584